Not Our Problem

'Today special interest groups are pressuring New Zealand's and other governments not to be so equitable. The special interests do not want to say "me first" in so many words, so they mount an attack based on "efficiency" and "waste of public money" or "inferiority of public vs private services".'

WILLIAM OMAN, 1996

Not Our Problem

Ian Cowan

iancowan138@gmail.com

Published by Ian Allan Cowan
PO Box 36-406, Merivale 8146
New Zealand

Copyright © Ian Allan Cowan, 2015

This edition published 2015
Reprinted November 2015

The moral rights of Ian Cowan to be identified as the author of this work in terms of section 96 of the Copyright Act 1994 is hereby asserted.

This book is copyright. Apart from any fair dealing for the purpose of private study, research, criticism or review, as permitted under the Copyright Act, no part of this publication may be reproduced, stored in a retrieval system, or transmitted in any form or by any means, electronic, mechanical, photocopying or otherwise, without prior permission of the publisher.

ISBN 978-0-473-32696-8

Designed, typeset and produced by Mary Egan Publishing
Artwork by Brendon Wright
Cover designed by Sophia Egan-Reid
Printed in New Zealand

This is a work of fiction in the sense that its characters are all imaginary, and any resemblance to any person living or dead is coincidental. To my knowledge there is no company called Health 4U operating in Nevada.

However, many of the things said by the characters, and actions taken by them, are based on actual events that occurred in New Zealand between 1987 and 1998. Where this applies I have provided references at the back of the book.

For the purposes of the narrative, the time scale has been foreshortened, and events described are not necessarily in chronological order.

Dedicated to everybody who helped to make it stop.

ACKNOWLEDGEMENTS

Many thanks are due to Geoff Walker and Sue Reidy for their invaluable comments and suggestions, and to Robin Gauld, Tim Hazledine and Ruth Spearing for their support.

Thank you also to the staff at Mary Egan Publishing for guiding me through the process of publication, and their professional skills in creating the final product.

Brendon Wright, at B & N Creations, was generous with time and ideas and produced the picture of somebody's Nanna for the half title page.

Most of all, I thank my long-suffering family who have lived with 'The Book' for so many years; especially my wife Stephanie for her unflagging generosity of listening time and for all her love and support.

The quotation on page 2 is reproduced with kind permission from Springer Science+Business Media: Health Care Analysis, 'Cultural Diversity, and Some Advice for the Minister', volume 4, 1996, page 143, by W H Oman, and from Professor William Oman.

INTRODUCTION

In the early 1990s, New Zealand endured one of the most concerted attempts anywhere in the world to impose an ideologically-driven market model onto the delivery of public health care services. What happened at the time and the ideas that drove the notorious 'health reforms' now, almost a quarter century later, seem inexplicable. The reforms were rooted in neo-liberal economics and private business principles as applied to public trading companies, such as electricity, post and telecommunications. These ideas and corresponding structural arrangements were then transplanted onto health with complete disregard for the possibility that health care provision and the nature of the health care 'market' might just be a little different from government trading or private sector services.

Even more astonishing from the health reforms era was the extent of absolute self-belief amongst those behind the reforms that what they were pursuing was right: they had the theory, which was correct, and this just needed to be pushed into practice. In turn, they created a network of devotees across the new organisations established to implement the reforms: the Regional Health Authorities (government health care purchasers), Crown Health Enterprises (public hospitals), and other bodies which feature in this book. Most were hired because they knew nothing about or had no prior experience working in health, as this would have meant they had a 'vested interest' in the status quo and were incapable of the objectivity and improved decision-making that allegedly sound economic and business analytical skills delivered. Health professionals were also, it was asserted, no good at management, unlike those from the private sector.

The health reforms were short-lived yet their impact prolonged. There were some benefits, mostly unforeseen, but these were vastly outweighed by negatives. The harms to patients and health professionals cannot be forgotten. *Not Our Problem* comes at an important time in health policy internationally as the focus on patient safety and quality improvement continues to grow in the face of ongoing financial and other challenges that potentially undermine standards. *Not Our Problem* is not only a great read as we experience the reformers' mentality through the lens of Dr Steve Cassidy, a surgical registrar who is the odd one out when he takes a job in the new management team at his Crown Health Enterprise (CHE); it is also a very timely reminder of what can happen when pure ideology overrides the practical importance of listening to front-line health professionals.

Ian has done a superb job of weaving together a story that explores the tensions between professionals and the reform ideologues that were ever-present at the time. He spells out the key theories in simple terms and, through his key management characters, accurately portrays the prevailing mindset (and I witnessed this first hand when interviewing several CHE Chief Executives and many other reformers in 1993).

Let us hope that politicians, policy makers, professionals and the general public read, enjoy, think deeply about and debate this book and never let another set of such 'health reforms' happen in New Zealand or elsewhere.

Professor Robin Gauld (author of *Revolving Doors: New Zealand's Health Reforms*, 2001; 2nd ed. 2009)
Department of Preventive and Social Medicine
University of Otago, Dunedin, New Zealand

CHAPTER ONE

November 1992. Paxton, New Zealand

Stephen Cassidy glanced at his assistant. 'Bring it close.'

He made a two-centimetre cut in the tough membrane and Helen pushed the suction catheter into the hole, silencing the hiss of air as the tube filled with rushing blood.

Cassidy enlarged the incision and put his right hand inside the abdomen. He pushed gently up towards the left diaphragm, his eyes half-closed, concentrating on the information coming back from his fingertips. Parts of his mind registered the warmth as blood surrounded his forearm, then the spattering as it streamed onto the floor.

Separate lumps of boggy tissue confirmed that the spleen had ruptured. He felt the blood pulsing from the splenic artery, and pinched it between his thumb and forefinger. 'Artery forceps. Keep that suction going. What's the blood pressure?'

'Ninety on sixty. Two more units of blood on the way.'

He gripped the long forceps in his left hand and slid them along the palm of his right until he felt the tip touch his thumb. He opened the forceps, eased them over the artery, and tightened them click by click until the pulsation stopped.

'We've lost suction,' said Helen.

Kylie, the circulating nurse, replaced the full suction jar with an empty one. 'One litre of blood loss.' She wrote it on the whiteboard then grabbed another towel for the pool beside Cassidy's foot.

'It's not all blood,' said Allan O'Connell, the anaesthetist and at thirty-two the oldest conscious person in the room. 'Smell the beer.' His eyes flicked over his monitors and he wrote something on his clipboard.

The blood level in the abdominal cavity was dropping quickly now that the biggest bleeder was controlled. Cassidy enlarged the wound so that he could see the other organs.

The liver had a small surface tear oozing blood and bile, and he packed gauze between it and the diaphragm. He began examining the small bowel, running it gently through his fingers, searching for holes or bleeding points.

'What ya got?' said a voice over his shoulder. Geoff Pierce, the night-shift orthopaedic registrar and Cassidy's flatmate, had finished stabilising a shattered ankle in the next theatre and was ready to start on this patient.

Cassidy's eyes stayed on the bowel passing between his fingertips. 'Hi, Geoff. He's forty-eight. Rib fractures, facial fractures, left pneumothorax, ruptured spleen, small liver laceration, and there's something else still bleeding in here. Midshaft left femur fracture, so he's probably bled a litre into the thigh as well as a couple into his belly. X-rays are on the screen. The vascular team know about him and the radiographer's on the way.'

'OK. Is this the guy from the accident on Warwick Road?'

'Artery forceps.' Cassidy had found blood pumping from one of the small arteries supplying the bowel.

'Yes, it is,' said O'Connell. 'They said he was doing 110 on the wrong side of the road, on that long corner just before you reach Westmere. A young woman and a baby in the other car were killed.'

Cassidy's shoulders slumped. His hands stopped moving and he stared at them for a moment before speaking. 'Does anybody apart from me wonder why we're all standing here in the middle of the night, using our combined skill to save the life of a *murderer?*'

The pulse recorder beeped seven times before O'Connell said, 'Come on, Steve. Not even as a joke, alright? Sort out the belly and then we'll get the leg fixed. The sooner we finish, the sooner we can all grab some sleep.'

'No, I'm serious. This guy chose to get drunk, then he chose to drive, and there are innocent people dead because of that. Why isn't that murder, can anybody tell me? How can it be right that we save his worthless life? We should—'

'Steve,' Geoff urged in a low voice. 'Stop this nonsense and finish the operation.'

Cassidy looked around the circle of faces.

'Morning everyone.' The vascular registrar hurried in, tying his facemask. 'How long since the accident?'

Helen shifted her eyes to the wall clock. 'It's 2:45 now, so an hour and thirty minutes. We've nearly finished in the abdomen, haven't we Steve?'

Cassidy shook himself. 'Sorry, er, yes we have. Hi Bernie, we won't be long. Get me a suture thanks Sis, I'll tie off that little jejunal branch now.'

The tension dropped away, and Kylie lifted the drapes over the man's left leg so that Geoff could paint the skin with disinfectant.

'BP's rising, a hundred and five on seventy-five,' Alan reported. 'We're running the fourth and fifth units of blood in now.'

'This *fucking* thing's died again!' said Cassidy in a voice tight with anger. The diathermy unit, which electrically burnt tissue and sealed off small blood vessels, had recently started cutting out at random moments. The engineers had been unable to trace the fault and requests for a replacement had been ignored. Then it had restarted after a kick from a frustrated surgeon, so now Kylie knew what to do.

'Ready for X-ray,' said a new voice. The radiographer had positioned the X-ray machine over the thigh, and Geoff got ready to make the contrast injection to show the arteries in the leg. Everybody except Geoff, the anaesthetist and the radiographer left the theatre while the X-rays were taken.

'Why the hell can't they give us decent equipment?' said Cassidy as they waited in the scrub room. 'How do they expect us to—'

'Are you alright?' said Helen.

'Does it look like I'm alright?' Cassidy hissed. After a pause he sighed. 'Sorry, it's not your fault. And I didn't mean what I said. It was strange, as if somebody else was talking. But I'm just so tired.'

'Yes, I know.' Helen took a deep breath. 'But that's the job, isn't it? Come on, Steve. Finish here, then the two appendixes, and hopefully that'll be it for the night.'

....

At 4:30 Cassidy fell asleep in the tiny bedroom for the on-call surgical registrar. He was called about a drug order at 5:15. His alarm woke him at 6:45, and by 7:30 he was showered and shaved, and had visited his patient in the intensive care unit.

Now he sat in the cafeteria drinking stewed coffee and glaring at today's outrage in the Paxton *Bugle*.

Another Diagnostic Botch-Up read the headline. Daniel O'Malley, pictured with his leg in a plaster cast, had been sent home from Paxton Hospital's Emergency department last week despite X-rays that showed he had a broken leg.

'*My taxes have paid to train these people, and this is the best they can do,*' said Mr O'Malley, 54. '*It's not good enough. The Government needs to step in.*' The Bugle *agrees. Turn to page 9 to read our editorial on the shocking state of New Zealand's public health care system.*

'Hi, Steve.' Helen put down her coffee and muesli and pulled a bundle of laboratory results from the pocket of her white coat.

'Morning. Look at how they pump things up to make a better story. Anybody would think he crawled home with his femur sticking out of his thigh, but I'll bet it was just a crack in the fibula.' Cassidy folded the newspaper and tossed it onto the chair opposite. 'The ED guys still shouldn't have missed it though.'

'Poor things,' said Helen. 'It's a zoo down there. Patients everywhere, not enough staff, not enough space. It's amazing they don't make more mistakes.'

'Amazing who don't make more mistakes?' Geoff sat down with a plate of bacon, eggs, sausages and tomatoes. He was wearing a white coat over his theatre scrubs, and had small dots of dried blood above his left eyebrow.

'Everybody,' Cassidy sighed. How'd you get on with the femur?'

'Which one? Oh, your man, Mr Bright. The irony of names, eh?' Geoff buttered his toast. 'I've put external fixation on and we'll rod it when everything else has settled down. The artery was torn, but Bernie did a good job, the foot looks fine this morning.'

He started shovelling food into his mouth with the speed of a man who has people waiting for him to come and make decisions. 'What happened to you last night?'

'What do you mean?' said Cassidy.

'Come on, Steve. I mean your little rant about murderers, in front of the nurses and everybody. Remember? I've never seen anything like that before, and especially not from super-cool Steve Cassidy. What's the story?'

Cassidy closed his eyes for a moment. 'I'm sick of this horrible job. Most people go to bed and sleep through, every night of their lives. But one night in four, and one weekend in four, I'm up most of the night groping around inside people's bellies using crappy, unreliable equipment that never gets fixed. And if anybody's on leave it's one in three.

'I know somebody's got to do it, and I know it's mostly not people's fault that they're sick. But this guy killed two people.'

'All wrong,' said Geoff firmly. 'It's not your job to make moral judgements about the clientele. Or are you saying we should sit down and consider their *niceness* before deciding whether or not we'd operate? Mark them out of ten, or something? No, of course not. So forget the philosophy, grab the experience, and get out once you've done your share.

'In a few years you'll have passed the exams and done the stint overseas, and you'll be back here as a consultant while some other poor bastards beaver through the night.'

'Yeah, probably kicking the same useless diathermy machine.'

'Probably. But you never know, things might improve once our bright and breezy Minister of Health finds all those extra dollars next year.' Geoff drained his coffee. 'People, today's first trauma case is already in Emergency, I've got to go. See you later.'

'Bye.' Cassidy turned back to Helen. 'They don't let airline pilots work huge hours, so how come it's OK for us to do it? Making me work when I'm chronically sleep-deprived is downright dangerous. If I make a mistake it could be much worse than missing a little fracture on an X-ray.'

'That's true.' Helen started gathering cups and plates. 'Come on, it's time for the ward round.'

'What's the Minister of Health going to do?'

'I don't know. They're talking about big reforms, but I don't understand it.' Her pager beeped and she went to find a phone. Cassidy yawned and stared into space until she returned.

'Steve, Mr Durham has fallen out of bed in Ward 14. I'll go and see him, but can you take these and start Mr Jackson's ward round? Thanks.' She thrust the wad of laboratory result forms at him and hurried away.

....

Usually Cassidy welcomed Ward 18's morning smell, a blend of coffee, toast, and disinfectant plus the occasional alimentary disaster; it told him where he was and got him set to deal with whatever the day might bring. But today he walked in feeling like someone else watching Cassidy go through the motions.

Mr Philip Jackson ostentatiously checked his watch as his registrar arrived. Tall, silver-haired and three-piece-suited, Jackson was the best upper abdominal surgeon in town, and the endless demand for his skills in the public and private sectors had given him a clear picture of the value of his time. 'Dr Cassidy, so good of you to join us,' he drawled. 'I don't suppose you happen to have Mrs Griffiths' bilirubin result there, by any chance? Sister tells me your colleague disappeared with all the results.'

Cassidy's respect for Jackson's expertise had immunised him against his boss's sarcasm. 'Morning Mr Jackson, morning everyone.' He searched through the forms. 'Helen is dealing with an emergency in

Ward 21 . . . Here we are. Bilirubin is coming down and the other liver function tests are nearly back to normal.' Cassidy smiled at the closest of the medical students standing at the foot of the bed, and hoped he hadn't been rude to her recently. 'Miss Shand, could you sort these and look after them for us, please? Thank you.'

Yesterday morning Mrs Griffiths, an overweight woman of thirty-five, had been deeply jaundiced and suffering attacks of severe pain. An ultrasound scan had shown two gallstones blocking her bile duct and others in an inflamed gallbladder. In the afternoon Jackson had passed a gastroscope down her oesophagus and through the stomach, then found the tiny opening of the bile duct in the wall of the duodenum. He made a small cut and the stones had fallen out followed by a gush of murky bile. It took less than an hour, and already the fever and pain had settled and her colour was improving.

'Will it happen again, doctor?' she asked as Jackson palpated her abdomen.

'I hope not.' He pulled the bedclothes up. 'But we've put your name on the semi-urgent waiting list to have your gallbladder out.'

'How long will I have to wait?'

'Not too long, I hope,' said Jackson. 'But the waiting list is quite long at the moment and it might be a year or more.' He smiled to soften the blow. 'You should be able to go home this afternoon. Dr Cassidy will come and see you after lunch.'

In the next room lay Mr Hodder, a ninety-year-old man with multiple medical problems who had come in seriously ill with a bleeding colon cancer. After a long conversation with his anguished daughters, the team had operated. He had surprised them and survived the expected post-operative storm in intensive care, but then his recovery had stalled.

'Did you have some breakfast, Mr Hodder?' Jackson asked, but there was no response. The old man's face had an unhealthy reddish tinge, and his breathing was wheezy.

Once he had been a bank manager and Paxton Valley Golf Club champion. Now he was a frail, unreachable old man, hovering between life and death.

'Alright,' said Jackson. 'Keep trying to get some food into him. Who's next, Sister?'

Next was Mr Lodge, a pale and weary man of forty-five. He had been admitted directly from the outpatient clinic yesterday after his GP had sent him for urgent assessment with a hard, irregular liver that could only mean one thing. A CT scan had confirmed the presence of cancer and shown other tumour deposits in the abdomen and the chest.

Mr Lodge was a policeman with a young family and a set of dreams like anyone else, but now his world had turned upside down, and he had only months or even weeks to live.

Cassidy slipped out of the room and leaned against the wall with his eyes closed, wondering again why on earth he did this job: horror in the night, tragedies in the daytime. Of course they had wins — Mrs Griffiths' turnaround was like a miracle when you thought about it. But Mr Hodder and Mr Lodge . . . and the constant fatigue, waiting to lull him into a serious mistake. He wondered how much more of this he could take.

After a moment he took a deep breath, straightened his shoulders and caught up with the team as Helen returned from Ward 14.

The ward round continued. Bellies were palpated, test results considered, and decisions made. Each patient was the centre of attention for a few minutes until everybody under Jackson's care had been reviewed.

'Anyone else to see?' asked Jackson as Sister MacKelvie pushed the notes trolley back into the office.

'Yes,' said Helen, 'we've got outliers in Wards 4, 11 and 14. And a multi-trauma in ICU.'

'Why can't I have all *my* patients in *my* ward?' Jackson grumped as they set off to find the rest of their flock. 'There are patients in Ward 18 who don't belong to us, why can't we do an exchange?'

'That would be logical,' said Cassidy, keeping up easily with his boss's agitated strides as Helen trotted behind. 'But this is a public hospital, so it doesn't happen.'

Jackson stabbed at the lift button with a much-scrubbed finger. 'But *why* doesn't it happen? It wouldn't even cost anything.'

In the other wards they struggled with harassed nurses who were not familiar with Jackson's patients. The great man was terse in Ward 14, monosyllabic in Ward 11 and darkly mute in Ward 4, where they could not even see their patient; he had disobeyed instructions and gone downstairs for a smoke.

The intensive care doctors expected to bring Mr Bright out of his induced coma in a few hours. His fractured face was heavily bruised, and his chest and neck were swollen by air leaking from a punctured lung. But the fluid in all his drainage tubes was slight and clear, his kidneys and lungs were functioning as well as could be expected at this stage, and his belly was soft. Jackson nodded his approval and they headed back towards ward 18.

They went into Sister MacKelvie's tiny office and seated themselves according to protocol: Jackson took the battered leather armchair, Cassidy swung back and forth in the desk chair and Helen perched on the windowsill as they waited for the kettle to boil.

Today's hospital tour had irritated Jackson more than usual. 'How many other wards have we been to?'

'Four,' said Helen.

'That's ridiculous. Who's got patients in this ward apart from us? Geriatricians! Urologists! While our patients sit in wards where they don't understand the conditions *we* treat. It's dangerous for patients and it's a waste of our time. Thank you,' as Cassidy handed him his tea. 'And what about our people? We can't do anything for Mr Hodder. Obviously he has to be in hospital, but not in an acute bed. Mrs Griffiths should have that gallbladder out six weeks from now, once the inflammation has settled. But no, she'll go on the waiting list. She might be back in a couple more times, quite ill again, as she waits for eighteen months to get the operation. If we operated at the right time we could save money on the avoidable admissions, as well as improving her life.'

'How do we fix these things?' said Cassidy. 'And get all the broken equipment repaired?'

'God knows.' Jackson stirred his tea. 'With multiple layers of bureaucracy and zero pressure to improve anything, nobody has to take any responsibility and it all just drifts along. Anybody with some basic common sense and the right level of authority could sort it out, but they'll need to be quick before these reforms start and everything gets a whole lot worse.'

'That's the second time today that somebody's mentioned reforms,' said Cassidy. 'What's happening?'

Jackson grimaced. 'Competition between hospitals for funding. Soon we'll be fighting for work with Warwick hospital, even though they're thirty-five kilometres away. Any hospital, public or private, will be able to tender for a contract to take out a hundred gallbladders or whatever, and the purchaser will choose the cheapest provider.

'And then, reading between the lines, privatisation of the public hospitals, American style. It's come from nowhere and it sounds spectacularly badly thought out, but — good Lord, is that the time? I'm due in clinic.' He finished his tea. 'You still OK for tonight's list?'

Cassidy looked up.

'Remember? I've got four cases in private, starting at seven o'clock. We discussed it last week. You'll be there, won't you?'

'Er, I'm — yes, of course.'

Jackson gave them a half-smile each, smoothed his waistcoat, and was gone.

'For goodness' sake, Steve,' said Helen. 'You were operating most of last night and you're seriously stressed. You need to be in bed at seven o'clock, not starting a theatre list.' She shook her head sadly and picked up her list of things to do.

Cassidy groaned and rested his head on the desk. 'I know. But I can't let him down at short notice. Plus he's set me up for a terrific fellowship year in the States, and I need his support.' He lay there for a moment with his eyes closed, then sat up and said in a quivering voice, 'Or I thought I did.'

He twirled the chair and stared up at her. 'Helen, would you say I had a reasonable amount of common sense?'

'Today, you mean? In the past five minutes? No.'

'But usually.'

She sighed, her eyes on her notes. 'Yes Steve, you have lots of common sense.'

'I'm good at finding solutions to problems? Or suggesting them, anyway.'

'I suppose so.' Helen underlined something and stood up to go.

Cassidy smiled. 'Well then.'

'Well then what? Sorry, I'm quite busy right now.'

'Please wait, this is important.'

'Alright.' Helen closed her notebook. 'Tell me.'

'Listen. Everybody agrees that management don't know anything about health care. So why don't I take a year off and help them out?'

She frowned. 'You've got final exams in a few months and then you're going to the States. You can't take a year off.'

'Why not? I have to do something, I'm not sure I'm safe at the moment. I'm burning out, actually. And I don't want any more dramas like last night, that was awful.'

He jumped up from the chair. 'But I could have a break, then come back fresh. And it would be great for the hospital, wouldn't it? Think of what we could fix: no more outliers, Mr Hodder in a more appropriate place, no more kicking the diathermy every few minutes. And that's just the start. We could get a decent computer system—'

'And you would stay in Paxton for another year,' Helen mused. 'Now I understand.'

Cassidy grinned sheepishly. 'Well, yes, that would be another benefit, now you mention it.'

Helen was happily married and a good listener, and she had heard plenty about her registrar's troubled love life. She knew about the abrupt ending six weeks ago of his two-year relationship with Zoe, a charge nurse in one of the other surgical wards. Zoe had finally stopped trying to share a perpetually distracted Cassidy with his ten-hour days and brutal call schedule, his impossibly high standards for himself, and the pile of textbooks on his bedside table.

One Sunday, after his whining had ruined another lovely lunch, she had cleared her belongings out of Cassidy's flat and he had fallen into a horrible, unfamiliar well of loneliness and self-loathing from which he had been unable to escape.

Now he was watching Helen like a puppy hoping for a walk.

'I suppose you could,' she said after a moment. 'It might be good for everyone, if you don't mind putting your surgical career on hold for a year.'

'And if they'd let me come back afterwards.' Then he frowned. 'But how would I get a job in management? Would they even want me?'

'They're unlikely to welcome somebody offering advice they haven't asked for,' said Helen. 'Although now might be the perfect time, as it happens — they're advertising lots of jobs because of these new plans. Have you seen the ads?' She opened the *Globe* on Sister Mac's desk. 'Yes, here's one. Steve, I've really got to go, I'll see you after lunch.'

Cassidy pulled the newspaper towards him and read the advertisement.

Key players in exciting new
Crown Health Enterprise Management Team

Paxton Crown Health Enterprise, which is anticipated to commence operations on 1 July 1993, has vacancies for outstanding professionals with the right skill mix, who would welcome the chance to showcase their capabilities free of historical external constraints. We make no apology for aiming to develop New Zealand's best Crown Health Enterprise.

You will have demonstrated capacity to inspire, enthuse and motivate others.

You will already have proven your ability to develop co-operation and support within large, diverse groups of highly opinionated stakeholders.

Now is the time to put your stamp on the future. Lead a multi-disciplinary team in a service-oriented environment, into the exciting future that will be Paxton Health!

He read it through again. Then he tore the advertisement out, folded it and put it in his pocket.

....

'This is Loretta Chapman, aged thirty-two,' said Jackson. He inserted a thin metal tube through a hole in the skin just below the sleeping patient's umbilicus. 'Two attacks of biliary colic in three months, no jaundice. Gallbladder stones and normal bile duct on ultrasound yesterday.'

Forcing himself to concentrate, Cassidy inserted further instruments under the ribs on each side. Usually he took advantage of the more relaxed evening atmosphere to probe Jackson's experience with technical questions, but tonight just being a competent surgical assistant would take all his energy.

'CO_2 on please. Thank you.' As he worked, Jackson resumed his criticism of the public health system. 'Did you see that piece in the *Globe* at the weekend? They're absolutely right, what's happening in the public hospitals is madness. Push that fat away, thanks.

'The Board gets a certain amount of money to spend on pretty much whatever they like, and the money keeps coming whether they do a good job or not. And if they overspend they get a top-up, so why wouldn't they overspend?

'And then you get this situation where management suddenly says, "Go and buy that CT scanner you asked for two years ago. Here's one and a half million dollars. But make sure you spend all of it, the money must be gone before the end of the financial year or we'll lose it next year. And by the way you've only got three weeks." Unbelievable. Diathermy that, thanks.

'Alright, that's the common duct, there's the cystic duct, and there's the cystic artery. You agree? OK.'

A few minutes later Jackson gently pulled the gallbladder out and laid it on a cork block so that he could cut it open and check for nasty surprises. There were three stones and some brownish sludge, but no surprises. 'She'll feel a lot better without that,' he said as he lowered it into a jar of formalin. Then after checking that all was well inside the abdomen, he and Cassidy removed all the instruments and closed the holes. They left the patient in the hands of the anaesthetist and the nurses, and went to the tearoom.

'And the strategic planning is non-existent.' Jackson sipped tea from the pink mug proclaiming "It's not easy being a princess", which Cassidy had chosen for him. 'Did you read the Gibbs committee's report? They found tremendous inefficiencies, and management completely out of their depth.'

'Nobody understands how medicine has changed and what can be done these days. Take this laparoscopic surgery we're doing tonight. It's the future — much less pain and discomfort for patients, faster operations and shorter patient stay so the equipment pays for itself very quickly. But the public hospital managers don't even know about it. Why is that?'

Cassidy continued to assist. 'They haven't asked the doctors?'

'Exactly. They never ask the people who know what's needed.'

'Interesting you should say that,' said Cassidy. 'I've been thinking—'

'And now they're heading off into this privatisation idea without any analysis of whether, or how, it could deliver better health care. It's unknown territory, with people's health at stake. Sure, the current system's got big problems, but it needs gradual application of common sense rather than ripping it all to bits then working out how to put it back together again. And who's given the ethical approval?'

'I want to get involved in management,' Cassidy blurted.

'Good God.' Jackson stared at him. 'What do you mean, "get involved"?'

Cassidy explained his idea.

Jackson listened with a frown, then sat thinking for a moment. 'No, that's crazy. Terrible timing. You've got exams soon, and what about the Cleveland Clinic? They're expecting you next July, and they might not have any vacancies in 1994.'

'I'd have to take a chance on that. Mr Jackson, I'm very grateful to you for putting me in touch with your colleague there, and it's an honour to be offered a fellowship. But I need a break. I'm exhausted, and I'm not sure that my surgery is safe any more.'

'Yes, they told me in the clinic about your outburst in theatre.' Jackson leaned forward. 'Snap out of it, Steve. Of course it's tough when you're coming up to exams, but we've all been through it. Take some leave if you want to, but then pull yourself together, knuckle down, and get on with it. That's my advice.'

This manly empathy only made Cassidy more certain that he was right. 'Sorry, it's not that simple. I'm scared I'll make a serious mistake, and it's getting worse. I can't sleep, I can't study, and I can hardly be bothered teaching the students. It's bad for everybody.'

'And it's serious enough to make you put everything on hold for a year?'

Cassidy nodded. 'But it's not just that. I think I could make a real difference to these stupid mismanagement things that we talk about so often.'

'Sleep on it,' said Jackson, standing up as a nurse came to tell them the next patient was ready. 'It sounds like an over-reaction to me, but if you're set on it I suppose I can talk to the Cleveland people. Let me know tomorrow.'

....

For the first time since Zoe had left, Cassidy found himself singing along with Paxton Gold FM as he drove to work the next morning. Last night he had enjoyed his best night's sleep in weeks, and today the world seemed a much better place.

The more he thought about his new plan the better it felt. He didn't doubt that he would eventually have a career in surgery, but it was unacceptable that he could be putting patients at risk. He really did need a good break and a chance to re-set his priorities. And fixing silly organisational obstacles around the hospital would be an exciting bonus.

And . . . Zoe. His smile faded as that horrible afternoon came back in vivid detail for the thousandth time. Her anger and her despair. And her words — 'I love you, Steve, but I can't take this any more. Let's call it a day, OK?' The slam of the kitchen door behind her.

After a stunned moment at the table, he had gone out to see her carrying an armful of clothes to her car. 'Zo, please don't do this. Can't we talk about it?'

She'd shouted, 'We *have* talked about it, Steve! We've talked about nothing else for weeks, and I can't get through to you any more. So I'm giving up. I'm going to get my life back.'

And then — his knuckles whitened on the steering wheel and he started humming loudly to drive the memory away — he had actually stood in her path with his arms stretched wide to stop her. The contempt on her face had shoved him aside, and as he watched numbly from the veranda she had loaded up her belongings and driven away.

They had not spoken since that nightmare and he didn't know if he would ever be able to win her back, but he was certain there would never be anyone else for him. And his chances of fixing things up would be a whole lot better if they were in the same city, rather than thousands of kilometres apart, wouldn't they?

Of course they would. But he did not start singing again.

Ward 18 brought him back to business as usual, and with Helen he went round the patients, checking surgical wounds, reviewing test results, and updating case notes.

The appendicectomy patients from the night before last were doing well. Mrs Griffiths had gone home yesterday afternoon, leaving a box of chocolates in the ward office, but Mr Hodder dozed on in the acute bed which could have been better used by somebody else.

They spent a sad and difficult time with Mr Lodge and his wife, explaining the situation and trying to give them some hope of a miracle cure from chemotherapy.

'Did you talk to Mr Jackson about your idea?' said Helen as they returned from their circuit of the outliers.

'Yes. He'll give me the go-ahead if I still want to go through with it today. And he'll talk to the people in Cleveland.'

'That's generous of him, isn't it? It'll be hard to find somebody to replace you.'

Cassidy frowned. Then as Helen got started on the never-ending paperwork, he went to the charge nurse's office to consult his old friend and mentor Sister MacKelvie.

Sister Mac, one of the pillars of the surgical service, had become a ward sister when Jackson was still a long-haired registrar in corduroy trousers. Her clinical instincts were legendary and over more than three decades junior doctors had learnt to listen when she said she was worried about a patient.

'I'm exhausted and I'm thinking of taking a year off and doing something that doesn't involve pain and tragedy,' Cassidy told her. 'But I don't want to let people down.'

Sister Mac had seen registrars come and go, but she'd always had a soft spot for Cassidy. 'Stephen, put that idea out of your head. If there's something that you feel you really must do, then you should follow your instinct. Nobody's indispensable, especially in a place this size. Of course we'd miss you, but we'd cope.'

He pulled the advertisement from his pocket. 'What do you think about this?'

She read it in silence and gave it back to him.

'At least you didn't fall off your chair laughing,' said Cassidy. 'I think it would be interesting, don't you? I might be able to do some good in a general way, as well as getting eight hours' sleep every night. And I would stay in Paxton.'

'What does Zoe think?'

'I haven't seen Zoe for a while. She got sick of listening to me complaining all the time, and she's left me.'

Sister Mac frowned. 'Oh Steve, I'm sorry to hear that. Zoe was one of the best staff nurses I ever had, and she's a real sweetie. You two were made for each other.'

'I know,' said Cassidy sadly. 'But I hope that if I'm around more we can patch things up.'

'Do you know anything about hospital management?'

'No, but it can't be very difficult, surely. And my common sense and inside knowledge would be really useful to them, don't you think?'

'Rather you than me,' said Sister Mac. 'But if it's what you want, that's all that matters.'

'You're almost there,' said Geoff. 'You only need a bit more study, then get through the quiz and you can tell them where to stick their seventy hours a week.'

Cassidy shook his head. 'No, I've got to have a break. You saw me the other night. The department of surgery will hold my job for up to twelve months if I do go.'

'Wow, you've moved fast, haven't you? So, a year off, you lucky bastard. What's the plan? I'd start with a couple of months of surfing in Bali, then on to Europe for a damn good holiday. But what'll you do after that?'

'I want to get a job in hospital management. They're—'

Conversation stopped as Geoff inhaled then sneezed a mouthful of the Pig and Whistle's Special Dark Ale, and there was further delay while Cassidy slapped him on the back, then wiped the table and chairs with a cloth from the bar.

Geoff wiped his streaming eyes. 'Hospital management? You?' He started laughing and coughed again. 'Sorry, it's not that funny I suppose.'

'I'm glad you enjoyed it. But why is it funny at all?'

'Do you read the stuff in the paper about the health reforms?' Geoff was an avid *Bugle* reader.

'Not really.'

'What about TV? You watch the news.'

Cassidy sighed. 'Yeah, but I often fall asleep these days.'

'Ever heard of the Green and White Paper?'

'I've heard of it,' said Cassidy. 'Come on, Geoff, we're not all political junkies like you. If I get a job I can learn all that.'

'I suppose so. Well, I don't want to spoil a nice evening with politics, but I think it's going to be tough in the next year or two. They're planning big changes to make everything efficient and fair and cost-effective, meaning cheap. Cuts everywhere, and people are worried about the effects on patient care. You must have heard about that, at least.'

Cassidy sipped his beer. 'Sure, but people always moan in health. There's never enough money, never enough staff, research grants, car parks, whatever. What's new?'

'Pretty much everything, this time.' Geoff paused. 'But on second thoughts . . . '

'What?'

'I just thought, you're completely ignorant about the health reforms because you've been head-down, bum-up for so long, but maybe that's a good thing because you'll see it all with fresh eyes. And you *might* be able to introduce some common sense into the system, although it'll be a challenge.' Then he laughed. 'But why would they take you on? They want to take control *away* from doctors and nurses — you won't even get an interview. Want another beer?'

....

The smell of new carpet greeted Cassidy as he stepped out of the lift at the top floor of the Paxton Area Health Board administration building. Behind a gleaming white desk sat a smiling blonde receptionist whose blue jacket and white blouse looked as new as everything else.

'Stephen Cassidy, here for an interview at 2:30. I'm applying for the position of key player, and hoping for a chance to showcase my capabilities free of historical external constraints.'

'Doctor Cassidy, welcome,' said a rich, booming voice. Cassidy turned to see a smiling man with perfect teeth and a luxuriant moustache.

'Gerald Turnbull's my name, Quality Management is my game!' He shook hands firmly while gripping Cassidy's shoulder with his other hand. 'Heading up Liaison and Contracting. Welcome to the soon-to-be Paxton Crown Health Enterprise. Come through and meet some people.'

They went into a large room, where two men sat behind a long mahogany table.

'Stephen Cassidy, this is Alex King, our deputy CEO.' A burly bald man with a flat face and hard, beady eyes nodded without speaking while subjecting Cassidy's hand to a vice-like grip.

'Harold Prattley. Harold heads up Finance.' Prattley had bushy silver hair and a jowly face. His nose was large, lumpy and red: rhinophyma, noted clinical Cassidy. There was an operation for that.

In the far corner sat another large man wearing a black suit and dark glasses. 'That's Mr Diamond,' said Turnbull. 'He'll be observing today. He's from the CHEEU, the Crown Health Enterprise Establishment Unit.'

'I see.' Cassidy waved at Diamond, who nodded slightly.

Everyone sat down, and Prattley started. 'Stephen. Tell us why this job appeals to you.' He sat back and gazed at Cassidy over steepled fingers.

'It was the advertisement,' Cassidy said. 'Put your stamp on the future, all that.'

'I see. You're familiar with the Green and White Paper?'

'I've heard about it, of course, but I haven't gone into it in depth as yet.'

'What about the Gibbs report?'

'Same thing. I've heard of it.'

'Can you explain the National Interim Provider Board's role in the reforms?'

'Gentlemen,' said Cassidy. 'I have enthusiasm, medical experience, and a first-class mind. You want someone with the capacity to inspire and enthuse, and these are things that I can do. I expect to pick up the details as I go along.'

'Why are you here, Doctor Cassidy?' King made no effort to hide his feelings about this waste of his time. 'Why aren't you at work in the hospital, doing what you've been trained to do?'

It dawned on Cassidy that telling these people that management lacked common sense might seem rude. But he had not rehearsed any alternatives, and now here he was with a whirring sound inside his head, and a large, lizard-like man staring at him with open hostility. His armpits prickled.

'I think hospital management could benefit from my perspective as a clinician. I can see many ways to make the hospital work better, and a job in management would make it easier for me to bring in improvements.' He told them about the uncooperative diathermy machine and the problems with bed allocations.

King leafed through Cassidy's curriculum vitae as if it was last month's TV guide. 'What do you think is the role of a doctor in a hospital?'

'Oh, diagnosing and treating patients, getting them better, I suppose, ha ha!' said Cassidy. No-one smiled. 'Um, yes, well, they do lots of other things too. Teaching, research, audit and so on. Lots of doctors do some administration — running departments, maintaining standards, and deciding about new treatment programmes and equipment purchases.' Good save, Steve. He felt his confidence rising.

'That's about to change,' said King. 'We're going to take over the non-clinical work and put health onto a business footing.'

'It'll support doctors into increased core-role productivity,' smiled Turnbull, 'passing the business side to people with more appropriate skill sets.'

'More managers, you mean?'

'Absolutely,' said Prattley. 'The days of doctors running the health system, whether as amateurs or exploiters, are almost over. On One July we commence a completely new model.'

'Yes,' beamed Turnbull. 'Health provision is going to become a business process. A whole new era of client-orientated service with transparency and accountability will deliver unprecedented efficiencies to the public health sector, extracting strong fiscal upside, and rewarding excellence in performance.' He leaned forward, his eyes gleaming. 'Steve, helicopter above your micro issues and see the bigger picture. Once we get the ducks in a row it's going to be sensational. And you can be part of that, if you want to.'

'It sounds terrific,' said Cassidy. 'But what would I actually be doing?'

Prattley nodded. 'Let me explain. The momentum is building but there are headwinds, and this is where you might fit in. You see, there are groups of people who are used to having their own way, calling the shots and being kow-towed to. We know we're creating something leading-edge and in many aspects unique. The fragments we've shared today are just the beginning. But these others just want to block the reforms and deny the people of New Zealand access to the health care they're entitled to! It's hard to believe, but it's true. Who am I talking about here?'

Cassidy frowned. 'Opposition politicians?'

Turnbull raised his eyebrows. King shook his head and frowned.

Prattley blinked, then forced out a chuckle. 'No, it's health care professionals — the nurses and, especially, the doctors — they're opposing changes that could unlock as much as *six hundred and one million dollars a year*. They need help to overcome their preconceived notions and understand how the system has to change, and how we can support them to work smarter, not harder, to meet the new goals.'

'And that's where you would come in,' added Turnbull. 'You're one of them, but you'd also be one of us, the link-man, handling perceptions and explaining real-world concepts to them in their language. This is a very key role, Steve. Do you have any other questions for us?'

'I don't think so,' said Cassidy.

Turnbull smiled. 'So. Thoughts? Does our scenario resonate with your agenda?'

'It does,' said Cassidy. 'I'm certainly interested.'

Turnbull nodded and smiled again. 'Perhaps you could wait outside for a moment? Thank you.'

Cassidy let himself out and wandered over to talk to the receptionist. 'I'm sorry, I don't know your name.'

'It's Dawn,' she smiled.

'How long have you worked here, Dawn?'

'This is my second week. Before that I was a receptionist at the Paxton Grand.'

'How's the new job?' said Cassidy.

'It's much better than working all hours being nice to grouchy tourists, and I like being part of something new. Mr Turnbull told us about it last week. We're building something big — the whole world's watching, he said.'

'That big, eh?'

'Yes. He said the system is bleeding money because the doctors are used to having it all their own — whoops, I'm sorry, Doctor.'

Cassidy shook his head with a smile. 'I expect some of that. And it's Steve, by the way. But I probably won't get the job, I hardly covered myself in glory in there.'

'Don't worry, they're appointing new people every day,' she said encouragingly. 'Oh, there I go again, that sounds rude too.'

But Cassidy wasn't listening. 'How many key players do they need, though? And who are these highly opinionated stake-holders? It sounds like surgeons arguing about the All Blacks at a barbecue, ha ha! But I'd better let you get on with your work.'

He went over to the window and its view of the Botanical Gardens, his smile fading. What had he been thinking? He should have at least read the Green and White Paper. If he was unsuccessful, he would relive this moment in nightmares for weeks.

But he wanted this job. What improvements could you make with Paxton's share of six hundred and one million dollars? And the idea of a bigger picture role was exciting too — he hadn't expected that. This was a real opportunity.

Turnbull opened the door and invited him back in.

'Doctor Cassidy,' said Prattley when they were sitting again, 'we would like to offer you the post of medical adviser (contracts) and staff liaison leader, subject to negotiation of a satisfactory package, with the possibility of other responsibilities in the future. Are you prepared to respond to this offer at this time?'

....

'You'll never last,' said Geoff, poking at the lumpy stir-fry on the stove. 'You'll be an alien — they talk a language that you won't understand, and they won't understand you. You'll come running back as soon as the thrill of working business hours has worn off and you realise what loonies they all are. I give you a month.' He went to the fridge. 'What else should I put in, do you think?'

Cassidy sipped his beer. 'I've signed up for a year. The Cassidys don't go back on their word, you know. We're renowned for our integrity and constancy.'

'Your bloody-mindedness and lack of imagination, more like. Three months, maximum. What are these — oh no, they've gone a bit furry.'

'You're wrong, Geoff,' said Cassidy. 'This is not some mad spur of the moment thing. I've committed to it and it's going to happen. I think I might be able to make some difference round here, but it won't happen overnight. Twelve months and then we'll see.'

'Bollocks.'

'Want to bet on it?'

Geoff laughed. 'Sure. A chocolate fish says you won't last twelve months.'

'Done.' They shook hands.

CHAPTER TWO

His new office contained two desks. One was reserved by the only personal item, a small framed photograph of an impatient-looking middle-aged man with silver hair and moustache.

Cassidy sat down at the other desk and switched on the computer, which demanded a password. He was wondering who to ask, when Turnbull put his head round the door.

'Morning Steve, welcome to the new job. Come for a quick tour of the building, and meet the CEO.'

There was another man in the corridor. 'Steve, this is—'

'Jim Bennett. We'll be sharing the office for now.' Bennett only came up to Cassidy's chin but he seemed to fill the corridor. His tight dark suit emphasised powerful shoulders, and he had black hair trimmed very short on a head like a cannonball.

'Is it your first day too, Jim?' asked Cassidy as they followed Turnbull into the lift.

'Correct. I'm heading up the surgical cluster. You?'

'Staff liaison and contract negotiation.'

'Two key players in a powerful team,' smiled Turnbull, pressing the top button.

'OK, the seventh floor, you've been here already of course. Hello

Dawn, could I have a copy of the Green and White Paper, please? Thanks.' He handed over a large paperback, its cover split vertically into green and white halves. 'Read this carefully, Steve. It's why we're here.'

'*Your Health and the Public Health*', read Cassidy. 'Why is it green and white?'

'A green paper is a government publication for discussion,' said Turnbull. 'A white paper tells you what decisions have been made.'

'Right. So green means grey areas and white means a blueprint.' Cassidy leafed through the pages. 'Are the different bits colour coded for junior readers?'

'Ha ha, very good, Steve. Alright, the boardroom, where you interviewed, is the venue for the Management Group meetings. The offices of the CEO-designate and Board Chair-designate are on this floor too. Dawn, is Mr Nesbit free?'

'Not at the moment, Mr Turnbull, sorry, but he has a window at 9:30.'

'Perfect, we'll come back then.'

They went down the stairs to the sixth floor, where large offices opened off a central atrium.

'These are senior management offices. Mine's over there, if you have any problems that you think I might be able to impact.'

'This one's empty.' Bennett had gone searching.

'Today it is,' said Turnbull. 'But we're recruiting so actively, there'll probably be someone in there tomorrow.'

The fifth floor. 'This is the breakout area at this point in time. The canteen is here, and some meeting rooms.

'Fourth floor: Contracts section. Our lawyers and some analysts are based here.' Turnbull opened a door onto a large open-plan office, smelling of coffee and filled with serious men and women working at desks or in murmuring groups around tables. Nobody noticed the visitors.

Turnbull closed the door softly. 'They're crystal-balling the funder-provider interface. So much to do, so little time.'

Most of the third floor was public relations, a single large space with benches at the edges and a central area with abstract sculptures and a small basketball hoop. Casually-dressed young men and women shouted out words as they lounged on bean bags or threw balls at the hoop, while a small older man stood with marker pen poised in front of the whiteboard. They were listing words that rhymed with 'health', and so far they had 'stealth' and 'wealth'. 'Elf' and 'shelf' had been crossed out.

'Fascinating, the creative process,' said Turnbull. 'I could watch it for hours.'

'How does this fit the big picture?' Cassidy asked.

Turnbull smiled kindly. 'It *is* the big picture, Steve. This is Paxton Health rebranding for the journey to market dominance. But not just fiscally — we need positive public perception, and that's what these people are about. That's the PR team lead, Ricky Russell, with the pen.'

'But who's paying for it? All those lawyers upstairs, and people like this. How can the country afford them?'

'The development costs are coming out of Paxton Health's budget. But don't worry, compared to the savings that we'll soon be realising, this is peanuts.'

They went into a meeting room, empty apart from chairs and a table still wrapped in plastic, but with big maps of New Zealand and the world on the walls. 'This is highly sensitive commercially,' Turnbull whispered. 'After One July it will be our strategic planning room for long-distance contracts, nationally and beyond.'

It made sense, thought Cassidy as they went down to the next floor. If you had the staff and you'd dealt with your local waiting lists, you could get work from elsewhere to bring in more cash. And international contracts? Why not, when you thought about it? He was in a different world, but an exciting one.

'Now, the second floor, this is of course your area, gentlemen, and also where the offshore people work out of.'

'Offshore?' said Cassidy with a frown. 'Are we drilling for oil?'

'Offshore means overseas, Steve,' Turnbull explained after Bennett's surprised snort. 'The new health business model is underpinned by offshore insights and it'll give us an edge to have on-site consultants in the early stages. It's expensive but it's worth every cent.'

They came to a door with *Hamilton Sheppard* on it in brass letters, but it was locked. 'Hamilton Sheppard,' said Turnbull reverently. 'They work with health maintenance organisations all over the States. And we're consulting with a number of other American experts as well.'

'Aren't there New Zealanders who can do the job?' said Cassidy.

'No. The conceptual platform is cutting-edge for New Zealand, so we have had to draw on the skills of offshore consultants.'

'Not for long,' Bennett added. 'Soon *we'll* be the consultants teaching the world how to make public health care work profitably.'

Turnbull smiled and nodded. 'That's exactly right. Now the first floor, formerly the ground floor, just has support services and the audit and accounting staff. We'll give them a miss today, and meet up again at 9:30, OK?'

'I need some stationery,' said Bennett as soon as Turnbull had gone. He went along the corridor and opened a large cupboard filled with office supplies. 'Help yourself,' he said, starting to grab one or two of everything that was there.

'How did you know this was here?' Cassidy chose a yellow A4 pad. He already had a pen.

'Every business has cupboards like this. I'll need a printer too, I'll get onto Supply.'

....

'I get the feeling you haven't worked in the real world before,' said Bennett, sorting his new belongings into drawers. 'Some sort of academic, are you?'

'In a way. I'm—'

'Yeah, thought so. Picked it a mile off, no offence. Not like me — self-made man I am, or I will be by the time I've finished.' Bennett nodded seriously. 'I held an executive position in the enclosure business, making outers for food and drink mostly. Chambers Limited, you've heard of them. But I said to myself one day, "Jim, you're climbing the ladder, you're doing OK. Might even get a seat on the board if you play your cards right. But long term, where's the future in cardboard boxes? Where's the upside going forward?"'

'You could feel trapped in cardboard boxes,' said Cassidy.

'Exactly. So I checked out the options. And bingo, the health sector! Annual budget nearly four billion, huge potential economies identified, and major opportunities for the right players once those economies start coming on-line.' He put his in-trays on the desk beside the photograph.

'And you really think there'll be lots of money saved?'

'Hell yes. These places are a joke — run Chambers the way they run the public hospitals today and you'd all be out of a job in three months.' Bennett paused to experiment with the tilt of his backrest. 'We know that if you managed all the hospitals in New Zealand as efficiently as the best ones, there'd be annual savings nationally of *at least* four hundred and fifty-one million dollars.'

Cassidy nodded. 'So I heard. Who did the research?'

'Arthur Andersen. Economic consultants out of Chicago. And that's minimum — it could be six hundred and one million if we do it right.'

'But do you really think that's possible? The hospital budget for the whole country is about two billion dollars a year. Do they think a quarter of the hospital budget can be saved?'

'Yup,' said Bennett. 'Arthur Andersen are world experts and if that's what they think, then it's what we think too. And anyone helping the Crown to claw back that much coin will be in line for some nice personal incentives, won't they?' He leered at Cassidy. 'It won't be easy though, the quacks have run the show for so long. Arrogant shits, screwing the system for everything they can get — I can't wait to tell them how things are going to be after One July. We'll make them accountable to a proper budget, for the first time ever. And then the squealing will start.'

'So doctors are screwing the system? All of them, do you mean?'

'I suppose there might be the odd one who doesn't have his snout in the trough,' Bennett conceded. 'Not many though, from what I've heard.'

'How can you say that? It's absolute rubbish.' Cassidy felt his face flushing.

Bennett shook his head. 'It's common knowledge. They're all up themselves because they know so much. And even the ones that aren't making a fortune in private practice have way too much control over how public cash is spent. But not for much longer, I promise you that. It'll happen very fast once we start putting the changes in place.'

·····················

Paxton Health's new Chief Executive Officer was an athletic-looking man in his late forties, wearing a pink shirt with a white collar, and a shiny tie that matched his gold cufflinks.

'Richard Nesbit. Look, it's *fabulous* to meet you, we have such big plans for you both. Let's talk.' He leaned over to the intercom on his large, cluttered desk and asked Dawn to bring coffee.

They sat down in brown leather chairs around a glass coffee table. 'So, Steve, how much do you know about the organisation of our health system?'

Cassidy felt Nesbit's attention on him like a sunlamp. 'I don't know much about the management side. But I do know how it works, or doesn't work, for the staff and patients. There's certainly room for improvement there.'

Nesbit laughed. 'I think it's fair to say that if we thought there was only "room for improvement" we wouldn't be here. We'd still be chasing a buck in the commercial sector, wouldn't we Gerald?' He leaned towards Cassidy. 'But we're going much further. We're putting in place the most radical transformation ever, of any country's health system.

'It's long overdue and desperately needed, everyone knows that. But it took Simon Upton and his colleagues to start forcing the changes that will make the system deliver. The challenges are big, but they are matched by the potential rewards. And when we succeed, the changes we have set in motion will be copied around the world.'

He moved to the edge of his seat, his eyes gleaming. 'Today the area health boards are pressured by politicians from above and by the public from below via the media, and they run around putting oil on whatever wheel squeaks loudest. Any problem that's bad enough, they just throw money at it, but nobody even tries to see whether or not that money has been well spent. It's a mess, frankly — runaway expenditure, waiting lists out of control, demoralised staff. The taxpayers aren't getting the quality health system that they've paid for, and they are disappointed and angry.'

Turnbull nodded gravely, and Bennett did too.

'But we'll bring *accountability*. People will be expected to take responsibility, meaning they know how much a service costs, and what they're achieving for the client, the service provider, the purchaser and the Crown. For the first time those parameters will be transparent.

'And the — oh, thanks Dawn.' Dawn put down a tray with chocolate biscuits and a steaming coffee plunger. Nesbit grabbed a biscuit and chewed rapidly. 'The other essential innovation is to split the providers off from the funders, and make a market. You see, at the moment the area health boards allocate funding *and* provide the services. They're buying from themselves, and that creates all sorts of problems.'

Cassidy nodded and hoped he was looking intelligent.

'But soon,' Nesbit continued, 'funding bodies will have the money, and they will choose the best provider from among competing bidders.'

'It's a standard business model,' said Turnbull. 'Watertight contracts, sanctions for those who fall short, and an expectation that elite providers will survive—'

'And prosper, Gerald,' Nesbit mumbled, wiping his fingers on a serviette.

'—and prosper, at the expense of weaker competitors.' Turnbull pushed the plunger and started pouring.

'Black, thanks,' said Nesbit. 'Great!' He sat back and sipped his coffee. 'And as the successful businesses thrive and innovate, we'll see the emergence of a health care industry that actually meets the public's needs — a win-win situation.'

'But setting it up to run properly will be a huge task,' said Cassidy. 'The contracts will be incredibly complex to write and monitor.'

Nesbit shrugged. 'Our leaders have diagrammed the vision, and the rest is detail. We're building an outstanding team of professionals with real-world experience and the right skill set such as yourself, Jim — hell, you can do this stuff in your sleep.'

Bennett nodded, with a smug little smile at Cassidy.

'The only box left unticked,' Nesbit continued, 'is bringing the professional resource on board. A few doctors have put their hands up for more autonomy and more transparency, but we want *everyone* resonating with us as we journey into the new era. You're tasked with facilitating that process, Steve, and your background will be key.'

'I'll do my best,' said Cassidy, feeling Bennett's stare.

'I know you will. Look, it's time to finish but it's been great to meet the pair of you and I know you're going to be an integral part of our success. Steve, could I borrow you for a moment?'

Turnbull and Bennett left, and Nesbit turned to Cassidy. 'Thanks for staying back, I wanted to touch base concerning your position in the company.' They stood facing each other.

'Confidentially, I've gone out on a limb to get you,' said Nesbit. 'There's been opposition — some people don't like the idea of somebody from the old power structure having access to management deliberations. But I stood my ground.

'In all my businesses I've always made sure there's at least one outsider forcing us to confront issues we'd rather avoid, and over the years they've been such a positive influence. So I want you to ask the tough questions, and keep asking them. It won't always be easy, but I'll have your back, and you can get in touch with me at any time.' Nesbit stared into Cassidy's eyes as if gauging the strength of his soul. 'Are you up for this, Steve?'

Cassidy's vague doubts about the funder-provider split were forgotten in his excitement that this charismatic man would have such faith in him. 'I certainly am.'

They shook hands.

....

'You're a doctor, aren't you?' said Bennett as soon as Cassidy returned to the office.

'Yes, Jim. I cannot tell a lie.'

'That's a mistake. We have to forcefully impose control on the vested interests, and you'll get in the way.'

'The organisation needs my perspective,' said Cassidy. 'I've got lots of ideas and I certainly want to get to win-win.'

'It's not what Sir Roger would do. But never mind, I've had my say.'

'What would Sir Roger do?'

For a moment Bennett tried to maintain silence, but the pressure inside his head was too great. 'He wouldn't give a shit about win-win. He never pandered to the opposition — he would ram the changes through as fast as possible, then wait for the vested interests to catch up. They always join in once they finally see the benefits to themselves.'

'Interesting idea.' Cassidy picked up the photograph from Bennett's desk. 'This is him, isn't it? Sir Roger Douglas. But he's not even in this Government.'

'Of course not. But he started it all, based on the pioneering work of Friedrich von Hayek — somebody you haven't even heard of.'

Cassidy shook his head. 'I've heard of Rogernomics, though. Not exactly a roaring success, was it? And he wanted a flat tax rate, but he lost his job before he could ram that one through.'

'He has lots of brilliant ideas,' said Bennett stiffly. 'He was ahead of his time back then, but now people realise how right he is.'

'Really? People I know think he's completely wrong and downright dangerous,' said Cassidy, remembering his father's furious monologues. 'But I don't follow politics all that closely,' he added as Bennett snatched the photo back. 'Anyway Jim, I hope we can still work together now you know my terrible secret. No? OK, I'll get on with some reading now.'

Bennett polished the glass with his sleeve before putting the photo back on the desk. Then he went out, slamming the door behind him.

Cassidy shrugged, winked at Sir Roger, and sat down to learn about his new job.

....

He had expected to find the Green and White Paper difficult to understand, but its description of the problems was clear enough.

Financially, New Zealand's public health system was a bottomless pit. Between 1980 and 1991 the Department of Health's budget had risen faster than the increase in consumer prices by a staggering twenty-seven per cent.

Despite gobbling this extra cash, the system remained in crisis. Standards of care were uneven across the country. Waiting lists were growing everywhere, but more in some places than others, and there were many stories of personal tragedy caused by the system. Meanwhile buildings and equipment were decaying because there was not enough money for maintenance.

The area health boards were responsible to the electors but as they did not raise the money, they could always blame the Government for not giving them enough. Politicisation of the system made it almost impossible for boards to innovate.

The Government was paying for it all but could never find out where the money was going because boards kept minimal financial records. But they did know that the hospital system kept taking increasing amounts of the overall health budget, at the expense of preventive services and general practice.

As a system supposed to deliver health services to all people fairly and equitably, it was an expensive failure with no obvious way to make things better short of radical change.

Cassidy closed the book and stared at its two-coloured cover. This was awful. He'd had no idea that things were so bad — a cost blowout of twenty-seven per cent was clearly intolerable. Or had he mis-read it? No, there it was in black and white.

That was enough for now, he decided. He could wait for an hour to see how it was all going to turn out, and he had to buy something for lunch anyway. It wouldn't do any harm to go over to the hospital and see who was around.

He went downstairs and out onto Seddon Street. Alongside the administration block Paxton Hospital dominated the skyline, its grey concrete walls extending to the distant traffic lights. High above him flags of steam from the boiler vents floated into the sunshine as a rescue helicopter came in towards the helipad on the roof of the surgical block.

It all looked just as solid and purposeful as it always did, but now he saw it through the Government's perspective: this hideously expensive, badly run, *failing* thing.

But he was going to help with that.

....

The main hospital corridor was as always filled by a cross-section of the human race, subgroup hospital occupants: patients, visitors and staff of all kinds. Orderlies pushing patients in beds with nurses walking alongside, an ECG technician with her trolley, a young man on crutches backing through the swing doors of the fracture clinic. In the distance a flock of white coats crossed the corridor between wards, hurrying to complete the morning ward round.

Cassidy strolled along, appreciating them all: ground level, everyone serious and busy. Most of them had never even heard of the Green and White Paper.

'Steve.' It was Allan O'Connell, Cassidy's anaesthetist friend, clutching his lunch of meat pie and chocolate milk. 'Did you hear my news? I'm leaving, I've got a job in Saudi.'

'Hi Allan. What on earth for? There's nothing in Saudi but sand, and you have to live in a compound — if you might want an occasional drink, that is. And that's all there is to do anyway, I heard.'

O'Connell smiled and shook his head. 'There's interesting work there. More responsibility, great facilities, and a lot more money than I can make here. No politics, no budget cuts. You should come too, before all the jobs get snapped up — it might help your stress levels.'

'Thanks,' said Cassidy, 'but I've just changed jobs here, it's very exciting.'

'So I heard. I don't get it — you know it's all nonsense, don't you? How can a big public hospital, taking everybody that comes through the door and teaching as well, get anywhere near to making a profit? It's so bizarre, there has to be something else going on that they're not telling us. A hidden agenda, as they say. So stuff it, I'll miss this place and most of the people here, but I've had enough of all the bullshit.'

'Allan, you don't understand. We can save—'

'Forget it, Steve. I've got to go, I'll see you around some time. Good luck with the new job.'

Cassidy leaned against the wall, gazing thoughtfully down the corridor. It was sad that New Zealand was losing Allan. Perhaps he'd be back after a few years —

He forgot about Allan and stood up straight as he caught sight of Zoe walking towards him. Zoe Sorensen, the love of his life, the woman he wanted to marry.

She was talking to her friend Sarah, giving Cassidy a chance to stare. The dark honey hair was in a new, shorter style that really suited her. He ran a hand through his own hair.

Sarah saw him and nudged Zoe. She looked up sharply, then came across to him. Her slim figure was disguised by the deliberately neutral nurses' uniform, but her face, those mesmerising brown eyes . . . Cassidy swallowed.

'Hello Steve.' Her voice and her half-smile were cautious, controlled.

'Hi Zo — love the new hairstyle, it really suits you,' babbled Cassidy. 'Have you got time for a bite of lunch?'

'No, I'm going to a meeting then straight back to the ward. We're short-staffed.'

'What about dinner tonight then? We could go to Scarlatti's, for old times' sake.'

She paused. 'Alright. But it'll just be dinner, it won't mean anything.'

'Of course,' said Cassidy, struggling to keep his tone friendly. Things must be very bad if she felt she had to say that. 'You're sure? I'm not forcing you — good. But I don't know where you're living now.'

'I'm back at Pitman Street,' she said in the same neutral tone. 'My old flat.'

'Right. I'll pick you up at seven, OK?'

He couldn't stop smiling as he joined the queue at the hospital café and bought a filled roll. Clearly there was a lot of work to be done, but she hadn't just told him to get lost. And she had come past within minutes of his arrival in the hospital — that had to mean something, didn't it? Thank you, whoever was in charge of these things.

Scarlatti's, here we come!

....

The solutions to the problems were more difficult to follow.

He understood that the area health boards had money difficulties. But why not help them find out what everything really cost, then allow them to keep their savings and re-use them? Yet that was nothing like the proposed solution, presumably because of the need for the funder-provider split. But it was going to add an extra layer of bureaucracy that would have to be paid for somehow.

Cassidy sighed. There were some things that you just had to accept you would never understand, and this funder-provider business seemed to be one of them. But if competition freed up half a billion dollars, who would care whether or not Stephen Cassidy understood how it worked? As long as nobody asked him to explain it, anyway. He pushed on.

Government health money would be given to purchasing agencies that would buy care from providers. The biggest purchasers would be the Government's four Regional Health Authorities, or RHAs. But large groups of people could get together and set up their own health-purchasing organisations, called Health Care Plans. They would get money from the Government, then choose providers, and so for the first time consumers would have a choice of health care provider.

The providers, meaning the hospitals, would be run by businesses called Crown Health Enterprises or CHEs. Most CHE board members would be business people appointed by the Government, rather than elected by the voters.

Better providers would win more contracts. And effective health professionals and managers would be given more autonomy, and be recognised and rewarded for delivering better health care — hence Bennett's excitement about it all, Cassidy realised.

After public consultation a committee would decide what specific health services the Government should buy.

Users of some public hospital services would be charged a small amount from their own pockets.

The new system would be fully operational on One July 1993, less than seven months away.

Cassidy sat back and stared out of the window. It was exciting, but then just about anything would be better than the shambles they had now. And savings of half a billion dollars would buy so many improvements, even after some was lost to management costs.

Yes, he was much better informed now. It was a shame that people like Allan didn't understand the background.

And he wanted Zoe to understand too. Poor Zoe — that flat tone of voice was so unlike the lively, challenging woman that he knew. God, she was lovely. Those eyes, those bones, the sophisticated new hairstyle — she wouldn't be by herself for long unless she wanted to be. What a fool he'd been.

But perhaps there was somebody else already, and she was going to tell him that tonight. At Scarlatti's, where they'd shared so many happy times. Perhaps—

A knock on the door: Gerald Turnbull, bearing gifts. 'I thought you might be running out of things to read.' He put a booklet entitled *Unshackling the Hospitals* on the desk. 'This is the Gibbs Report, from the Hospitals and Related Services Taskforce. It was published in 1987, but it's still key.'

A small white booklet. 'This is the Health and Disability Services Bill, setting out legal obligations for RHAs and CHEs. Read Section 25 anyway, that's our area.

'Here's the National Interim Provider Board report, which is more philosophical, but worth a glance. And the Danzon report, on the commercial options.' He added two thin A4-size books to the pile. 'How are you going with the Green and White Paper?'

'Just finished,' said Cassidy briskly. 'It all makes sense, except the bit about—'

'Excellent. And we've got more briefings for you and Jim later this week. How are you two getting on?'

'He doesn't like doctors very much.'

Turnbull smiled. 'Pure market men always have strong views about vested interests.' He saw the photo on Bennett's desk. 'Good Lord, is that Roger Douglas? Well, well. Anyway, check the briefing programme with Dawn — we need you up to speed as soon as possible.'

....

Cassidy parked his ancient Jaguar and walked into the driveway of Zoe's flat. The flatmates were sitting on the veranda and his breath caught as Zoe stood up and separated from them in the golden evening sunshine.

She smiled at his stuttered compliments and thanked him as he held the car door open, but they travelled in a wary silence that lasted all the way to the best table at Scarlatti's.

Cassidy watched her as she gazed down at the swans on the lake. It had to be a hopeful sign that she was wearing the gold necklace that he'd given her on their first anniversary. And the elegant black dress, following her curves and showing plenty of warm summer skin — she knew it was one of his favourites. How many times had he helped her take it off?

He frowned as happy memories were driven out by the scene of her departure, and the way he'd behaved.

'Good evening. Would you care to see the wine list, Sir? Sir?'

Cassidy blinked. He chose something and then he and Zoe sat looking at each other.

'Hi, Steve,' she said softly after a moment. 'Thank you for inviting me here.'

'Thank you for accepting the invitation. Zo, I—'

But the wine waiter was back and Cassidy had to approve the label, wait as the cork was pulled, tell the man it was fine thank you, and wait again while their glasses were filled.

Zoe sipped before he could propose a toast. 'Well, is it true what people are saying?'

'I don't know what they're saying. But I've taken a year off from surgery and joined the management team. I'm going to do staff liaison, and I'll be a key player in contract negotiations with the Regional Health Authority.'

She frowned. 'OK. But why have you done this?'

'Several reasons, but mainly because I was burning out. After you left I tried to study in every spare moment, but I couldn't concentrate and I was getting nowhere. I struck a run of crazy on-call nights including some extra shifts because people were away. Everything just compounded and I started to worry that I might be turning into a dangerous surgeon. And then I had a weird episode in theatre one night.'

'Yes, I heard. So you ran away.'

'No,' said Cassidy carefully, 'I stepped back and I'm having a break before I carry on with my career. But it will be an exciting year.'

She raised her eyebrows and waited.

'I can make the hospital run better, and they need somebody like me to show them how to do it. I've put the exams and the fellowship in the States on hold for a year.' He had to pause as a waitress appeared. Zoe ordered linguine, and he followed her. Neither of them had looked at the menu. 'And because of the reforms, I'll be able to influence decisions while it's all still fluid. The timing is perfect.'

'Oh, Steve,' Zoe sighed. 'You're so innocent. It's part of why I — why everybody likes you so much. We're in a desperate state, and every time we think it can't get any worse it does. But now we can all relax because the great Cassidy will make both sides see reason, and everybody will kiss and make up? Is that what you think will happen?'

'Of course not. But do you know how much money is being wasted because nobody knows what's going on? Experts from Chicago say we could save up to six hundred and one million dollars a year. That's an awful lot of money, Zo.'

She raised her eyebrows. 'But if they don't know what is going on, how do they know that we could save six hundred *and one* million dollars?'

While he was frowning at this, she continued, 'And what makes you think that the savings will go back into the health system?'

'Well, I haven't read anything that says it won't.'

'There's that innocence again. But seriously, Steve, I don't want to see you caught in the middle of all this and getting hurt.' She held up her hand as he started to speak. 'I know you very well. You expect to succeed — you always do, don't you? Dux of Paxton Boys' High, cricket captain, the debating team, the golf team . . . and all those prizes at medical school.'

'I remember some pretty impressive sporting trophies in *your* wardrobe.'

'Sure, but I was never anywhere near your level.' Zoe sipped her wine. 'You make it look easy, but I know how hard you work to get what you want. You set your goals, put your head down and go for them — and you reach them, no matter what's in the way. It can make you a pain to be around sometimes.' She paused while he thought about that. 'But is it possible that this thing might be a bit big, even for you?'

'I'm not expecting to fix it all. But I can be a bridge between the two sides.'

'A bridge?' she laughed. 'From what's happened so far, I think you'll be more like one of those old tyres they hang between ships and wharves.'

Their meals arrived and she got started, but Cassidy was too much on edge to eat. 'The potential benefits are *massive*. Imagine half a billion—'

'Listen, let's make a deal. No more talk about all that tonight, OK? You know what I think. But I'm pleased that you're excited, and I suppose it's good that there'll be somebody on the inside trying to limit the damage. I just hope you don't get chewed up and spat out, that's all.'

There was still something Cassidy had to say before he could think about food. 'And Zo, I won't have to leave Paxton for at least a year. I'll be working nine to five, and I'll be free in the evenings.'

'That's nice.' She took another mouthful. 'You can go to woodwork classes.'

'I want to spend more time with you. Show you I can change, I know I can, and win you back.'

Her eyes glowed for a moment, then she sighed and shook her head. 'Maybe you should let go and find somebody else, for both our sakes. Get over this idea that you still own me. You — you did before, but then it got too hard. Remember? I can't risk going through that pain again.'

Cassidy frowned and picked up his fork. 'I don't like who I've been.'

'Steve,' she said gently, 'we'll always be friends. But beyond that, I just don't know.' She put her hand on top of his for a moment. 'If you've really done this huge mad thing even partly to get us back together again, well, I'm extremely flattered. I'm stunned, actually. But it puts a lot of pressure on me, doesn't it?'

He stared at her, afraid to speak in case he said the wrong thing.

'You can't expect me to swoon into your arms the moment *you* decide everything's going to be fine, no matter how magnificent the gesture is. Can you? Steve?'

'I wasn't expecting that,' muttered Cassidy.

'Let's see how it goes for a while,' she said after a silence. 'We can go out together sometimes. But if either of us wants to spend time with somebody else, we should.' She swirled the wine in her glass. 'And between us it will be strictly platonic until you've qualified as a surgeon, alright? I still — have feelings for you, but I won't just go back to where we were, and I need to keep things simple while we make up our minds. Do you agree to that?'

'I do,' he said solemnly, and they both laughed. The tension fell away and they gossiped about friends and the hospital for the rest of the meal, before he drove her home in companionable silence.

As they stood outside her house Zoe asked, 'Have you met someone called Jim Bennett?'

'Yes, we work out of the same office, as we managers say. I would have thought we worked in it, but never mind. Why do you ask?'

'He's going to be the manager of our *cluster*, in the new language they all use. Is he nice?'

'No, he's not,' said Cassidy. 'He's aggressive and rude. For some reason he's all wound up about doctors, and probably nurses as well. So far he hasn't stood on his desk roaring and beating his chest with his fists, but I sense it's only a matter of time.'

Zoe pulled her wrap tighter round her shoulders. 'Well, perhaps it is good that you're there to give some balance.' She stepped back as he moved in for a platonic kiss. 'Good night, Steve, thanks for dinner.'

'My pleasure, Zo, any time. What are you doing on Saturday night? How about going out, maybe to a movie? Or Black Mambo. Or both, if you'd like.'

She hesitated. 'I'll think about that and let you know.'

Not too bad on balance, thought Cassidy as he started the car. Naturally she was cautious, and the formal platonic thing made it seem as if he was taking a lot for granted, which was unfair. But at least she didn't already have a date with somebody else on Saturday night.

Or perhaps she did, and was even now weighing up two offers. He sighed, and drove home thinking about the past and wondering about the future.

CHAPTER THREE

'We're getting up to speed as fast as we can,' said Turnbull next morning. 'We need to hit the ground running on One July with a portfolio of signed RHA contracts. But we're starting from scratch with the business data, because previous management hardly monitored any of the financials.'

Bennett nodded. '"A total lack of proper costing information" they said in the Gibbs report. Unbelievable.' He glared at Cassidy.

'It's been a slack, no-accountability environment,' agreed Turnbull. 'But we'll turn that around, we've put in place a team of analysts to observe and quantify the entire process.' He paused. 'Steve, here's something you can help with — some staff members are refusing to talk to our people, or even supplying deliberate misinformation. That's childish and unhelpful, and it has to stop.'

'They're understaffed and overworked,' said Cassidy. 'They've seen lots of analysis and planning over the past few years, but none of it's made any difference. They're sick of it.'

Bennett popped a knuckle. 'We'll soon flush out the troublemakers.'

'Please do what you can.' Turnbull turned to Bennett. 'Now Jim, please tell Steve how you would deal with a failing business that you've just acquired.'

'Sure,' said Bennett, glancing condescendingly at Cassidy. 'First you examine the accounts to see which lines are profitable, and which are losers. If loss-making lines can be salvaged, you make the changes. If they're hopeless you dump them, lay off surplus staff, and sell the plant.

'You reduce overheads — raw material costs, salaries, consumables — and inventory. That's stuff that's sitting waiting, either to be made into something or sold, Doctor. You cut out the fat. You create monitoring systems and make everyone accountable. Then you start scoping new opportunities.'

'Thanks, Jim,' said Turnbull. 'Steve? Any questions so far?'

'That's how you'd do it for an ordinary business,' said Cassidy. 'But what's it got to do with public hospitals? You can't discontinue a "line" if it involves people, rather than baked beans or something.'

'That's a common mistake,' Turnbull smiled. 'But the notion that a hospital can't be put on a business footing is yesterday's thinking.' He leaned forward. 'This is confidential, Steve, OK? We've created a paradigm that will inform all our planning going forward. Stop titling health service users patients — it clouds the vision. They're either an RGU or an RLU.'

'Not clients?'

'Modern management requires more precision than that. The RHA will be our client going forward. Think RGUs: Revenue Generating Units. That focuses you on the key business aspect, and strips out the emotion.

'For example, take a fit man, fifty years old, who needs a hip replacement. This is *elective* surgery, meaning you choose to do it — oh, of course, you know that. Anyway, he has an X-ray and goes to a specialist assessment clinic, then goes on the waiting list.

'When he's called up off the list, he has a pre-admission visit plus any tests he might need. A week later he comes in and has the procedure. We have operating theatre costs, price of the new hip itself, related consumables, an X-ray to check it's OK, physiotherapy, seven to nine days in hospital with associated overheads, and he leaves. One follow-up clinic appointment a month later.

'Soon we'll know *exactly* how much all that costs, so we can work out how much to charge the RHA to generate revenue for the CHE. Right? That's good business.

'But take an eighty-five-year-old. He's confused, falling over, whatever. He's admitted under a fixed cost contract, elderly care. We put him in a bed and feed him, standard daily overheads, nice and steady. He's still an RGU at this stage. We could even sub-let him to a nursing home.

'But then somebody notices he's got — what's another thing he could have? Dignity?' said Cassidy.

'No, something medical. Let's say a cough. The doctors do tests and decide he needs to have extra money spent on him. Maybe a lot extra. They say, "My patient needs to have this done, I don't care how old he is. The money is not my problem." You lose control of overheads, and your RGU transitions into an RLU. A revenue-*losing* unit. So the game is to pick the units that carry the lowest investment risk, and avoid the rest.'

'I can work with that,' said Bennett.

'Avoid the rest?' Cassidy shook his head. 'Sorry, Gerald, that's all wrong. A publicly-funded hospital deals with everyone, no matter what it costs. But this plan would exclude the people with the most need, especially the elderly. It would be indefensible to deny people care, even if you could separate them out. I mean, how could you possibly pick the good *investments* when they're lying on trolleys in the Emergency Department?'

'We don't know yet,' said Turnbull, 'and that's why you're here. How would you do it?'

'No, no, no. I'm not getting into this. You'll have to think of some other way to run the business.'

Turnbull frowned. 'Listen, Steve. You don't understand the big picture, but you don't have to. You're here to provide medical insights, remember? You need to get used to working on your part of the big plan, and being the best medical adviser you can be. So, how do we separate the winners and the losers at the front door?'

'It would be impossible,' said Cassidy. 'More often than not you're not sure what's wrong before you admit them and work them up, and even then you can't predict how things will go in hospital. Patients can surprise you.'

'Business success comes from minimising surprises. How would you do that? Give us a scenario.'

Cassidy considered the proposition. 'This is crazy. But I suppose if you really wanted to go that way, and somehow ignore all the people needing acute care, in theory you could close the Emergency Department and only take elective surgical patients. Then you'd be like a private hospital. And even they get surprises sometimes, although they often send those patients here.'

'After they've taken their cash,' Bennett added. 'Those guys have got it sorted.'

'But what about the people you've turned away? Who would care for them?'

There was a knock at the door and Richard Nesbit came in. 'Sorry to interrupt, Gerald. Oh, terrific — I'm bringing the new chairman of the Board round to meet some key players, and here are three of you together.'

They stood up as Nesbit ushered in a silver-haired man in his late fifties.

'Hello, everyone. Ross Frankton is my name,' he said in a plummy voice. 'Please, carry on.'

'We were discussing health management paradigms,' said Turnbull after the introductions.

Frankton beamed. 'Excellent.'

'Ross, I particularly wanted you to meet Steve,' said Nesbit. 'He has a medical background and is taking on staff liaison.' He winked at Cassidy.

'Excellent. You'll be the one confronting the lies and misinformation coming from clinicians, and I promise you my full support.'

'Thank you,' said Cassidy. 'I'm looking forward to it. But we can't refuse to treat patients based on age and diagnosis.'

'Steve's just getting up to speed on the new environment,' Turnbull explained after a startled silence. 'We haven't finished our briefing.'

'Fantastic,' said Nesbit. 'Well, we'd better keep moving.' And with more nods and smiles the leaders withdrew.

'I've got another meeting now,' said Turnbull, 'we'll continue this later. Steve, I need you to keep reading and thinking — it's important that you adapt to basic business paradigms, even though you're new to them. Please keep an open mind, and work on dovetailing your ideas in with what we're about here.'

....

It was clear that Cassidy would need to help management with some blind spots about ethics and decency. But he was in the right place to do it, thank goodness.

His excitement about improving the system increased as he read the Gibbs report. This was the raw meat from which the reforms had been cooked, and it had been marinated in righteous wrath.

The system was crippled by years of government and local mismanagement, and by an 'absolutely extraordinary' lack of costing information. The management structure was 'over-centralised, bureaucratic, inflexible, and confused'.

Hospitals were paralysed as proposed innovations were either derailed by vested interests or stifled by the requirements of central bureaucracy. Some doctors were trying to work as managers but were hopelessly conflicted, while others took advantage of the chaos to build personal empires.

Waiting lists existed 'despite the demonstrable fact that there are enough overall resources in the public hospital system to treat all those currently waiting'.

And here on page 13, a little table, just six lines and three columns, showing the Arthur Andersen savings projections. Cassidy felt as if he had arrived in a holy place and was looking at the glowing source of the reforms, tiny but very powerful. But he searched unsuccessfully for details of the methods underlying the conclusions.

'What happened to the Gibbs report when it came out?' he asked Turnbull over coffee.

'Nothing. Roger Douglas commissioned it, but his Labour colleagues didn't support it when it appeared in 1988. It took the vision of the

National Government, after they were elected in 1990, to realise its importance. Gibbs is vital because they commissioned the Arthur Andersen report, with the real data on potential savings.'

'Do you have a copy of the Andersen report?'

'No, we weren't given visibility of that, all we have is what's in Gibbs. But that table of costs and possible savings is key.'

'But where's the detail about which hospitals they studied and how they worked out their numbers? You'd need that to judge the quality of the conclusions.'

Turnbull shrugged. 'It convinced the Gibbs committee, and they're no fools. Arthur Andersen is one of the largest accounting companies in the world.'

After the lubricating rage of Gibbs, the Danzon report was dry and long. As Cassidy finished it, twitching from the extra coffee he'd had to drink, he realised that most of it had gone over his head.

He put Danzon aside and started on the National Interim Provider Board report. This was meant to set out the pathways for implementation, but it was oddly lacking in substance. There was nothing to summarise, although it was reassuring to read that the reforms were 'based on proven principles that work'.

He yawned and stretched. Five o'clock, time to go home — what a great system. But he put all the papers in his briefcase, planning to have another crack at Danzon during the evening.

'These are fascinating,' said Geoff later. He had been studying the reports while Cassidy and Claire, who was Geoff's sister and the other flatmate, watched television. 'It's easy to see the real agenda.'

'What do you mean, the real agenda?' said Cassidy.

Geoff sighed. 'If you'd been paying attention over the last few months, you would have heard lots of people saying it, and it's not about improving health care for the public. All the recommendations are from business people or American experts in health privatisation — the Government got the answers they wanted by choosing who they asked, and discouraging public submissions. They're going to try and sell our public hospitals to private companies.'

Cassidy frowned. 'I didn't pick that up at all.'

'Are you sure, Geoff?' said Claire.

'It's there all right. But they couldn't say it too loudly, could they? Not in New Zealand.'

The temptation to tell them about revenue losing units was almost overwhelming, but Cassidy had been told confidentially and that battle would have to be fought and won in secret. 'But however they do it,' he said slowly, 'if we get a more efficient service and no more waiting lists, that's got to be good, hasn't it? As long as nobody misses out.'

....

In his first week as CEO Nesbit had sent a memo inviting all Paxton staff to send comments and complaints directly to him. But his good intentions soon disappeared under an avalanche of work, and the growing file of incident forms had become an embarrassment. Turnbull solved it by handing all the paperwork to Paxton's new staff liaison person.

Cassidy was dismayed by the number of forms. Complaining took time and effort, and most hospital staff would rather look after patients than spend time on paperwork; these bulging ring binders were a sign of widespread frustration.

He leafed through the most recent entries. Three from the last four weeks featured familiar confident handwriting and were about a broken laundry bag holder, with increasingly furious underlinings and exclamation marks.

Cassidy took them out of the folder and put them to one side, smiling as he pictured Zoe writing them. He had taken her to see *A Few Good Men* last Saturday night, then on to Black Mambo where they'd danced until very late. They both loved dancing and he knew she was having a great time, but at the end of the evening she had bid him a chaste good night and quickly closed her front door on him.

He stared out of the window, remembering the silver dress that he liked so much, and how it had felt to touch her again as they danced. He wasn't about to mess things up a second time, but that didn't mean it was easy to—

Someone spoke in the corridor, and Cassidy shook himself and returned to staff liaison.

A recent cluster of forms, including more from Zoe, concerned the behaviour and attitudes of one K Renshaw, who seemed to specialise in annoying the staff. 'K Renshaw prevented Student Nurse Arlidge from performing her duties.' 'K Renshaw was reading patients' notes and refused to stop until Dr MacFarlane threatened to call the police.' 'K Renshaw was hiding in the linen cupboard, causing a shock to Nurse Holland when she opened the door.'

Who was K Renshaw? This was something he could start with, and he would have to visit Zoe's ward to get more information. But first he needed coffee.

....

It was early and the canteen was almost empty, but three managers were huddled at a corner table. Turnbull beckoned Cassidy to join them.

'Steve, this is Randy Steinberg from Hamilton Sheppard.' Cassidy shook hands with a chubby, smiling man with curly blond hair.

'Harry was telling us about the part charges,' said Turnbull.

Prattley grunted. 'It cost us a quarter of a million to set up the charging system, and about the same in annual running costs. Treasury calculated that by charging inpatients just fifty dollars a night, and even less for outpatient visits, Paxton Hospital would take in about 8 million dollars a year in cash. So they took 2 million out of our allocation. According to them, we should have collected over 3 million already, but so far we've got less than half a million.'

'Whoa,' said Steinberg. 'That's a lot of free riders.'

Turnbull nodded. 'The Government's had to exempt heavy users, but lots of people just refuse to pay, and a whole lot seems to go missing even if we do go after them. Some of the debt collection people might actually be gang members, it was on TV.'

'You can sure tender low if the business plan includes stealing most of the money,' said Steinberg. There was a thoughtful silence.

'Patients hate the charges,' said Cassidy. 'Some of them give the staff a hard time about it, as if it's their fault. And now you say they're making Paxton bleed money as well. Why on earth were they started?'

'They're meant to stop people overusing the system,' said Turnbull. 'If something's free people take it for granted. "To make them mindful of the most economic use of health resources" was how the Minister put it.'

'Does he think people *choose* to get ill?' said Cassidy. 'They can choose whether or not to go to the GP, but they don't choose to come into hospital — that's a doctor's decision based on need.'

Turnbull shrugged. 'Well, at least the prescription charges are working. People are visiting their GPs less, and they're getting less of the medicine that's been prescribed. So that's good.'

'No Gerald, it's bad. Bad for the patient and the system. If you don't treat illness early when it's cheap to fix, you have to treat it later when it's more expensive and the patient is more ill.'

'That's tough on a few folks,' drawled Steinberg. 'But this is not about getting a couple hundred dollars out of peoples' wallets, it's about changing attitudes. Once it's normal to pay some for health care, it's easier to ramp it up. You watch, pretty soon the whining will be about the *size* of the charges, not whether it's right or wrong. And the other clever thing they've done is this poor card—'

'Community Services Card,' Turnbull corrected.

'Right. So poor people can avoid the charges. Then other folks decide they don't want to pay either, especially when the charges start hiking up, and so they get themselves some insurance. And once most people are insured, you're set for a full-on market situation and some serious commercial opportunities.'

'Maybe,' Prattley sighed, 'but right now we're going backwards.' He got slowly to his feet. 'I've got a meeting. See you later.'

'What are you actually doing over here, Randy?' asked Cassidy.

'I'm consulting on some aspects of the reforms.' Steinberg leaned back in his chair. 'But it goes the other way too, I'm observing and reporting on the experiment.'

'Experiment?'

'Sure. What's going down here is unique — not in the changes themselves, but in the speed of it. Britain is phasing in similar reform over five years, but if you guys can crack this in about two, other places will start jumping right in behind you.'

He finished his coffee. 'Nobody could get away with anything like this in the USA, we have too many layers of government. But here? Single-chamber Parliament, single-party Government with a big majority — they can do whatever they want to. And boy, have they grabbed the opportunity.' He shook his head in admiration. 'It's like "OK, people, everything's changed," and it all just starts happening.'

'It's not *quite* that simple, Randy,' Turnbull smiled. 'There's vested interest noise. But we'll deal with that.'

'Hmm,' said Cassidy. 'What does "vested interest" actually mean, Gerald?'

'People who profit from the current system and don't want it to change.'

'I see. And what do you call people who profit from the new system once they've got the politicians to change it?'

'Visionaries,' laughed Steinberg. 'Steve, you need to understand that this little country is on the way to the best health care system in the world. Once you've dealt with the resistance and there is genuine competition, costs will tumble, waste will be eliminated, waiting lists will go. I tell you, it's a privilege to be a part of this.'

'How will you know if the reforms have been a success?' Cassidy asked.

Turnbull considered. 'Vigorous competition between viable providers, satisfied shareholders, and everything at arm's length from the Crown.'

'It's pretty hard to satisfy the public. Individuals who have a bad experience—'

'Steve, the shareholders are the Minister of Health and the Minister of Crown Health Enterprises. We don't answer to the public.'

'Yup, key concept,' said Steinberg. 'Change this big is a lot more difficult if you have to worry about what Joe Public might think.'

Sister Sorensen was making a bed when Cassidy arrived in Ward 21. He enjoyed the view as she bent forwards to tuck in the blanket, and her brief knowing smile as she walked towards him.

'Hello, Mister Manager.' She pushed a loose strand of hair back behind her ear. 'What have we done wrong now?'

She looked tired and Cassidy felt a surge of affection, quite different from his feelings a moment earlier. He wanted to put his arms round her, but instead he said, 'Who's K Renshaw?'

'Kenny? He's on your side.'

'I'd never heard of him until I saw all the incident forms.'

Zoe looked along the ward. 'In that case we should find him so that you can shake his hand. He might be hiding though — I expect you saw the one about the laundry cupboard.'

'I did. What on earth was he doing inside a laundry cupboard?'

'Counting towels or something, I suppose.' She smiled at Cassidy's puzzled frown. 'Kenny just appeared one day and started pestering us with questions. We said we were all too busy, which was true. So now he ferrets out the information for himself, peeping into places, reading patients' notes, and scribbling on his clipboard. He gets on everybody's nerves, but if you ask him what he's doing, he just says, "If you can measure it, you can manage it."' She glanced at Cassidy. 'Are you sure he's not a friend of yours?'

'I've never met him. But I can talk to his boss about it.'

Zoe grimaced. 'Jim Bennett, yes. Isn't he horrible? He's never been near the wards, but he thinks nursing is just making beds and emptying bedpans. He made a mean little speech at the Surgical Section nursing meeting — first he told us we shouldn't put so many patients through because it costs too much. Then he said there's no money for equipment replacements, let alone any extra relieving nurses, so we needn't bother asking.'

She paused to check on a patient who was being wheeled back from the operating theatre. 'And what about his clothes? Somebody should tell his mummy not to wash his suit in hot water.'

Cassidy laughed. 'I know. Anyway, I'm here to find out about this equipment that needs repairing.'

'Thanks, Steve. Come and see.' They went into the sluice room, where metal frames on castors held the bags for dirty linen until they were full and ready to go to the laundry. One of the frames had lost a wheel, and obviously would tip over if there was any weight on it.

'We need at least two working properly,' said Zoe. 'Only having one wastes precious time. Jerry the theatre orderly tried to fix it, but he says it needs a new piece welded on.'

'Isn't it a job for Engineering?'

'Most of them have been laid off, and the ones left behind are run off their feet.' She sighed. 'Not exactly a big-ticket item, is it? But after his royal smugness had told us there was no more money even for little things like this, I thought I would try the incident forms.'

'It's ridiculous that we can't fix something like this,' said Cassidy. 'I'll see if Ron can help.' He picked the damaged holder up and stood ready to go.

'My hero!' With a brilliant smile, Zoe took the wheel from the windowsill and put it in his pocket. Cassidy decided he should do more liaison, it was very rewarding.

....

Ron and Carol Higgins were Cassidy's neighbours, and Ron knew all about metal things; he had worked as a fitter in the Railways workshops until they closed ten years ago. He had emphysema and the young doctors helped by mowing his lawns, often receiving unsolicited fresh vegetables in return.

Cassidy knocked on the back door.

'Hello, Steve. What have you got there?' Ron stepped back inside and switched on the porch light, then put on the glasses that always hung on a string round his neck. He inspected the underside of the metal frame.

'It's from Zoe's ward at the hospital. They can't get anyone to fix it.'

Ron snorted. 'This is easy. You've got the wheel? Come on.' He pulled the door shut and they went across to the immaculate little workshop behind the garage.

Cassidy laid the frame on the bench while Ron, wheezing softly, rummaged in a box for a suitable piece of steel.

Half an hour later the holder stood upright, and all the tools were back in their places.

'Thanks so much for this, Ron,' said Cassidy.

'It needs chrome plating to finish the job.'

'No, it's great as it is.'

Ron nodded. 'Give young Zoe my love. When are you going to make a respectable woman of her?'

'I live in hope,' said Cassidy lightly. 'But talking of respectable women, how's Carol these days? I haven't seen her for a while.'

'She's crook actually,' said Ron, wiping his glasses with his handkerchief. 'She's been having chest pain, and it turns out she's got high blood pressure. Dr Stone sent her to the hospital and they did some tests, and now she's on the urgent waiting list for heart surgery.'

'Oh, I'm sorry to hear that — is there anything I—'

'She's asleep now, but I'm sure she'd love a visit at some stage. Perhaps at the weekend.'

'Sure. Give her my love, Ron. And thanks again.'

······················

'Got a minute, Jim?' said Cassidy.

Bennett stopped outside the door of Turnbull's office.

'I'm getting complaints about one Kenny Renshaw, he's getting in everybody's way in the surgical wards. Does he work for you?'

'No, he works for *us*,' said Bennett. 'How do you think we know anything about costs when there's zero legacy data? Most of what we do have has come from Kenny and his colleagues.'

'But he's annoying and obstructing the staff.'

'He's doing his job and they're obstructing *him*, you mean.' Bennett glowered at Cassidy. 'How dare they, when we're progressing reform on behalf of the Crown?'

'But Kenny—'

'Kenny and all the other analysts will stay in post until Paxton is operating in a business-like manner, meaning we have the financials we need, the computer system is up and running and staff are complying with data entry requirements.'

Cassidy nodded. 'But please can you at least ask him to back off a bit? And he can't read patients' notes unless he's involved in their care, it's illegal.'

Bennett rolled his eyes. '*Illegal?* Under what, the Doctors are God Act of 1756 or something? This is business now, do you get that?'

'But patients' notes are—'

'Gentlemen,' said Turnbull from his office doorway. 'Are we meeting now or would you rather carry on out there?'

'No, we've finished,' said Bennett.

Cassidy started to speak, but changed his mind and followed Bennett into the office. He would save his strength for the bigger battles to come.

Turnbull made no comment on the conversation. 'Steve, I want to bring you up to speed on some scenarios, so that you'll be on the same page when we interface with the RHA.' He leaned back and ordered his thoughts.

'As you know, in future we won't be taking every unit requiring hospital care, we'll only handle those that come under an RHA contract. So we need to define our core business and proactively define the services that we will tender for, stripping out the RLU work and expanding the RGU side. This innovation will free up capacity. We plan to eliminate the surgical waiting list within six months, and—'

'Six months?' said Cassidy. 'We haven't got anywhere near the capacity for that. Two years, maybe, if we took on extra staff.'

Turnbull smiled. 'No, we just have to leverage productivity with evening shifts and night shifts, using the operating theatres that are currently idle after hours — a ridiculous waste of precious resource. And when we've cleaned up the RLU situation we'll have ward capacity for the extra units who have been operated on, plus de-positioned staff competing for the new jobs.

'Once the waiting list is zeroed we'll enter the main RGU market, elective surgery. It'll be simple to just carry on with evening operating sessions for RGUs who would currently go to a private hospital.'

'And that's when the cashflow starts ramping up,' added Bennett. 'That group will require superior accommodation, of course.'

'I've got a team running the numbers,' said Turnbull.

Cassidy frowned. 'What do the insurance companies think about private patients in public hospitals?'

'I'm meeting up with some of them next week. I don't foresee problems there — competing providers will benefit the insurers, big-time. And Steve, can you confidentially interface with the surgeons and sound them out about working evening sessions, please? We'll pay fee for service, based on current salaries plus a little extra.'

Cassidy was certain that no surgeon would leave the freedom of private practice to work evenings in this place for a third of the fee, but he didn't feel like telling Turnbull that. 'I can ask one of the surgeons, and if he wants to take it further he can contact you. But Gerald, what about Warwick? Surely most of the competition will be with the other public hospital, rather than private.'

Turnbull nodded. 'Absolutely. Regardless of RGU income, we'll struggle long-term unless we hurt Warwick more than they hurt us. It's going to be rough — we'll need to be visionary and agile to outsmart them.'

'Outsmarting's not enough,' said Bennett. 'We have to drive them out of business so that we score a local monopoly. Then we can dictate terms to the RHA, while we scope out other RGU-rich scenarios.'

'You're right Jim, that's the big picture. Anything else? Jim? Steve?'

'War between hospitals sounds insane to me,' said Cassidy. 'Literally insane. And who do you think would look after the elderly patients that you've abandoned?'

Turnbull sighed. 'Steve, nobody's being "abandoned". Paxton is reconfiguring its work streams to maximise shareholder return, but the RHA remains responsible for purchasing health on the public's behalf.

They'll simply go to the market and find another provider who can turn our RLUs into RGUs. The market will sort it out.'

'But what if it's some unscrupulous rest-home operator who scoops up the contracts nobody else wants, and treats helpless old people like cattle?'

Bennett laughed. 'If they keep out of the *Bugle*, there's no problem. But if they're bad enough, word gets out, they close down, and the RHA goes back to the market.'

'That's right,' said Turnbull. 'And next time round, we might be in the market ourselves. Nobody's going to tender for revenue-negative work, but we would have done the modelling and worked out a price that guaranteed profitability. Maybe we'd add a levy for units aged more than fifty.'

'But what if everybody's price is too high, and the RHA refuses to buy?'

'Won't happen,' said Bennett. 'They must buy all the care, or the Minister will be on their case.'

'But the Health and Disability Services Bill says the CHE must, hold on a moment' — Cassidy got the booklet out of his briefcase — '"exhibit a sense of social responsibility by having regard to the interests of the community in which it operates."'

'That's 25 (d), Steve,' said Turnbull patiently. 'What does 25 (a) say the CHE must be?'

'"As successful and efficient as comparable businesses that are not owned by the Crown." (b) is about ethics, and (c) is about being a good employer.'

'Correct. 25 (a) means staying solvent, and it's top of the list for a good reason. There's no point in us "exhibiting a sense of social responsibility" then going bankrupt, is there? We'd all lose our jobs. Another team would come in and start again, and if some services were still not viable, they would just cease to be provided.'

Cassidy gaped at him. 'What do you mean, *cease to be provided*? If people need a particular service—'

'Listen, Doc,' said Bennett. 'RLUs bleed money. So we'll try and avoid their risk, but somebody will pick it up. So dry your eyes and put your hanky away, alright? It's all going to work out fine.'

....

Nesbit had invited the management team for a barbecue two weeks before Christmas, and to Cassidy's delight Zoe accepted his invitation to go with him. She got into his car wearing a new golden yellow sun frock with matching strappy sandals.

'I'm so pleased you could come, Zo. You look wonderful.'

'Thanks. I'm excited about meeting your new friends. Will Jim Bennett be there?'

'I expect so.' A warning light clicked on in his head. 'Listen, you've got to be nice, OK? This is a friendly social gathering, and it's very kind of the Nesbits to invite us. It would embarrass me if you made a scene.'

'As if I would do that! Especially when your management career is just beginning.'

'Zoe—' He pressed gently on the brakes.

'Best behaviour, I promise. Isn't it a gorgeous day?'

....

The CEO's house was a large ivy-covered Georgian-style residence, basking in the sun at the end of a long drive. Cassidy rang the bell and Nesbit came to greet them, looking just right in cream moleskin trousers, white shirt and paisley cravat.

'Merry Christmas, Richard,' said Cassidy. 'This is my friend Zoe.'

Nesbit beamed. 'Hi Steve, and welcome, Zoe. Merry Christmas to you both. Come through, everyone's out here.' They followed him through the house and into the crowd on the back lawn. He gave them champagne and agreed that the weather was fabulous, before leaving to greet the next arrivals.

Something bumped into Cassidy's legs, and he turned to see Jim Bennett beaming down at a small tottering replica of himself.

'Sorry. This is Nathan. Say hello to Steve, Nathan.' But Nathan was already wobbling off in another direction. 'OK, we'll catch up later.'

'There you go,' said Cassidy. 'Jim Bennett has a human side.'

'Hmm,' said Zoe. 'But isn't it scary to see a midget Jim? Soon he'll be at kindergarten, beating up the other kids and stealing their lunches.' She sipped her wine then inspected it appreciatively.

They walked over to Gerald Turnbull and Randy Steinberg, and Cassidy introduced everybody.

'Ain't this something?' Steinberg was dappled in the shade of ancient chestnut trees. 'Two weeks from Christmas and it's the middle of summer. Back home right now it's minus two, snow on the ground and a wind that could cut you in half.'

'Randy's from Chicago,' Cassidy explained.

Zoe was impressed. 'What are you doing so far from home?'

'He's observing the experiment,' said Turnbull with a wink at Cassidy.

'Oh?' Her voice had risen in pitch and Cassidy went onto full alert. 'What is the experiment?'

'Your health reforms. Proper management of hospitals and application of market principles. It's never been done before — not so fast or so completely, anyway. The whole world's watching and waiting to learn from what happens.'

'I hadn't known that it's an experiment,' said Zoe. 'What are the possible outcomes?'

'I don't think we should talk shop at a lovely party like this,' Cassidy cut in. 'What are your plans for Christmas, Gerald?'

But Steinberg was enjoying this beautiful woman's attention. 'Best case: everything goes as planned, you make those savings, and New Zealand gets an efficient, high-productivity health system.' He smiled and drank some wine. 'Worst case: the math is wrong, and the model doesn't work. The Government picks it all up again and deals with the debt.'

'And lots of jobs get lost.'

Steinberg shrugged. 'Jobs will be lost either way, that's how you get savings. What's your pick, Gerald?'

'If we stay on message, we transition to a better health system,' said Turnbull. 'We know it's a mess at this point in time, and there's still lots of flab to trim. But once that's done and we have a lean, mean enterprise then the market is wide open for us.'

'What if I told you that it was lean before you started, and now it's becoming just mean?' said Zoe. She finished her champagne in a single gulp.

Turnbull twirled his moustache. 'I'm not sure I understand.'

'I'm a nurse at the hospital. We're short-staffed and overworked, and it's dangerous. Overworked people make mistakes. Lots of good people are leaving because they can't stand it any longer, so it keeps getting worse. And we can't get anything fixed — a small thing was broken, I asked and asked but nothing happened until Steve took it home and his kind next-door neighbour fixed it.'

Turnbull frowned. 'Of course things are tough at the moment, Zoe, but that's what we're working to change. We just have to make the difficult time as short as possible.' He gave her his best toothy smile. 'And we will.'

Nesbit appeared, smiling round the group. 'Steve, have you got a minute?' Cassidy followed him to a quiet patch of lawn. 'I haven't had a chance to catch up since you started. How's it going?'

'I'm learning a lot.' Cassidy glanced back to check that Zoe wasn't punching Turnbull. 'But some of the plans are unethical, and that will be a political disaster.'

'Like what?' said Nesbit with a frown.

'This RLU idea. You can't deny people care because you think they might be unprofitable.'

'Oh, that.' Nesbit sipped champagne. 'Don't worry, Steve, the market will come through there. One man's RLU is another man's RGU, you'll see. But it's good that you're challenging us, it's exactly what I want you to do.'

'And the idea of forcing Warwick to fail as a business—'

'Mr Nesbit,' said one of the waiters. 'There's a phone call for you from Wellington.'

'Thanks. I'll have to go, Steve.' Nesbit gave Turnbull a conspirator's smile. 'Keep it up, you're doing well.'

Zoe was in full flight as Cassidy re-joined the group under the trees. 'Did you read the piece in this morning's *Globe* about the cost of the reforms so far? Over seventy-three million dollars, when they'd budgeted less than fourteen million, and by the end of 1995 administrative costs might reach 350 million. How do you feel about that?'

'It's over budget, but acceptable given the overall scale of the plan,' said Turnbull. 'You need to trust us, Zoe, we do know what we're doing.'

Cassidy moved them to a more neutral topic. 'I wonder what Richard did to be able to buy this gorgeous place.'

'He's built up several companies over the years, mostly in apparel.'

'Really,' said Zoe in the same tense, clipped voice. 'Please explain how a background in *apparel* qualifies him for an important job in health.'

'It just means he knows how to run a business.' Turnbull was frowning now. 'The detail of his previous experience is irrelevant, in fact it's better that he's come to this position content-free so that he can be objective.'

'Content-free?'

'That's a key principle in modern management. Content is a distraction at the top level. CEOs are there to make the big decisions, leaving the micro stuff for others to address. It's policy, Zoe. Of the twenty-three CHE CEOs around the country, more than half are from the private sector with no health background. Same with the new directors on the CHE boards — they've been appointed because of their knowledge of business and their communities. It's quite logical.'

'Well, nice to talk,' said Cassidy. 'We'd better move on.'

'An experiment!' said Zoe in her high, clear voice as they got new glasses of champagne from a passing waiter. 'And we're all guinea pigs.'

Cassidy saw the Bennett family under a sun umbrella, with Nathan temporarily concentrating on a sausage. 'Let's say hello to Jim.'

'Jim, yes, why not?'

Bennett got to his feet as they arrived. 'This is my wife Jenny, and that's Erin, who's eight weeks old today,' he said proudly.

Jenny Bennett, sitting cradling the sleeping baby, smiled up at them. She had dark wavy hair and a confident, open face.

'Can I get you a drink?' said Cassidy.

When he returned, Zoe was in the camp chair smiling down at the sleeping Erin in her arms, and Nathan wanted to get moving again. Jenny produced a cloth from a large bag and Bennett wiped his son's face and hands before they set off.

Cassidy handed Jenny a glass of orange juice. 'It's a full-time job.'

She smiled. 'It is, but it's fun too. Jim's a great dad.' They stood and sipped their drinks for a moment. 'He talks about you often, so it's good to meet you. He says you're a bit of a dreamer.'

'Is that bad?' Cassidy asked lightly.

'Of course it is, when there are hard, real-world decisions to make. He was amazed that they appointed a doctor to the management team.' She turned to check on Erin.

'So doctors don't understand the real world, despite dealing with suffering people every day?'

'Obviously it's vital work,' said Jenny, 'and you have to be smart and well-trained to do it. But without financial responsibility you're not in the real world. Doctors in hospitals don't have to worry about all that, do they? They get whatever they want. And if they don't, they just throw a tantrum and more money appears and the health budget gets a bit bigger.' She glanced at him. 'That's why we need people like Richard and Jim and the others to straighten things out.'

He swirled the champagne in his glass. 'And you think they will straighten things out?'

'I don't know. But it's a big opportunity, and Jim's going to take full advantage.'

Cassidy thought he would rather be a bit of a dreamer than someone who takes full advantage, but he let it go. 'Jim's a very confident person, I've noticed. Does he ever admit that sometimes he might be wrong?'

She looked across to where father and son were playing peek-a-boo round a tree trunk. 'He hasn't yet, but I'm sure he would if he really thought he actually was wrong.'

'You see, it's possible that despite all the clever people involved, and all the money that's being spent, these reforms might never work.'

'But that won't be Jim's fault,' said Jenny. 'He'll give it all he's got, and then he'll move to the next project. Everybody does that.'

'Jenny,' Zoe called softly.

Erin was gumming her knuckles and frowning at Zoe with deep blue eyes. 'Time for a feed,' said Jenny.

'For all of us.' Cassidy sniffed the smells of the barbecue.

The two women swapped places again, and Cassidy and Zoe came back out into the sunshine.

'That was beautiful,' Zoe said quietly. 'All that life and potential, just beginning.' Her face hardened. 'But everybody else—'

'I know. Did you hear what Jenny said? Oh, we're being summoned. I'll tell you later.'

Nesbit, now wearing a butcher's apron over the landed gentry outfit, was beckoning with his tongs from behind a small aircraft carrier, its flight deck covered in squadrons of onions and every sort of meat. 'Take lots, Zoe, I don't want to be eating sausages every day until One July! Just a kebab? Sure? You're welcome.' He loaded Cassidy's plate with steak, sausages and onions. 'There you go, Steve. Enjoy.'

'I'm Patricia,' said Mrs Nesbit at the salad bar. 'Steve, hello. You're the doctor aren't you? How nice to meet you. Richard is very pleased to have you with us. And — Zoe? Lovely. Do help yourselves.'

'Jim Bennett's wife told me he thinks I'm a dreamer,' said Cassidy after they found a spot on the steps and got ready to eat.

'What does that mean?' asked Zoe.

'It means he's doing what has to be done, and I'm soft for thinking our first responsibility is to the patients.'

She turned to him, her eyes tigerish in the sunlight. 'My God, the smugness round here is so thick you could cut it with a knife. How can you bear it? It's so *bloody* unfair. Little people like us care so much and work so hard, and these others just turn up and — and . . .' She put her plate down. 'Can you take me home now, please? I don't feel like eating their food.'

Cassidy had just taken a mouthful of astonishingly succulent steak. 'Are you sure? Won't it seem a bit—'

'I'll wait for you out on the street if you don't want to come now. Or I can get a taxi.'

Cassidy stood up and took their plates back to Mrs Nesbit, mumbled an apology, and followed Zoe through the house and down the drive.

'Feel good?' he said as they drove away.

Her face was flushed with anger. 'I shouldn't have come, it's better not to meet these people face to face. Then we wouldn't have to listen to them talking down to us like that, all smooth and patronising and with zero interest in what it means for patients and the people looking after them.'

She wound her window down and let some cooler air into the car. 'That creep Turnbull. How can you stand being round them all day? Or perhaps you really agree with them — you hardly said anything when they were being so full of themselves.'

'For God's sake Zo, you know what I think. But this wasn't the place or the time for a shouting match. And Richard Nesbit said he thinks I'm going OK, so that was good.'

'Oh, come on, Steve, he's using you! You're just window-dressing — they can tell everybody they're consulting with the medical profession, while they ignore everything you say.'

'It's early days, Zo. Give me time and I will make a difference.'

She snorted and stared silently ahead, then after a couple of minutes she stretched and relaxed. 'Oh well, I'm glad it's your job not mine. Erin was lovely though, wasn't she? It was worth going just to meet her, it's not her fault she's the daughter of Jim Bennett.'

'Poor wee thing,' agreed Cassidy as they drew up outside Zoe's flat. 'Zo, there's plenty of the day left, let's go to the beach. I brought my togs just in case, and now I need to dive into some cool, clean salt water.'

She smiled a rueful smile and squeezed his arm. 'Me too. Give me five minutes to get changed.'

....

Over a slice of Sister Mac's familiar Farewell Party Lemon Sponge after Cassidy's last ward round, Jackson had invited him to continue assisting in private, and since then he had spent most Monday evenings at St Luke's. This kept him in touch with surgery and Jackson's teaching, while Jackson got a reliable assistant and felt that he was supporting a promising junior colleague through a temporary period of insanity.

This evening the boss was mellow as they walked out of theatre, as well he might be: four procedures safely and skilfully completed, four patients who would soon feel much better, and the world put to rights for another week.

'I've got something to ask you,' said Cassidy once they were in the changing room. 'In my management role.'

'Sure.' Jackson sat down to take off his gumboots.

'Would you be interested in doing extra operations at the hospital? On private patients?'

Jackson sat back with his hands on his knees, looking up at Cassidy. 'No.'

'Right. Thanks.'

'I knew this would happen.' Jackson put the boots on top of his locker. 'They've just realised they can't make a profit from complicated public hospital patients, haven't they? So they have to try and find otherwise healthy, single-issue patients, who will pay cash, because the insurance companies won't pay for treatment in a public hospital.' He threw his scrubs into the laundry bag and reached for his shirt. 'Have they thought this through?'

'It's still at the concept stage.'

Jackson grunted. 'I suppose they *could* do it, if they could find surgeons willing to do the work. But it would be a political minefield — most Kiwis still believe we have a pretty fair society, and nobody likes queue-jumpers.'

'They were planning evening surgery and separate private wards,' said Cassidy. 'That's not really queue-jumping.'

'The *Globe* would tear them to shreds all the same. Money would be diverted from other areas to set it up, and that would be exposed.' Jackson pulled on his trousers. 'Then there's the fact that the theatres and equipment belong to the public. Would they charge me to use their facilities on my private patients?'

'I don't know.'

'And finally there's my personal view,' Jackson continued, lacing his Italian brogues. 'Why on earth would I be interested even if they could fix the chaos in the hospital? They'd have to offer me a lot more than I make here before I would even consider it.' He took his tie off its peg. 'Do they know how much a surgeon earns in private?'

'They have no idea.'

'They want to make some money on the back of my work, but they couldn't possibly afford to pay my private fee and still get something for themselves. They're dreaming.'

'They're trying to grow the business,' said Cassidy, feeling a bit sorry for Turnbull.

Jackson ran a comb through the distinguished silver hair, then put on his suit jacket. 'They'll have to find other ways to do that, won't they?' He put the comb in his pocket. 'Goodnight, Steve. Thanks for your help tonight.'

·····

The year 1992 was winding down, but the RHA contract negotiations were due to start in February and Paxton staff were hard at work developing proposals. The canteen buzzed with conversations about fixed and variable overheads, depreciation, and opportunity.

A sensational rumour came and went: the Warwick CHE Board-designate had apparently tried to buy Paxton Hospital outright, but someone in a very high place had stepped in before negotiations could begin.

Cassidy's offer of medical advisory help with setting up contracts had been politely declined, but the surging flow of incident forms and phoned complaints kept him busy listening and investigating, even though mostly he could only provide a sympathetic hearing to angry staff.

His regular hours still gave him guilty pleasure. A full eight hours' sleep every night was a wonderful luxury even if he was sleeping alone, and most of his weekends and evenings were free for television or reading. He renewed the Paxton Valley Golf Club membership that had lapsed after he became a doctor and normal life had disappeared.

Although he spent time with Zoe when he could, often at the beach or playing tennis, the barrier between them showed no sign of weakening. So it was a welcome surprise when she rang and invited him to join her and her mother for Christmas dinner.

He arrived at the Sorensen family home in Westmere bearing strawberries and wine, and a large bunch of flowers for his hostess. Isabel Sorensen welcomed him in and led him to the kitchen.

'Thanks Steve, that's wonderful. Put it all on the bench so that we can have a proper hug. It's lovely to see you again after all this time.'

'You too, Isabel, I've missed you.' He sniffed the Christmas cooking smells. 'Thank you so much for inviting me.'

She smiled. 'It was Zoe's idea, but I'm very pleased you could come. Can you reach up to the top cupboard and get that big vase for me, please? Thanks. Zoe just rang, she's been held up at work but she said we should have a drink and she'll be here soon. So please open your wine, then I'll get you to shell the peas.'

Cassidy pulled the cork on the chardonnay and poured two drinks.

'How long since you were last here?' said Isabel as she arranged the flowers.

'About six months, I think. Too long. As I'm sure Zoe's told you we broke up, and now we've started seeing each other again. But it's not the same as before.'

'So I understand.' Isabel picked up her glass. 'She was very upset, you know. She's had boyfriends in the past, but you were different, and I was sure that you were going to be the one. I was pleased for you both. But then you gradually changed into somebody else, and she couldn't bear it.' She sighed. 'Anyway, Merry Christmas.'

He stood up and they drank and smiled carefully at each other, and as usual when around Zoe's Mum, Cassidy thought about genes. Mr Sorensen's illness and death when Zoe was at secondary school had inspired her to become a nurse, but her ballerina mother was the source of her grace and beauty. If Zoe looked this good in her late fifties, then that would be fine with him.

If it was him in the end, said a voice in his head. There had been no thawing of their relationship as yet, and recently he had started to wonder if there might be somebody else.

'Are you OK?' She had seen the frown flitting across his face.

'Not really,' said Cassidy. He paused. 'Isabel, do you ever wish you could have some times in your life back again, so you could do them differently?'

'Good Lord, of course I do! Everybody does.'

'Well I'd like about a year, if that could be arranged. I can't believe how stupid and insensitive I was to Zoe. And since then I've been burning out at work. But now I'm trying to deal with all that and become . . . a better person, I suppose. I've made this big change in my work for a year, I've put my study on hold, and I'm available more. But I don't know where I am with Zo, I can't tell what she's thinking.'

Isabel shouted with laughter. 'Oh, Steve. Do you honestly expect her to show you what she's thinking after about five minutes? She doesn't *know* what she's thinking, and I'm not surprised. You treat her badly until she can't bear it any longer, and now you're telling her you've practically thrown away your career for her — who wouldn't be confused?'

'It's not quite like that,' said Cassidy.

'And what'll happen after you've got this other thing out of your system? Are you going to go back to being Mr Top-of-the-Class again, and shutting out the person who cares most about you? It *scares* her to think that maybe the cold, boring Cassidy — no, let me finish — is the real one. And it scares me too, Steve. But you need to understand, Zoe's everything I've got and I won't let you hurt her again.'

Cassidy's face was burning. Slowly, frowning, he sat down and picked up a handful of peas and stared at them.

After a moment she tapped his hand and said gently, 'And don't eat before the meal, it'll spoil your appetite.'

He laughed and let the peas fall back into the bowl. 'Alright. But how can I fix it? I mean, *I* know I can change, and I will, whatever it takes. But how can I get her to believe me?'

'That's for you to sort out,' said Isabel, picking up a pod and shelling out the peas. 'You're a lovely guy most of the time, but you need to control your need to chase professional perfection at the expense of everything else. Ask her to help you. And take it slowly and respectfully.'

They heard Zoe's car coming up the drive. 'Thanks, Isabel. I will.'

He had a wonderful evening. The meal was perfect, and Zoe was funny and affectionate. She told her mother to feed him up because he was their champion and he would need all his energy for fighting the forces of evil in 1993, but otherwise they talked about anything except work.

They all did the dishes together then played Scrabble, a Christmas tradition in the Sorensen family. Zoe was determined to win, and she did after some spirited challenges and frequent use of the ancient family dictionary that had none of the words that Cassidy wanted to use.

Barefoot, her white dress gleaming in the moonlight, she walked with him to the street. It was a warm, still night and they leaned against his car for a while and argued lazily about which star was which.

Finally he said, 'Thank you, Zo. For everything. And your Mum too, she's amazing.'

She smiled. 'Yes, she is. I know she had a great time tonight, and that means a lot to me.' She took his arm from around her waist, stood on tiptoe and kissed his cheek. 'Good night, Steve. It was a lovely evening — thanks for coming. And sorry about the Scrabble.'

'"Fax" is a perfectly good word,' said Cassidy as he got into his car.

'Local rules, young Cassidy. They didn't have faxes when the dictionary was printed, so it's not allowed,' said Zoe, leaning through the window.

'And it would have been a triple word score. I demand a return match.'

'And *your* dictionary?' laughed Zoe, stepping back as he let in the clutch. 'Not a chance.'

He drove home feeling better than he had for a long time.

They saw the New Year in together, in the happy boozy crowd in Paxton Plaza. Then it was 1993, and the final countdown to One July began.

CHAPTER FOUR

Cassidy's phone rang before he had finished reading the first of 1993's complaints. 'Gerald here Steve, good morning. I'm with Richard Nesbit, could you spare us a minute?'

Nesbit and Turnbull were sitting at the coffee table in the CEO's office, examining a letter. Nesbit jumped up to shake hands. 'Steve, happy New Year, and welcome to 1993. What a year it's going to be, eh? Have a seat. Listen to this — the CHEEU have forwarded briefing papers, setting out a raft of KPIs, and they want *us* to create them.'

'Fantastic,' said Cassidy. 'What's a raft of KPIs?'

'A whole lot of Key Performance Indicators, Steve,' Turnbull explained. 'Measurable standards, so that providers can demonstrate that they meet agreed goals.'

Nesbit was beaming. 'And we'll set the standards, so if we design leading-edge but achievable KPIs then meet them, every time, the contracts will just pour in.'

'"Measure quality of patient service and significantly improve this,"' Turnbull read. 'And "Measure quality of clinical services and introduce a system that comprehensively reviews these services."'

'Straight away, I said "Steve Cassidy's the man for those". Didn't I, Gerald?'

'You did, Richard. And rightly so.'

'It's certainly exciting,' said Cassidy, 'but why can't their medical advisers set the standards?'

'The CHEEU don't have medical advisers,' said Turnbull. 'Their brief is strictly commercial.'

'So how can they decide whether our clinical KPIs are appropriate?'

'They can't — they just need to be able to tell Treasury that Paxton has clinical KPIs in place. They define general principles, and they want us to provide the innovative thinking. Here, Dawn's made a copy for you.'

Cassidy realised why he felt confused. 'But we're already doing quality clinical work. Of course we could always improve, but I think we do brilliantly considering the difficulties in the current system.'

'With respect, Steve, that's out-dated thinking,' said Turnbull. 'Your people probably are producing quality. But how do *we* know? We need proof, that we can pass up the line — monthly reports, the trend analysis and projections. Without KPIs and accountability to them, we're nowhere. "We think we do a pretty good job" doesn't hack it when you're competing for multi-million dollar contracts. This is where skilled managers value-add by professionally supporting frontline staff.'

'That's very true,' said Nesbit. 'But today we also start managing client perceptions, and that's key in this early, fluid stage of the game.' He stood up. 'Steve, we want you to lead this. Be creative. Tell us things we didn't know, and show us how to convert them into visionary policy.

'But time is tight. I've set up a meeting of the Management Group ten days from now, and I need a quality action plan from you within a week. Run it past Gerald first, could you? Excellent.'

···

Cassidy was so excited that he could barely wait for the lift. This was a key part of the future health system, and Richard Nesbit, the CEO himself, had demanded visionary policy. His moment had arrived.

It was good that Bennett had finally moved up to a sixth-floor office, as Cassidy needed space and quiet to think. He put the folders of incident forms on the other desk and started leafing through the Green and White Paper.

Time passed quickly as he pondered and scribbled. He rushed to the canteen just before lunch service closed and came back with a plate of fried rice, but forgot to eat it until much later.

The message was everywhere: in the new system providers would compete on quality, in facilities and in clinical care.

Quality was difficult to define, but it was obvious when it was missing. He only had to think back a few weeks to see what needed changing.

The outpatient clinics, with their cramped, noisy waiting areas and poky consulting rooms. The lack of privacy for serious conversations with patients and their families.

The muddle of the patient notes. The computer system that had promised so much and delivered so little. The waiting list with all its unfairness and uncertainty.

Then the wards, understaffed and poorly equipped. Staff were chronically near to breaking point, and that increased the risk of mistakes. Mostly the threats to safety were caught in time, but sometimes . . .

How good could it be with enough staff for safe work? The effect on quality would be magical. And what if — Cassidy started pacing — what if staff were actually rostered to research and audit, instead of doing it in their spare time? Paxton would become like the Mayo Clinic, it would lead New Zealand. And as its reputation grew, people from all round the country would start demanding to be treated at Paxton. People with cash, from other RHA areas, drawn by quality.

But what did 'enough staff' mean? He needed some numbers.

Zoe was in a meeting when he arrived on Ward 21, so he sat in the corridor outside and got started on a list of KPIs for clinical work.

'Hi, Steve, what's happening?'

Cassidy jumped up with a big grin. 'Zo, I've got the opportunity I've been waiting for since I started this job. The Government has asked how we will obtain quality and how we'll measure it. Richard Nesbit has passed the question on to me, and I'm going to tell them that we need *more* staff, especially nurses, not less. But I need to know how many people that means. Have you got a minute?' He stopped. 'What's the matter?'

'I haven't seen you this excited for a long time and it's nice,' she smiled. 'Come down to my office.'

'My brain is fizzing, it's an amazing feeling,' he said when they were alone.

'I'm so pleased for you. But Steve, please listen for a moment. This is probably not going to work, and you need to be ready for that. Yesterday Kenny was asking why we don't re-use syringes and catheters, so — more staff for the wards? What are the chances of that happening?'

Cassidy shook his head. 'This is different, it's come from the CEO himself. There'll never be a better time to put things right. Now please sit down and pay attention. Question one: how many staff nurses do you need to run a ward like this to the highest standards of safety and quality? Think carefully before you answer.'

Still smiling, Zoe answered all his questions.

'OK,' said Cassidy, 'that's all for now. I've also got to build a *raft of KPIs*, at the request of the Crown. Do you know what that means? You do? You're more than just a pretty face, I see. But don't worry, the raft is half-built already.'

He checked his list of questions and answers, and put it in his pocket. 'Thanks, Zo. Would you fancy a spot of tennis on Saturday, when this is all over? As long as you don't mind losing, of course.'

'I'd love a game,' said Zoe, who had played in the Paxton under-18 women's team. 'Loser buys dinner, how does that sound?'

Cassidy was smiling as he left the ward. He would almost certainly be paying for dinner, but Zoe had suggested an evening together, and that was progress.

Back in his office, he typed, considered, deleted and typed again. He stared out of the window. He paced.

'Quality of patient *service*'. That meant friendly and professional staff, good food, a pleasant environment generally, everything clean and fresh. Recent magazines in the waiting areas.

That was the easy part; making sure that people got the right diagnosis and the best treatment was infinitely more important. He made a list of fifteen KPIs and the number of staff needed to carry out those more challenging audits.

A short waiting list was a mark of quality, and that would require more staff too.

After three exciting days the document was finished and had been approved by Zoe, Sister Mac, and his flatmates.

He put it aside for the weekend, and as expected Zoe thrashed him at tennis without raising a sweat. She was happy and a little bit flirty at the Happy Snail and Black Mambo, and even though they remained platonic, Cassidy was delighted with his day.

He made final corrections to his document on Sunday. On Monday he loaded it onto a floppy disc and took it into town, where he paid for three copies to be printed and bound with a black cover showing the title in gold letters: *A Quality Plan for Paxton Health, S Cassidy, January 1993*. He couldn't stop smiling as he thumbed through them in the bus on the way back — this was a significant achievement, his best so far in the new job.

He left a copy on Turnbull's desk, and went downstairs to start cleaning up the mess of papers and dirty dishes in his office.

....

Ten minutes later the phone rang. 'Steve?'

'Gerald, hi. Did you see my paper?'

'How many copies of this are there?'

'Three. But I can print more if you—'

'Get up here now please.' The phone went dead.

Turnbull had the report open in front of him. 'Come in and shut the door.' He flipped over a couple of pages, then looked up at Cassidy. 'What's this?'

'It's a blueprint for winning on quality,' said Cassidy. 'Real quality, not just painting over the cracks. It's visionary. This is how we deal to—'

'No, this is how we commit business suicide!' Turnbull shouted. 'You want a hundred more staff nurses, twenty-five more orderlies, and *how many* more doctors?'

'I understand it could be a bit of a shock when you first see it, Gerald. But everybody says they want quality service, and this is what it will take to get it.'

'Sit down.' Turnbull massaged the bridge of his nose for a moment. 'Clearly there's been a misunderstanding. Why on earth would we hire more staff after we've worked so hard to increase productivity?'

'Firstly for baseline patient safety,' said Cassidy. 'As your medical liaison person I'm telling you that the hospital is dangerously short-staffed already. But once that's taken care of the extra staff will boost the quality, and that's the visionary part because when everybody knows that Paxton has the highest quality in the country, the outside work will flood in.'

Turnbull shook his head. 'I understand the concept. But we could never tender competitively against a stripped-down Warwick if we did this — we would go belly-up, not them. And how do you suggest we would pay for it all?'

'From the savings,' said Cassidy. 'The Arthur Andersen money, the half a billion dollars.'

Turnbull stared at him. 'I don't know where that idea came from. Most of the Arthur Andersen money, as you call it, will only appear through productivity maximisation, and it'll go into the Crown's general account. It'll probably help pay for the Navy's new frigates.'

Cassidy opened his mouth but no sound came out.

'So come back from fantasy-land and reconfigure this in light of political reality and our budgetary environment. Find the low-hanging fruit, things that our analysts can measure cost-effectively. And for the rest, we'll redecorate here and there to get the sort of quality that we can measure with customer surveys and keep the CHEEU happy. As Richard said, as much as anything else we're managing perception here.' He closed the folder and held it out. 'But we can't afford this crazy dream.'

Cassidy made no effort to take it. 'You told me you wanted quality, and now you're saying that none of the savings will be ploughed back in. You'll cut services to the bone, let the money go, and then tell the public you're providing quality service? Why not tell them the truth?'

'That's enough,' said Turnbull. He dropped the folder into the rubbish tin. 'The Crown are our clients and we know what they want. And you need to now get on board or get off the bus, OK? Think about that.'

'Yes, I will think about that and I'll get back to you shortly.' And Cassidy slammed the door behind him with a force that Bennett himself could not have beaten.

....

He clattered down six flights of stairs, ran through the lobby and arrived wild-eyed in sun-baked Seddon Street, startling pedestrians and treading on somebody's dog. Turning away from the yapping animal he walked quickly towards the hospital, then through the silent sliding glass doors and into a cool and familiar world.

It was Monday afternoon, so Geoff would be doing the huge fracture follow-up clinic that he always whined about. Cassidy bought a chocolate fish at the volunteers' shop in the lobby, then went down the corridor and into the orthopaedic department waiting room.

Dozens of faces turned towards the newcomer. There were people everywhere — people with crutches, bandages and slings, patients in wheelchairs, a man asleep on one of the benches with his foot in a battered plaster cast. Everybody all squashed together as they waited, with small kids running and shouting around them.

Cassidy had done a three-month sentence here a long time ago and never really thought about what it was like for the patients, but now he saw the queue at the reception desk, the disgraceful lack of space, the feeling of time standing still. Quality? Gerald Turnbull should come and see this before handing money to the Navy.

Geoff came out of Consulting Room 4 and walked quickly behind the reception desk, looking fierce and holding a patient's notes. Cassidy watched as he punched some keys on one of the computers, then smacked the top of its monitor.

Clearly this wasn't a good time to tell Geoff about his problems. Cassidy quietly returned to the main corridor, and then without any conscious decision he found himself walking into Ward 21. He found Zoe at her desk, frowning over another incident form.

She smiled and sat back in her chair. 'Hi, Steve. What's in the bag?'

'A chocolate fish,' sighed Cassidy. 'I bet Geoff that I'd stay in the new job for a year. But he's flat out in Fracture Clinic so I couldn't give it to him.'

'What? You've resigned?' She got up and closed the door. 'Or have you been fired?'

He slumped into the armchair. 'Neither yet, but there's no point in staying on. I've just been told that all the money they save in health care will probably be used to buy ships for the Navy — can you believe that?' He remembered what she had said at Scarlatti's about the money. 'What an idiot I've been. It was never written anywhere that the savings would be sucked out, and I never asked — I guess I wanted the job too much.

'And our blueprint for quality, from last week? It's in the bin.' He told her about his beautiful document and its demolition by Gerald Turnbull, then sat staring at his hands.

Zoe stood looking down at him for a moment. 'And now you're just going to give up.'

'What else can I do? That stuff that you said about me always winning, that's a joke. There's nothing like going up against the big government machine to make you realise how small you are.'

'But don't you think—'

'It pisses me off,' said Cassidy. 'They asked me how to get quality because I'm their "expert adviser". But as soon as I tell them, they don't want to know.' He snorted bitterly. 'It'll make them think twice if I resign.'

'It won't, Steve.' Zoe came and sat on the arm of the chair. 'Put yourself in Gerald Turnbull's position. He's been hired to turn the hospital into a successful business, right? And that's what he's trying to do. He doesn't make policy, so when you suggest a whole different policy instead of some management ideas, he can't evaluate it and he won't. And if you go, he'll just shrug and get on with his job as if you've never been there.'

Cassidy groaned and closed his eyes.

She put her arm round him. 'The quality plan is fantastic, but it's too much too soon. You have to be more patient — and you must stay on the inside. Yes, I know I've changed, but I hadn't met Jim Bennett when we were first talking about it.

'We really need somebody who can tell them every day how dangerous all this is. And if you resign they won't get another medical adviser, will they? So please hang on for all of our sakes, do what you can, and wait for the chance to make a difference.'

After a moment she went back to her desk, and Cassidy sighed and got to his feet. 'You know what, Zo? You're a very wise person. You'll make somebody a wonderful wife one day.'

'I know I will,' said Zoe. 'But now I've got work to do, and you must go back over there and carry on saving the world, OK? But just one step at a time for now — save the leaping over tall buildings for when you know you can. And eat the fish, it'll cheer you up.'

....

'Good morning,' said Nesbit. 'Welcome to this special management group meeting to consider the CHEEU's key performance indicators.' He smiled at Cassidy. 'We'll go through the list in order. Number one: "Increase patient throughput using expenditure savings." Harold.'

'Throughput is increasing alright, but we're going further into the red,' said Prattley, who was getting gloomier every day. 'The staff just keep on treating as many units as they can, and it's impacting massively on the overheads, especially in consumables.

'We've suspended routine maintenance and slashed capital expenditure. But we won't get into positive cashflow until we divest revenue-losing work and cut salary costs by rightsizing the workforce. And we'll still need to somehow compensate for the part-charges budget cut.' He sighed. 'Did you notice that they've changed 25(a) of the Act from "a successful business" to "a profitable business"?'

'Don't worry,' said Turnbull, 'we'll soon be saving millions and millions.'

Nesbit nodded. 'Absolutely. Thanks, Harold. Success remains ahead of us there, but ongoingly of course, everyone must do all they can to force economies.

'Number two. "Measure quality of patient service and significantly improve this." Steve.'

Using handwritten notes, Cassidy trundled through the easy topics — the décor, the magazines, the food. 'Staff friendliness is one area of concern. The nursing staff are overworked and stressed, and sometimes they can be abrupt towards patients. But the public understand the situation, and if a nurse is rude they blame the organisation, not the nurse.'

'We don't want them blaming us,' said Terry Goldsmith, the deputy director of Finance.

'We need more nurses.' Cassidy glanced at Turnbull. 'But if you won't do that, we're stuck.'

'Rubbish,' said Bennett in a loud voice. 'We're not stuck at all.'

Nesbit smiled. 'Tell us, Jim.'

'We'll do another customer satisfaction survey.'

'Okay,' said Cassidy cautiously. 'And we'd tell the CHEEU that we'll act on any suggestions.'

'Sure, Doc,' Bennett sneered. 'Then if some whinger demands a new innovation, we're expected to actually provide it. How stupid would that be? No, just informing CHEEU that we're running a survey lets them tick the box on commitment to quality.

'And meanwhile the nurses need to get some clarity around downward flexibility in workforce numbers. Once they understand they can't change that, and they adapt to the new industrial landscape, then quality will rise.'

'Thanks Jim,' said Nesbit. 'Number three, also yours, Steve: "Measure the quality of clinical services and introduce a system that comprehensively reviews these services."'

'It's not easy,' said Cassidy. 'Measuring clinical quality properly takes time and money.'

'How would you do it?' Turnbull asked as if the black folders had never existed.

'By auditing patient records. You'd have a team going through notes and counting, say post-operative infection rates. And you'd do the same for patient falls, drug administration errors, radiological misdiagnosis and so on. I've got a full list here.'

Nesbit grimaced. 'It sounds terribly labour intensive. Are there any more cost-effective suggestions?'

'What about the number of deaths in hospital?' King suggested. 'That would be easy to count.'

Cassidy shook his head. 'The raw data is misleading. A big hospital gets the more difficult cases sent from smaller hospitals, including the sickest people, so they have a higher death rate.'

'Numbers on the waiting list,' said Bennett after a pause.

'Don't forget the client feedback forms,' Turnbull added. 'They're a cost-effective indicator of quality.'

'Sounds good,' said Goldsmith. 'Counting waiting list numbers and monitoring client feedback should be enough perception-wise.'

'As long as we don't kid ourselves that we're actually measuring quality,' said Cassidy.

Nesbit nodded and smiled. 'Good work everybody. Now, number 4 is "Introduce an accurate set of performing statistics." There are some standard parameters to be reported, numbers going through clinics, that kind of thing. We're progressing this — Jim, you've got your people gathering data? Excellent.

'Now, number 5: "Increase the status and respect of the CHE." Ricky.'

Ricky Russell, the head of public relations, grinned. 'My people have developed some exciting perception management concepts.

'First thing: Paxton Crown Health Enterprise. Bit of a mouthful, isn't it? And the average person has no idea what it means. So we brainstormed it. "Paxton CHE. P CHE,"' he said in a dreamy voice, his eyes half-closed. 'Then it hit us. PCHE . . . *Peachy!* Suggestions of softness, warmth, summer. A fluffy, cuddly image. How could we capitalise on that?'

He passed round photographs of Paxton Hospital, with its familiar weather-stained concrete slab walls. Then came pictures with it painted the colour of a peach, and a ten-metre high peach painted on the end wall. 'People, this is the Peachy hospital promoting itself.'

'Great branding,' said Goldsmith.

Other people agreed. 'This leaves Warwick nowhere.' 'It'll position us closer to the community.' 'Go Team Peachy!'

'How much would it cost to paint the outside of the hospital?' said Prattley grimly.

'Not just the outside, Harold,' said Russell with a mischievous smile. 'We see the peach theme following through into the corridors and wards, staff uniforms — everything. Bed linen, too.

'And there's more. We brainstormed all those harsh medical names. "Accident and Emergency"? Such negative words. Why not accentuate the positive: "Quick Help"!'

People laughed.

'Fracture clinic : "Take a Break". Radiology: "See Through".' Russell raised his voice over the excited chatter. 'Operating theatre: yuck. How about "A Stitch in Time"? Let's make people *smile* as they head off for their operation.'

Nesbit was beaming. 'Inspirational work, Ricky. Money invested in that kind of development would repay itself many times over. That's how you become a market leader.'

'The only way you'll get more business is by winning more contracts with the RHA, based on cheapness,' said Cassidy. 'This is money down the drain.'

'No, Steve, this is about consumer power. Ricky's vision positions us commandingly for the long term, when people will be choosing their provider. I think it's brilliant.

'Alright everyone, thanks for that excellent work. We'll finish there, but I just want to say that another of the performance indicators that we haven't discussed is to "create an effective management team". I will be telling the CHEEU that Paxton — sorry, Peachy — already has such a team in place!'

The meeting broke up but Cassidy stayed in his chair, his body suddenly too heavy to lift.

'Well done, Steve,' said Turnbull. 'You're getting the hang of it now.'

Then Cassidy was alone in the room. He rested his head on his hands and stared at the table. One step at a time, he told himself. One step at a time.

CHAPTER FIVE

In early February the Paxton Health/RHA interface team drove to Warwick for a preliminary RHA workshop on contracting.

Paxton took up one side of the boardroom table with Warwick's people lined up opposite. Cassidy had been hoping for an ally on the Warwick team, but he was disappointed to see no familiar faces in the enemy ranks.

The RHA chairperson was Bryce Bailey, a dapper little man with receding sandy hair and a neatly-trimmed beard. 'Welcome, everybody. Today we commence a game-changing transition. The introduction of market forces into the public health system will deliver a cost-effective, consumer-driven, transparent system.

'For too long we have heard that health is "different": business rules somehow don't apply, and it can only be understood by the people who profit from it. In other words, please leave the foxes in charge of the chook house!' He chuckled. 'Well, we beg to disagree.

'Arthur Andersen showed us the potential for enormous savings. We'll get a better health system *and* significant opportunities for elite players. Through your business skills and the new structures we're workshopping today, I know we will achieve something . . . extraordinary.'

After a pause he said, 'Are there any other providers represented here, apart from the two CHEs? We're expecting a broad range of interested parties.' He waited. 'Nobody? Alright, let's cut to the chase.

'First, the obligations of the various parties under the Health and Disability Services Bill. I'll ask Thomas Evans, who heads up our legal team, to give us an overview.'

A three-piece suited man stood up, and Cassidy tuned out. He noticed the woman sitting next to Evans; she was striking, with a pale, intelligent face, and shiny black hair that curved over her red leather jacket. She turned as she felt his gaze on her, and he looked away.

Evans finished talking and Bailey asked for questions.

Turnbull raised his hand. 'The National Interim Provider Board has written that "RHAs will stringently monitor the quality of the care delivered by all providers". How will you do that?'

'Let me first emphasise that quality is paramount,' said Bailey. 'Implementing quality in health care is a major goal of the reforms, and any provider neglecting quality will soon start losing contracts.'

'But how will you assess it?'

'We will require from providers a firm undertaking that their quality is of the highest standard, and that they are committed to maintaining that standard, before we contract with them. That's not negotiable.' Bailey paused for emphasis. 'And if quality issues come to our notice, for example if we keep hearing about a provider's poor service in the media, we may cancel the contract. That's a powerful incentive to implement quality, don't you think?'

'But will the RHA be checking our service quality?' Turnbull asked.

'No we won't,' said Evans. 'That's your job.'

Bailey pushed on into a profound silence. 'Scope of Purchasing. We face challenges here. We have yet to hear from the National Advisory Committee on Core Health Services, but we need their list of the services we'll be purchasing before we sign off on funding arrangements with the Crown and providers.

'It's frustrating, but meanwhile we can start with conditions that will obviously need purchasing, such as heart attacks and hip replacements, and we can clean up the more obscure items when the list appears. In a worst-case scenario, if no local core services list appears we might adopt the Diagnosis Related Groups list that the United States Government uses for Medicare reimbursements. It has 467 basic items on it so it's pretty comprehensive.'

'Four hundred and sixty-seven different contracts?' said one of the Warwick people.

Bailey laughed. 'Don't worry, we're hiring plenty of people!'

'Excuse me,' said Cassidy. 'The Green and White Paper said that RHAs would consult their own communities and respond to local needs. Will you be carrying out community consultation?'

'Certainly not. We answer to the Crown, not local pressure groups.'

'Don't forget,' Evans added, 'The Bill requires only that we consult "as we consider appropriate".'

More hands were raised, but Bailey looked at his watch and said, 'We'll continue questions after morning tea.'

After queuing for coffee and pastries the Paxton team huddled in a corner, away from Warwick ears.

'No RHA quality audit,' Bennett whispered. 'Thank you, God!' Turnbull had his back to the room and was grinning from ear to ear.

'Game on,' said Steinberg around a mouthful of Danish. 'Your salary budget will take a dive now that you can trim out over-qualified nurses and suchlike.' He shook his head wonderingly. 'Didn't we have Christmas already?'

'What do you know about DRGs, Randy?' asked one of the analysts.

'They've operated for nearly ten years in the States. Uncle Sam pays a set amount, say for a hernia repair: the surgery and the related overhead, based on real costs. Get the guy out on schedule, and you make a profit. Discharge him early, you have less overheads, same fee, there's a real incentive to get him up and out. But if things go badly, say some infection that keeps him in longer, then the hospital wears the extra cost.' He laughed. 'That sure focuses folks on pushing them through.'

'It sounds very sensible,' said Turnbull.

'In theory, sure,' said Steinberg. 'But DRGs cause huge headaches. Why? Two reasons. One, unless you incentivise them the docs don't co-operate and they just keep on treating clients however they feel like, same as here. Drives management crazy. And two,' licking cream from his fingers, 'DRG creep. Let's say hernia guy is taking medication for asthma. It's under control, but when he's in his hernia workup you can have an asthma doc come by and check him out. And then you've got two things you can charge for.

'So yeah, DRGs. Great theory, but they sure as hell favour the provider. You guys are having a pretty good morning, I'd say.' Randy backed out of the circle. 'I need another Danish. They're damn fine, must be the cream down here.'

After morning tea Bailey introduced the woman in the red jacket. 'This is Claudia Donaldson, our expert in contract law.'

'Thanks, Bryce. I know most of you are familiar with this, but I need to be sure we're all on the same wavelength about RHA contracts with providers.

'Initially we will contract for your existing work patterns, to put our systems in place before we transition to the full competitive contracting environment. We'll be using a cost-and-volume model where you tender to provide a fixed number of treatments for a specific illness at a certain cost, and we negotiate a contract. That gives the best balance of risk for both players.'

'A fixed number?' said Cassidy. 'That won't work. If we have a contract for eighty lung cancer operations per year and one year we happen to do eighty operations in the first ten months, what do we say to patient number eighty-one?'

Claudia passed it to Bailey, who shrugged. 'Not our problem. The provider would have to decide whether to roll the client over to the next year—'

'But he's got cancer and he needs treatment quickly.'

'No budget, no treatment,' said Bennett.

Bailey nodded. 'That's true in principle. But the provider can always elect to operate anyway and take the loss. Or they might negotiate cost retrieval from the client — small weekly payments perhaps.'

'You'd ask a patient to pay for treatment in the public system?' said

Cassidy. 'That would get you onto the front page of next morning's *Globe*, for sure. No, we need flexibility, so that you agree to pay for up to ninety, say, and we give you a refund if we do less.'

'A *refund?*' laughed one of the Warwick people.

Bailey smiled. 'I think your proposal would see us paying for ninety "lung cancer" operations a year even if only eighty genuine lung cancer cases were actually treated. Or seventy, for that matter.'

Claudia was staring at him with amused curiosity.

'In reality,' Bailey continued, 'You'll tender for those eighty operations based on current costs, naturally less your discount to make it competitive. If you secure the contract you'll then get busy and trim your overheads — we know there's plenty of fat there — and that will give you the flexibility to do the extra work.'

Another hand went up. 'Yes sir, you have a question for Claudia?'

....

Cassidy was eating his lunch at the edge of the Paxton group when Claudia Donaldson appeared in front of him.

'Hello. I need to be sure you understand contracts — I take it you're a doctor? That's easy, nobody talks about patients round here.' She started eating. 'The health business model requires robust rules. Your refund idea might work if everybody was as honest as you are, but that's not how modern business works. We can't give any player a chance of ripping us off — imagine trying to administer special agreements like that across hundreds of contracts.'

Cassidy frowned. 'But isn't the new system going to be more flexible and responsive?'

She shook her head. 'At operational level you must *eliminate* flexibility. Your staff must be made to comply with negotiated contract quotas and ignore the externalities.'

'Externalities? What are they?'

'An externality is an effect on somebody else that results from you doing business. Not being able to treat clients outside your contract is an externality.'

'And you think I'll tell somebody with a new cancer that we can't treat him because of an *externality*, do you?' Cassidy laughed. 'I don't think so. No Paxton doctor would do that.'

'Why not?'

'Because it would be immoral. And unethical. And unfair . . . don't you agree?'

She chewed for a moment. 'I don't have an opinion on it.'

'What? How can you not have an opinion on something as important as that?'

'My job is to make sure the RHA is protected from risk,' said Claudia, 'and that's what I do. If they had employed me to debate ethics I would, but they didn't so I don't.

'And you need to think that way, too. If you're confused about your role, it makes you unreliable and damages your employer. So if you can't commit to what Paxton Health want, you should get a different job.'

Bailey was calling for everyone to return to their places.

'Thanks for the advice,' said Cassidy.

'You're welcome.' She gave him another of those pitying smiles, and he went to get coffee.

....

'Check this out,' said Geoff, showing Cassidy the *Listener*. 'This article rubbishes the figure of twenty-seven per cent for the relative increase in health care costs between 1980 and 1991, which they used in the Green and White Paper.

'Public health sector costs went up by 242 per cent in that time, and the Consumer Price index went up by 215 per cent. Take one from the other and they got a twenty-seven per cent difference, which is nonsense. Would Treasury think the difference between 300 per cent and 200 per cent is 100 per cent?

'Listen to the chairman of the Medical Association: "A curious piece of arithmetic of which a sixth-form schoolboy would be ashamed." How about that?'

'What's the right answer?' said Cassidy.

'On those numbers, eight point six per cent, it says here. But it gets worse — correct for inflation and the increase in population over that time, and the relative cost of health care actually *fell* slightly. Isn't that amazing?' Geoff laughed. 'That's a central plank of the Green and White Paper, and Simon Upton talked about it before the election. They'll have to stop the reforms, I reckon.'

Cassidy shook his head. 'That's what you or I would do, Geoff. But these guys will have some explanation.'

························

Cassidy handed photocopies of the *Listener* article out at morning tea in the canteen the next day.

'Who cares?' said Bennett after glancing at it.

Turnbull nodded. 'I agree. Obviously once they'd committed, they were in a hurry and the maths wasn't checked. But if the end goal is right, the odd little mistake doesn't matter.'

'*Little* mistake?' said Cassidy. 'It's one of the headlines in the Green and White Paper.'

'These things can happen when you're running at full speed, but that's the only speed to go when you're implementing change.' Turnbull smiled at Cassidy's expression. 'Relax, Steve, there are bigger things to think about than that. And anyway, what can they do about it? We're well down the reform path now, and the underlying logic is sound. The Minister can't suddenly say "Sorry everybody, we got it wrong, we're back to the status quo next week." Politically, that would be disastrous.'

'But they might not have won the election if they had used the real figures,' said Cassidy. '*This* is a political disaster. What do you think, Randy?'

'I see it a little differently,' said Steinberg with a wry smile. 'Dollar to a dime they deliberately put that wrong number there.

'Think of it as the first stage of a space rocket. It's essential for getting things moving and pointed in the right direction, but after that they trash it. They don't need it any longer, and by now the boys are on their way to the moon.'

'Same with this twenty-seven per cent. It got people thinking there was a crisis, so big changes must be needed. They'll still think that because they've kinda got used to the idea by now, and some noise in a magazine won't make any difference. It's the news cycle, my friends — give it a week and folks will be stressing about something else, you'll see.'

'What? You can't just dismiss it like that,' said Cassidy, his voice rising. 'Deliberately lying is much worse than making a mistake. It's cynical manipulation of the voters. Can't you see that?' he looked round at the group. 'Anybody?'

'Listen, Steve,' said Turnbull. 'You're attacking the wrong people. We're managers, right? Our job is to put in place the system that has been designed, and that's what we're doing. If you have a problem with the design then you've got two choices. You can walk away, or you can think about the bigger picture of what we're doing here, get over your objections, and carry on with the job.'

'Yup, that's how it is, Doc. Deal with it,' said Bennett with a patronising smile.

'Jim Bennett told me to deal with it, and that was it,' Cassidy told Zoe on the phone later. 'I felt like punching him in the face. How can they support such dishonesty?'

'They're just doing their jobs, I suppose,' she said with a sigh. 'Anyway, Steve, you do have to deal with it for now, and keep working away at them.'

Cassidy put the phone down and stared at it, envying Zoe's simple faith in him and wondering if he was ever going to make a difference.

But how could he make a difference when he was working with people like Jim Bennett?

······································

Building a dynamic and effective team takes time, and it was late February before the Paxton minibus went to Warwick for the first RHA/Paxton contract negotiation meeting.

Turnbull was sitting next to Cassidy. 'Steve, I want to run something past you, a key part of our plan for attacking Warwick.'

'Sure,' said Cassidy, pleased at this first consultation since the quality plan incident. He hadn't even seen the agenda for today's meeting.

'We're bidding for high level paediatric services today.'

'Paediatrics? How would that work? Paxton sends all its complicated paediatric patients to Warwick because they have the ultra-specialised staff and facilities. We can't possibly compete in paediatrics.'

'Who's competing?' said Bennett from the seat in front. 'We're *eliminating*. Paediatrics is their big thing, so we take it out.'

'"Take it out"? How?'

'The market, Steve,' said Turnbull. 'Remember? Everything comes back to the market. We win the contract and some Warwick people are de-jobbed. But guess what? Paxton's got a nice new department and we're hiring.'

Cassidy was still struggling to understand. 'So Warwick's expert paediatric doctors, nurses, physios, speech therapists and everybody else would lose their jobs.'

'Unless they can get work with us. Naturally at lower pay rates, because going forward we've got all the paediatric work in the area.'

'Most of them will go to Australia,' said Cassidy. 'I would.'

Turnbull shrugged. 'We'll be making fewer hires anyway, to increase productivity.'

'At the expense of quality.' Cassidy thought for a moment. 'You'd have to build a new specialised children's unit in Paxton, duplicating everything they've got now.'

'Not duplicating,' said Bennett. 'We scoped out their facilities and there's plenty of fat there — playrooms, fairy tale pictures on the wall, even a pretend schoolroom. We wouldn't need all that nonsense.'

Cassidy stared out at the normal world moving past the peach-coloured minibus. 'No, this is an RBI.'

'An RBI?'

'A really bad idea. Patient care will definitely suffer. And all the extra travel for patients and their families. Parents of chronically sick children sometimes move house to Warwick so that they can be close to the hospital, did you know that?'

Turnbull smiled and shook his head. 'Steve, you're expert in your field, and we value that. But you still don't understand how business works and you're thinking like a mouse. You need to soar like an eagle and see the opportunities over the horizon. Once we've converted Warwick hospital for long-term, low-level RGUs on age-adjusted contracts, we'll get serious economies of scale. And then we start seriously growing the business, in line with the Crown's expectations. Remember that office with the national and international desks? That's the future.'

'Maybe,' said Cassidy. 'But this uprooted, stripped-back paediatric idea would certainly harm patients so it's unthinkable. And even if it wasn't, have you considered how it would go in the *Bugle* — crying kids, angry parents, Peachy's not so fluffy after all?'

Bennett shook his head. 'Collateral damage is just part of the change process. People will get over it.'

....

'First item, tertiary paediatric services,' said Bryce Bailey. 'This is an exciting proposal, gentlemen. It's bold and visionary, and we love the aggressive pricing. Congratulations on a great piece of work.'

He closed the folder. 'But we're only awarding one-year contracts. I thought you knew that.'

'Bryce,' said Turnbull with a frown, 'the proposal envisions major capital expenditure, and it'll take us three years to recover upfront costs. We need an exception, otherwise we risk big fiscal downside.'

Bailey shook his head. 'A three-year contract carries unacceptable risk for *us*. It's policy that all contracts are for one year so that we maintain the market. Warwick must have a chance to come back in with a more cost-effective bid, and new providers will also be entering the arena. That's much trickier if everything's stitched up for three years.'

'But we can't innovate competitively on one-year contracts.' Bennett's face was red. 'Nobody can.'

'You'll find a way,' said Bailey, picking up another folder. 'So we'll put that one aside pending receipt of your bottom-line price for a one-year paediatrics contract.

'What's next? Yes, the general surgical services categories. This will be easy, it's all diagnosis-based. You've used our draft contract form, that's good. You've defined the service you're providing, the number of times you'll provide it, and your best price. We specify penalties for non-compliance, and then we negotiate. That's all clear. Let's—'

'Excuse me.'

'Yes, Mr Cassidy.'

'These categories are too vague.'

'Vague?'

'Yes. Take hernia surgery for example. There are many different types of hernia, and they can be simple to repair or much more difficult.'

Bailey shrugged. 'No problem. Your price could incorporate a consideration for more difficult hernias. You could restrict your tender to specified types of hernia. Or perhaps you won't tender for hernias at all, if you perceive unacceptably high downside risk. Anyway, let's—'

'And what about complications?'

'Of course you must consider all the risks,' said Claudia Donaldson. 'Do you include complication costs, tender high and risk missing out, or do you exclude them, tender low and risk making a loss? You'll need to find that balance.'

'Your surgeons will be more careful if they know we're not paying for complications,' Bailey added. 'Otherwise we'll be incentivising sloppy work.'

'You'll be incentivising avoidance of difficult cases, if you can make the surgeons come into line with what you want,' said Cassidy. 'Patients needing more complex surgery or people with other illnesses will get stuck on the waiting list, while a fit younger person goes straight through.'

Bailey shook his head. 'That's a hypothetical.'

'It's a certainty. And another thing: if somebody gets pneumonia after a hernia repair, would that be paid for under the hernia contract, or the pneumonia contract? Assuming one provider holds the contracts for both those categories.'

Bennett made a low hissing sound and started popping knuckles.

'Mr Cassidy,' said Bailey, 'are there any diagnostic categories here that you could see Paxton tendering for? What about appendicitis, surely that's straightforward.'

'Well, that brings up another problem. You could call it a can of worms — it's actually the "vermiform" appendix, Latin word meaning it's like a worm, ha ha! Sorry, yes, the time. You're going to pay by diagnosis, correct? Hernia, large bowel cancer, appendicitis and so on.

'But most of these patients come in because they've got a sore belly. Some will have appendicitis, lots will have something else. The clinicians try to sort out why they're sore, and fix it when they can. But there are people who get better and go home without a clear diagnosis.'

'That would be rare,' said Bailey.

'No, it's about one person in three with abdominal pain. And I don't see "abdominal pain, cause unknown" on this list. That group will need a separate contract, otherwise Paxton will bleed money.'

'Do you think *any* contracts can be signed off today?' Bailey asked with exaggerated patience.

'No I don't, because what you're trying to set up won't work. The contract should be for all of general surgery. Then you could—'

'Steve,' muttered Turnbull. 'Have a rest, OK?'

'I'm fine thanks, Gerald.'

'No, let some of us say a few things. Alright?'

'Oh. Sorry.'

Cassidy sat back with a little smile. Zoe was going to be proud of him.

···

'These negotiations will be challenging,' said Turnbull on the way home. 'The RHA will be tough, and we'll need a lot more analysts and lawyers.'

'Who'll pay for them?' asked Cassidy, remembering the simplicity of the Green and White Paper.

'All new hires come out of our budget, of course.'

'But how can you afford them?'

'We should start by laying you off,' said Bennett, popping his knuckles. 'What was the point of all that crap about hernias and appendixes?'

'That's my expertise, Jim. Contracts set up by people who don't understand what they're signing are bound to fail. I urge you to start communicating with the staff who understand the actual work, and believing what they tell you.'

Bennett snorted. 'No, doctor, they just have to learn who's the boss. Why is it so difficult to get normal employer-employee relationships, for God's sake? We're in charge now, and a hernia's a hernia, end of story. And the sooner they understand that, the better.'

'This is exactly why the health sector needed reforming,' said Turnbull as they drove into the car park. 'But nobody said it was going to be easy.'

....

One Saturday morning Cassidy and Les Marriner, an old classmate who was training in pathology, were warming up on the practice putting green at Paxton Valley when a shadow darkened the turf in front of Cassidy's ball.

'You Cassidy?' said a large and vaguely familiar white-haired man. The veins in his neck were bulging, and his pink sweater toned well with the deep maroon of his furious face.

Practice-green etiquette had been grievously breached, but Cassidy had been well brought up and it was a lovely day, so he straightened up and smiled. 'Yes, I'm Stephen Cassidy.'

'What the hell do you think you're playing at?'

'Pardon?' said Cassidy. 'I'm practising my putting.'

'Don't get smart with me, young man. I'm talking about your work, if you can call it that.'

Cassidy glanced across at Les, who stopped trying to pretend that nothing was happening and came to the rescue.

'Hello, Professor Calhoun,' he said. 'Steve, Professor Calhoun used to be the head of pathology.'

'I'm retired now but I hear what's going on,' said the pink and purple man. 'There's a bunch of pumped-up administrators trying to take the place over. Somebody's told them the American way is best, and that's what they're aiming for — insurance for everybody who can afford it, bugger-all for the rest, and worse patient care than we've got now.' He glared at Cassidy. 'Is that what you want?'

'Certainly not,' said Cassidy.

'And you're making it easier for them. You're a disgrace to your profession!'

Over Calhoun's shoulder Cassidy could see people waiting to use the green, some staring at him and others apparently enthralled by the beauty of the clubhouse. 'No, Dr Calhoun, I'm making it harder for them by being there for the patients. Every day I tell the managers about the complexity of medicine and the dangers of not listening to the professionals.'

'Lance,' said one of the men in the audience. 'We're teeing off next. Or do you want to let the next group go first?'

Calhoun was still glaring at Cassidy. 'Stupid bloody do-gooder. You should get out of the way and stop protecting these people.' He turned and stumped off.

Cassidy went back to his putting practice, but his arms had become strangely stiff and the hole seemed to have shrunk to half its size.

Les sank a four-metre putt and picked up his ball. 'OK, big guy, time to front up.' As they walked off the green, he put his arm round Cassidy's shoulders. 'Would you like to talk about it?'

'No.'

'Great, neither would I.'

....

'I played really badly,' Cassidy told Claire later. 'This big angry face kept coming between me and the ball, it was a nightmare. People have told me I'm wasting my time and it won't make any difference, but this is the first time anybody has attacked me personally. "A disgrace to your profession" he called me. Is that what I am?'

Claire laughed and sipped her tea as they sat on the sunny back step. Like her brother Geoff she was relaxed and funny, but unlike him she was small, neat and sensible. She was used to being consulted by large male flatmates.

'Of course you're not, Steve. You're definitely doing the right thing. Who knows what might happen if we all just put our heads in the sand and left the managers to do whatever they want? It would be chaos.'

'I know,' said Cassidy. 'But they all have this weird certainty that they know exactly what's needed.'

Claire shook her head. 'Your knowledge and common sense are what's needed, even if they don't know it yet.'

'Thanks, Claire,' said Cassidy. He finished his tea and stood up. 'You're wasted in oncology, you know that? I'm sure it's not too late to switch into psychiatry if you felt like it. No? Think about it anyway. And I'll go and mow Ron and Carol's lawns.'

....

Carol was sitting on the veranda in her dressing-gown. She raised her face to the sun as Ron lifted her sadly swollen feet onto a stool and covered them with a tartan blanket.

She looked exhausted, but she still had a smile for Cassidy. 'Hello Steve, lovely to see you. How's Zoe?'

'She's great, thanks,' said Cassidy, kissing her cheek then casually feeling her pulse as he sat down beside her. 'But what about you, Carol? Are you taking all the tablets they've prescribed? The pulse is a bit irregular, and those feet—'

'They want me to take about five extra medicines,' Carol laughed. 'I'd rattle when I walked if the doctors had their way.'

'But you *are* taking them all, I hope.'

'Steve, stop worrying, I'm doing fine. I'm getting lots of rest like Dr Stone said, and Ron's been wonderful. He's quite a good cook you know.' She smiled at Ron, whose brief smile did nothing to hide his anxiety. 'I'll be good as gold after the operation, although I'm not looking forward to it. They've put me on the urgent waiting list and I'm expecting a call any day. Anyway, how's the new job?'

'It's been a bit of a struggle so far,' said Cassidy, 'but I'm not about to give up.'

He imagined his new colleagues assessing this overweight woman with the narrowed arteries and the swollen feet, who was so kind and wise and who was now asking her husband of almost fifty years if there were any potatoes ready for Steve to dig.

She had worked hard all her life and paid her taxes, and she was surely entitled to a few more years to enjoy her grandchildren in the best health possible. But Turnbull and Bennett would only consider her effect on the balance sheet, and he feared their verdict would not be favourable.

Cassidy shivered and stood up, and a few minutes later the clippings were flying as he pushed the old hand mower along as fast as it would go.

....

The next day Cassidy attended his first regular Management Group meeting.

'RHA negotiations and related matters,' said Nesbit. 'Gerald.'

The team was pleased when Turnbull described the RHA's view on its quality obligations, but there was a mutter of disappointment when he told them about the lost paediatrics tender. 'There could be other headwinds here,' he continued. 'Steve has raised some issues.'

King glared at the medical adviser. 'What sort of issues?'

'With respect,' said Cassidy, 'you're expecting to make sickness nice and neat. That would be great if it was possible, but real life is often more complicated.' He outlined the dangers of simple contracts, ending with the "abdominal pain, no diagnosis" situation.

'Really?' said Nesbit. 'Doctors sometimes don't find out what's wrong with their clients? That's quite a downside. We'll have to budget for that and tender higher to cover those losses. But if Warwick don't know about this, they'll bid low and land the contracts that we want.'

'No, wait!' Bennett banged his hand on the table. 'This is game on, it's just the break we need.' He leaned forward, his eyes gleaming.

'We tender only for high RGU percentage scenarios, and leave the rest. Warwick don't know about the multi-diagnosis situation, let alone this zero-diagnosis thing, so they underestimate the risks and bid low. Soon they're leaking money, and about to go belly-up. We do a hostile takeover of Warwick, using equity from the Crown who are begging us to help them out because there aren't any other local players. And then we're in the box seat with a regional monopoly provider situation.'

'We'd have to decide how much pain was bearable while we were sitting out,' said Prattley.

'There certainly would be pain in Paxton,' Cassidy agreed. 'Patients stuck even longer on the waiting list because we'd stopped doing that work, or having to travel to Warwick while they're acutely ill.'

No, I mean financial pain for us if our facilities are idle while Warwick is overloaded but still operational. We'd lay off as many staff as we could, but there are still huge fixed overheads.'

'Yeah, all those beds are a problem,' Cassidy agreed sarcastically, 'especially when there are sick people in them. Less beds would mean less patients. Less overheads. In fact, why not take *all* the beds away and be done with it?'

'That's an intriguing idea,' said Turnbull thoughtfully.

But Bennett was ecstatic. 'I'd say it's a *brilliant* idea. Fewer beds with unchanged demand will mean that units have to be moved through faster so that we still meet quota. We can downsize the nursing workforce and save a bundle on salaries. Plus it gives us capacity to expand, to handle the extra work from Warwick after they fail. Nice work, doc — who would have thought you'd come up with something like that?'

'Sorry, everybody,' Cassidy raised his hands to calm the chatter round the table. 'That was a joke, OK? Having fewer beds wouldn't make doctors push patients through any faster, because they can't. It would just increase the waiting lists.'

'I disagree,' said Nesbit. 'Once we have incentives in place and staff know what's expected of them, they will surprise you. Great brainstorming everyone, that was very useful.

'Next item: a message from the Crown's Communications Strategy group. This is Mr Smithson, from the Health Reforms Directorate in the Prime Minister's department.'

A man with short bristly hair and thick, black-framed glasses stood up at the back of the room.

'Thanks, Richard. Look, thanks for your time, I know you're all busy people. But as you're aware there's public negativity about the reforms, due to media and health professionals' misinformation, and this is setting the wrong stage for the next few months.

'We need you to be proactive on this. If you hear anyone criticising what's going on in health, you should confront them and say, "True. Things aren't ideal. In fact, right now New Zealand's health system is a disgrace." Mention cost blowouts, waiting lists, provider capture — all the failings of the current system.

'And then you say, "But that's exactly what will start to improve after One July. Work has begun on developing a health system that works properly, and delivers more consumer choice." That will help us tremendously in the fight for public understanding.

'We will require staff groups and associations to attend Health Reforms Directorate briefings on the reform process. And watch out for when we commence informing the public with innovative television advertisements.

'And remember, this comes from the highest level in Government. Are there any questions?'

There were no questions. Faces were sombre and jaws clenched as the group mentally prepared themselves for the battle ahead.

Smithson nodded. 'My people will be in touch to arrange dates for staff briefings, starting soon. The longer people believe that the health service should be above economic and fiscal reality, the longer the distortions and resentment smoulder, and the more difficult it will be to progress into the new era.'

'Thank you, Mr Smithson,' said Nesbit as the PM's man headed for the door. 'Alright, we'll finish there, unless — yes, Steve.'

'We should start regular briefings for our senior medical staff anyway,' said Cassidy. 'I'll arrange a meeting, say next Wednesday lunchtime? It would be useful for the doctors to meet the CEO.'

Nesbit seemed genuinely disappointed. 'I'll be out of town on Wednesday, otherwise I'd love to be involved. Alex, would you be able to go along?'

'I've got far more important things to do.' King glanced contemptuously at Turnbull. 'We have yet to sign a single contract with the RHA, four months out from One July.'

'It's not our fault,' said Turnbull. 'The RHA are being very difficult. They refuse to provide ballpark costings to help us frame our proposals, they challenge every tiny detail, and once they make an offer they refuse to negotiate.'

Bennett shook his head 'Don't worry, it's routine bum-sniffing. They're trying to force us into win-lose, and we're not blinking. The market will find its level eventually.'

Nesbit chipped in before King could reply. 'Alex, I'm with Steve on this one. I know you're incredibly busy but he's right, it's becoming urgent that we get the medical people on board, start sharing some ideas, and slow down the rate of resignations. It needs somebody senior. And you can do a better job than some outside person when the goal is a strong Paxton team.'

'Very well,' said King, 'I shall say a few words. But it will be a waste of time.'

'I can be there,' said Turnbull.

'I'll come and share the Peachy vision,' said Russell. 'They'll love that.'

Nesbit smiled. 'Good idea. Let me know how it goes, and I'll prioritise coming to the next one. Thanks, everyone.'

······································

'Key concept,' said Cassidy. He was on the couch in his flat, with Zoe beside him and the remains of an excellent veal cordon bleu, one of his favourites from the good old days, in front of them.

His heart thumped as she turned towards him. She was glowing in the yellow sun-frock after a late summer day at the beach, and they were alone in the flat.

'OK, I'm ready,' she said, smiling at the look on his face.

Cassidy reassembled his thoughts. 'The current system isn't exactly a roaring success, is it?'

'What system might that be, my sweet?'

'You can't call me that if we're still being platonic. Unless you—'

'We certainly are. Sorry. All right, what system might that be, Steve?'

'The current public healthcare system, Zoe. Everybody complains about it. But listen. The reforms haven't even started yet, have they? Today's problems reflect the old mismanagement. Once the new system is running, things will rapidly improve as people start pulling together as teams, with strong support and high morale, aiming for clearly defined goals.'

She stared at him. 'And you believe that.'

'No, I don't,' sighed Cassidy. 'But it's what the Prime Minister says we should tell everybody, and I wanted to see what you thought about it.'

'It's nonsense — nobody that I know would ever join a "team" if Jim Bennett was the captain.' Zoe smoothed the skirt over her thighs, and watched a few moments of *Wheel of Fortune,* which had gone unnoticed during the meal. 'But apart from that, how are things going on your side of the wall?'

'I'm getting some traction now, thanks to your advice about taking it slowly. I definitely made a difference at the RHA meeting when I explained the complexities of the acute abdomen. And I've arranged a meeting next week between the deputy CEO and senior doctors to talk about the reforms. It'll be the first time that both sides are in the same room and able to have a decent conversation.'

'That's good, although I wonder if anything we say or do will have any real effect. Who's the deputy CEO? Was he at the barbecue?'

'A hard man called Alex King. He was there but you didn't get a chance to meet him.'

'After I made you take me home.' Zoe poured the last of the wine into his glass by way of atonement. 'Sorry about that, Steve, although it doesn't seem to have damaged your career. But let's get outside, it's too nice an evening to be thinking about managers.'

'Good idea.' Cassidy finished his wine and started to clear the dishes, but the TV caught his eye.

Wheel of Fortune had finished and the first commercial featured a woman in a pink tweed suit, standing in an empty operating theatre. She held a clipboard in one hand and rested the other on the operating table.

She moved slightly towards the camera and started speaking about the health reforms: they were about to improve health care access for all New Zealanders, and bring choice to the health consumer.

'No thanks, lady.' Zoe grabbed the remote and flicked to TV1, but the same woman was there, continuing the same speech in perfect synchronisation. 'Oh *yuck*, get away from me.' But without missing a beat, there she was on TV3 as well. 'She's — my God, how can they *do* that?'

She cycled through the channels again, then pressed the off button and threw the remote onto the couch. 'They're trying to brainwash us!' She glared up at Cassidy, who had jumped to his feet in horror. 'Did your mates do this?'

'Don't call them my mates — and no, I didn't know anything about it,' he said in a trembling voice. He glanced at the window, wondering for a mad moment if the tweed-suited one might be there as well. 'They said there would be some advertisements, but they didn't tell us about this, this *propaganda* exercise. Where do they think this is, Nazi Germany or somewhere? I can't believe they would do that in New Zealand.'

Zoe shuddered. 'Let's get out of here, I need to walk.'

They went quickly along Wakefield Road, then more slowly, soothed by the calm summer evening, up the long slope of Jasmine Street. Soon they were breathing in the smell of newly mown grass at the wrought-iron gates of Victoria Park. They crossed the silent cricket fields, with Cassidy remembering school-day triumphs, and sat down on the old bench at the edge of the park.

Paxton basked in the golden light below them, and beyond it the deep blue of the ocean stretched to the cloudless horizon.

Zoe spoke for the first time since leaving the house. 'We're so lucky to live here. Is there anywhere else as beautiful as this?'

'Possibly,' Cassidy murmured. 'But I've never been there.'

'I've never imagined leaving before,' she said quietly. 'This is my home, it's where my family and friends are.' She took a deep breath while Cassidy stared at her. 'But knowing for sure that they're taking the money away from the hospitals, rather than using it to make them better, has knocked me right back. I can see what it's going to be like as they keep cutting and cutting.

'And now those advertisements — what a smack in the face. Why would anybody stay here, when the people in charge can treat us like that and get away with it?'

'They can't get away with everything while I'm fighting them,' said Cassidy. 'And I wouldn't still be there without your support.'

'I know, Steve. And thank goodness you are. But I personally can't do anything, unless there's a strike or something I suppose. I hate feeling so useless.'

'Useless?' He put his arm round her waist. 'Every day you're helping people who really need you.'

'But that would be true wherever I work. It doesn't have to be here.' She glanced at his face. 'Don't worry, I'm not packing my bags. I wouldn't leave unless it was unbearable, but recently—'

'Zoe Sorensen,' said Cassidy. 'Will you marry me?'

'What?'

'I'm serious. I haven't got a ring or anything, but you've just made me realise how much I love you. I couldn't bear to see you go.' He stood up. 'Would it help if I went down on one knee?'

She frowned and laughed at the same time. 'No! It's very sweet of you to ask, and I believe you mean it, but we don't even know if we're right for each other. That's why we're keeping our distance while we think about it. Remember?'

'While *you* think about it.' Cassidy sighed. 'All right. But I'm pleased that I've told you my true feelings.'

'Feelings noted,' she said with a smile. After a silence they stood up and started walking back. 'You know the deal, Steve. I need to be certain that I can trust you not to turn into a brute again. It may seem harsh, but good intentions aren't enough until you're doing your usual work and being your usual self.'

'I'll resign tomorrow and we'll go away together,' said Cassidy. 'This is much more important than a ridiculous job.'

She gave him another of those heart-bumping smiles. 'That's

beautiful, but right now, your job is more important than us.'

'You're amazing, Zo. Complicated, but amazing.'

She stopped and faced him. 'Not really. But there are lots of people who want you to keep on doing what you're doing, and I'm one of them.'

'Then don't leave me,' Cassidy pleaded. 'I really need your support. Geoff and Claire are great, but I hate being treated as if I've betrayed one side or the other, you should see some of the letters I get. And anyway it's only a few more months until the year is up.'

They walked in silence for a moment before Zoe stopped and sighed. 'I shouldn't have talked about leaving. I'm sorry, that's not fair to you, although work is tough at the moment and I'm dreading what might be just ahead.' She smiled again. 'But right now, I'm here. The president of your fan club. Let's just take it day by day, OK?'

'OK. Does the fan club have rules about holding hands while walking with the subject?'

'Sometimes it's permitted,' said the president.

·································

Cassidy, Turnbull and King sat beside the podium of the hospital's main lecture theatre and waited for the clock to reach 12:30. Facing them in the front row, Russell leafed through his overhead transparencies, and behind him the seats were rapidly filling with men and women in theatre scrubs, white coats, or suits. There were many more senior doctors than Cassidy had expected.

'Harry Prattley's resigned,' said Turnbull.

'Really? Why?'

'He's been struggling for a while, he's not convinced that savings will materialise. The Peachy plan was the last straw — it's exciting and visionary, but it will mean even more borrowing.'

'Has he got another job organised?'

'Not yet, but anyone with his skills will soon get snapped up.'

'That's good,' said Cassidy. 'By the way, were you watching TV the other evening when they advertised the reforms simultaneously on all three channels?'

Turnbull smiled. 'Yes, wasn't that great? It stops people switching channels then saying nobody told them anything. Roadblock, they call it.'

'Everybody I've talked to thought it was horrible. It was propaganda, actually.'

'You call it what you like,' growled King. 'I'd say it's a powerful way to confront ignorant resistance.'

'Well, on that note, let's start winning hearts and minds,' and Cassidy stood up and walked to the podium.

The room was packed and everyone was staring at him. People he had worked for, other senior people who he only knew by name, and many of his friends. Claire waved from the crowd standing at the back.

Cassidy swallowed. 'Good afternoon. Thank you all for coming to this first briefing on the health reforms. I hope it will be the first of many meetings to improve communication within the organisation, and raise our standards of patient care. Now I'm going to ask Mr Alex King, the deputy Chief Executive Officer of Paxton Health, to speak and I would ask that you keep any questions until he has finished.'

King walked heavily to the podium and stood there, motionless except for his beady eyes, until every face was turned silently towards him.

'I am a businessman appointed by the Minister to senior management of the Paxton Crown Health Enterprise, which will commence operations on the first of July. As you know, it has been decided that health providers in this country will become successful businesses, through management by people with the appropriate expertise.

'This is a significant departure from current practice, but it's clear that substantial efficiency gains can be made through implementing a business model.'

The room was silent. Even the hospital's early medical giants, framed for eternity, seemed to be leaning forward and waiting to hear what was coming next.

'We need your informed cooperation for a successful outcome. Today I will describe aspects of the competitive health care model, to help you place your trust in our vision and skills for making the business work.'

Murmurs of conversation started. 'Mr King,' said the professor of anaesthetics, 'people who have worked here for decades know this is a very good hospital, but it can never become a true business.'

Cassidy jumped up. 'Professor Leeson, I wonder if we could keep questions—'

'I disagree,' said King. 'To people with the right skills, running a hospital is no different than running an aluminium smelter.'

'An *aluminium smelter?*' said another voice. 'You can't see any differences between a patient and a heap of bauxite?'

'If we could just save the comments—' Cassidy's plea vanished into the hoots and shouting.

'In business,' King continued in his normal voice then paused so long that people started to call for quiet, 'in business, success comes from standardising and measuring — something that this organisation urgently needs help with — then making objective decisions. Systems, in other words. We are starting to measure the real costs of hospital activities. Soon we will know how many days each client is in the hospital, what is done to them, how much it costs, and how they feel about the experience. With those metrics—'

A storm of boos and laughter broke out. Cassidy waved his arms and shouted as loudly as anyone, and the noise subsided. 'It seems questions can't wait, so we'll take them as they come. Dr Walsh.'

Tony Walsh, the head of cardiology, was a competent-looking man in his fifties. 'Of course we need better business systems. But we also need more rigorous clinical measurement — of what was wrong with our patients, the appropriateness of treatment, and any side effects or complications, for example. Can you pledge, here and now, to help us set up comprehensive, hospital-wide clinical audits? That would help everybody, and we could share the data with others to advance medical knowledge.'

King almost smiled. 'With respect, your suggestion shows how far away from commercial reality you stand. Clinical data and research results are commercially sensitive, and in the new business structure sharing that information with competitors will be prohibited.'

There was a roar of anger and dissent. White-haired professors of international distinction were on their feet and shouting along with the rest of the audience.

Cassidy went across to the podium. 'What about personal details? Allergies, for example,' he shouted. King shook his head to indicate that he could not hear, and they waited until the noise dropped.

'Thank you,' said Cassidy. 'I have asked Mr King to consider exchange of patient details between CHEs, in the event of someone being admitted somewhere away from their home. Would an enquiry from another CHE about possible allergies and other history be refused?'

'I suppose we could make an exception there,' King said. 'But in a competitive environment, giving secrets away to the opposition could put the business, and hence all of our jobs, at risk. Who wants that?'

'Mr King,' said Walsh after the reaction had peaked. '"Secrets" like that aren't how we work, I'm sorry. But I have another question: whose idea was it to make hospitals that have co-operated efficiently for more than a century suddenly start competing with each other?'

'Competition underpins the business model,' said King. 'It drives efficiency, and we are well set up with Paxton and Warwick placed as they are. Competition will help managers develop and reinforce the team spirit of their staff, in line with the best traditions of professional care and good service of their clients.'

A chorus of groans followed this statement, and about a dozen people stood up and walked out, some pausing at the door to shout comments. King watched them go, his initial astonishment hardening into contempt.

The last footsteps echoed on the back stairs, and some oxygen seemed to return to the room. The people left behind looked expectantly at the chairman. Cassidy glanced towards Russell, but the Peachy champion had hidden his transparencies and covered his face with his hands.

Tony Walsh raised his hand. 'Mr King, we both know the answer to my question. It's all come from the Minister of Health and his political colleagues, along with people at Treasury and the Business Roundtable, huddled with their American consultants and feeding off each other's ideas without any practical input whatsoever.' Sounds of agreement and applause rose behind him.

'The reactions from my profession show the scale of the chasm between the political and medical views of the world. But now you've got to try and enforce the dangerous fantasies of your masters, while ignoring the informed concerns of the people who actually make a hospital run.

'So I would like to express my sympathy to you all for the mess you're in, and ask you what you plan to do next.'

King gave Walsh the angry lizard stare for a long time, his jaw muscles working as if he was chewing.

'We will succeed,' the big man finally ground out. 'We know there are massive efficiency gains to be made, and we are used to achieving business success. We would prefer to do it with your support, but if this group continues assuming that you alone know all the answers and are refusing to enter any debate or consultation, we will do it the hard way by gradually bringing in people who align with our goals.'

Walsh shook his head. 'You can't succeed without us, Mr King. This meeting should finish now.'

'I nominate Tony Walsh as the spokesman for the senior medical staff,' shouted Leeson. 'All those in favour . . . Carried!'

'Thank you,' said Walsh as the applause died down. 'Mr King, I invite you and your colleagues to visit us in the hospital to learn about what it is you are attempting to reform.'

'I don't have time for that,' said King. 'My whole day is taken up with meetings.'

'Surely you could spare an hour,' Cassidy urged as the groaning started again. 'You could go for half an hour right now, there's time left. It would make a huge difference.'

'No,' said King. 'It would be a pointless exercise.' He turned to the audience. 'It has been enlightening for me to observe the attitudes and behaviour of this group of highly paid professionals. Apart from that, I predicted this meeting would be a waste of time, and I was right.'

He walked to the door and let himself out, amidst more groans and boos. Turnbull and Russell got up and followed him.

Cassidy was left facing the audience. 'Thank you all for coming. We'll finish there for now, but I will continue to do everything possible to improve the communication between management and the clinical staff.'

'Thank *you* for what you're doing, Steve,' said Leeson. 'We need you on the inside, so don't give up!' He started clapping, and everyone joined in.

Cassidy hurried out to catch up with the managers. After a silent lift journey he went back to his office and wondered how many days or hours he had left.

CHAPTER SIX

Two hours later Turnbull knocked and came in as Cassidy was reading a memo from the CEO: Simon Upton had been replaced as Minister of Health by Bill Birch, and the part charges for hospital inpatient and outpatient services had been abolished.

'Hi, Gerald. Isn't this great about the part charges?'

'It's a pragmatic response to events in an election year, I suppose,' said Turnbull as he sat down. 'But it's a setback to the reforms because it will damage the embedding of the user-pays culture that Randy talked about.' He smoothed the moustache, then took a moment to examine his fingernails. 'Steve, Alex was upset after the meeting with the doctors. He thinks you set him up, and you didn't support him. He has suggested that you should be dismissed.'

'That's not fair,' said Cassidy. 'The meeting wasn't a great success, but it was the start of communication. Can you imagine how it would be received if I was fired for trying to bring the sides together?'

'Calm down, you're safe. The CEO still sees you as a useful team member and he wants you to stay in post. But your job description has been slightly reconfigured.'

'What does that mean?'

'People think it would be better if you didn't come to the RHA meetings any more.'

'But I brought up some really important issues last time.'

'Maybe,' sighed Turnbull, 'but at the end of the day, a big string of objections is unhelpful when we're trying to get contracts signed off.'

'Objections?' said Cassidy with a frown. 'I was trying to suggest contracts that stand a chance of working.'

Turnbull shook his head. 'People feel your game is better suited to the in-house situation. We certainly need you in the Management Group meetings — you earned this month's salary just with that suggestion of removing beds. Simple but powerful. Why hadn't we thought of that already?'

'Gerald, please listen, that was a joke. It would be madness to take beds away.'

'It's that different way of seeing the world that's so refreshing,' Turnbull went on. 'And your link-man role will be vital going forward. You're going to help Jim with the orthopaedic surgeons next week, aren't you? Good. Not to mention all this,' he added, pointing to the incident forms on the desk as he stood up. 'Anyway, I've got to run. See you tomorrow.'

'We *mustn't* take beds away, for Christ's sake!' Cassidy shouted as the door closed.

···

'Congratulations Steve, you're almost halfway there,' said Geoff as the flatmates sat down for dinner a few days later. 'Five months now. I didn't expect you to last nearly this long, even before I had seen the awful Mr King. How can you stand being around people like him all day?'

'Well, Geoff, this is the moral fibre of the Cassidys coming through,' said Cassidy. 'The stubborn bloody-mindedness, remember?'

'But it has its better moments. There is a certain morbid fascination in watching them gradually realise what they've got themselves into. We had a terrific meeting today, with a report from an outside consultant they'd engaged to tell them how to stop all the doctors leaving.'

'A consultant?' said Claire, serving out mushroom risotto. 'They could have saved lots of money if they'd just asked you.'

'I know, but they trust people who come in content-free, find out whatever they can in a few days, and become the instant expert.'

'They've been doing that since Arthur Andersen got off the plane,' said Geoff, sniffing his food. 'Claire, this smells so good.'

'Thanks. So how did the expert presentation go?'

'Rather badly,' said Cassidy. 'He started by describing the long medical training and the toughness of the job, but nobody was interested in that. They laughed when he said that because doctors are smart and powerful, they tend to think they can run a hospital department or a business.'

'But they can,' said Geoff. 'There are lots of doctors successfully running private practices.'

Cassidy nodded. 'I know, but nobody was about to show any sympathy for doctors. And after that things went downhill, starting with information asymmetry.'

'Information asymmetry?' said Claire.

'Yes. The government seems to think it can create a fair market for health. But a fair market needs symmetrical information. For example, you know what bread you like, and you can see if the price is fair by comparing with the other brands sitting next to it. If you don't like my bread or you think it's too expensive, you can buy somebody else's, and if that happens a lot I have to increase quality or drop my price. So we do have a genuine market in bread.

'But in a conversation between a doctor and a patient it's different, because only one person knows lots about health and illness. And patients can't easily shop around. So it's asymmetrical, there's no proper market as such, and instead it needs trust. And it's not just the patient trusting the doctor's knowledge and skill — the employers have to trust doctors too, and pay the bill for whatever they do, even if it is expensive.'

'And there's nothing they can do about it,' said Claire. 'Poor things, it must be very frustrating for them.'

Geoff nodded. 'And anyway, why should doctors strain to save money when the reward for coming in under budget is to lose funds for next year?'

'That's right,' said Cassidy. 'I wish I could cook meals like this, Claire. Would you be able to teach me, do you think?'

'Steve, don't put yourself down,' said Geoff seriously. 'You fry a very fine sausage, and there's nobody in Paxton better than you at heating a mince pie. Nobody!'

'I'd be happy to show you some things, Steve,' Claire smiled. 'This is easy.'

'Thanks very much. Anyway, where was I? Yes, then he said that the doctors needed to align with management's goals, they needed to be fully *engaged* with their employer. And that was where the managers could be influential by setting the tone of the organisation, fostering a sense of community, and creating excitement around common goals. And everybody was writing it all down as if it was the Holy Gospel, even though it's the exact opposite of what they actually do. It was a beautiful example of cognitive dissonance.'

'The doctors *are* fully engaged,' said Claire. 'They're engaged in looking after the patients.'

Cassidy nodded. 'I pointed that out, but nobody listened. To these people, employee engagement means helping them cut services to dangerous levels so that Paxton hospital can win RHA tenders, destroy Warwick hospital and get a monopoly.'

'What a mess,' Geoff sighed. 'Did the instant expert have any concrete suggestions?'

'Yes, he did. He said we need lots more doctors, so that the bad ones would lose their jobs and there would be people to replace them.'

Geoff nodded slowly. 'Intriguing. How would we get lots more doctors?'

'Get rid of the Colleges, shorten undergraduate and postgraduate training time, and lower the bar for immigrant doctors. I know — I asked him how he thought the public would feel about a sharp drop in quality, but Jim Bennett assured me that doctors would be sued or struck off or both, if they were bad enough. "The market will fix it," in his words. They're setting up a Health Commission to scrutinise the health professionals.'

Geoff was frowning. 'Sorry, slow down a bit. A surgeon who screws up people's lives by choosing the wrong operations, or doing them badly, would be dealt with *eventually*?'

'Yup. Everybody seemed happy with that. They'd rely on the media for their information, as far as I could gather. I said that new doctors should be of the highest possible standards before they started treating people, but nobody was interested.'

Claire sighed. 'Were you able to inject any common sense at any stage?'

Cassidy shook his head. 'I did try. I suggested getting senior doctors involved in management again, but that got the only other laugh of the day.' He squeezed the last grains of rice onto his fork. 'After that I gave up, but there was one last gem. He said that when Hong Kong becomes part of China in 1997, all kinds of professionals will leave Hong Kong, and we'll be able to hire as many new doctors as we need.'

'You can see the way they think, can't you?' said Geoff. 'They're desperate to make it all work, but they keep getting hit by facts that don't fit their plans. So they flail around searching for one Band-Aid after another, rather than face the fact that it's a complete crock. Wouldn't you love to know how much that report cost?'

·································

Cassidy had been serious about wanting to learn to cook, and at lunchtime the next day he walked into town and bought a copy of the *Edmonds Cookery Book* as Claire had suggested. He had some spare time these days and he was ready to learn a new skill, especially with a kind and willing teacher.

He was back at his desk and reading page ten about the different types of flour, when there was a knock on the door. With a guilty glance at the clock, Cassidy put the book into a drawer and opened the nearest folder of complaints.

It was Zoe, in her nurse's uniform. 'Hi, Steve. I hope I'm not interrupting?'

'Zo, goodness, of course not. Come in, I'll make tea.'

'No thanks, I can't stay.'

'Well, er, have a seat. What brings you to enemy headquarters?'

'We've just had a meeting of senior nurses,' said Zoe. 'I said you should be there, as the staff liaison person, but I was over-ruled. But I came to tell you before the official announcement — we're going on strike.'

'Really? All the nurses?'

She nodded. 'Yes. And other groups — physios, radiographers, orderlies. Even the kitchen staff. That's if there is a majority vote for it at the stop-work meetings, of course.'

'Wow. That should get their attention, shouldn't it? Who's leading it?'

'There are quite a few of us on the committee but Paul McAlister from fracture clinic will be the spokesman.'

'I guess it had to come to this,' said Cassidy. 'But it'll be bad for the patients.'

'I know,' said Zoe sadly. 'But it's tough on them already. There was another near-miss last night, in Ward 15. The house surgeon had made a mistake with a prescription, and they didn't have the usual staff on so nobody picked it up until the very last moment. A patient with renal impairment almost got a double dose of gentamicin.' She nodded at the look on Cassidy's face. 'Yes, she could have had permanent hearing damage.'

'Will I get an incident form?'

'I expect so. But . . .' Zoe stopped and looked away.

'You're right,' said Cassidy softly. 'What difference can Steve Cassidy make?'

She came round behind the desk and put a hand on his shoulder. 'Sorry but it's true, isn't it? This is getting too big for us to solve ourselves. They're talking about "downward flexibility" which is code for employing less-skilled nurses so that they can pay less — patient safety doesn't come into it. And they'll get away with it if we don't expose them to the public through TV and the papers.'

Cassidy took a deep breath. 'I agree. It's time for a bigger audience now. Well done for making a hard decision, Zo, I know your views on striking. I'll support you wherever I—'

But Zoe was gazing at the framed picture of herself that stood on the desk. 'I didn't know about this, Steve. That's lovely.'

'I kiss it a hundred times a day,' said Cassidy. 'I got the idea from Jim Bennett.'

She laughed. 'Jim Bennett? I can't tell if you're being serious or not.'

'I know. It makes me even more adorable, don't you think? But now we must both get back to work, unless you really would like a cup of tea? Alright, I'll see you at the weekend. And thanks for letting me know.'

....

Cassidy conscientiously made up the time he had used to sample the *Edmonds Cookery Book*, and left work a little later than usual.

He planned to throw himself into learning how to cook, with his usual enthusiasm for any new project. But he would keep it a secret from Zoe until he was good enough to put on a really special meal for her. He should have proper lessons as well, he decided as he drove home. She'd been sarcastic about woodwork lessons, but she was right again. What a woman! He should find out about evening classes.

There was an ambulance in Ron and Carol's driveway.

Cassidy parked and ran, to be met at the front door by the reversing back of an ambulance man carrying a stretcher. Carol was lying on it, her face pale beneath the oxygen mask. Her eyes were closed.

They rolled the trolley into the ambulance and locked it down. The driver closed the doors and ran to the front, and the siren began.

Ron stood in the doorway, his eyes wet and fearful. 'She cried out,' he gulped. 'I went in and she was — she was—'

Cassidy put his arm round the trembling shoulders. 'Come on, I'll take you to the hospital. Where's your jacket?'

A nurse directed them to the Coronary Care Unit waiting room. Cassidy asked Ron for the names and phone numbers of their children, and went to the pay-phone down the corridor to let the family know. Then they sat together, Ron's eyes fixed on the doorway, the quiet whistling of his breathing the only sound apart from the softly ticking clock.

The minutes went slowly by until a young man in a white coat, with a stethoscope around his neck, knocked gently on the doorframe. 'Mr Higgins?' He came in and sat beside Ron, recognising Cassidy with a quick smile — Warren Davison, one of the cardiology registrars. 'We'll bring you in to see her now, but I warn you she's very unwell and we've put an airway tube in to help with her breathing. She's had a major heart attack and the heart is struggling.'

'Is she going to be all right?' Ron quavered.

'It's too early to tell, Mr Higgins.' Davison paused. 'we've found that her blood pressure is very high. Was she taking all the tablets that had been prescribed?'

'Well no, doctor, she wasn't because — because it was so expensive,' said Ron in the same tremulous voice. 'With the extra charges on doctors' visits and prescriptions and that, we hadn't been able to afford everything.' He sniffed.

Davison sighed. He was a year behind Cassidy, but he already had some silver hairs and the steady, straight-mouthed face of someone who had seen plenty of suffering.

'Come on, let's get you in to say hello for a moment. You've let other family members know? That's good.'

Cassidy and Davison left Ron holding Carol's hand, and had a drink of water in the ward office.

'Is she a relative of yours?'

'Next-door neighbour. I knew she was unwell and on the waiting list, but I hadn't realised how bad things were.'

'The blood pressure?'

'Yes, and not getting the tablets because of the part charges. Christ, I would have paid for the bloody things if I'd known.' Cassidy blinked.

'There's been a lot of that going on, with God knows how many deaths and how much unnecessary suffering,' said Davison. 'Why aren't these people investing in prevention? Honestly it beggars belief. But Tony Walsh is getting more and more angry about it, so we'll see what happens.' He finished his water, crushed the plastic cup, and spun it into the bin. 'I've got to go. Take care.'

'Thanks Warren,' said Cassidy. He went back to the waiting room to wait for Ron and Carol's children to arrive.

....

Cassidy stayed until Carol's family had arrived, then left as there was nothing more he could do. He slept badly and rang the hospital at six a.m. to learn that Carol had died during the night.

He pulled on his robe and eased the front door open. Then he sat on the old couch on the veranda, staring across at the neat little house and garden next door.

'Steve?' It was Claire, holding out a cup of tea. 'I heard you talking on the phone. Is Carol alright?'

He told her the news, and swung his legs round so that she could sit beside him.

'I guess we shouldn't be surprised,' he said after a silence. 'She had a lot of risk factors, and she wasn't taking all the anti-hypertensives.'

Claire blew her nose.

'She could have gone at any time, I guess,' sighed Cassidy. 'But if I'd listened a bit more carefully the last time I saw her, she might still be here now.'

They sat in silence again, then Cassidy snorted. 'Jim Bennett would call this "collateral damage" from the part charges. He should come and explain that to Ron.'

....

'I come over here as little as possible,' said Bennett as they walked along the main hospital corridor. 'Hardly know my way round.'

'That's stupid,' said Cassidy. 'How will you get people's respect and cooperation when you hide from them all the time?'

Bennett glanced in surprise at this new, rude Cassidy. 'I just need them to do their jobs, Doc.'

They came to the Ward 25 seminar room, which was empty. Bennett took a file marked 'Hip replacements 1993/4' out of his briefcase and put it in front of the chair at the end of the table, then wandered round the room. He flicked on the X-ray viewer and glanced at pictures of broken bones. He read about hand-washing technique.

He looked at his watch. 'Bastards. They're keeping us waiting to try and get us on the back foot.'

'They'll still be in their earlier meeting,' said Cassidy.

'No, this is tactics. I've seen it all—'

The door opened and a dozen men came in, all talking at once. Two were in theatre scrubs and the rest in dark suits. A small group went to the X-ray viewer and started examining pictures of rods and screws in someone's spine.

'Good morning,' Bennett shouted from the head of the table.

The surgeons noticed him and soon they were all sitting, most of them with crossed arms and hostile stares.

'Good morning. My name is Jim Bennett, and I'm the manager of the surgical cluster.'

'Where's the CEO?'

Bennett smiled. 'I represent the CEO and the Board. On One July we enter a new environment where procedures are purchased by the Regional Health Authority through negotiated contracts. If this particular tender is successful, the RHA will purchase from us 120 hip replacement operations over twelve months. Then before One July 1994 the contract will be readvertised, and if we achieve a positive result the 1994/95 volumes and pricing structure will be signed off.'

'And you think this is good,' said Patrick Parkes, the director of orthopaedic surgery, who as a registrar had just missed out on an All Blacks trial.

'Certainly.'

'Who sets the price?'

'We have a negotiating team.'

'What is the medical experience of the team?'

'Their experience is in negotiation,' said Bennett.

Parkes over-rode a burst of incredulous laughter. 'How have you set prices? Nobody's asked me about this — I bet they haven't even asked Butch.'

'Butch?'

'Cassidy.'

'He's not involved.' Bennett spoke slowly and clearly. 'The analysts have considered all factors and calculated the price.'

'Do the analysts know the difference between a Charnley and an Exeter prosthesis? Do they understand that the technology improves constantly, and six months from now we might be using something different, with a different price?'

Bennett shook his head. 'There will be no more cost blowouts.'

Parkes snorted. 'You're dreaming if you think we'll compromise patient care so that you can collect your productivity bonus. We work to get the best outcome for each patient, and if it costs a bit more, well tough.'

Bennett shook his head. 'Once the quota and budget are fixed, they're fixed. And when our obligations are fulfilled you will have to tell the next client that they'll have to wait for the new contract year to begin. Assuming our 94/95 tender is successful.'

'Maybe,' said Parkes. 'Or we could do the operations that need to be done, and you and your bean counters could get stuffed. Because we're dealing with people in pain. And for your information they're patients, not clients. Lawyers and hookers have clients.' The surgeons laughed.

'Listen to me,' said Bennett. '*There is no more money.* I can't stop you doing what you want to day by day, but once the money is spent there will be no top-ups — from One July everyone will be held accountable to their contracts.'

He paused. 'There is another aspect. How many hip replacement sets are in stock?'

Silence.

'There were 180 yesterday morning,' said Cassidy. Bennett had got him to count them.

'Thank you. On One July, inventory will be carried over from the Area Health Board budget and entered on the books at zero cost. So you can start the new year that much ahead.'

'But hold on,' said one of the surgeons, 'some of those will be B-83s.'

Cassidy checked his notes. 'There are thirty-one B-83s.'

'Well, you can forget them,' Parkes sat back, folding his burly arms. 'They've had a five per cent annual dislocation rate in overseas trials, and we've stopped using them.'

'So who ordered that many, when the technology changes so fast?' said Bennett. 'There's a good example of your management skill levels. But they must be used up before any new sets are bought.'

'*Must be?*' Parkes' face turned the colour of raw steak. 'Who the hell do you think you are? I was an orthopaedic surgeon when you were in kindergarten.'

'You're very senior,' Bennett agreed. 'But the days of ignoring financial reality are over.'

''This is completely unacceptable!' shouted Parkes. 'I shall lodge an official complaint!'

'Feel free. None of this is my decision.'

'Let's *pretend* for a moment,' Parkes mimicked, 'that we believe you, and that our professional life is going to be invaded like this. Do you think anyone will want to work here any more? I warn you, people won't stay.'

Bennett stared at him and said nothing.

'I've heard enough,' said one of the surgeons. 'I've got patients waiting.' He got up and the others followed, slamming the door behind them.

Bennett closed his diary. 'So we tick off another so-called consultation with the medical profession. And they wonder why people despise them.'

'Who despises them?'

Bennett paused from stuffing folders into his briefcase. 'Everybody I know. Those guys got very expensive training for nothing, and they think that somehow entitles them to behave exactly as they please.'

'The patients think the surgeons are terrific,' said Cassidy. 'What will you do if they all leave?'

Bennett shook his head. 'They won't leave, they just need to look tough in front of their friends. This often happens when people first hear about accountability.'

They walked back in silence until they reached the administration block. 'Come upstairs for a moment,' said Bennett.

His new office was the same size as the one he had shared with Cassidy, but up here he and Sir Roger were alone and the view was better. They sat down.

'So, Butch, tell me about these things dislocating.'

Keep calm, Cassidy told himself. 'There's a metal ball on the thigh bone component that fits inside a cup in the pelvis, and it can sometimes pop out. It's very painful. And it seems the B-83s are more likely to do that than the others.'

'Then what? Another operation?'

'No, they get put back in by manipulation under a quick anaesthetic. They might need surgical revision if it keeps happening.'

'So it's not the surgeon's fault?' Bennett was doodling on a pad.

'No. It's mostly a problem in older people who aren't very strong. They walk less because of pain before the operation, making the muscles even weaker so they don't hold the new hip in very well.'

'It's the client's fault.'

'It's not anyone's fault. It just happens sometimes, and it's why they keep designing new ones that they hope are safer.'

Bennett underlined 'B-83' on his pad. 'Do you think other CHEs would have a few B-83s lying around?'

'Probably . . . Oh no, I see what you're thinking. '

'We could buy them all, anonymously of course, or they might even give them away. That would change the maths. We could increase the number of operations we bid for, and seriously undercut Warwick. We might even get *all* the hip jobs for the whole area.' He started drawing dollar signs around 'B-83'.

'Except that our surgeons won't use the B-83s.'

Bennett shook his head. 'With the savings on overheads we'll pay an incentive for using them. That'll get them off their high horses, you watch.'

'Forget this, Jim,' said Cassidy. 'It's unethical and it would be legally indefensible. It's not going to happen.'

'Have a nice day, Butch.'

CHAPTER SEVEN

'Your new staff representative won't last long if he carries on like this,' said Bennett, throwing the *Bugle* onto Cassidy's desk a few days later.

Senior Doctor Attacks Health Reforms, Cassidy read. Walsh's picture led an article describing the effects of inadequate prevention, then the prescription part charges, on a patient who was not named, but was almost certainly Carol Higgins.

She would probably still be alive today if our health system was anywhere near an appropriate standard. But New Zealand proportionally spends less per person on health than almost all the OECD countries, so failures like this are not surprising.

What is surprising is the method the Government has chosen to try and improve the situation. Managers, lawyers and analysts are crowding into an underfunded health system, taking salaries out of it, then telling us we need to economise. They couldn't have got it more wrong, and it's very dangerous.

'He's absolutely right,' said Cassidy. 'But what's it got to do with me?'

'You need to do some staff liaison. Find this blow-hard and remind him that media contact is restricted to the CEO and the Board chair. If he doesn't like working here he can leave, but hanging round and then whining in the *Bugle* just shows him up as a loser. Is he a mate of yours?'

'I hardly know him. But Tony Walsh is a legend, he's extremely good at his job and he gives this place 110 per cent. He's the opposite of a loser.'

'Wow,' sneered Bennett. 'But even if he walks on water, he can't mouth off in public every time he doesn't get what he wants. It's a breach of his contract with us and it could negatively impact the reforms.'

'What he's saying is true though. You should listen.'

'No, *you* should kick his arse and explain the rules, liaison man. And that's an order from Alex King.'

....

Cassidy trudged towards the Coronary Care unit, remembering Carol sitting on her veranda that last sunny morning, and Ron's breakdown at her funeral.

He asked for directions, then knocked on the half-open office door before realising that Walsh was on the phone.

Walsh beckoned him in and pointed to a chair. Cassidy moved a pile of patient notes onto the desk and sat down.

'No, I'm saying that political decisions are causing hardship and poor outcomes at a personal level, and people need to know what's happening . . . Deaths? Yes, people are dying because of these policies . . . I can't answer that in a sound-bite, but I'd be happy to spend more time on it later . . . You're welcome. Goodbye.'

He put the phone down and smiled at Cassidy. 'I seem to have caused a bit of a stir.'

'You have. Dr Walsh, I've been sent to ask you to stop talking to the media, apparently it's a breach of your employment contract.'

Walsh shrugged. 'It would be a breach of ethics not to warn the public, so that's easy. But thanks for the feedback.' He looked at Cassidy. 'What's your role in all this? I was surprised to see you running that meeting the other day — aren't you a surgical registrar?'

Cassidy explained his temporary career path.

'Good for you. Are you having any effect?'

'It's hard to tell. I'm constantly explaining that health care is complicated, but they prefer to think about nice neat units.'

'Yes, they're the generals back at headquarters, sticking coloured pins in maps, and we're in the front line dealing with all the sweaty and unpredictable detail that they would rather ignore. But we have to keep educating them, so it's good that you're on the inside.'

'Carol Higgins was a friend,' said Cassidy. 'I'm kicking myself for not seeing what was going on. I hadn't realised how sick she was.'

Walsh sighed. 'So many people are suffering consequences because they stopped taking their medication. Which is not something the honourable Mr Upton had considered — I hope, anyway — when he decided to give people some pain.'

'Well, at least they've stopped the hospital charges now.'

'Yes, that's good,' said Walsh, 'even if it is only because there's an election coming up. But somehow we have to get them thinking beyond the short term. Keeping a cardiac patient alive and out of hospital with angina rehabilitation and some education about diet and exercise costs the country about five hundred dollars, but time in Coronary Care plus bypass surgery costs about eighteen thousand dollars. Hardly a bargain for the taxpayer, is it? And what kind of a "first-world" health system is it when somebody like Mrs Higgins dies a preventable death?

'No, we have to keep at them. This strike will be awful, but at least it will bring the issues out into the open. But for now, I'd better get back to the ward round.' He stood up. 'It's been good to meet you, Steve. Keep chipping away. Speaking of which, I've seen you at the golf club, haven't I? We should have a game some time.'

....

'I hope you gave him a good slapping.' Bennett lathered tomato sauce over his pie.

'He definitely understands the issues,' said Cassidy.

'Good. We're being very nice about it, considering. People upstairs wanted us to review his contract.'

'Fire him, you mean?' said Cassidy. 'What people upstairs?'

'The CHE Advisory Committee, CHEAC. They're developing Paxton's detailed establishment plan.'

Cassidy started buttering his roll. 'I've never heard of them. But they don't see a place for Tony Walsh in the detailed establishment plan?'

'Only if he does what he's paid to do, which is cardiology.' Bennett stared at Cassidy. 'I really do hope you made that crystal clear to him.'

Gerald Turnbull unloaded his tray and sat down. 'Good afternoon, gentlemen.'

'Hello, Gerald,' said Cassidy.

'All Walsh needs to know,' Bennett continued, 'is that apart from a few whingers like him, everybody is pulling together to develop a world-class health system.'

'Huh! Tell the RHA that,' said Turnbull. 'They're still being obstructive, even though the Crown has brought in external consultants to force contracts through. We can't even get them to commit to service definitions.' He started his soup.

'I can help there,' said Cassidy. 'Half a dozen doctors could whack out all the service definitions in a week or two.'

Turnbull shook his head. 'No, Steve, we can't have medical capture. But did you hear what happened yesterday? We'd completed the negotiations on hip replacements for this year, and we only had to sign the contract. Then the RHA announced that the Crown is building a reserve for re-allocation to areas with most need and will be holding back two per cent of every contract fee, so they would be adjusting the final price accordingly.'

Bennett had just taken a big mouthful of pie, but he emitted a low growl and rolled his eyes.

'What? That's not how the market works,' said Cassidy. 'Shouldn't hospitals just go belly-up if they can't make a profit?'

'They should,' said Bennett as soon as he could speak. 'Sir Roger would never interfere with the market like that.'

'This is a setback for the model,' Cassidy continued with mock seriousness. 'A most unwelcome intrusion of reality. Although it is good news for patients in those areas.'

Bennett growled again and stabbed a potato.

'At least we got the contract,' said Turnbull. 'Hip replacements, a nice neat job that we can measure and control. And even minus the two per cent we've got a healthy margin, thanks to the B-83s.' He laughed as he saw Cassidy's frown. 'You're allowed to take credit where it's due, Steve. When business courses all over the world are studying our work in years to come, the B-83 play will be a nice case report, and it'll have both your names attached.'

'I would sue if my name appeared anywhere near it,' said Cassidy. 'But what about the increased pain and suffering from the extra dislocations?'

'We can live with that,' said Bennett.

'But the surgeons can still refuse to use them.'

Bennett shrugged. 'Their choice. I spelled it out in the meeting, and I've put it in writing to their knuckle-dragging boss: when they run out of the other types they can either start using up the B-83s, or tell the units that they'll just have to wait a bit longer.'

'You see, Steve,' smiled Turnbull. 'Right there, Arthur Andersen's economies are starting to work.'

'Congratulations,' said Cassidy. 'Let's get to work on those frigates, eh? A bit of rope here, a handrail there, it'll soon add up. All we have to do is ignore the agony of the little old lady arriving in the Emergency department with her fifth dislocation.'

'What?'

'*Little old lady?*'

'Sure.' Cassidy put milk into his coffee. 'It's mostly older people in the public hospitals.'

'Little old ladies are *RLUs*!' Turnbull's voice quivered. 'Hip replacements are for RGUs, aren't they?'

'That's what you said in the briefing, Gerald,' said Bennett, his face twitching.

'Two broad groups of patients have hip replacements.' Cassidy nibbled a piece of icing off his pink bun. 'There are the relatively young, fit people that you described in the briefing. They often have insurance and have the operation in private. Then there are the uninsured, who come to the public hospital after extra years of pain. The elderly get most of the hip replacements in the public system, either for bad arthritis or after a fracture.'

Bennett slumped back in his chair and stared at the ceiling. After a moment he said tonelessly, 'We calculated it down to the last toilet roll. Hip replacements were going to cross-subsidise heart surgery and close Warwick out of that, but instead we'll be spending all our time battling RLU cost blowouts . . . this is a bloody disaster.'

'One among many,' Cassidy agreed. 'But remember what Randy said about DRG creep. You can always cash in on the comorbidities: diabetes, high blood pressure, niggling infections. Sometimes even cancer.'

'Hmm, I'd forgotten that,' said Turnbull. 'So we'd just say that as well as the hip replacement contract, the unit comes under the diabetes contract, or the infection contract. Or better still, she's under both.' He started smiling. 'This could be seriously cashflow positive for us, even before we punch her ticket for the hip replacement.'

'Only if we secure those contracts,' said Bennett. 'What happens if they're all awarded to Warwick? We can't have their people snooping around over here.'

'Don't worry,' said Cassidy. 'Diabetes is so common that every CHE will get a diabetes contract. And it should include a ring-fenced budget for diabetes prevention.'

'Prevention?' Bennett laughed. 'I don't think so. Why would a health-care business ever want less illness?'

'Yes, you've got those shareholders to think of haven't you?' said Cassidy. 'But what will happen if hip replacement RLUs suck all the money out of the diabetes contract?'

'Then the Crown bails us out or we stop providing a diabetes service.' Bennett was looking a lot more cheerful. 'Either way it won't be our problem.'

'Exactly,' said Turnbull. 'Thanks for pointing all that out, Steve.'

....

It was Geoff's thirtieth birthday, and the little Wakefield Road house shook as the Rolling Stones blended with the laughter and shouting of young doctors, nurses and friends.

Zoe was at a family dinner party for her grandfather and was going to come as soon as she could afterwards. The minutes dragged for Cassidy — strike committee meetings had kept her busy after a unanimous 'yes' vote at the stop-work meetings, and he had not seen her for a week.

He danced with Claire for a few minutes before somebody whisked her away. Left alone again, he made his way through the crowd towards the kitchen to get a drink.

Among the tubs of iced beer bottles sat the large bowl of Geoff's famous secret-recipe punch. As a courtesy to the birthday boy, Cassidy filled a glass and drank half of it immediately.

A heavy hand fell on his shoulder. 'Hi, Steve.'

Cassidy shuddered as the fiery brew hit his stomach. '*Whoo!* Hell. Rob, have you tried this? It needs a No Smoking sign.'

'No sane person would drink punch made by a surgeon,' said Robert Dow, who had recently qualified as a physician. 'Can I talk to you for a minute?'

Groaning silently, Cassidy topped up his glass and led the way to the back garden. There would be a frost tonight but it was quieter there, despite the melancholy vomiting sounds coming from behind the garage.

'Have you seen the employment contracts your mates have been offering us?' said Dow.

'They're not my — No.' Cassidy drank more punch. 'This stuff is awful.'

'The collective contract has expired, and they produced new individual contracts with seriously decreased leave and allowances. And they wanted us to let them drop our salaries by up to five per cent "if the fiscal needs of the Board require it"!' We challenged the salary reduction clause, and they said it was to give us "protection".'

'Who were you dealing with?' asked Cassidy.

'A louse called Bennett, mostly. Anyway, they came back with the next version that gave the CEO the right to alter salaries "as he or she sees fit"! That's what they'd been offering protection against, but of course now that offer is history.'

The vomiting had finished, and they moved aside to let the reveller wobble back to the party.

'They said it meant they could increase the salaries of good performers. What a joke.' Dow finished his beer. 'Don't they understand the damage they're doing?'

'No, Rob, they don't. They're under pressure from above, and sometimes the details get — I'm not sticking up for them, I'm just explaining.' Cassidy sighed. 'Anyway, I'll see what I can do.'

'Thanks mate,' said Dow. 'It's good to know we've got somebody on the inside, we all appreciate what you're doing. But you'd better get cracking or they might run out of senior doctors.'

Cassidy followed Dow back into the warmth of the kitchen. He decided the punch wasn't too bad once you got used to it, but tipping his head back to empty his glass made his head spin. He sat down at the table.

'Steve,' said Geoff a moment later, 'why are you lurking back here? I've got someone who wants to meet you. This is Clive Maxted — you know, *Maxted's Morning*? We were talking about the reforms and I said you're fixing everything for us. Clive, this is Steve Cassidy. I'll leave you boys to it.'

Cassidy stood up with some difficulty and shook hands. 'Excuse me a moment.' He went to the sink and drank two glassfuls of water. 'Would you like a drink, Clive?'

Maxted silently held up a bottle of beer.

'Oh, OK. I always read *Maxted's Morning*, it's good. Let's sit down.'

The *Maxted's Morning* column was the best part of the *Globe*. A consistent advocate for battling Kiwis, it was strongly opposed to the health reforms and was sometimes quoted by the opposition in parliamentary debate.

Its author was in his forties, with greying hair curling over the collar of a battered brown leather jacket, and shrewd eyes in a plump, humorous face. 'Geoff tells me you're single-handedly resisting the full force of the reformers.' Maxted peered at Cassidy with a scientist's curiosity.

Cassidy started to shake his head, then waited for the room to stop spinning. 'You mustn't believe everything Geoff tells you.'

'What's your job exactly?'

'Staff liaison officer. I'm trying to make the transition into the new system easier for the hospital, and to explain to management why the staff respond the way they do.'

Maxted nodded. 'How's it going so far?'

After that, Cassidy's evening improved. Maxted was an interested listener and it was a relief to talk to someone without feeling attacked. Pizza appeared, and they ate as they talked.

Then suddenly Zoe was there, exclaiming at how hot it was inside the house and unzipping her ski jacket to reveal the favourite silver dress.

'Sorry I'm so late.'

'No problem, Zo,' said Cassidy, helping her out of the jacket as Maxted stared with open admiration. 'This is Clive Maxted, you know, from *Maxted's Morning*? Zoe Sorensen. I'll just hang this up.'

When he came back, they were sitting close together and Zoe was talking fast in a low voice while Maxted listened intently. Cassidy got drinks for all of them, and joined in.

There was lots to say, but the flow of talk finally slowed and Maxted finished his beer, shook their hands and said goodnight.

Cassidy stretched and sat down again. He was with his favourite person and soon they would be dancing, but she still had some wine left and there was no rush. 'How was dinner?'

'I left them all having a great time. Granddad was in good form for an old bloke who turned eighty last week.'

'And your Mum?'

'She's good, she sends you her love.' Zoe sipped her wine. 'Do you think it was alright talking to Clive Maxted like that?'

'Probably not,' said Cassidy. 'But as it was all true, I don't care. Do you know what I heard tonight about the doctors' employments contracts? Evidently . . . no, that's enough about all that.' He stood up. 'Young Zoe, let's have a little holiday from work and politics. Come and dance with me, please.'

With a smile she took his hand, and they went towards the happy noise in the lounge.

Much later, Sinatra was crooning softly and they were dancing slow and close.

'I should go,' Zoe said huskily. 'It's been a lovely evening but it must be very late.'

'You don't have to rush away. You're not working tomorrow, are you?'

He smelt her scent as her head moved against his shoulder. 'No.'

'I don't think it would be safe for you to drive,' said Cassidy. 'There might be ice, and you've had a few wines. I'd hate to think of you falling asleep on the way home.'

'I'm almost asleep now,' she murmured. 'I'll get a taxi. There's a joke about that, isn't there? "Call me a cab." "Okay, you're a cab."'

'You'd wait for hours for a taxi at this time of night. It would be easiest just to stay here.'

Her back muscles tightened under the thin material as she lifted her head and looked across the room, but then she snuggled back against him. 'There's somebody on the couch already.'

'You could sleep in my bed.'

'Really.' He had to lean down to hear what she was saying. 'And where would you be?'

'That's Andy Green on the couch. I'll put him in a taxi, and I'll sleep there. Zo?' He staggered slightly as she leaned against him, then he reached down and picked her up and carried her to his bed. She was dead to the world and did not waken as he pulled the sheets back, gently laid her down and unclasped her hands from his neck.

He took her shoes off and put them neatly beside the bed. Then he stood for a long time watching the moonlight and its shadows on her face and body. The temptation to slip in beside her was almost unbearable, but they'd come so far and the thought of losing her again was infinitely worse.

Cassidy sighed wistfully and pulled the bedclothes over and up to her chin. She muttered something and turned on her side, and he closed the curtains and tiptoed out of the room.

CHAPTER EIGHT

July 1993

Cassidy welcomed the end of the waiting when One July finally arrived, although he was increasingly worried about what the next few months would bring.

He had just started on the day's feedback forms when he was joined by Keith Stratford, the hospital's veteran mailman and a mate since Cassidy's house surgeon days. Keith was always eerily well-informed, possibly because the internal mail envelopes mostly had their flaps tucked in rather than gummed down.

He handed Cassidy one of the brown envelopes. 'Morning tea at ten o'clock to celebrate the official start of Peachy.'

'Thanks, Mr S. Today's the big day, eh?'

Keith sniffed. 'The bosses think so. They'll be scoffing their lamingtons and patting themselves on the back for a "smooth rollover", meaning nothing's changed. But then it'll start hitting the fan as they lay off everybody they can to make their cuts. By the time this little lot's all done we'll be down at around six and half per cent of GDP spent on health, the lowest in the OECD. Lower than Greece, for God's sake. Of course that's before people bring it back up again by spending their own money.'

Cassidy frowned. 'How do you know that stuff?'

'A little birdie told me. And here's something else — Mr Nesbit's resigned, he's going to Wellington to advise the Minister.'

'What? When?'

'Last day today,' said the oracle. 'Mr King will be the next CEO, and God help us all.' He looked at Cassidy. 'And what about you? How much longer will you be running round trying to steer the *Titanic* away from the iceberg?'

'As long as it takes,' said Cassidy. 'I'm right inside the organisation now, and when they realise how badly they need my help, I'll be ready. I've already made a difference in—'

'Dr C, you're farting against thunder, pardon my French. These boys are playing on a different court from you. It's not about improving health care for people like me, it's about creating wealth for people like them. You watch what happens, then tell me I was wrong.' Keith nodded seriously. 'You're doing your best, and we're all grateful, but you'll never get them thinking your way. Do yourself a favour and get out early, is my advice.'

'Maybe,' said Cassidy absently. He had just realised that there would be no more Nesbit between him and King. 'But you're not always right, you know.'

'That's true,' said Keith. 'I did make a mistake once.'

'There you are, then. What happened?'

'I thought I had made a mistake, but it turned out I was wrong about that. Anyway, don't forget, morning tea at ten. Enjoy the lamingtons.'

....

'Is it true that Richard Nesbit is leaving?' Cassidy asked over the chatter of the canteen.

'How did you know that?' said Turnbull with a frown. 'He's making an announcement here at 10:30. We'll certainly miss Richard's enthusiasm and vision, but Alex will step up. He's perhaps more of a fighter, which could be useful going forward. But whatever happens, this is a special day. Take it all in, everyone — years from now you'll remember where you were when it all officially began.'

'Yes,' said Cassidy. 'Fifth floor, administration block of the P CHE.'

'Partly right. It's the first day of Peachy, of course. But it's not the administration block any more, it's the Leaders' Building. More brilliance from your team, Ricky.' Russell beamed as Turnbull raised his peach drink in a toast. 'One July, gentlemen. A smooth rollover then onwards and upwards. We have an elite corps of professionals—'

'And the Doc,' boomed Steinberg, slapping Cassidy on the back.

'—and we'll soon have all the ducks in a row to commence highly productive work and permanently change the ways in which health is delivered in this country and eventually the world. Cheers!'

'And what a mandate the people have given you,' said Steinberg. 'Did you see that poll showing that seventy-seven per cent of New Zealanders were dissatisfied with the system before the reforms started?'

Cassidy frowned. 'That doesn't mean they wanted *this* new system though.'

'Maybe, but what can they do about it? The show's on the road. Nice job, guys!' They raised their glasses and drank again.

'How did the first strike negotiation go?' said Cassidy.

Bennett laughed. 'It couldn't have gone better.'

'They gave us all the usual stuff,' said Turnbull. '"We're short-staffed — safety is threatened — patients will suffer".'

'"We won't take it any more,"' moaned Bennett. 'But they always do. Your girlfriend was there, Butch. She got really cross, something about laundry bags, I couldn't follow it. Then as I was explaining market realities, she goes "That's irrelevant. This is about *professional standards!*"' He smirked and took a bite of lamington.

Cassidy could imagine Zoe's face as she said that, and a lump came to his throat. She could usually beat him in an argument because he was reasonable. But Bennett was not reasonable, and because she cared so deeply she would keep on fighting until she was badly wounded. At least Gerald—

'She was with you at Richard Nesbit's barbecue, wasn't she?' said

Turnbull. 'I remember she got worked up then, too.'

Cassidy looked at their smiling faces. 'Did anything they said make sense to you?'

'Steve, it *all* made sense to us. It was textbook vested-interest behaviour.'

Bennett nodded. 'Vested people always go on about principles or professionalism when they're actually fighting for power or money. It would save so much time if they tried the occasional moment of honesty.'

'They're transparent to us though,' said Turnbull. 'And the path ahead is just as clear.'

'One part's definitely clear.' Cassidy could feel the anger tightening his throat. 'Fewer trained nurses will put sick patients at risk.'

'We're set for a long strike that will eventually *force* attitudinal transformation,' Turnbull continued. 'We'll wear them down until they give in on our terms. With a senior nurse in charge of a team of contractors and juniors the work will still get done, and way more cost-effectively.'

Cassidy decided he had had enough peach juice. He would miss saying goodbye to Nesbit, but that was not the priority. He went back to his office and rang ward 21.

The ward clerk answered and he asked to speak to Sister Sorensen. 'I'll put you through.'

'Hello.' Zoe sounded harassed.

'Zo, it's me. I heard you'd been in the strike meeting with the managers, and I was wondering how it went.'

'If you know I was there you probably know how it went. Jim Bennett is just *evil* — we're definitely doing the right thing, even though I hate it.' After a silence she said, 'What does RLU stand for?'

Damn, thought Cassidy. Turnbull had said the RLU concept was confidential. 'That's just management jargon, Zo, don't worry about it.' She had to be protected from the more gruesome aspects of Turnbull's plan or she might leave before the year was over.

'So you do know what it means. Why haven't you told me about it already?'

'It's confidential,' said Cassidy. 'I'm sorry.'

'Come on, Steve. When people trust each other it means no secrets.'

'We trust each other. But if something's confidential, it's confidential. You have to be able to tell me a secret and be sure that I won't tell everybody else, don't you? And I have to try and keep the secrets that these people tell me, otherwise they'll stop telling me things and I won't be able to tell them they're wrong.'

'As long as you're not turning into one of them.'

Cassidy sighed. 'I'm definitely not doing that. But please don't ask me to compromise my integrity, Zo.'

He could feel her tension coming down the wire, but after a moment she said in a different voice, 'Fair enough. And I love your integrity. Jim Bennett wouldn't have put me in his own bed and left me to sleep, would he?'

Cassidy raised a joyful fist. 'We don't know that, but please don't ever do the experiment. Anyway, you'd better get back to work.'

'Yes. And I'll find out what RLU stands for one way or another, while you keep your lily-white reputation.'

'Thanks, Zo. Don't forget, *Jurassic Park* on Friday.'

....

'Thanks for coming, Dr Walsh,' smiled Turnbull, 'we know you're very busy. This is Quentin Dixon from Contracts, Melanie Keating his assistant, and David Hobson from Legal. And you know Dr Cassidy. Would you like tea or coffee?'

Walsh chose tea, and Turnbull continued. 'Dr Walsh, we're struggling to reach agreement with the RHA on service definitions for our contracts. And there's increasing pressure from the shareholding ministers — we're already past the deadline for inking the contracts, due to negotiational issues. So I hope that by the end of this meeting we will have at least one clear set of definitions to use with the RHA.'

'Well,' said Walsh. 'A heart attack contract. It's an intriguing idea, and I'll be interested to hear how you think it would work.' He noticed the man at the far end of the table. 'Excuse me.' He walked down and held out his hand, forcing Diamond to stand up. 'Tony Walsh.'

'Diamond, Crown Company Monitoring and Advising Unit.'

'Really. Who do you advise, when you have monitored?'

'Treasury. They run the hospitals now.' Diamond sat down.

'Yes, I believe it's a world first,' said Walsh. 'So what's the plan? Will we end up like America, with their health maintenance organisations making huge profits, lower standards of health care for most people, and millions of Americans with no health insurance?'

'We don't comment on that,' said the CCMAU man.

'I'll bet you don't.' Walsh went back to his seat. 'And you couldn't just modify the current system?'

Diamond shook his head. 'When we have the right solution we go for it one hundred per cent.'

'But how do you know it's right? Is anybody in Treasury expressing even the tiniest doubt about the wisdom of all this?'

'We don't comment on that either.'

'Gentlemen, I wonder if we could—'

'How's it all going so far?' said Walsh. 'The whole "more private, less government" thing, under Labour since 1984, and now under National. Are you pleased?'

'There was no alternative in 1984. The right measures were put in place to strongly kick-start the economy.'

'But that was eight years ago, and since then Gross Domestic Product has gone down, not up, with massive unemployment and rising crime rates. The country's collapsing because of these policies — the kick-start has failed completely.'

'Good things take time,' said Diamond. 'Some people are doing well, and in the long term the wealth will trickle down to the rest of the community.'

'Oh please, Mr Diamond. Trickle down *never* happens. Does Treasury expect us to believe in the Tooth Fairy as well?'

'I wonder if we could come back to contract definitions, please,' said Turnbull.

'Right.' Walsh switched his attention back to the main group. 'Well,

I think "heart attack" is too vague. Let's use "myocardial infarction", meaning that some heart muscle has died.'

Quentin started writing.

'Not angina, that's heart pain, but without muscle death. You'd need a separate angina contract if this is how you want to do it. And one each for pericarditis, oesophagitis, pulmonary embolism, musculoskeletal chest pain. Then there's "chest pain, no cause found". Any of those can put somebody into coronary care.'

'This is great,' smiled Turnbull. 'We need as much detail as possible so that the RHA can't take advantage of us.'

'Right. So, one contract for management of each of those conditions? Plus the complications of myocardial infarction. Let's see: septal rupture, acute mitral regurgitation, pericardial effusion plus or minus tamponade, acute heart failure, rhythm abnormalities, embolic injuries. Dressler's syndrome. That's a quick list, there will be others. I assume you'd need a separate contract for each of those, and all the various combinations.'

Quentin put down his pen with a small click.

'Then there are different degrees of severity,' Walsh continued. 'One patient might have a small infarct and be back home in four or five days, while the next suffers a complication and dies after ten days despite all our efforts.'

'Those four-day ones would suit us best,' said Turnbull with a light laugh. 'How can we get all of them, and as few as possible of the other kind?'

Walsh glanced at Cassidy. 'What would happen to "the other kind" if we took as few as possible of them, Mr Turnbull? We treat everybody, of course.' He finished his tea. 'But how are you expecting to measure all this?'

'I've done this work in factories,' said Quentin. 'We'd carry out observational studies of worker time and consumable use, followed by a multivariate analysis for each diagnostic combination.'

'If you can measure it you can manage it, apparently,' said Cassidy. 'But you'd have to do it for a year to get anything useful.'

'A year!' Turnbull shook his head. 'That's impossible. We need hard data for our tenders in the next month at most, otherwise the RHA could rip us off.'

'Steve's right though,' said Walsh. 'This is not a factory where you can change one variable and see what happens in the next few minutes.'

Diamond broke the awkward silence. 'Dr Walsh, commercial reality can be challenging for outsiders, and we understand that. But you need to get over the idea that health is "too hard" to manage responsibly, and start owning the problem.'

'We do own the problem,' said Walsh with a frown. 'We deal with all the cardiology patients.'

'The new problem,' Turnbull said, rather too loudly. 'The challenge of achieving cashflow positivity. Perhaps it will help if Quentin tells you about the cost modelling he's done on your service.'

Quentin nodded. 'Assuming the same income as last year, you could right-size your overheads by replacing one senior nurse per shift with a new graduate, and taking out two coronary care beds. That would bring you close.'

'Then cutting the length of stay, a day here, a day there, would get you over the line,' Turnbull added. 'Assuming we get a suitably powered contract from the RHA.'

'And with that would come accountability, of course,' said Hobson.

'Meaning?'

'Meaning we monitor the unit's throughput and outcomes, and we hold you to an agreed level of productivity.'

Walsh nodded thoughtfully. 'So if we treat less patients, or more patients happen to die in one month than in the one before, you can punish the staff.'

'Underperforming individuals or teams can be sanctioned,' the lawyer agreed.

'Sorry,' said Walsh. 'Let me explain how hospital medicine works. I know cash is short, and I save money wherever I can. But the first priority is patients' needs. And expertise, professionalism and trust give you quality of care, not fear of being "sanctioned".' The veins in his neck started to enlarge. 'The thought of being accountable to some bizarre contract signed between—'

'Sorry, going to stop you there, doctor,' said Turnbull. 'You're going too micro, just like Steve does.'

Cassidy nodded. 'You have to soar like an eagle, Dr Walsh.'

'That's right. You see—'

'Or a helicopter, either would do.'

'Thanks, Steve. You see, what we're after here is *market edge*. In the business era of health, through increasing cost-effectiveness, Paxton will secure more contracts. Best case: with our input, you blow Warwick's heart attack service out of the water. Then you'd be asked to set up a regional service — more equipment, more staff, whatever you needed to handle the extra load.'

'Imagine having the chance to double the size of your service,' said Hobson with a smile. 'And of course there would be substantial personal incentives for successful individuals such as yourself.'

'Extra money for me, you mean?' said Walsh. 'As long as I cut staffing levels and bed numbers, even though we're barely managing with the staff numbers we have now.'

He shook his head then stood up and tucked his chair under the table. 'Sorry, I'm not interested. You should tender for the whole coronary care service on the current budget plus five per cent, and leave it at that. Thanks for the tea.' And he was gone.

'Shit!' said Turnbull.

'He was guarding his empire,' snorted Hobson. 'He doesn't give a damn about the business.'

'No thanks to the medical adviser,' Diamond growled. 'Where was *your* support, Mr Cassidy?'

Cassidy shook his head. 'It wasn't needed. You all explained the new paradigm beautifully. He saw the risks — they're obvious to most people — and he doesn't want to be part of it.

'But as it happens I'll be seeing Dr Walsh at the weekend. I can have an informal chat with him and see if there's anything we can do going forward, OK?'

'Thanks Steve,' muttered Turnbull, his eyes closed. 'Do your best. We need this one.'

....

Next Monday the strike began, and Turnbull called Cassidy to his office. 'Steve, I want you to keep a watching brief in the hospital during the strike. Monitor the situation and report back if there are any concerns.'

'OK. By the way, I played golf with Tony Walsh yesterday, and I asked him about the heart attack contract. He doesn't want another meeting, but he repeated his suggestion about tendering for the whole service.'

Turnbull grimaced and shook his head. 'He just doesn't get it, does he? The RHA would never go for that idea. And neither can we — it would set us up for another budget blowout, instead of making any savings. How do we incentivise stubborn actors like him, Steve? What would it take?'

'Beats me,' said Cassidy, and leaving Turnbull staring moodily out of the window he went to get started on monitoring.

The hospital could never close completely because of very sick patients and new acute admissions. But the echo of his footsteps in empty corridors, and the padlocks on usually-open doors, were strange and unsettling.

In Ward 18 he found Sister MacKelvie and a skinny youth in John Lennon glasses, struggling to get a large patient out of bed and onto a commode chair.

'Try and get your arm — Oh, thank goodness, here's Steve,' she gasped. The three of them got the man onto the commode easily enough, and John Lennon wheeled him off to the shower.

'Not on the picket line, Sister Mac?' said Cassidy as they walked back towards the office.

She snorted. 'Don't think I don't want to show these people what I think of them. But I'm happy to mind the ward while the others go. Just a minute, Steve.' She went to investigate a call light above one of the doors, leaving Cassidy wandering slowly along.

'Help,' someone said calmly through a doorway beside him. He hurried into the room and found an elderly woman sitting comfortably in bed, with her forearms loosely tied to the side rails by thick cuffs of bandages. She tugged half-heartedly at the restraints. 'Help,' she said in the same conversational tone.

He read the name card on the end of the bed. 'Hello, Mrs Brand.'

'Who are you?'

'I'm one of the doctors. Can I help you?'

She turned to stare at the doorway again. Her snowy hair had been beautifully brushed, but she had an old lady's papery skin and her forearms were heavily bruised despite the softness of the bandages. 'Are you there, Norman?'

Cassidy found Sister Mac washing her hands.

'Sis, what's wrong with Mrs Brand?'

'They removed a colon cancer after she came in with bowel obstruction. She's recovering, but she's not yet ready to go back to her nursing home. She's demented and still a bit confused, and we've had to use restraints because she keeps getting out of bed. Is she calling for Norman again?'

They came to the old lady's room. 'Violet, are you alright?'

'Violet Brand,' said Cassidy. 'I had a teacher called that in standard two at Oakville Primary, she retired the next year.'

'She used to be a teacher. Violet, do you remember Stephen Cassidy?'

'She was lovely,' said Cassidy. 'She had a rabbit, called Squiffy. He stayed with us in the holidays.'

Mrs Brand was frowning at her arms. 'Poor Violet,' said Sister Mac quietly. 'I wonder if fixing the cancer was best for her, but still, here she is.'

John Lennon appeared in the doorway. 'Sister, there's been an accident!'

Cassidy started towards the door, but Sister Mac put a hand on his arm. 'I'll deal with it Steve, I'm sure you've got other things to do. Thanks for coming to see us.'

Cassidy strolled along, his visiting done.

It felt almost like a holiday if you forgot the background. But dozens of operations, procedures and clinic appointments had been cancelled, and that meant frustration and extra suffering for those people, and no progress on the waiting lists.

It sounded as if there was a football crowd outside.

Fancy remembering Squiffy the rabbit after all these years. His sweet, stupid face and the red glow in his ears when the sun shone through them.

The shouting was very close now, and he could see shadows of people through the frosted glass windows of the side entrance door. Without thinking he pushed against the door and it suddenly opened, so that he stumbled and fell. His chin hit the edge of the top step and his teeth clashed together. He swore. He was surrounded by feet and legs.

'WHAT DO WE WANT?' boomed a metallic voice.

'RESPECT!'

Hands under each shoulder pulled him up. He tasted blood and grit.

'WHEN DO WE WANT IT?'

'NOW!'

'Steve, are you alright?' It was Zoe. She pulled a handkerchief from her pocket and dabbed at his lip as he leaned against her. Goodness what a lot of people. And placards.

'WHAT DO WE WANT?'

'RESPECT!'

His head was spinning and his face hurt. The concern on her face. Her white handkerchief was dotted with his blood.

'WHEN DO WE WANT IT?'

'Zoe, will you marry me?'

'NOW!'

No reaction; perhaps he had only thought it. 'Thanks, Zo. I shouldn't be here, I'll slip away. Sorry.' He stumbled towards the door, but one of the orderlies stood grinning in front of it.

'WELL, LOOK WHO'S HERE.' The loudhailer user was a big man

with a greying beard: Paul McAlister, the charge nurse in the fracture clinic and the chairman of the strike committee.

'Hello Paul, I'm just going.'

'PLEASE WELCOME DOCTOR STEPHEN CASSIDY!' The crowd stood silent apart from a few ironic cheers. A baby was crying. TV vans waited in the background, and beyond them the traffic moved indifferently past.

'IN CASE YOU DIDN'T KNOW, DOCTOR CASSIDY HAS JOINED MANAGEMENT.' Boos and laughter. 'DOCTOR CASSIDY, IT'S SO GOOD OF YOU TO DROP IN' — more laughter and shouts — 'ON BEHALF OF MANAGEMENT WHO HAVE NOT YET DONE US THE COURTESY OF COMING TO HEAR OUR VIEWS.' He held the megaphone towards Cassidy. 'Over to you, Steve.'

'I'm not here on behalf of management. I've just been seeing how they're getting on in the wards.'

'HE'S NOT HERE ON BEHALF OF MANAGEMENT. SO WHO *IS* COMING TO ADDRESS THE WORKERS?' McAlister switched off the megaphone. 'You're not leaving without giving us a few words, so go for it before the mob gets out of hand. They're not very happy today.'

'Thanks, McAlister. You're a real pal.'

'Button's on the side there.'

'HELLO, CAN YOU HEAR ME?' Cassidy boomed. A line of seagulls rose from a TV van's aerial and flew away. 'I, ER, THANKS FOR COMING — OH, STUFF THIS.' He handed the megaphone back. 'Can you hear me alright?' he shouted. He dabbed at his cut lip.

'We have to find a way through this, er, difficult time. Health care reform can save millions, but the money must—'

'THANKS STEVE, THAT WAS VERY WELL PUT!' Amplified McAlister drowned him out. 'LADIES AND GENTLEMEN, A BIG HAND PLEASE FOR THE MORNING'S COMEDY TURN, DOCTOR STEVE CASSIDY!'

Cassidy felt his face flushing as the boos and yells increased. 'Wait a minute. You invited me to speak, then you cut me off before I could say anything. That's not fair, Paul.'

'WHAT DO WE WANT?'

Cassidy turned away. This time he was allowed through the door into the deserted corridor, and he went round the back way and across the car park to the Leaders' Building.

··

Cassidy sank gratefully into Turnbull's armchair. 'Somebody should go and talk to the strikers.'

'Have you been in a fight?' said Turnbull. Bennett rolled his eyes and shook his head in mock despair.

'I fell over at the strikers' meeting, it was an accident. Then they asked me to speak.'

'But you didn't, of course.'

'No, I — well, I said a few—'

'Steve, please tell me you didn't address them. Before we get down to understanding why you were anywhere near the strikers in the first place.'

Cassidy checked with his tongue. At least there weren't any broken teeth. 'I hadn't planned to be. I was in the corridor and I heard the noise, so I opened the door and somehow managed to fall flat on my face in front of everybody — it must have been funny to watch.

'They wouldn't let me go without saying something, so I thought I could try to help them understand a different point of view.' His lip had started oozing again and he dabbed at it with Zoe's handkerchief.

'How did it go, Steve?' Bennett asked in a caring, counselling voice. Turnbull buried his face in his hands.

'They didn't want to listen. I started talking about the potential savings, but they stopped me and I left. Somebody should go along and at least show that we respect them.'

'But we don't respect them,' said Bennett. 'And we won't until they start being a whole lot more adult and cooperative, rather than constantly telling us how important they are and how ignorant we are.'

Turnbull nodded. 'Going out there to be harassed and mocked wouldn't serve any useful purpose, but it could make things worse. And we're certainly not going to argue in front of TV cameras. It's best just to let them blow off steam and go home.' He smiled. 'Besides, the strike is saving us bucket-loads of money, and the longer it lasts the better it is for us.'

'Significant fiscal upside going forward,' Bennett agreed. 'Thanks guys.'

'But people are missing out on operations and clinic appointments,' said Cassidy.

'That's sad.' Bennett shrugged in wide-eyed innocence. 'But it's not our fault.'

'How were the wards?' asked Turnbull.

'Pretty scary. I was in Ward 18, with a charge nurse who's a bit old for heavy lifting, helped by volunteers who naturally don't know anything. They're getting by but it won't be sustainable for long.'

'That's disgusting,' said Bennett. 'How can we win public sympathy if do-gooders keep helping them pretend everything's OK?'

'But without them the wards would fall over.'

'That would be a *positive* outcome perception-wise,' said Bennett as if explaining to a child. 'Why is this so difficult for you to understand?'

'What if somebody you knew was involved, Jim?' said Cassidy. 'Would you mind them suffering so that you can look good?'

Turnbull raised his hands for calm. 'Collateral damage happens, and that's just how it is. Of course we'd be unhappy if it was one of us, but it isn't so there's not much point talking about it.' He glanced at Cassidy. 'Was there someone you knew in there?'

'Yes, there was. One of my teachers from primary school.'

'Small world, eh? Was she was pleased to see you?'

'She didn't recognise me. She has dementia.'

'Really. Dementia,' said Bennett, drawing the word out. 'Why is she in hospital during a strike?'

'She came in with an obstructing colon cancer. She's still recovering from the surgery, so she can't go back to the nursing home yet.'

'And she would have died if they hadn't operated?'

'Yes.'

'How much is it costing us for them to save this demented unit?' said Bennett softly.

'I don't know. Thousands of dollars.'

'Could they have let her die?' asked Turnbull as Bennett groaned.

'Yes, sometimes that's the kindest thing to do when someone's really sick and there's no chance of getting them back to good health. But whoever it was decided not to do that. It's easy to be critical afterwards, but they did what they thought was best for her at the time.'

'Maybe.' Bennett was glowering. 'But it was a lousy business decision.'

'Well Jim, that's how it is,' said Cassidy. 'And even though you'd like to, you can't over-rule the judgment of the senior doctors.'

'For now, Butch,' said Bennett. 'For now.'

·····················

Five o'clock finally came and Cassidy drove home looking forward to some time on the good old couch in front of the good old TV, then an early night.

Claire had been home all day, and the flat was warm and fragrant with curry.

He put his arm round her as she stood at the stove. 'Claire, you little beauty, what's all this?'

She dipped a teaspoon into the pan and tasted the sauce. 'Mm, that's quite good. It's chicken jalfrezi, I found a new recipe. And I'm making some bhajis to go with it.'

The talk turned technical. Cassidy was making good progress under Claire's guidance, and he had already had four French cooking lessons, on Wednesday evenings at Paxton Girls' High.

'Anyway, how was your day?' said Claire as Cassidy got a beer from the fridge.

'I didn't do much apart from injuring and humiliating myself in front of several hundred people, and possibly the whole nation on TV tonight. Oh, and I proposed to Zoe again.'

'Goodness, it's becoming a habit, isn't it? What did she say?'

'Nothing.' He told her the whole story as she finished cooking and served the meal.

'Poor old Steve. Ooh quick, it's news time.'

'Industrial action brings Paxton Hospital to a halt,' said the announcer over a long shot of the morning's strike meeting.

There he was, with Zoe dabbing his lip with her handkerchief.

Suddenly his face filled the screen. 'We have to find a way through this, er, difficult time. Health care reform can save millions, but the money must—'

They cut to a short clip of Alex King giving nothing away, then moved on to an item about President Clinton.

Cassidy groaned and turned the sound off. 'Why did they show that? Did it enlighten anyone about the issues?'

'Have something to eat,' said Claire, 'you'll feel better.'

He would have preferred to punch somebody, but after a few mouthfuls he began to relax. 'Great curry, Claire.'

'Thank you. Was your speech before or after you proposed?'

'After. Did you see the way she was looking at me? I wish I could see that again.'

The phone rang and he went out to answer it.

'Steve, Clive Maxted. Did you see yourself on TV?'

'Hello Clive.' Cassidy was surprised; this was the first time they had spoken since the party. 'Yes, I did.'

'Excellent. Now, I'm hoping to get a favour. Would you mind if I came round for a moment?'

'Now? No, that would be fine. You can try some of Claire's curry. See you soon.'

'It was good television, Steve,' laughed Maxted fifteen minutes later. 'People would have had a giggle, which goodness knows doesn't happen very often these days. It doesn't all have to be grim and earnest — talking about the funder-provider split would just make people change channels.'

'And that would annoy the advertisers.'

'Correct. This curry is delicious, Claire.'

'Thanks,' said Claire. 'I'd better get going, I'm helping out at the hospital until midnight. Nice to meet you, Clive.'

'You too. Goodnight . . . But they wanted to show that a strike is going on, the hospital is empty, and management who have caused it are heartless and uncaring. Do you want that last bhaji? Thanks.' He devoted himself to eating for a moment. 'This is amazing. Has Claire got a boyfriend?'

'You'd have to ask her that, Clive. You said you wanted some help.'

Maxted wiped his hands on a serviette. 'I need to get some photos for an article I'm writing. Can you get me into the hospital, please?'

'No, sorry,' said Cassidy.

'Do you mean you can't or you won't?'

Cassidy sighed. 'I don't like what's happening any more than you do. But I want to keep my job, and if I'm caught helping you I'll be history.'

'How could that happen? And anyway, this is for the public good, I assure you.'

'And you promise to keep me out of the spotlight?' Cassidy considered. 'No, it's still too dangerous.'

The public good, Steve. Why else do we turn up to work each day?'

....

The only way into the hospital after hours was through the Emergency entrance. Cassidy showed his ID badge to the security guard, and in they went.

'I want a shot of empty corridors, this'll do nicely.' Maxted waited for some nurses to walk past then rapidly took three photos. 'Can we see inside a ward?' Ward 17 was empty. They went in and turned on the lights, and he took more photos. 'Now. Where would the dirty laundry go?'

'Why do you want to see that?'

'Just for background.'

Cassidy showed him. 'When there is any, this is where it's bagged up for the orderlies to take away. But why are you interested in dirty laundry?'

'Can you take me to a ward that is working please?'

'Clive, I—'

'Come on Steve, this is how we make a difference. Trust me.'

Ward 18 had a handful of patients' names on the whiteboard. There was no-one in the office. Feeling like a burglar, Cassidy led the way to the sluice room.

One laundry bag in its holder was half-full, one was almost full, and two full bags lay on the floor, sealed up and ready to be taken away. Everything as usual.

'That's not what I want,' said Maxted. He loaded all the dirty laundry into one bag and stood back to check the effect. 'Not enough. Open those other ones, can you?'

'What?' said Cassidy. 'It's dirty hospital linen, there could be all sorts of—'

'Could you help me please?' Maxted was already tugging at the string of one of the bags. Cassidy watched for a moment then silently started on the other.

A minute later they stood back. Both bags were now overflowing, and there were crumpled sheets and towels on the floor in front of them. Maxted took three photographs.

'OK, I've got what I need. Let's go.' He stood and watched Cassidy tidying up then washing his hands.

The door swung open and a nurse backed in, colliding with Maxted. She screamed and dropped a bundle of bedding.

'Janet, hello,' said Cassidy. 'This is my friend Clive, he's doing a story on the strike for the *Globe*. We're not stealing anything, I promise.'

'Hi Steve. Goodness, you gave me a fright,' Janet laughed. She picked up the sheets and dropped them in a bag, then started washing her hands.

'How's it been going?'

'No problems. The volunteers have been great, and we've only got eight patients this shift.' She turned to go. 'Sister Mac said that you knew Mrs Brand. Would you like to say hello again?'

Clive and Mrs Brand? Some things the public did not need to know. 'No thanks, we'll just slip away. Good night.'

They went along the silent corridor and Cassidy pressed the lift button. 'That was great,' said Maxted. 'Those laundry bag ones—'

The lift doors opened and there beside an empty hospital bed stood Jim Bennett, wearing an orderly's grey coat. He lunged to close the doors but Cassidy beat him to it.

'Well, who says managers are heartless? Here's one helping out during the strike in his own time. Clive, this is Jim Bennett. Jim, Clive Maxted.'

Bennett swallowed. 'What are you doing here?'

'Mind if we join you?' The doors closed and they started going down. 'It was good of Barry to lend you his coat,' said Cassidy, nodding at the name tag on the coat stretched across Bennett's muscular shoulders.

They arrived at the hospital basement after a silent journey. 'I'm working for the public good!' said Bennett as the doors opened.

'When do you not, Jim? Can I give you a hand?'

They pushed the bed out and parked it beside seven others in the loading bay.

'Why are you removing beds? And why are you doing Barry's work? And why are you doing it in the middle of the night?' Cassidy shook his head. 'So many questions.'

'I'm cutting overheads, Butch.' The usual Bennett was back. 'Remember how you suggested that, then pretended it was a joke? But I saw the vision, and I'm following through.'

Maxted lifted his camera. 'Would you mind if I took a photo of the two of you together, perhaps in front of the beds?'

'Certainly not.' Bennett stepped quickly into the lift and the door closed.

'What an interesting man,' said Maxted. 'He seemed tense.'

'The proverbial coiled spring,' agreed Cassidy. 'I suspect he would like us all to think that the beds had been removed by market forces, so this was an embarrassing moment for him. But he'll get over it, nothing bothers Jim for long because he knows he's always right.'

They went back through Emergency and out to their cars. Maxted headed towards the *Globe*, and Cassidy went home. There was still time to unwind with a bit of TV then get an early night.

....

He turned on the television and sat down, then remembered that he had no shirt ironed for tomorrow. Sighing, he found a clean shirt, got the ironing board from behind the couch and switched on the iron.

'Nurses and other staff at troubled Paxton Hospital started strike action today.' Cassidy put the iron down. Please don't show him again. No, there he was, and there was Zoe looking beautiful and — loving, was the only way to describe it. There was Paul McAlister.

Paul McAlister, yes. I need to have a chat with you one day, my old *mate*.

Then as if by magic, that very person appeared on the screen again, alongside another familiar face. Cassidy abandoned the ironing and sat down.

'We're joined in the studio by Mr Alex King, the new Chief Executive Officer of the Paxton Crown Health Enterprise, and Mr Paul McAlister, representing striking nurses, paramedical staff, kitchen staff and orderlies.'

King displayed his usual contemptuous expression. His understated grey suit, crisp white shirt and silver tie made it clear he was a serious man with big responsibilities.

Next to King, hairy McAlister was a nervous but determined Wild Man of Borneo. He wore a mustard-coloured shirt and matching knitted tie, but no jacket.

'Gentlemen, thank you for joining us,' said Langdon Doherty, one of the country's most important interviewers. King nodded slightly, and McAlister reached for a drink of water.

'This strike will cause significant suffering in Paxton, as many patients will miss planned surgery. Given that waiting lists are already horrendous, isn't there an urgent need to solve the dispute? Mr King.'

'Paxton Health deplores the strike action and urges strikers to return to work immediately, so that normal service can be resumed and negotiation can begin.'

McAlister shook his head. 'He knows as well as I do that we've been asking to talk to them for months, but management haven't even bothered to answer our letters. We've had to strike to get their attention, and now we expect them to make some serious offers about staffing levels.'

'Mr King?'

'The world is changing,' said King. 'New Zealand has had one of the best public health systems in the world, but it's now failing, and successive governments have not confronted that reality. This government has rightly determined that only sweeping reform based on successful business techniques can deliver what is needed. There is no alternative.

'The days of medical people dictating how things will be run for the benefit of themselves and their cronies are over, and we will not be going back there.' He held up his hand to stop McAlister replying. 'The nurses are trying to take us back to the 1970s, to suit their own ideas. They seem to want everyone whose job it is to make beds and empty bedpans to have had at least three years' training for which they claim a large salary. The business model—'

'That treats skilled staff with contempt!'

'—takes a more rational approach. Of course we need some highly skilled senior nurses. But we need more lower-skilled people doing the simpler tasks to free the senior nurses for the top-end work. No private business could survive the top-heavy staffing pattern of our public hospitals.'

'Are you saying that Paxton Health is going to lay off nurses?' Doherty asked.

'How you get the results is a blend,' King said in his gravelly monotone. 'However, that is not a topic for public discussion, given the competitive commercial environment.' He folded his hands and leaned back into Buddha-like repose, his eyelids drooping.

Despite his dislike of the man, Cassidy had to admire King's performance. "How you get the results is a blend" — in other words yes, we will lay off nurses, and that's not all. But he hadn't actually said that, had he?

'Mr McAlister?'

McAlister's purple face clashed unhappily with the mustard shirt. 'It's unbelievable that you can voice those insulting opinions in front of the New Zealand public. You seem to be completely unaware that nursing is a complex job demanding high skill levels, and New Zealand nurses have those skills. They're in demand in Australia, in Britain, in Canada—'

'Perhaps they should all leave then,' murmured King.

'And how would the health system run then? Tell me that.'

'I regret I am unable to discuss any more than I already have.'

'Mr King,' said Doherty, 'waiting lists are growing and highly skilled staff are leaving at an unprecedented rate, but you're suggesting that *more* should go. Isn't that the exact opposite of how the public views the situation?'

King opened his eyes fully, but kept his hands folded in his lap as if he was supervising mat time in kindergarten. 'That's very well put and it shows why people are confused about what is happening. You see,' now he leaned forward to explain, 'we have different ideas about who the public actually is.

'Mr McAlister here sees the public as the clients who are in front of him when, or should I say if, he is at work. Also the individuals about whom he reads in the newspaper when they have not been able to get what they believe they're entitled to.

'But in reality, the public is the *whole* population, and that's who we're responsible to, through the shareholding Ministers. Is it fair that forty-two per cent of people in one city wait more than two years for orthopaedic surgery while in another city it's just two per cent? Is it right that it should cost more than ten times as much per night for a hospital bed in one city as in another? Is it?'

'He's fudging it!' Cassidy shouted. 'Ask him about costs of teaching hospitals.'

'Of course not,' said Doherty. 'But how does that affect—'

'The Arthur Andersen report indicated that the health sector could save half a billion dollars a year if all public hospitals were as efficient as the best ones. *Half a billion* taxpayer dollars per year — do you think that's worth trying for?'

'It's a lot of money, certainly.'

'Do you think we should try and claw back excess spending, for example by reviewing out-dated staffing levels in our big hospitals, and learning to work smarter, not harder?'

'Well yes, if it really is excess spending.'

'"Really?"' said King. 'What do you mean by that? Arthur Andersen is a highly respected and trustworthy multinational consulting firm. Are you suggesting their report might be wrong? What about the Gibbs report? The Danzon report? These are from top business experts — would you like to criticise them as well? I assume you're familiar with them.'

'Well, not really, I — Gentlemen, we're almost out of time,' said Doherty. 'Mr McAlister, would you like to have a final word?'

McAlister's face was taut with frustration. 'Yes I would. If this man is representative of health care management everywhere, God help us all.'

'Hear, hear,' said Cassidy. He turned the sound down and went back to his ironing.

Bloody hell. King had won everything. McAlister hadn't laid a glove on him, and he'd even hunted Doherty into a corner as well, *Langdon Doherty* for God's sake.

The phone rang, and he went out into the cold hall and turned on the light.

'Steve? Did you see that interview?' Zoe sounded as angry as McAlister.

'Hi, Zo. Yes, I thought—'

'If he was saying what they all think, it's hopeless, and our professionalism doesn't count for anything. Why on earth would anyone want to work for somebody like that?'

'You don't work for him, you work for the patients,' said Cassidy. 'And you're doing the right thing with the strike, it's how you'll make a difference. Do you remember saying that when we were in the park? It's on TV now, Langdon Doherty's talking about it, and Clive Maxted is going to have something in tomorrow's *Globe*. It would be a terrible mistake to walk away just as things are warming up.' Unlike the hall, he thought. Perhaps if he crouched down it wouldn't feel so cold.

Her sigh came down the phone. 'Yes, I know. But after seeing that, I've decided I need a break. I'm leaving tomorrow morning for a couple of weeks on my cousin's farm at Connemara. They don't know yet, but I've got a standing invitation there. She's got two wee boys that I haven't seen for ages, and—'

'Auntie Zoe. I'll bet you're their favourite.'

'—I need to do some serious thinking about my life. Listening to that horrible man made me realise that these people have made me do something that I don't want to. I hate being on strike. I don't owe him anything, certainly not loyalty. So why stay here?' She paused. 'You're still working away, but you don't need me for that. I'll miss you of course, but we can't resolve our issues until you've—'

'You could resolve them, Zo,' said Cassidy. 'Did you see yourself on TV, helping me after I'd fallen over? The look on your face? That's what's real between us, not this idea that I've still got this Frankenstein side to my nature. That's gone, and it won't—' He had noticed a burning smell. 'Damn! Zo, I think I've left the iron sitting on a shirt. Hold on a minute, will you?' The phone banged against the wall as he struggled to his feet.

When he picked it up again only seconds later, she was gone. He dialled her number three times but she must have left the phone off the hook.

He pulled his jacket on, intending to go to her, but then he paused. There was nothing more he could say or do while she still insisted on this cruel and unnatural platonic punishment.

Zoe, Zoe, Zoe. Cassidy sighed and hung the jacket up again. Best give her the space she needed. She knew what his feelings were.

He let out a loud howl of rage and frustration, then went to his bedroom to find another shirt.

CHAPTER NINE

Maxted dominated the front page of next morning's *Bugle*. The laundry bag spilled its sheets and towels under the headline 'Hospital Struggles to Provide Basic Services'.

The article praised the staff and the volunteers, then described stresses within management and in the RHA contract negotiations, and the hostility between management and the medical staff. It ended by attacking King's 'arrogant' performance on TV and demanding a referendum on the reforms.

Cassidy's face burned as he read about 'sources close to the issues'. He and Zoe had been foolishly indiscreet when they had been chatting with the nice man during Geoff's party. And sitting at this very table, too! Good work, Steve.

But perhaps no-one in the Management Group would make the connection between him and Maxted's 'sources'.

....

People clapped as King walked in, but then they saw the look on his face as he held up the *Bugle*.

'We are under attack! We are working towards beneficial change but the public are being told they are victims. We must confront this media manipulation.' He sat down. 'I need suggestions.'

'Alex, I must say you did a great job last night,' said Turnbull. 'More interviews like that would be helpful.'

'No. All that happened was that I confronted the insinuation that we are mindlessly downsizing the workforce. The prejudice against us is much wider than that.'

'But you gave the public something to consider.'

King grunted.

'The TV advertisements will be helping,' said Goldsmith. 'The road-blocking will force people to think about what's being said.'

'And we're all spreading the message personally whenever we can,' Russell added. 'But it's hard to resist that laundry bag picture — it's eye-catching, powerful. Great technique, you have to admit.'

'It's dishonest though,' said Cassidy. 'The staff are coping well with help from volunteers. There's no laundry problem.'

'How do you know?' Bennett asked. 'Have you been there recently?'

'I came in yesterday evening. It's part of my job to keep an eye on the wards.'

'Yes, we bumped into each other, didn't we? And I met your friend with the camera.'

'A camera?' said King. 'Who was this person?'

'Clive Maxted,' Bennett told him.

'What was he doing?'

Cassidy swallowed. 'He took the photo and he wrote the article. He has deceived me and betrayed my confidence, and I apologise to everyone here.'

King's eyes bulged. 'You helped a journalist to enter the hospital and take pictures, knowing that he would damage the company?'

'I'm sorry,' said Cassidy. 'He just said he wanted to describe the strike. It was for the public good.' No-one said anything. 'But there's no real harm done, this will be wrapping fish and chips tomorrow and we can move on.' Or out, he thought.

King was staring at him. 'You have been completely irresponsible. I will see you in my office immediately after this meeting.'

'Why were you in the hospital, Jim?' said Turnbull.

Bennett gave a coy little smile. 'I wasn't going to tell anyone, but I was following Steve's suggestion for downsizing and this seemed the perfect time to action it. I removed beds from empty wards and took them to the basement, so we now have fewer beds. Only twelve less out of five hundred at this point in time, but there will be further opportunities if the strike continues.'

'Good work, Mr Bennett,' said King. 'Next — "Travel Agent". What's this about?'

Turnbull passed him a letter. 'This is from a travel agency, Good Vibes Travel. Because so many health employees are purchasing one-way tickets out of New Zealand, they will offer a discount if we nominate them as preferred travel agent.'

'For God's sake!' King tore the letter into pieces.

'Sorry, Alex,' muttered Turnbull. 'I was thinking about licence fees.'

'Absolutely not,' said King. 'What kind of message would it . . . ' His voice was strange, tight. He tried to loosen his tie as sweat broke out on his face. 'It's terribly hot—' With a horrible gurgle he slumped sideways onto the floor.

Cassidy rushed to the head of the table. King was now unconscious. 'Get the chair away, lie him down on his side. Call an ambulance!'

Once King was clear Cassidy knelt over him and felt his neck. No pulse. 'Roll him onto his back. Does anyone know CPR?' He thumped King on the sternum and felt for the pulse again. Nothing. He threw off his jacket and started sternal compression.

'You pump, I'll breathe.' It was Bennett.

'OK. Five compressions, two breaths. Get his legs up on a chair.' *Pump, pump, pump.* 'Somebody note the time.'

'The ambulance is on its way,' said Dawn a moment later. 'I'll go down and wait for them.'

Time passed. One, two, three, four, five, pause. In hospital, a cardiac arrest team would be running towards them with a trolley of equipment and drugs, but right next door they had to wait for an ambulance to come several blocks.

The lips were less dusky. Still no pulse.

'Carry on.' One, two, three, four, five. 'How long have we been going?'

'Twelve minutes.'

Suddenly an ambulance man was there, with others close behind bringing a stretcher and cases of equipment. 'Well done. We'll take it from here.' His badge said Colin, Team Leader.

Cassidy moved away, then sat back against the wall with his eyes closed as others pumped and breathed. Within seconds King had a tube in his trachea and a drip line running into a vein.

'Run the bicarb flat out. Adrenaline please.' Colin was watching the trace from the ECG leads placed across the chest.

King's colour improved quickly, but the blood pressure was very low. Colin signalled to the others that they needed to go. 'Now, we'll lift him onto the trolley. Watch out for the drip and the oxygen. On the count of three . . . Good.' They strapped King to the stretcher and put a blanket over him, without stopping the cardiac massage. 'OK, we've got contact details? Somebody hold the lift please.'

The team hurried him towards the lift as the leader gathered the last bits of equipment.

'Is he going to be alright?' Goldsmith said in a quivery voice.

'He's got a chance,' said Colin without slowing his work. 'Lucky we don't have to go far. Might be different in future though, eh?' He winked at Cassidy and snapped his case shut. 'Good work, guys.' Then he was gone.

'Steve,' said Turnbull over a babble of voices two minutes later. 'I know where the CEO's emergency supplies live.'

Cassidy stood up slowly, his back muscles screaming after their unaccustomed exercise, and took the glass of brandy that Turnbull was offering. He went over to Bennett, who was staring out over the rooftops of Paxton.

'Thanks, Jim.'

Bennett nodded. 'Think he'll make it?'

'Maybe. It'll depend on what's happened. You did a great job — where did you learn CPR?'

'My Dad collapsed, just like that,' said Bennett, his eyes bleak. 'Mum was at the shops. I was fifteen, my sister was twelve. We didn't have a bloody clue what to do, couldn't even remember the number you had to dial.' He snorted softly. 'So I went on a course. I had to do something, even though it seemed pointless at the time. But maybe it was worthwhile today.'

'Damn right it was. You know, I wasn't going to drink this, but cheers.' They clinked their glasses.

People drifted back to their places. There weren't enough glasses and people were drinking the CEO's cognac from cups. 'Wasn't it awful?' said Quentin. 'His face just before he fell over.'

Turnbull leafed through King's papers. 'Public perception, RHA negotiations update, performance incentives. Nothing too urgent. Look, we'll cancel this meeting.'

···

'Maxted speaking.'

'Hello, Clive.'

'Steve, hi. How did the article play in the corridors of power?'

Cassidy remembered King's mottled blue face. 'It caused major stress.'

'Excellent.'

'No, it wasn't excellent. And I'll probably lose my job for letting you in.'

'Really? That's a bit rough.'

'Surely there's enough to write about with what's actually going on at the moment without having to make things up? I would have thought you would have had enough material from what Zoe and I told you at the party. The picture was just plain dishonest.'

'Everybody colours in a bit from time to time,' said Maxted. 'Everybody. Can you put hand on heart and tell me you never tell a lie, not even a little one? Never a slight shading of the truth?'

'Of course I do. But only to avoid hurting somebody I care about.'

'OK. So even the righteous Cassidy tells the occasional little porky to keep things happy in the home. And yet he objects to a journalist doing his job?'

'Clive,' said Cassidy, 'it wasn't true.'

'As a symbol the laundry bags were true,' said Maxted. 'No, listen — I need the image to grab people's attention, to make them pause to think about the badness of strikes in general then be curious enough to read what I've written. Don't forget, oh exalted one, that we're in a daily struggle to lead the debate, and that the print media are always, always playing off the long tees.

'TV can bring on the awful Mr King and let him punch the other people up for a few minutes, and everybody thinks it's good to watch. And so it is, especially if old Langdon cops a few. But that's just entertainment, it's an easily digested, low-residue diet. It doesn't have enough substance to make people think and start demanding change. Like more honesty from their politicians, for example, and a whole lot more respect from management for their nurses.

'And that's where I come in. I want you to see the picture, read the headline, then buy the paper to take a few minutes to learn what's really going on.'

'And you don't lie in what you write?'

'Never, Steve. I swear.' Maxted laughed again. 'But I'm sorry it's caused you trouble. Oh, while you're there, I've heard a rumour that the Paxton CHE is planning to set up a branch in Saudi Arabia. Have you heard anything about that?'

'Good-bye, Clive.'

....

'That's good,' said Jackson. 'Now find the short gastric vessels. And check for small branches coming off the diaphragm.'

Cassidy moved his fingers along the outer edge of the stomach and lifted it forward until he could see the tiny arteries that Jackson had described. He cauterised them before getting ready to tighten the gap in the diaphragm that let the oesophagus into the abdomen.

'Derek, can you put the bougie down when you're ready?' said Jackson. 'Thanks.'

Derek Watson, the anaesthetist, gently opened the mouth of his sleeping patient and passed a soft rubber cylinder into the oesophagus, pushing it further until Cassidy felt it entering the stomach.

'All set?' said Watson. 'Good. By the way, I had a postcard from Allan O'Connell in Saudi this week. Says he's having a great time. They're hiring surgeons as well, apparently.'

Jackson was watching as Cassidy dissected the tissue away from the front of the oesophagus. 'Make sure you're well clear of the anterior vagal trunk. Yes, that's fine.'

'They have good diving there, I was surprised,' Watson continued. 'It might suit you for a while, Steve, once you've got this management thing out of your system. Allan said there's plenty of interesting work.'

'We'll have the Babcock clamp now, thanks Sister,' said Jackson. 'I tell you, if I was young and free, I'd be thinking about a job like that. Just about anywhere would be better than our public hospitals right now. They're on a knife edge as far as patient safety goes.'

'Did anybody else hear that rumour about Paxton planning to set up a branch in Saudi?' said Watson. 'That would have to be their best idea yet.'

'Nothing surprises me any more,' Jackson sighed. 'These clowns promised that hospital waiting lists would shorten but instead they're getting longer. Shouldn't that be a priority before they start some bizarre adventure somewhere else? Steve, did you know about this Saudi idea?'

'Not specifically.' Cassidy was working the clamp between the oesophagus and the posterior vagal trunk. 'But they're keen to expand.'

'I suppose they're desperate to get some outside cash,' said Watson as he adjusted the flow of oxygen slightly. 'But it's very risky, surely. As soon as the RHA know that Paxton has an outside income source, they could start paying them less. And if the Saudi thing falls over—'

'As it surely would,' said Jackson.

'—they might struggle to get the same local rates again.'

Jackson nodded. 'Absolutely right. I very much doubt that they'd be able to get anything set up over there anyway, but it's instructive about how the medicine-as-business mind works, isn't it? Alright, we're ready to suture the wrap now.'

'Who allows stuff like this to happen?' Watson continued. 'I can imagine a boardroom full of new-age businessmen having a collective brain explosion, but it's the CEO's job to calm everybody down and keep them in the right lane, surely. Who is the CEO at Paxton? Isn't it some guy who's made a fortune in the clothing business?'

Cassidy was concentrating on some tricky work with needle and thread. They were operating to cure reflux symptoms, and this part was critical. Once he had carefully adjusted the sutures, as Jackson monitored the tension, he was able to relax a little. 'No, Richard Nesbit has gone and his successor is on sick leave. They're re-advertising the job at the moment, actually. Perhaps one of you should apply.'

'Right, Derek, bougie out thanks,' said Jackson. 'It's an interesting idea, but not for old codgers like us. I'm sure we could do the job a damn sight better than it's being done at the moment, but we're already fully occupied and anyway we don't understand how they think.'

Watson nodded. 'It needs a sensible person who's already on the management team but also understands how hospitals work.'

Jackson looked at his assistant, who was closing the abdominal wall. 'What about you, Steve?'

Cassidy laughed and continued placing sutures.

They finished the operation, but Jackson would not let the idea go away. 'Don't just write this off,' he said as they walked towards the tearoom. 'I could be a referee, and I'm sure my colleagues would support your application.'

'I couldn't possibly do it,' said Cassidy as he filled the kettle. 'I'd need at least an MBA and ten years' management experience.'

'You don't know till you've tried. Somebody in the hierarchy just might have insight into how far out of their depth they are. They need a medical CEO to start steering the reforms towards a structure that could possibly work. If you gave it a couple of years, it would be a bigger contribution to Paxton than passing your surgical exams.' Jackson shook his head in wonderment. 'And the fact that it's me saying this shows you how important I think it is.'

'Sorry,' said Cassidy, pouring the water into the mugs. 'They would think it was a joke. And anyway, I expect I'm about to get kicked out.' He told Jackson about his drunken conversation with Maxted at Geoff's party.

Then he paused, remembering Zoe coming into the kitchen that evening. Her bare shoulders easing out of the ski jacket. 'And besides, I've got other things to do. I'd never want a career in management.'

....

Cassidy picked up his mail and tried not to think about his immediate future. He had not had many jobs in his life so far, but he had left them all on his own terms and he hated the idea of being given the boot — the words 'embarrassment' and 'humiliation' kept floating into his mind and crowding out 'relief' and 'freedom'.

Nobody had spoken to him about the *Globe* article since King's crisis, and the silence was beginning to gnaw at him. He decided to do something about it as soon as he'd sorted these letters.

Notice of an upcoming conference on *Evolving Business Opportunities in the New Zealand Health Care Scene*. 'Participation *Essential*, Or You Risk Being Left Behind!'

Bin.

Letter to Judas Cassidy.

Bin, unopened.

Letter to Stephen Cassidy, staff liaison, from a charge nurse describing her fears for patient safety.

Put aside for consideration and action.

Invitation from Gerald Turnbull for Stephen Cassidy and a guest to hear Jason Hockley, Associate Minister of Health. Subject: 'The Health Reforms: Where Are We Up To?' Venue: the Nikau Room, Paxton Grand Hotel. 6 pm, Monday 2 August 1993. Refreshments to follow.

Hmm. Hockley was a local man. He was often in the Paxton Valley clubhouse on Saturdays, slapping backs, shaking hands and sharing his and the National Party's views on life. It might be interesting to hear what a politician had to say. And right now, the invitation gave him an excuse to go and find out what was happening about his future. Cassidy went upstairs.

'Steve, come in,' said Turnbull. 'I was just going to come and see you. I've been visiting Alex in the hospital, and he sends you his best wishes.'

'Thanks, Gerald. How's he getting on?'

Turnbull frowned. 'I'm not sure. Can heart surgery make you go off your head?'

'You can get a bit of memory loss, probably from tiny strokes. Or you could have confusion and even delirium if there was infection anywhere. Why do you ask?'

'Alex had the operation a week ago, and I understand it went well. But now he's talking nonsense about the hospital, while seeming perfectly normal in other ways. It's spooky. Could you go along and see what you think?'

'Yes, I will,' said Cassidy. 'Am I going to be fired?'

Turnbull put down his pen. 'Alex did want to see you after the meeting, didn't he? But of course that never happened, and in all the excitement I guess we lost sight of the original problem.'

'The leaks to the *Globe*.'

'Yes indeed,' said Turnbull slowly. 'That's pretty serious stuff, isn't it?'

'I know.' Cassidy hung his head. 'I shouldn't have helped Clive Maxted get into the hospital, but he told me the public have a right to know and I support that idea. We are going for a transparent and accountable health service, aren't we?'

'I think it's really a decision for the next CEO, whoever that might be,' said Turnbull after a moment of thought. 'But in the meantime, since you have shown remorse—'

'Oh yes.'

'—and I have such respect for the ideas of Richard Nesbit, I think we should give you another chance.' He waved away Cassidy's thanks and picked up a letter. 'Now, this is what I was going to talk to you about. It's from some group called the Coalition Against Waiting Lists. They want to address the Board and obviously that's not going to happen, but we need somebody to give them a sympathetic hearing while preventing any bad publicity. It would be right up your alley.'

Cassidy read the letter and handed it back. 'I'm not the person for this. I know how it'll go — they'll be reasonable and well-informed people with graphs that reflect badly on Paxton, and I will have to agree with them that the situation is intolerable. Then I'll come back here, and you'll tell me nothing can be done. What's the point?'

'The point is to give them a sense of closure so that they stop pestering us. Management often uses MDPs like this.'

'MDPs?'

Turnbull nodded. 'Meetings with disempowered people. Nothing can possibly happen as a result of this meeting. But if a senior staff member gives them a sincere hearing and promises he'll do what he can, they feel respected, and that's a good outcome. If you want you can suggest they talk to the RHA, that's where the money is. But however you work it your job is to tell them to get lost in a way that sounds like win-win, OK?'

'I'll do my best,' sighed Cassidy, picking up the letter again. 'But there's something else I wanted to ask you. I've just got your invitation to the reception next Monday.'

'Good. Will you be coming?'

'Yes please. Do you mind who I bring as a guest?'

'I'd have to veto Zoe,' said Turnbull. 'Lovely girl and everything, but she might start shouting and we can't have that.'

'I was thinking of Tony Walsh, unless you've already invited him.'

'Tony Walsh? I can't imagine him wanting to learn about the real world.'

'It would give the medical staff representative another view of the reforms,' said Cassidy. 'And I'm sure he'd appreciate the attempt to communicate.'

'Alright,' shrugged Turnbull. 'As long as he behaves himself.'

'Thanks, Gerald. I'll see if he's free.'

··

King was dozing in bed in the cardiac surgery ward. He opened his eyes as Cassidy walked in, and smiled a smile of most un-King-like warmth. 'Ah, Steve, good to see you. Have a seat.' His voice was weak, but his handshake was firm. No stroke on that side anyway, thought Cassidy.

'Alex, this is wonderful. Things were pretty grim when I last saw you.'

'I can't remember anything about it. I remember driving to work, but after that it's a blank until I woke up in Coronary Care.' King cleared his throat. 'I understand you saved my life.'

'We just kept you going until the experts arrived,' said Cassidy. 'Jim Bennett did a great job.'

'I don't know how to thank you.'

'No need, Alex. If you want to make it worthwhile, make sure you behave yourself in here and don't come back to work until you're ready.'

King smiled the unfamiliar smile again. The lizard seemed to have disappeared. 'Ross Frankton has told me they'll have to appoint a new CEO because there's so much happening. So there's no rush for me, is there?'

He levered himself up in the bed, grimacing with pain. 'Steve, do you know what? I've had time to think during the last few days, to watch and listen. And I think everybody should experience this place before they start making decisions about health care.'

'What do you mean?' said Cassidy.

'The people who work here are amazing. I've never met a group like them. Their jobs are complicated and demanding, and often emotionally tough. But they just get on with it, and they think nothing of staying on after work to do whatever has to be done, or even just to have a bit of a chat.

'Tony Walsh and the coronary care people were so kind and so skilled. And my surgeon, Mr Keegan, comes in and we talk about all sorts of things. I've learnt so much. We should be giving these people our full support, not fighting them — I can't wait to tell everyone about it.'

Bloody hell, thought Cassidy. Now he understood Turnbull's concern. 'That's quite a change, Alex, if you don't mind me saying so.'

King laughed softly. 'Trust me Steve, there's nothing like almost dying and then waking up in a place like this to make you sort out what's important in life.' He smiled at the student nurse who brought in a cup of tea and a biscuit.

'The pressure on the nurses, it's not good. It's quiet now because of the strike, but I understand that normally every bed is in use. They can be two nurses short for a shift, so they get agency nurses who might or might not know something about this side of the job. Everybody's feeling the strain. Then somebody else leaves, and it gets a little bit worse for the staff, and for the patients. We need to stop that happening.'

'I couldn't agree more,' said Cassidy. He absolutely had to be present at the first meeting between this new King and Jim Bennett. 'But what about the reforms, and half a billion dollars that can be saved?'

'Mr Keegan challenged me on that,' said King. 'He said the data didn't support the conclusion reached by Arthur Andersen, and their original report should be revisited. We agreed that things could be done better, but half a billion dollars to be saved? I doubt it.' He winced again as he changed position. 'And here's another thing: in a competitive environment this operation would be done by the CHE that had won the contract for heart surgery. And because price is the over-riding criterion, that would mean that the operation would usually be done by the lowest bidder, wouldn't it?'

'Yes.'

'Who might be cutting corners because they bid so low to get the contract.'

'Possibly.'

'I remember saying harsh things about the staff on television,' King mused. 'I gave them no credit for their skill and compassion. Or their integrity. I don't blame them for being angry — I'm ashamed of what I said. And it's frustrating that I've lost the chance to do something about it, now that I'm not the CEO.'

A minute passed, while Cassidy listened to the familiar sounds of the ward.

'Simon Upton should be a patient,' King murmured. 'Bill Birch. All of them. Who'll be the new CEO?' he said in a stronger voice, as Cassidy stood up to go. 'Gerald Turnbull? Jim Bennett? Good business people, but they don't have the bigger vision. I suppose it could be somebody from outside, but that would be risky at this stage because there's so much to catch up with and start managing straight away. If only there was somebody already in Paxton management who really understands about hospitals.'

'Alex,' said Cassidy gently, 'your job is to get lots of rest and recover fully, not to sit here worrying about Paxton Health.'

'It could be you,' said King. 'I'll admit I opposed your appointment, but Richard Nesbit is smarter than I am. That's why he's so rich, I suppose. I understand now what you've been saying in the meetings, and why you wanted us to come and visit the wards. It makes sense. People sense, political sense, and — I never thought I'd hear myself saying this — business sense as well. We can't keep treating the staff the way we do and expect to get a successful business out of it.'

Cassidy nodded. 'That part's certainly true.'

'You wouldn't have to know about balance sheets and so on, there are people to help you with the administrative detail. No, you'd be there for your vision and your integrity. You could be Paxton's only hope for a long-term future.'

'You're very kind, Alex, but I'm not qualified and I'm not available.'

King nodded and seemed to drift off again but he suddenly said, 'You'd be able to do something about the food here. I understand market forces, but patients are sick people who need good food to help them get better. Some of the stuff they serve, I wouldn't feed it to pigs. I'd be starving if Hazel wasn't bringing food in for me.'

'I've had a lot of complaints about the food,' said Cassidy. 'But what you've said will give me extra ammunition for the next Management Group meeting. Alex, I'll come and see you again soon.'

....

The Nikau Room was filled with conversations as Paxton Health managers and guests waited for the Associate Minister's address. Beside

Cassidy, Walsh was engrossed in a journal article that he had started reading as soon as they had sat down. Cassidy glanced across, saw 'sub-units of lactate dehydrogenase', and read no further — better to conserve his brain cells for more relevant tasks such as getting better food for the patients. He saw Bennett sitting in the front row, and wondered if he would ever get any empathy into that hard, round head. He exchanged a wave with Turnbull, who was sitting four seats along. At least Gerald would consider another point of view sometimes. But Jim Bennett . . .

Ross Frankton stood up and the conversations subsided. Walsh folded the article and put it in his pocket.

Frankton introduced the speaker. Jason Hockley had a commerce background and had entered Parliament after several years in Treasury, so he was well qualified to lead the exciting developments in health care. He was a very busy man and they were fortunate to have him with them tonight.

Hockley walked to the podium, looking tough and confident as always. 'Thank you Ross, and good evening to you all. Tonight I want to reflect on where we have come from, then spend a few minutes painting a picture of where we are going.' His rich voice filled the room and he looked along the rows of faces as if engaging personally with each of them.

'When National received the mandate of New Zealand voters in October 1990, we knew we had heavy work ahead of us to set the country back on the path to prosperity. But we were, quite frankly, appalled when Treasury briefed us on the state of the nation's finances. From Labour we inherited massive debt; the health system was a black hole into which billions of taxpayers' hard-earned dollars were disappearing.'

He took them over well-worn ground: ineffective area health boards, no-one with any idea of costs, no accountability, waiting lists growing by the day. The twenty-seven per cent 'cost blowout' did not feature.

Hockley piled up the bad news, then paused. 'However, there is a way forward, as you all know. It's started already, and we're moving onward and upward to a system where free play of market forces will put the consumer in the driving seat and ensure a fair deal for everyone.

Where individual industry and excellence are rewarded as they should be. And where public hospital inefficiency and the dreaded waiting lists are consigned to history!'

Murmurs of approval came from all sides. Turnbull caught Cassidy's eye and gave him the thumbs-up. Cassidy smiled back, until his view along the row was blocked as Walsh stood up.

'Minister, sincere apologies for interrupting,' he said as the room fell silent. 'You said that you'll put the consumer back in the driving seat. Can you explain how patients are in the driving seat when their needs are judged for them by the RHA, that doesn't have to consult anyone about anything? Wouldn't it be more accurate to say that consumers have been tied up and stuffed in the boot?'

Hockley stood silently as angry murmurs came from the audience. After a moment Walsh sat down.

'Predictably, we've been criticised,' the Minister continued. 'Visionary plans always attract attacks from vested interests. But we knew we were right, and we had the mandate of the people.

'The opposition thinks it's all wrong,' he smiled, shaking his head slightly. 'Give Labour half a chance and they'd return health administration into the hands of huge bureaucracies wasting money and running hospitals into the ground. But we know New Zealanders don't want that.

'Other people have accused us of cutting taxpayer funding to the public health service. But we have not cut one cent! We . . .' He hesitated as he saw Walsh standing again.

'Minister, sorry,' said Walsh. 'The Prime Minister and the Minister of Health both denied health funding cuts too. But do you remember the Minister of Finance's comment in late July 1991? She said, "We have cut something under one hundred million dollars, if you want to be particular." I just thought I should mention that.'

Hockley shrugged with a faint smile that did not reach his eyes, and Walsh sat down again.

The Minister continued. 'Reform will bring inter-regional equity. Market forces will ensure that services cost the same wherever you live, unlike the present situation. Arthur Andersen told us that a geriatric client in an acute bed could cost the taxpayer anything from sixty-four to a hundred and ninety-nine dollars a day in a small hospital, and in the big hospitals it's ninety-nine to six hundred and fifty-seven dollars a day. Who thinks that's fair? I certainly don't.'

'Minister, with respect,' came Walsh's voice again. 'You told us earlier that nobody knows what any service costs. But those Arthur Andersen numbers have been calculated down to the last dollar. If they could measure real costs, why can't you?'

Frankton waved urgently to somebody at the back of the room. Diamond appeared at the end of the row and reached across Cassidy to grab Walsh's arm.

'Let me guess,' said Hockley. 'Are you a doctor, by any chance?'

'Yes I am.' Walsh shook off Diamond's grasp, but Cassidy stood up and they moved into the aisle.

'Well, Doctor, now everyone here can understand what's going on.' Hockley raised his voice as he moved away from the podium towards Walsh. 'You think a medical degree entitles you to criticise those making the tough decisions — decisions that will repair the damage caused by your irresponsible, unaccountable spending. But, before you leave' — he returned to the podium as people laughed — 'I *will* reply.

'Our vision extends far beyond the current situation. Once the RHAs are in full operation, more health purchasers will enter the arena: Health Care Plans, private insurers, and other risk management organisations, national and international. Then the market will work and the consumer will truly be in charge. Does that answer your question?'

Everyone stared at the trio standing in the aisle. 'Please come and visit my ward, Minister,' said Walsh. 'You would find it instructive and I could explain the Arthur Andersen numbers to you. And that invitation applies to everyone else here tonight.'

Hockley said nothing. Walsh turned and walked towards the exit, accelerating to keep a gap between himself and Diamond.

The mellow, practised voice started up again. 'Now, a vision of the future.'

The door closed behind them. Diamond stayed inside, to Cassidy's relief — he had wondered if CCMAU might physically throw them off the premises.

Staff were setting out plates of nibbles on tables in the foyer. Walsh, apparently unruffled, went to the bar and brought back two glasses of wine. 'That was fun. Cheers.'

'Thanks. Do you think you'll have had any effect?'

Walsh shook his head. 'No, they can easily ignore the occasional little flare-up of resistance. He's sure he's right and he's preaching to the choir, so it was never going to be a real conversation. Interesting to watch their minds at work, though, isn't it? Here, have a sandwich.

'Trot out the same old lies and half-truths, and if someone calls you on them, just keep talking. Then use the Andersen numbers, without any explanation, to conclude that one hospital is fantastically efficient while another is a complete mess. And if anyone challenges you, get them thrown out.' He sighed. 'It'll take more than a few little pinpricks from me to force any change.'

'They're looking for a new CEO,' said Cassidy, 'so there's just a chance we could get somebody who understands. Would you apply?'

'Not after tonight, Steve,' Walsh laughed.

'You should think about it. No, I'm serious. People are saying there must be a medical candidate, they're so desperate that Philip Jackson even wanted *me* to apply. Then Alex King did too, it was bizarre. He's changed his views on the reforms completely.'

'Yes, I've seen him a couple of times since the operation,' said Walsh. 'People often change their ideas after a near-death experience, but he's done one of the bigger turnarounds that I can remember.' He paused. 'Cassidy for CEO, eh? What do you think about that idea?'

Cassidy smiled and shook his head. 'Even if I was anywhere near to being qualified, which I'm not, I wouldn't be interested. I'll be gone when my year is over.'

Walsh wandered over and got some more sandwiches. 'What about if we supported your application?'

'Who's we?'

'All of us. Every doctor in the hospital. Everybody on the staff. I'll talk to Phil Jackson about it. We'll get Alex and Phil as referees. I'll be another, and we'll get a staff petition going tomorrow.'

'But I don't want the job,' said Cassidy.

Walsh smiled. 'It's unlikely that you'll have to face that problem, but at least we'll send a powerful message that we want things to change. And if you did suddenly get a chance to make the world a better place, I think you might be interested.' He put down his glass. 'I'd better go, I've got some phone calls to make.'

With a rising sense of being swept along by a big wave, Cassidy drove home and consulted his flatmates.

'It's a mad idea,' said Claire, 'but what have you got to lose?'

'Do it, Steve,' Geoff agreed. 'It'll be good for staff morale even if you don't get it. You have to put your hand up.'

Claire nodded. 'That's decided then. Now, are we all set for Saturday?'

....

When Zoe came back from her holiday she found Cassidy's formal invitation to dinner at his flat on Saturday at 7 pm.

She arrived on time, wearing the black dress as requested. Geoff, in jacket and tie, took her coat and ushered her into the lounge where the fire glowed and the candle-lit table was set for four, with quiet Chopin on the stereo.

He pulled out her chair, then smoothed a napkin across her lap. He was pouring wine as Cassidy and Claire, also formally dressed, brought in bowls of fragrant soup.

The meal began, and Zoe looked round at the conspirators' faces. 'What's going on?'

'It's a welcome-back dinner,' said Cassidy. 'We've missed you. Have some garlic bread.'

'How was the holiday?' Claire asked.

'Perfect,' sighed Zoe. 'It was such a complete break. I couldn't believe how peaceful it was up there, all you could hear were the birds and the animals. Millions of stars — we sat out on the veranda one night, all rugged up, and drank Irish coffee. Ellie and Tom were so welcoming, and the boys are gorgeous. And I delivered three lambs!' She looked at Claire. 'This soup is delicious, but what's the flavour?'

'*Marrons,*' Cassidy told her. 'Chestnuts. It's French.'

'Really? It's very good.' Zoe's smile faded. 'But yesterday afternoon I was back listening to Jim Bennett in another farcical strike meeting. And I couldn't help thinking that I would much rather be listening to the sheep out in the country, and looking across at the mountains.'

'I can understand that,' said Claire. 'Is there any progress in the negotiations?'

'None, as far I could tell.'

'It sounds lousy,' said Cassidy, remembering the managers' smiles at the savings that a long strike would bring. 'I'll take your plate, and we'll be back in a moment. Are you warm enough? Good.'

Zoe's eyes got bigger as Cassidy and Claire brought out the next course: camembert chicken, with cauliflower *au gratin* and fresh green beans. 'What's going on here? I feel as if I'm in a French restaurant.'

'*Encore du vin?*' Geoff filled her glass. 'So your unexpected leisure continues. What will you do next, when you're not fighting the forces of darkness in strike meetings?'

'I'm going to help Mum paint her kitchen. She's been putting it off for ages, so it's good to be able to help.'

'A silver lining, excellent,' said Geoff. 'And speaking of silver linings, there was a piece in the *Globe* this morning that's good for a laugh.' He jumped up and brought the newspaper to the table. 'Listen to this. Our leaders blew 2.8 million dollars on those simultaneous TV ads for the health reforms. Remember the woman with the clipboard? God knows why they had her standing in an operating theatre in street clothes, but never mind. Here are the results: people believing the health system would improve went from twenty-two to thirty-four per cent. People believing it would get worse, twenty-five to seventeen per cent. I'll bet the corks are popping in the Beehive about those numbers.'

He took a sip of his wine. 'And that's the good news. "Don't understand the role of the Regional Health Authorities" went from fifty to fifty-six per cent, and about the same for the CHEs. And listen: "Don't know" was the commonest answer to *almost all questions.*' He threw the paper back onto the couch. 'That's got to be one of the great propaganda triumphs, hasn't it?'

'They must be so disappointed,' said Claire. 'But how could they possibly have thought that bullying everybody like that would make people listen?'

'It certainly didn't make us listen,' laughed Zoe, 'all we could think about was turning it off. I don't suppose they'll try that again. How's the strike affecting you, Claire?'

'Not at all — the oncology wards haven't stopped, cancer patients can't wait. But poor old Steve's got the worst of both worlds, haven't you?'

Cassidy nodded. 'Yeah, I have to turn up, but with most of the wards closed there's less liaising. Most of the people over there' — he would never call it the Leaders' Building — 'are working flat out on the RHA contracts, but that doesn't involve me.'

'You should be writing the RHA contracts,' said Geoff. 'Without any medical input they're going to be a joke. But when you're the CEO you can change all that.'

'That's right,' laughed Cassidy. 'After I've fired a few people and given everybody else a pay rise.'

'CEO?' said Zoe.

'He's applied for it,' said Geoff. 'There are no limits to what this guy will do to get you to stay, Zo.'

After a silence Zoe started clearing plates. 'Thanks Claire, that was an amazing meal. You must have—'

'Not me,' said Claire with a smile at her pupil. 'Steve cooked it all.'

'Steve?'

'It was your idea,' said Cassidy. 'Sort of. Do you remember at Scarlatti's, saying I should do woodwork classes? Well, I took French cooking classes instead, after Claire got me started. She's a great teacher. And *voila*! But sit down please, there's still dessert to come.'

'We'll get it,' said Claire. 'You two sit and chat.' Geoff got the hint and they cleared the plates and left Cassidy and Zoe together.

'Steve. CEO? You said you would give this a year, then start a new life.'

'I know,' said Cassidy. 'But don't worry, I've got a snowball's chance in hell of getting it.'

She frowned. 'Sorry, I must be missing something here. Why did you apply?'

'People I respect asked me to apply. Even Alex King — he's changed completely since the heart attack, it's wonderful.'

'And you couldn't have said no?'

'I did at first, but then I thought — even though it's a long shot, you never know, and I shouldn't walk past such a huge opportunity.'

Zoe nodded. 'Right. A huge opportunity to sit in lots of meetings, and to be the old you again, too busy and important to do normal things and spend time with—'

'It's not like that, Zo,' said Cassidy urgently. 'Imagine what we could do if a miracle happened. If I got the job, it would mean that some important people wanted things to change, wouldn't it? There would be *support*. So we'd work on getting decent staffing and better information about everything, and we'd use people's ideas to make the place run as it should.'

The doubt on her face made him hurry on. 'It would be the *opposite* of the old me, I promise. And if the old, grouchy, silent Cassidy ever came back, well, you could whack me over the head and make me stop. But only you, that would be a rule.'

At least that made her smile, just as the door opened and Geoff brought in the French apple tart.

They ate and chatted, and the strain left Zoe's face. 'That was great, Steve,' she said as they finished their coffee. 'I'm so impressed.'

'Thank you. The chicken was a bit overcooked.'

'Hey, that's old Cassidy talk. Do I get to smack you on the head now?'

'It really was very good, Steve,' said Geoff. 'And best of all, now we can have a break from bloody chestnut soup after all those practice runs.'

CHAPTER TEN

'Dr Cassidy, this is Dr Dominic Snow from Treasury,' said Frankton. Cassidy shook hands with a sleek middle-aged man in a beautiful suit, and they all sat down.

After a brief pause Snow said abruptly, 'It's not going to happen. We would never appoint a vested outsider to a situation of this importance.'

'In that case, why are we here?' said Cassidy in a similar tone.

'It's about respect. Alex King gave you a reference, and even though he's clearly unwell after his illness, his involvement obliges us to at least spend some time in conversation. And as it happens, I would value your opinion on a number of matters.'

'Alright.' In Cassidy's mind anger and relief were swirling around in equal concentrations, but he was surprised to notice some disappointment in there, too.

Snow straightened his waistcoat. 'Dr Cassidy, evidence worldwide makes it clear that competitive provision of health care will give New Zealand a much more dynamic and more diverse health care industry that will be increasingly responsive to the needs of the public. So why are hospital employees being so negative?'

'You've got evidence?' said Cassidy. 'Fantastic, we must make it public immediately. Pass it to me if you like, journal articles, book titles, whatever, and I'll gladly—'

'Oh, good Lord, no,' Snow chortled. 'Health workers don't understand economics and markets, that's our territory. You should stick to your areas of expertise, and leave policy-making to us.' He sipped some tea. 'What is annoying the *caring professions?*'

'Management don't seem to trust the staff,' said Cassidy.

Snow frowned. 'That's entirely appropriate — in business, trust gets in the way. What is trust anyway? Can you bottle it? Can you measure it? Of course not. So how can you manage it? Relying on everyone to "do the right thing" just invites abuse of the system. To maximise productivity you need solid contracts, incentives for compliance and punishment for failure to deliver.'

'Really,' said Cassidy. 'So it's either money or fear — you can't see that people might work in healthcare for other reasons.'

Snow exchanged an amused glance with Frankton. 'What other reasons could there be?'

Cassidy frowned. Nobody had ever asked him that question before. 'For most of us the "incentives", once you're getting a fair salary, are the challenge of the work and the chance to make a difference for someone who's worse off than you are.'

'Oh, you're talking about *altruism*,' said Snow. 'Can you explain that to us, please? It's a concept I've never understood.'

'I just did. I'm not saying everybody feels that way, or even thinks about it very often, but it's there.'

'Nonsense! Next you'll be telling me you do things for other people for no extra reward, just because "it's the right thing to do".' Snow's face was turning purple. 'Is this based on some God-given guidance, or mysterious revelations of some kind? Please tell me.'

'I'm sorry, you've lost me,' said Cassidy.

The Treasury man clenched his fists and breathed heavily for a few moments, then resumed in a calmer voice. 'Relying on people to do "the right thing", whatever that might mean, is hardly a basis for a rational system, is it? Everyone's out for themselves — you are, I am, that's normal, it's how the world works. You need to come into the real world, and the sooner the better so that we can set up these reforms and start to reap the benefits. Yes, Dr Cassidy, the real world!' His eyes narrowed. 'You need to read Hayek — yes, good idea, write the name down. Start with *The Road to Serfdom*. And then *Atlas Shrugged*.'

'Is that by Hayek too?'

Snow rolled his eyes. 'My God, you applied for this job without knowing about *Atlas Shrugged*! It's by Ayn Rand, of course. I re-read it every couple of years, to make sure I'm staying on track. You need to read *Atlas Shrugged* before you start taking the moral high ground with me, by God.'

'Thanks for the advice,' said Cassidy as he stood up. 'I'm sorry that you feel the way you do. But why don't you come and see *our* real world? I'd be happy to take you on a tour of the hospital.'

'Don't be ridiculous,' sniffed Snow.

'OK. Well, good luck with finding the right person.' Cassidy walked out, surprising Dawn with a dazzling smile as he waited for the lift.

....

Turnbull had been on leave since the evening of the Associate Minister's speech, but Cassidy found a chair next to his boss before the next Management Group meeting.

'Well, Steve, that's the last time you bring a friend to any function involving me,' said Turnbull.

'What? Oh yes. Sorry, Gerald.'

'Doesn't matter, it was just pathetic in the end. It's a shame you left though, the Minister shared his vision for a health system based on fairness rather than socialism.'

'Really? Fairness meaning equal access for everybody?'

'No, fairness meaning it's unfair that my tax money should be spent on you if you break your leg, because fixing it doesn't benefit me. So everybody should have private insurance to make it fair.'

'Gerald, we pay taxes so there's *public* insurance for broken legs.'

Turnbull smiled tolerantly. 'Did you get a chance to see Alex?'

'I did. He's got a new outlook on life, but that can happen after a near-death experience. Otherwise he was in great shape, considering.'

Turnbull shook his head. 'He was completely off message when I was there last. But perhaps he'd recovered by the time you saw him.'

'Let's hope so,' said Cassidy. 'We wouldn't want Alex to become an RLU, would we?'

But Turnbull was staring as Bennett and Frankton came in together.

'Morning everyone,' said Frankton. 'I have two announcements. First, it's no secret that the business is encountering headwinds, both fiscally and attitudinally. So it's been decided that I will sit in on these meetings going forward, to support this great team in any way I can.

'And second, the difficult decision has been made to put Alex King on indefinite sickness leave. He is suffering complications of his illness that rule him out as a suitable CEO for the moment. We have been through an exhaustive recruitment process and interviewed a number of outstanding applicants, and we have appointed Jim Bennett as the new CEO of Paxton Crown Health Enterprise.'

Bennett slid into the chair at the top of the table, and Frankton sat down beside him to the sound of applause. Turnbull closed his eyes and did not join in.

'Thank you, Mr Frankton,' said Bennett with a grin. Cassidy felt a lurch of panic as he realised that his short-term future was now in the hands of his worst enemy.

'I'm honoured by this promotion and will work tirelessly to ensure the success of Paxton Health.' Bennett stopped smiling. 'But I must make something clear. The CEO's package is incentive based, so if the organisation doesn't meet its targets it would cost me personally a lot of money. And that's unacceptable.' He stared at the silent faces around the table.

'Those deliverables *will be* delivered. I want focus and aggression as we deal with the RHA, and I want to see our competitors ground into the dust. Through next week I will be interfacing with each of you individually to discuss how you'll help me make that happen.' He paused as if daring anyone to question him, but no-one spoke.

'Good. Let's get to work.

'We're back to full throughput tomorrow. The staff have withdrawn their claims and the strike is over.' He nodded as a few people clapped.

'Thank you. Next: Finance report.'

'First, let me introduce the new Deputy Director of Finance, Ruth Stokes,' said Goldsmith, smiling at a pinstriped and shoulder-padded woman in her forties. 'Welcome, Ruth.

'Now, the 93/94 business plan. Two months into the financial year, we have no signed-off plan because the RHA have not yet finalised their purchasing requirements for the year. So we've based it on a rollover of existing work from last year. It's the best we—'

'Mr Chairman,' said Diamond. 'This plan falls short of expectations. You risk defaulting on your legal obligation to operate profitably.' He looked even tougher than Bennett, and behind him loomed the mighty shadow of Treasury.

'But how can we plan when they don't tell us what they want to buy?' Goldsmith whined.

'You've got plenty to work on,' said Diamond, 'particularly staff costs and consumables. We have people ready to work alongside you if necessary.'

'Moving on,' said Ruth after a moment, 'our modelling shows big potential upsides from earlier discharges. Average length of hospital stay currently is 8.7 days. Cutting that by one day across the board will save millions.'

'How would you do that?' Cassidy asked. 'Order that everybody be discharged a day earlier?'

'Big PR potential there,' chirped Russell. '"Choose Peachy — they'll whizz you through".'

'But doctors make discharge decisions based on what's best for each patient.'

'The paternalistic medical model no longer applies,' said Ruth.

Cassidy shook his head. 'You need to think this through. People who are discharged too soon often come back into hospital, and then it's usually for more than one day. But even if they manage to stay out of hospital, caring for them will put an extra burden on families and the community. That's a big hidden cost.'

'Shifting costs to users is key,' said Goldsmith. 'Arthur Andersen predicted savings of at least 180 million dollars from shortening length of stay.'

'And if they're re-admitted we can bill the RHA for a separate admission,' Ruth added.

'I like what I'm hearing,' said Diamond. 'But *you've* got to make it happen.'

'Here's something that will help,' said Cassidy. 'Day surgery decreases length of stay by many days. The operations are faster, and there's much less discomfort for patients. They're using it in private already and we should be too.'

Goldsmith shook his head. 'No capital expenditure, Doc.'

'This is not expensive, it would only need some new surgical instruments.'

'Forget it.' Bennett glared at Cassidy. 'If we start doing something a lot more cost-effectively the RHA will pay us less. There's no incentive there. What's next?'

'The hospital boilers need a major overhaul,' said Turnbull.

'Why bring that here?' Bennett glanced at his watch. 'It's Engineering's problem.'

'It's illegal for anyone without a steam ticket to work on the boilers. We de-jobbed the last qualified engineer a while ago, but he's already taken another position in Queensland and I couldn't entice him back. He was quite rude when I rang, actually.'

'So get an outside provider.'

Turnbull shook his head. 'We've had a quote, but it would mean more borrowing.'

Bennett considered. 'The boilers still work, right?'

'Barely enough to heat the building in winter, according to the Chief.'

'Add it to deferred maintenance.'

'A cold hospital would help your early discharge programme,' said Cassidy helpfully.

'What's next?' snapped the CEO.

Goldsmith looked at a letter. 'We've had a withdrawal-of-service threat from the Friends of Paxton Hospital.'

'Never heard of them.'

'They're the hospital volunteers,' said Turnbull. 'They operate the hospital shop and fundraise with cake stalls, and use the money to buy new equipment for the wards. And they run Meals on Wheels — the hospital cooks the food and the volunteers deliver it, in return for their petrol costs.'

'Would withdrawal damage the business?' Frankton asked.

'Absolutely,' said Cassidy. 'Helping elderly people stay in their own homes is better for them and it saves you heaps of money.'

Goldsmith shook his head. 'It's costing us upfront, and we have no contract for community work.'

'You can't just pull the plug, though — people would suffer. Some might actually starve in their own homes.'

'Ew.' Russell wrinkled his nose. 'Perception nosedive!'

'What's their problem?' Cassidy asked.

'They say they won't keep giving their time and effort to help us make a profit.'

'For God's sake,' snapped Bennett. 'Alright, liaison man, you go and explain to them that "profits" go back to the Crown, which in the end is the taxpayers.'

'Alright,' said Cassidy. 'But while we're discussing food, I have received complaints from patients, including Alex, about the quality of the hospital food.'

Bennett looked at Turnbull. 'Who won the catering contract?'

'A firm called Lobid. They tendered well under the others.'

'Ricky, any PR implications here?'

'People might grumble,' said Russell, 'but not enough to affect overall perceptions.'

'Just make sure your own health insurance is up to date, everyone,' laughed Goldsmith. He stopped as he caught Bennett's eye. 'Er, next item, we're searching for revenue raisers. Anything that would get more money coming in will be considered.'

'What's happening with the Saudi project?' someone asked after a silence.

'On hold pending improvements in the balance sheet,' said Frankton.

The meeting ended on that gloomy note, and Cassidy turned to Turnbull as the others left. 'Gerald, I'm sorry you didn't get the job. I had thought you would be first choice.'

Bitterness flickered across Turnbull's face, but then he shrugged. 'Thanks Steve, but it's probably time for a change anyway. I've been here for eighteen months, and that's long enough.'

···

Cassidy knocked and walked in for his scheduled CEO interface, then stopped in amazement.

The room had been transformed. The floor was of shining black and white tiles and the walls glared in high-gloss white. Nesbit's welcoming armchairs and rug had been replaced by black leather and chrome chairs surrounding a black coffee table. The black glass desk held only a computer, a white telephone, and the photo of Sir Roger, and in the black leather chair behind it sat the man of the moment, Jim Bennett.

'That was quick,' said Cassidy.

'I got people in over the weekend. I didn't want to be working with painters everywhere.'

'It's crisp.' Cassidy thought it was sterile and cold, but that might just have been because of the open windows, releasing paint fumes into the frosty morning.

'Yup. It symbolises the way forward, for me and for the organisation.'

'Shouldn't you have used peach?'

'Butch, that remark shows why this is my office and not yours.' Bennett caressed the edge of the desk. 'The Peachy concept is premium opinion-shaping, it sends a powerful message of care and love into the hearts of the public. But warm and fuzzy doesn't work when you're about to grab the opposition and beat the crap out of them.'

'Got it,' said Cassidy. 'Anyway, congratulations on the promotion.'

'Thanks. Sit down.'

They considered each other across the gleaming desktop. 'We need to consider your position,' said Bennett. 'It's show time and I need an elite management team, all pulling for me.'

'Of course.'

'So where does that put you? You have no training in change principles and management theory, but you're sure that you're right and we're wrong, and you constantly criticise and obstruct. You delay progress in meeting after meeting — no, let me finish. You're friendly with a *Bugle* reporter and you helped him attack us. If I'd been in charge that day I would have fired you, Alex or no Alex.'

Cassidy shivered and said nothing.

'But. You have the best chance of getting current clinical employees on board until we find some team players, and you sometimes say things that are useful. So I have decided to keep you on for now.'

'That's very kind,' said Cassidy.

'It's nothing to do with kindness. I expect you to help me solve problems caused by your snotty colleagues, and in any other area where your knowledge value-adds. But from now on I require a positive, problem-solving approach and no more whining. And to help you take this on board, as from today your package will be performance-based.'

'Performance-based?'

'Help me meet my goals and you'll share the rewards. Your base salary will drop but the bonus, if awarded, will bring it back to just above your current level. It's the same for me, in case you're feeling sorry for yourself. Dawn has the contract for you to sign.' Bennett popped a knuckle. 'I'm facing financial imperatives that you can't imagine, but—'

'Let me try,' said Cassidy. 'You've been told to find more savings or lose your job.'

'Don't poke your nose where it doesn't belong, Doctor.'

'And you're starting to wonder whether more savings really can be made without crippling the hospital, but CCMAU won't listen.'

'And don't try to piss me off,' Bennett growled. 'I think you might still be helpful to me, but if cutting you loose will make my job easier I'll do it in a second.'

'Alright,' said Cassidy after a moment. He stood up to leave, but suddenly a beaming Alex King appeared in the doorway.

'Marvellous, the two people I most wanted to see.' He stepped in as Dawn smiled apologetically behind him. 'May I join you for a moment? I hope I'm not interrupting anything important.'

Bennett somehow found a smile, and jumped up to shake King's hand. 'Alex, how are you? Steve's just going.'

'I would like him to stay, please. I know you were both involved, and I wanted to thank you.'

Bennett was still catching up. 'Yes, yes, of course. Have a seat, Alex.'

'Well, just for a moment,' said King. 'I don't want to take up too much of your time.'

They moved to the chairs around the coffee table. 'You're looking great, isn't he, Steve?' babbled Bennett.

Cassidy was dismayed to see King here so soon. He should have been at home in front of the fire or in bed, but his voice was strong and his eyes had a missionary's gleam despite the dark rings under them. He was trembling, perhaps with excitement, but Cassidy got up and shut the windows anyway.

'I know what you're thinking,' said King. 'It's only been a few weeks since my heart attack, and I'm supposed to be resting. But the things I have to say just can't wait.' He turned to Bennett. 'Gerald told me you're CEO now. Congratulations.'

Bennett nodded and smiled.

'I've come to help you. I was telling Steve earlier on about the marvellous people I've met in the wards. They work so hard, and yet we're treating them badly. Staff cuts are dangerous, Jim — we need more staff, not less.

'It's clear to me now that we've approached these reforms back to front; we should have started with the people at the coalface. The doctors and nurses have great ideas for doing things better, and we'll continue to struggle until we start treating them with respect and using their suggestions.'

Bennett was frowning. 'But Alex, you said on TV that doctors were running the service for the benefit of themselves and their cronies. Didn't you?'

'You're right, I did say that.' King shook his head in disbelief. 'But that was before I spent time seeing it all first-hand.' He reached over to pat Bennett on the knee. 'I urge you to get into the wards today and see for yourself, then start harnessing the energy. Go for win-win alongside these wonderful people, and you could make Paxton truly great.'

Bennett managed another polite smile.

'And another thing,' said King. 'Remember the National Party's campaign theme, "The Decent Society"? What do you think that means? To me, it means that we care for everybody as well as we can, especially the most unlucky people in society. What else can it mean?

'I can't see how a hospital labelling a person as a Revenue Losing Unit, and trying to avoid caring for them, can possibly call itself part of a decent society. Can you?'

Bennett seemed to wilt under King's earnest stare, but then he rallied. 'Alex, thanks so much for coming, great to see you. Sorry, but I've got a meeting in — no, I'm meant to be somewhere else now, actually.'

King stood up. 'Oh, that sounds familiar. I hope I haven't held you up too much.'

'Not at all,' said Bennett. 'Best of luck with the recovery.'

'Please don't forget what I've said. Any help I can give you, Jim, just give me a call. Dawn has my home number. And thank you both, once again.'

'Sure. Goodbye.'

Cassidy started to follow King out.

'Hey!'

He turned back, closing the door.

'What the hell was that all about?' Bennett snarled.

'Pardon?'

'Did you put him up to this?'

'Absolutely not. And it would be fantastic if you listened to him actually, although I do seem to detect a hint of—'

'"Decent Society"? Jesus!' Bennett popped a knuckle.

'Yes, it's definitely there, a sense that you aren't quite resonating with Alex on this. Am I right? That's a pity, he's talking good sense. But anyway, I must go and focus on the company's needs going forward. And you've got a meeting to go to.'

'I *haven't* got a bloody meeting to go to,' said Bennett in a seething whisper. 'How else could I get rid of the old fool? Much longer and he would have started singing "Kumbaya"!' He glared at Cassidy. 'What's so funny — are you sure you didn't set this up?'

'Quite sure, Jim. Have a nice day.'

....

'This is one of the best meals on the planet,' Cassidy announced. He had taken Claire and Zoe to see *The Fugitive* on a wintery evening, and now they were eating toasted cheese and drinking hot chocolate. 'And wasn't that a great film?'

'Yes,' said Zoe. 'The part where Harrison Ford saved the child's life in the emergency department.'

'Any part with Harrison Ford in it,' Claire added dreamily.

'No,' said Cassidy, 'I'm going to be Tommy Lee Jones when I grow up.'

Claire put more pine cones on the fire. 'Is it good to be back at work, Zo?'

Zoe paused before she answered. 'It's good to be getting some money again. But the strike didn't fix anything, and the managers seem to have more power now than they did before we started.'

'I don't know how we can force them to listen,' said Claire. 'Even when they do formally "consult" it feels like nothing's happening.

'I went to one of the Core Services public meetings a couple of weeks ago, and it was weird. The committee wanted a decision on public funding for varicose vein surgery, as if you can make things that simple, but all people wanted to talk about was the new system and what a disaster it is. It was a circus. They never did discuss varicose veins, but I wonder if they considered the feedback they actually did get.'

'Seems unlikely, doesn't it?' said Cassidy. 'It would be "outside their brief" I expect. But public consultation about core services was doomed from the start.' He reached for the jug and topped up their Milo. 'Oregon spent a fortune trying it a while back, and look where it got them.'

'What happened?' said Zoe.

'The public of Oregon produced some spectacular ideas — they ranked tooth decay above ectopic pregnancy, which even I know can be fatal. And they wanted open-heart surgery to have uncapped funding, so now Oregon does four times as many heart operations per thousand of population as we do. Moral of the story? You can't ask the public for their opinion about technical things and expect a useful answer. I wouldn't have a clue about the best way to build a bridge or run an airport, would you? No. I'd ask the experts at those jobs.'

'The public know what they really want, though,' said Claire. 'It was quite clear at the meeting: Kiwis expect their health system to give everybody a fair go, even if it does mean the odd person getting something they shouldn't.'

'Sounds good to me.' Zoe cupped her hands round her mug and stared into the fire. 'But now that we've got Jim Bennett as CEO, who knows what the future will bring?'

····································

Cassidy yawned silently and held the phone further away.

As more people learnt about their liaison person, he had become busier as an interpreter between the warring tribes. Earlier he had told the new manager of We've Got it All, formerly known as Supplies, that the Intensive Care Unit's request for new ventilators did not mean extra wall fans. Now he was agreeing with an orthopaedic surgeon that managers could not actually dictate which prosthesis he put into a patient's hip, while reminding him that the hip replacement budget was fixed and not negotiable.

He put the phone down and yawned again, then decided it was coffee time.

Somebody knocked on the door just as he was about to open it. 'Hello, Dr Cassidy.' It was Claudia Donaldson, the RHA's contract lawyer, today in a formal suit, but with the same amused, thoughtful expression.

'Claudia, how nice. But what are you doing here? Shouldn't you be hunting down contract-breachers or something?'

'I've got a few minutes before a meeting and I thought I'd drop by and say hello.'

'Great, come and have a coffee.' Cassidy led the way to the lift, and ushered Claudia in. 'So how are things at the RHA? I heard the negotiations were stalled until the Crown sent in the bottom-kickers.'

'There are challenges, but that's natural in a ground-breaking project, particularly one of this size and complexity.'

'Complexity? No, no, business techniques eliminate complexity. You just get the client into hospital, measure how long they stay and count the costs of what you do to them, and then ask them how it went. What could be simpler?'

'That's what we thought,' she said wearily.

'Here we are. Ms Donaldson, you sound low. You need strong coffee — and something to eat perhaps? I recommend the pink buns. My treat, of course.'

They found a table, and Cassidy smiled at his glamorous guest. 'Have you got good medical advisers?'

'Come on, Steve. Surely you understand about capture by now.' She took a bite of her pink bun.

'You're consulting with the community though. That would give you a useful perspective.'

Claudia shook her head. 'That would be capture too.'

'Hmm,' said Cassidy. 'Let me make sure I understand. You should be identifying people who need help, but if anybody actually tells you they need help you cross them off the list. Is that the technique? It must save lots of money.'

She was not amused, although that might have been due to the bun. She put it to the edge of her plate and sipped her coffee. 'We're caught between the Crown requiring us to save every cent possible, and providers telling us they won't survive on what we can afford to pay them. All the contracts should have been signed off by now, but we've only completed a few.'

'But you're still the boss, right? Peachy is scared of the big bad RHA.'

Claudia grimaced. 'No, we're at the mercy of the providers. They know more about the market than we do, and they do all sorts of tricks to drive the price down artificially and kill competition. They add clauses about other illnesses—'

'They have to do that. Comorbidities are everywhere, and putting your heads in the sand won't make them go away.'

'All that's bad enough. But the legal side is a quagmire.'

I'm in a Meeting with a Disempowered Person, thought Cassidy. How sad to see Claudia, of all people, so demoralised.

'The Commerce Act prohibits contracts that lessen competition. So if we give, say, the total hernia surgery contract to Warwick, Paxton could sue us for anti-competitive behaviour. Then there's the Consumer Guarantees Bill, but what health care provider can guarantee an outcome to somebody with a major illness? It makes no sense. And don't get me started on the Fair Trading Act . . .' She drifted into despairing silence, then had another sip of coffee.

'So round and round we go, with each side concentrating on protecting themselves rather than providing the best service possible. And the Crown has introduced enforcers to push things through, even though we're still learning about all the hazards.'

Cassidy smiled. 'We've come a long way from the times when people trusted each other and the job got done, haven't we?'

'Would those be the times when costs kept blowing out and waiting lists grew, by any chance?' Claudia stood up. 'Thanks, Steve, I'd better go. Sorry I went on a bit there, but it was good to chat.'

'Yes it was,' said Cassidy. 'Give my regards to Bryce Bailey.'

'Bryce has left the RHA, he's doing consultancy work now.'

'Good for him. Anyway, Claudia, keep believing. Market forces, that's the ticket.'

CHAPTER ELEVEN

The Management Group had assembled, and Bennett made his entrance.

'Right. Nurses' packages. Post-strike we're increasing the downwards flexibility of individual employment contracts. Mr Goldsmith.'

'We've had a cycle of voluntary redundancies,' said Goldsmith. 'Now we're commencing disestablishing positions then inviting re-application for the same positions with flab removed, for a smaller package.'

'Flab?' said Cassidy. 'What flab could there possibly be in a nurse's package?'

'Continuing education outstandingly,' said Ruth. 'Uniforms. Non-annual leave.'

Goldsmith nodded. 'In the medium term we will further right-size by eliminating charge nurse positions and—'

'*What?*'

'—replacing them with a small, agile team of client care advisers working out of a central location, each managing a cluster of wards.'

'No!' shouted Cassidy. 'That would be a disaster. Has the Board approved this?'

'Certainly, and the sooner the better,' said Frankton. 'The financials are overwhelmingly in favour.'

'Stuff the bloody financials,' said Cassidy, momentarily disregarding the company's needs. 'A ward without a charge nurse would be like a ship without a rudder. As your medical adviser, I insist that you abandon this plan.'

Bennett tried to ignore him. 'Next, the draft financial—'

'Or there will be severe consequences for patients and, believe me, for the people who over-rode professional advice and made such a colossal mistake.'

'What do you mean, severe consequences?' asked Frankton with a frown.

'Something as serious as this couldn't stay secret. The public would hear about how you had messed things up to save a few dollars, and you — everybody here today — would become liable for mistakes made in the wards. Are you ready for that?'

'Is that a threat?' said Bennett.

'Absolutely. You have to listen to me on this.'

Bennett exchanged glances with Frankton, and sighed. 'We'll put that concept on hold pending further study. Next, the financial plan for the next two years. You have a copy in your agendas. It includes the nursing productivity enhancements discussed before Dr Cassidy's outburst, and is close to signoff. I will—'

'It's nowhere near close to signoff,' boomed Diamond from the bottom of the table. 'Treasury requires another ten per cent to be trimmed.'

Another ten per cent?' Bennett gasped. He glanced at Frankton, but the Board chair was engrossed in the balance sheet. 'That's not possible.'

'It's the decision of Treasury after reviewing this draft,' said Diamond. 'The RHA has been as flexible as possible on your tender prices, but it cannot keep adding upside. There's still substantial inefficiency out there and it's your task to eliminate that and enable Paxton Health to operate as a profitable business.'

He took off the dark glasses. 'And if you are non-compliant ongoingly, CCMAU may recommend replacement of senior Paxton management, starting at the top.'

There was a long silence.

'Mr Chairman,' said Turnbull. 'This would be a good time to announce the new external surgery initiative. It's been top secret until now.'

Bennett's mouth was slightly open. He nodded without moving his stare from Diamond's granite face.

'Yesterday we inked a contract with another RHA for waiting-list surgery worth four million dollars.' A buzz of excitement started up. 'Yes, it is good news. This is a fee-for-service contract, delivering outside cash, and if we perform well we can expect more of this work in future.'

'It's wonderful to have positive news at last,' said Frankton.

'What about quality?' asked Ruth. 'Could they potentially dump high-risk units on us?'

Turnbull nodded. 'They could, but we'll be sending a team to assess unit quality. And when our RHA buys work from CHEs outside this area we'll send our suboptimal—'

'Sorry Gerald,' said Cassidy. 'Are you serious? Patients from here will go to another part of the country to have surgery, and patients from there will come here. Why? What about patients' families? Everybody will lose, except airlines and motels. Why don't we just do our work, while the CHEs in the other areas do theirs?'

'This will be a genuine market,' said Turnbull. 'There will be buying and selling, and negotiating on price for the best deals. That's what markets do.'

Diamond nodded approvingly. 'Good work, people. This approach is just what's needed. Tell your staff to continue seeking opportunities for non-RHA income, and reinforce again the need to eliminate all overheads not directly related to contract obligations.'

....

'Don't look at me like that, young Marriner,' said Walsh while Cassidy counted their scores. 'You think that holing my bunker shot at the twelfth was just lucky. But as another famous golfer said, the more I practice the luckier I get.'

Les snorted. 'It's the other way round for me these days. I'm thinking of taking up lawn bowls instead.'

'Poor chap. I'll still take that beer off you though, and we can drink a toast to the handicap system.'

They handed in their cards and went upstairs to the bar. Walsh started counselling Les about his swing as Cassidy sat enjoying the cold beer and warm sun.

A braying laugh caught his attention and he saw Jason Hockley working the room, meeting and greeting, patting backs and shaking hands, scanning the room to plan his next move.

Hockley noticed Walsh and came across to their table. 'Hello, how was your round?'

'Don't get him started,' said Les, not recognising the Associate Minister of Health.

'Mind if I join you?' Hockley sat down across the table from Walsh. 'You're the man who tried to spoil my address at the Grand, aren't you? But then you had to leave. Jason Hockley,' and he held his hand out across the table.

'Tony Walsh. This is Stephen Cassidy, and Les Marriner.'

'Morning. You're an angry man, Dr Walsh.'

'Most people who work in health are angry.'

'I don't see why.'

'Don't you? Then perhaps you can explain why it's illegal for citizens to lie to the Government, but OK for the Government to lie to the citizens.'

Les stood up. 'Time to go. Thanks for the game, guys.'

'See you, Les,' said Cassidy.

'What do you mean?' Hockley had not noticed Les.

'The old system had problems—'

'At least you admit that.'

'—but it was improving. Before the election you promised to keep the status quo, apart from making a few changes related to private practice. Didn't you?'

The Minister smiled and nodded.

'You won the election. Then after secret consultations you tipped the system upside down, hoping to fit it into a commercial fantasy based on suspect and highly selected advice. And we will have years of expensive chaos and poorer quality health care as a result.'

'Tony,' said Hockley, 'we did what we had to do to get the mandate. We knew people wouldn't understand what had to be done.'

'But you lied.'

'If people are stupid enough to believe parties' promises, then they don't deserve a vote.'

'*What?*' said Cassidy. 'Say that again?'

'You heard, Steve.'

'So if you fool enough stupid voters with your lies, you can then do whatever you like?'

'No, we can do whatever is *right*,' Hockley drawled, pushing his chair back and crossing his legs. 'The end justifies the means, have you heard that saying before?'

'It's your certainty that you are right that's so bizarre,' said Walsh. 'Especially when you're surrounded by sophisticated people telling you that you're making a huge mistake.'

Hockley picked a piece of lint off the knee of his green Jack Nicklaus trousers, then smiled tolerantly at Walsh. 'When the model is fully operational, you'll see it differently because you and the other elite players will be looking at some serious incentives.'

'Are you planning full privatisation?' Cassidy asked. 'It's never been said officially.'

'Think about it,' said Hockley. 'Food is supplied by private companies, giving us good food at fair prices with no waiting lists. Why shouldn't health be the same?'

Walsh rolled his eyes. 'Well, Minister, that's because there's plenty of food. But it's rationed when it's scarce, for example during a war.

'But health care services are always scarce, and they can't just be left to market forces because people miss out if you do that. And that's immoral, although I appreciate that might be hard for you to grasp.'

Hockley stood up. 'I'd better keep moving. Tony, you've got to move past this "we know best" Nanny State idea where the health consumer has no responsibility.'

'Ah yes, the Nanny State,' said Walsh. 'What does that expression actually mean? What is a nanny, Mr Hockley?'

Hockley snorted. 'A woman who looks after young children.'

'Why do young children need looking after?'

'Obviously, because they can't do it themselves.'

'And she would bring them back onto the right track if they're naughty?'

'Yes,' said Hockley, scanning the room to find his next contact.

'So a nanny looks after people who can't help themselves, and stops people from doing wrong things.' Walsh paused. 'That describes a government's responsibility — something that most people think we should build up, rather than demolish.'

Hockley shook his head with the pitying smile that Cassidy knew so well. 'You're ten years behind the times, mate. Developed countries everywhere are moving into smaller government, with people taking personal responsibility for their lives. The modern government's job is to maximise opportunities for wealth creation.'

'And to hell with the people who never get the opportunities?'

Hockley laughed. 'Now that's socialist talk, Tony. Forget it.' He shook hands with them both. 'If there's anything else I can help you with, please don't hesitate to get in touch.'

Cassidy stared at the politician's retreating back. 'I've never seen him out on the course, have you? I think this is work for him. And he's probably doing the same at some tennis club in the afternoon, then with the theatre crowd in the evening. What a life.'

'If you want to feel sorry for anybody,' said Walsh with unusual venom, 'remember Carol Higgins. Not people like him. "If people are stupid enough to believe parties' promises" . . . My God.'

....

Bryce Bailey, handing Cassidy his business card, was transformed in a crisp blue blazer, white shirt and striped tie. Even his hair seemed younger.

'"Bryce Bailey, consultant",' Cassidy read. '"Across The Board Quality Management". Have a seat, Bryce. How's business?'

'Best move I ever made,' smiled Bailey. 'People can't get enough about quality these days. I'm meeting up with Paxton management staff this afternoon to brainstorm Monday's workshop on growing the business, and there's the New Paradigms, New Horizons seminar next week.'

'Goodness. Is all your work with Paxton?'

'Oh, no. Later this month I'm leading a weekend Enhanced Leadership retreat with Warwick's management, then I'm helping them choose colours for their outpatient clinics.' He laughed at Cassidy's expression. 'Don't worry, Steve, it won't cause World War Three if you know Warwick are refreshing their décor, but I swear I don't pass any important information around. That would see me out of work in five minutes, and rightly so.'

'Sounds like you're not missing your old job,' said Cassidy.

'Definitely not. It's no secret that the RHA is struggling. The CHEs are playing dirty, fighting every clause and pretending they can't deliver at fair prices. They seem to think nobody knows about all the slack in the hospitals.'

Cassidy sighed. 'There really isn't any slack left, Bryce. And now CCMAU wants another ten per cent cut out of the business plan — they have no idea how dangerous that is for patients, and they don't seem to care about it either.'

'It can be done,' said Bailey. 'Across the Board could work alongside your people to achieve results that would amaze you.'

Cassidy shrugged. 'I doubt that, but anyway I don't have authority to hire you. These days I mostly advise at management meetings, and deal with complaints from staff and patients.' He pointed to the pile of folders. 'And there's no shortage of those.'

Bailey frowned. 'High complaint volume is an AMI, an Adverse Morale Indicator. Low morale impacts negatively on productivity.'

'They've got real problems, like staff shortages, or faulty equipment not getting fixed,' said Cassidy. 'They're not just trying to annoy management.'

'Do they feel disempowered?'

'Definitely.'

'Do they see themselves as internal customers of management?'

Cassidy laughed.

'I see potential here,' said Bailey. 'Why don't I share a couple of suggestions at no charge? And if they work out, you and I could partner effectively going forward.'

'Don't worry, Bryce.' Cassidy had strong feelings about free riding.

'Let's see now. You can quickly raise morale by showing that staff are appreciated. How do you do that? Find outstanding staff members, reward them, and give it a bit of publicity. Call them Health Champions — simple but effective, you'll see.'

'I'll pass it on,' said Cassidy diplomatically.

'And what about an event to enhance the sense of community among staff?'

'Bryce, you don't need to do this.'

'I know — a fun run. Some laps of the park, sausage sizzle afterwards, people renew old friendships and make new ones. Different age groups, get the kiddies along too. Fun runs always go down well.'

Cassidy wrote 'fun run' and 'sausage sizzle' under 'health champions' on his yellow pad.

'What's the MDR, the management/doctor relationship, like here?' said Bailey.

'Terrible.'

'Well, why don't the managers challenge the doctors to some kind of competition? Perhaps a race, or a tug-of-war. That would break down the barriers. And get the *Globe* along to make sure the community sees what a great employer Paxton Health is.'

'Thanks,' said Cassidy, adding 'docs vs mgrs' to the list. 'I'll pass this on, and I'll mention that they're your suggestions.'

'That's great, Steve.'

Cassidy paused. 'Bryce, can I ask you something? As an insider, how do you think the reforms are going?'

'Off the record?'

'Absolutely.'

Bailey checked that the door was closed, and leant over the desk. 'They can't possibly succeed,' he murmured. 'Nobody knows how to contract for what actually happens. And some people go through hospital and get better, with *no diagnosis*. Did you know that? Oh yes, you did.

'All the contract forms we'd drawn up were based on a single diagnosis, they were useless for everything except the most straightforward cases. It falls over when people have more than one thing wrong with them — you can't possibly write a contract beforehand for every combination, let alone different degrees of severity, although I hear they're still trying to do that. And then, how do you monitor it?

'We didn't know if the hospitals were being straight with us, so every contract was a potential loser for the RHA. But we couldn't ask any experts because of the risk of—'

'Capture,' whispered Cassidy.

'Yes. The analysis and legal costs were astronomical, and it was all coming out of our health purchasing budget. We couldn't even fund the current purchasing, let alone make any savings. And cutting funding to the CHEs would be politically unacceptable. So where do you go from there?'

'How's it all going to end up?'

Bailey glanced over his shoulder at the door again, then leaned even further towards Cassidy. 'It's heading towards a very expensive train wreck. But you didn't hear that from me.'

Cassidy shuddered, thinking of *The Fugitive*. 'But Bryce, what should we do? We're talking about sick people here. We can't say there's going to be a train wreck, then do nothing.'

Bailey shrugged. 'You and I can't stop it — this is politics. All you can do is get off the train while there's still time.' He stood up and adjusted his tie. 'Great to catch up, Steve,' he said in a normal voice. 'I hope those suggestions are useful. Let me know how you get on.'

....

Bennett began the next Management Group meeting by welcoming keen new managers of medicine and paediatrics, each replacing someone who had lasted less than six months.

A grim Turnbull was next. 'The external surgery contract is cancelled. Our surgeons said it would be "unethical" to operate on units from other areas, as it would disadvantage those on our waiting list.'

'That's a good point,' said Cassidy. 'But did they agree, then change their minds?'

'No, they refused to cooperate after hearing about the deal.'

'So you didn't consult them before tendering.'

'We don't need to consult them,' Bennett snapped. 'They work for the Board, and the Board decides what work they do.'

'In theory,' sighed Frankton. 'I met with their representatives, but they wouldn't budge.'

Turnbull continued after a silence. 'We're subcontracting forty hip replacement operations out to private providers. We can't meet our contracted quota of elective operations because so many surgeons have terminated their employment with us, so those same surgeons will now do the operations at private hospitals for a significantly higher fee.'

'Good for them,' said Cassidy. 'Let's watch that wealth trickle down, eh Gordon?'

Frankton tried to rally the troops. 'We will not be defeated,' he said in Churchillian tones. 'We must enhance our corporate image, so that skilled people fight to come and work at Paxton. Are there any ideas?'

'I have two,' said Cassidy after waiting for anybody else to speak. 'First, Philip Jackson's surgical team had a major triumph last week. It's the first time this operation has been done in New Zealand, and it was a success. You could publicise it as a win for Paxton. It involved — wait, I'll draw a diagram.' He got up to go to the whiteboard, mentally revising Jackson's description from Monday evening.

'Sit down.' Bennett's voice was weary. 'We don't care what was done, and we can't publicise it anyway because it's commercially sensitive.'

'Mr Cassidy,' said Diamond. 'If this was the first time in New Zealand, was it cleared with the RHA?'

'I don't know.'

'If it wasn't specified in a contract, it took resource that should have been used for meeting contractual obligations, and that's inappropriate. I will need a report.'

Cassidy nodded. 'Glad to oblige. It was a brilliant innovation, and they saved somebody's life.'

'You can't do the report,' said Bennett. 'Who's managing the surgical cluster?'

'Simon Keesing, but he's on stress leave.' Turnbull sighed. 'I'll do it.'

'Are there any usable suggestions for corporate image enhancement?' Bennett looked hopefully round the group before nodding to his medical adviser.

'I had a meeting with Bryce Bailey, of Across the Board Quality Management.' Cassidy went through the suggestions for the fun run, the sausage sizzle and the tug-of-war between managers and clinicians.

'Nice,' said Goldsmith. 'I'll be there — let's all go along and crush the bloody doctors.'

'Mr Peachy will come,' said Russell. 'This will be a boost for employee engagement, it's a great idea.'

Even Turnbull was smiling. 'It'll break the ice between the Leaders' Building and the hospital, while moving us towards the community. How many would come, do you think? Say, three hundred? I'm sure we can find a few dollars to hire a marquee and barbeque some bangers.'

'That is unacceptable,' said the voice of CCMAU. The chatter collapsed.

'The Act states clearly that this entity's responsibility is to its shareholders. If you can make a business case for marquee hire as an investment, then I will consider it. Otherwise I forbid the use of Crown equity on a venture whose benefits cannot be measured.'

'Perhaps the Friends of Paxton Hospital could help,' suggested Frankton in a hollow voice.

The door opened and Dawn wheeled in the tea trolley, and with it a welcome waft of coffee. Cassidy joined the queue for the scones with cream and jam that made the business meetings bearable. He took his coffee and scone over to the window, where Ricky Russell joined him.

'Steve, love the fun run concept.'

'Good,' said Cassidy. 'Bryce had another suggestion too, but it was so ridiculous that I didn't mention it.'

But the perception manager loved the Health Champions idea as well. 'We could have a monthly newsletter, highlighting staff members who've done something special. And there would be a badge, Mr Frankton could pin it on them at a special ceremony. Leave this with me, Steve, I'll get the team onto it, build a scenario. Health Champions, I love it!'

'Finance,' said Bennett as the meeting resumed.

Goldsmith's despair was almost at pre-departure Harry Prattley levels. 'The lost surgical contract is a heavy blow. Our debt is increasing daily. We can make repayments only by borrowing more, and a large tax bill comes due on the twentieth of the month.' He turned to Frankton. 'Is there any news about tax relief?'

'What Terry is alluding to,' Frankton explained, 'is legislation to put all health providers on an equal footing for tax obligations. The National Interim Provider Board proposed this and they were going to issue another report when they had completed their investigation. This would have levelled the playing field because unlike us, the private providers are mostly non-profit organisations paying no company tax, which gives them a massive advantage. But we've heard nothing more about it. Mr Diamond, have you? — no.'

'We're considering every option for debt reduction,' Goldsmith concluded, 'but at this point in time I have nothing more to advise.'

'Business plan,' said Bennett grimly. 'Mr Frankton and I have spoken to many of you since the last meeting, and you have not yet come up with enough cost-cutting measures to meet Treasury's requirements.'

He went through the proposals: lay off more staff here, close a clinic there, keep working at reducing the length of patient stay. And sell as many assets as possible.

Nobody had any new ideas, and the room fell silent. It was clear that Peachy was going to fall short of what CCMAU was demanding.

Diamond took off the glasses. 'You have one more week. And if the business plan still fails to meet Treasury requirements, we will have no choice but to put Paxton Health into *workout*.

'That means I will bring in CCMAU experts who will drive the business planning process and ensure that all appropriate steps are taken to bring the organisation to commercial viability. Managers who are unable to adequately perform these tasks will be replaced by CCMAU appointees. There will be weekly meetings with CCMAU, at which the balance sheet of the organisation will be reviewed and action adjustments made as needed. There will be an external observer to enforce compliance.'

The dark glasses went back on. 'One week, Mr Chairman.'

....

Cassidy opened the fridge and inspected the contents. Claire was working late tonight, and he didn't have the energy to do anything fancy for himself and Geoff. He got potatoes, carrots and cauliflower out of the fridge and two mince pies out of the freezer, and started filling the kettle.

He heard footsteps outside. Zoe looked round the door and came in.

'Zo, hi, terrific! Just a minute,' said Cassidy over his shoulder. 'Have you eaten? I can put another spud in the pot.' He plugged the kettle in and turned to greet her. 'We've got lots of pies — hey, what's the matter? Come here.'

He was shocked by how thin she felt as they hugged. He gently pushed her away so that he could see her face. 'Zo, what's happened? Here, use this,' as he gave her a handkerchief, 'it's the one you rescued me with in the strike meeting, I've been meaning to give it back to you anyway.'

She wiped her eyes and blew her nose, then rested her head on his chest. 'Anna Blakelock resigned today — the best of the staff nurses that I had left. So now I can make a safe roster only if I work two extra shifts a week myself. Yesterday we had twenty-one patients on drips, and we can't run a safe shift with just one IV-certified nurse.' Her voice was muffled and tearful. 'I'm so tired, I'm terrified I'm going to start making mistakes myself, if I haven't already.'

He pulled out a chair and sat her down, then opened a bottle of wine and gave her a glass. 'Is there anyone you can talk to about this who will understand?'

'Lots of people understand, but none of them can do anything about it.' She looked up at him. 'And that includes you, doesn't it Steve?'

They heard a car in the drive. Geoff came into the kitchen, red-eyed and crumpled after working for a night and the days on each side of it. 'Hi Zo, Steve. Guess what happened yesterday.' He threw his bag in the corner, got a beer out of the fridge and slumped into a chair beside Zoe.

'What happened yesterday?' said Cassidy.

Geoff drank deeply. 'Thank God for beer at times like this, eh? Well. Patrick Parkes had booked one of his major pelvic reconstruction and total hip replacement procedures. The man's seventy-four, colon cancer treated five years ago, now he's got a big secondary deposit just above the right hip and going into the joint. They can't give any more radiation treatment. He's in terrible pain, can't weight-bear, and the whole pelvis could collapse at any moment. No tumour anywhere else, as far as we know.

'Yesterday morning Parky walks into theatre and sees the whiteboard. "Where's my big case, Mr Richards? He was first on the list." I had to tell him what I'd just found out myself, that Trevor Hoskins had cancelled Mr Richards' operation and put in two knee replacements instead.'

'Trevor Hoskins? The manager?'

'That's the one. Well, you can imagine. Parky makes a noise like a bull with its balls caught in — sorry, Zo. He heads off to find Mr Hoskins, and I follow along.

'Parky shoves open the door of Trev's office, grabs him by the shirt and lifts him off the floor. Trev's screaming, Parky's shouting, but I somehow manage to push them apart.'

'Lucky you were there,' said Cassidy.

'Yeah. Parky gives Trev another mouthful, then punches a hole in the notice board. He goes back to theatre and changes out of his scrubs, and he's gone for the day. They had to get Andy Bishop out of his clinic to do Parky's list, and he was *not* happy.

'Meanwhile somebody gets Trev a cup of tea, and I ask him why he did it.'

'Why did he do it?'

'Because he couldn't find a cost code for the procedure in the RHA contracts.' Geoff nodded slowly. 'Yes. Acting on instructions, this guy, who doesn't know his arse from his elbow, didn't check with anybody but just went ahead and overrode a major clinical decision.'

'Wow,' said Cassidy, musing on the limitations of content-free as a management model. Zoe silently sipped her wine.

'Previously it's gone the other way. A while ago Trev started choosing random patients off the waiting list and squeezing them onto full operating lists "so that we can meet quota," before he was politely requested to stop doing it. I can't see him lasting much longer.' Geoff drank more beer.

'And that was the day's entertainment. The rest of it is just awful. People are saying they're going to make a *ten per cent* cut in our funding, on top of what's been taken already. So we'll have more layoffs of everybody except the surgeons, who've mostly gone already. We're losing so many good people, and they're taking truckloads of experience with them. It'll take the unit years to recover.'

Cassidy sighed and shook his head.

'And there's another rumour,' Geoff continued, 'that they're planning to get rid of the charge nurses. I mean, at that point the imagination just blows a fuse, doesn't it? Wards without ward sisters? Time to ring *Good Vibes*, I'd say.'

'That was just a proposal,' said Cassidy. 'I've got them to reconsider it, for now at least.' To hell with confidentiality. 'What do you mean, ring *Good Vibes*?'

Geoff started laughing. Neither of them noticed the tears rolling down Zoe's cheeks.

'You didn't hear about that? The guys in fracture clinic made up this bogus travel agency, with a proper letterhead and everything. They wrote a letter to management offering a discount for Paxton staff leaving on one-way international tickets, it was hilarious. They never got a reply of course, but now if anybody's feeling really pissed off about life round here, we just say "I'll think I'll talk to *Good Vibes*," and everybody knows — Zo, are you alright?'

Zoe shook her head.

Cassidy sat down and put his arm round her shoulders as Geoff muttered about needing a shower and left them alone.

She managed a trembly smile. 'Sorry about this. It's not like me, is it?'

He kissed her gently, her salty cheek.

'I know we should keep fighting them,' she said in a steadier voice, 'but after my day today I was ready to give up. And then listening to Geoff and you I saw it clearly — they're going to win, aren't they? As long as we somehow keep things going when we *know* it's dangerous, we're protecting them and making it easier for them to keep cutting. And the more we do that, the longer it will be before everybody understands what a disaster it all is.

'So then I thought, why am I doing this?' Zoe was folding and unfolding the handkerchief as she spoke. 'It's not normal to work this way, and it's only here that it happens — because of New Zealand's *experiment*.

'But if I go somewhere else, I can do what I'm trained to do properly, the work that I love. And I can probably earn more and maybe buy a little house. That would be nice.'

Cassidy swallowed. 'What about us?'

'I don't know.' Her face was bleak. 'Maybe there isn't an "us" in our futures. You've been sweet to me in so many ways since we've been back together, and you've respected my need to keep it platonic—'

He groaned and put his head in his hands.

'It's been just as hard for me, Steve. Do you think I didn't want to go back to what we had? I'm so grateful that you didn't try and get me into bed, because I would have given in and that would have made it even more complicated.' She touched his cheek. 'I'll never care for anyone more than I used to care for you.'

'God, Zo!' Cassidy jumped up with clenched fists. 'What happened happened, and I can't bear thinking about it, especially after these months of rebuilding. But how can I get away from it?' He opened his arms out wide. 'I've changed. I want to marry you. If you have to leave your job, I understand and respect that, and maybe we have to be apart for a while. But I'm begging you, please don't write us off.'

She stood up. 'It's right for me to get away from here. And as for us, they say that if you love something, you should let it go. And if it's real—'

'Rubbish. I love you and I never want to let you out of my sight.'

She shook her head. 'No. You stay here and keep on fighting, and I'll write to you when I'm settled somewhere. If we are meant to be a couple, it will happen somehow. Goodbye, Steve. Thanks for everything.' Then the door was closing behind her.

His mind shut down for a moment and he grabbed the edge of the table to steady himself as he stared at the neatly-folded handkerchief. He shook himself and got his limbs working again, but when he reached the street her car was gone.

Cassidy stood among the traffic yelling like a madman. Then he walked away and kept on walking for hours, hardly knowing where he was.

At 2 am he came home, chilled to the bone, had a shower and fell into bed.

....

'Paxton Health has failed to produce a business plan that is acceptable to Treasury,' Diamond told the Management Group. 'So workout begins and Paxton will follow a work programme drawn up by the Ministry. With CCMAU's help you will finalise RHA contract negotiations, control costs, and produce a revised business plan that meets shareholders' expectations of profitability.'

Cassidy was back from two days of sick leave. He still felt hollow inside, but somehow he had a bit of fight left. 'I strongly recommend that you consult senior doctors on the new business plan. My information is that no more cuts can safely be made without serious patient risk.'

Diamond's lip twitched. 'With respect, Doctor, your information is worthless in this forum.'

'If Dr Cassidy's information was worthless he would not be working here,' said Bennett. 'But we won't be consulting staff — the details of this plan could cause a public relations backlash that could be difficult to manage.'

Diamond nodded. 'The new plan will remain strictly confidential until after the election. It could give ill-informed critics a field day.'

'What about well-informed critics?' said Cassidy.

'There are no well-informed critics. Next, you will re-negotiate your teaching contracts, and you may withdraw from contracts for uneconomical services.'

'No more RLUs,' said Turnbull. 'That's a huge bonus.'

Cassidy snorted. 'No, it's unacceptable. "Uneconomical services" means some of our most vulnerable patients, and withdrawing that care would be unethical and dangerous.'

'The market will provide for them, Mr Cassidy,' said Diamond with exaggerated patience. He ignored Cassidy's loud groan. 'And now, moving on. These are my CCMAU associates, who will assist with implementation of the new business plan.' He indicated three stern young men in dark suits sitting behind him. 'Mr Reid, Mr Boyle, Mr Marshall. Mr Boyle has been analysing league tables of CHE performance.'

Boyle, a smaller and hairier version of his boss, stood up and handed round folders of graphs. 'Thank you Mr Diamond,' he said in a high, nasal voice. 'These bar graphs depict the current financial situation of every CHE in the country. This is highly sensitive information and identifiers are deleted, but Paxton Health is the blue line.'

There were several graphs. Boyle told them about net tangible assets, current and projected revenue, and debt-to-equity ratios. Cassidy was soon out of his depth, but it was clear that despite their difficulties, Paxton was far from the worst of the CHEs.

'What about absolute debt levels?' asked Bennett.

'All the CHEs are in debt but comparison of debt levels alone is misleading owing to the spread of sizes of the businesses.'

'What?' said Cassidy. 'All the CHEs are in debt?'

Boyle nodded. 'At this point in time, that's correct. Some providers have reduced overheads, and two or three are in positive cashflow. But all CHEs are carrying debt, and several, including Paxton, have received equity injections from the Ministry. Five CHEs are borrowing just to maintain services.'

'But if all the CHEs are in debt, that proves that what the Government wants can't actually be done.'

'Not at all,' said Frankton. 'Business success is still ahead of us, but that only means we must roll up our sleeves and push on. We can't turn back after all that's been achieved to date.'

'We need more RD,' added Goldsmith.

'Research and development?' said Cassidy. 'We need more money.'

Bennett sighed. 'RD is Roger Douglas.'

Dawn knocked and wheeled in the coffee. Everybody gratefully seized the chance for a break, but to their dismay the golden scones had been replaced by miserable little biscuits. Welcome to workout, thought Cassidy. He went over to talk to Boyle.

After the numbers man had offered no views on the progress of the meeting or the comfort or otherwise of his motel room, Cassidy said, 'Can you tell me, confidentially of course, which CHEs have positive cashflow?'

'Why do you want to know?'

'We should try and learn from the successful hospitals.'

Boyle told him two names.

'Hmm,' said Cassidy. 'They're both small. Not full teaching hospitals.'

'That's right.'

'And they send all their complex cases to bigger hospitals, which will help the balance sheets in the small places while increasing costs at the big places. So you can't use the small hospitals to say there's a lot of waste in the big hospitals.'

'The market will operate and the problems will be solved,' said Boyle firmly after a pause. 'The model is sound.'

'The model is disastrously wrong,' said Cassidy. 'It gets more like *Alice in Wonderland* every day, and I seem to be Alice.'

Boyle frowned. 'But Arthur Andersen—'

'Never mind,' said Cassidy heavily as Bennett called them back to their places.

'We have a problem with the hospital roof,' Turnbull reported. 'There are significant leaks, requiring buckets in Wards 23 and 24 whenever it rains. We've had quotes for repairs, but there's no way we can afford them.'

'Forget it,' said Bennett. 'Not this financial year, anyway.'

Cassidy looked at Diamond. 'A leaky roof needs fixing immediately. Surely even you would agree with that.'

But the CCMAU man shook his head. 'You'll attain profitability only by maximally reducing outgoings. Put it on the deferred maintenance list.'

'Next,' said Turnbull. 'We have learnt that one of our clinicians, Philip Jackson, recently worked at Warwick for several hours without management permission.'

Bennett stared at Cassidy. 'Well?'

Cassidy shrugged. 'Our top specialists often go to Warwick, or their people come here, to advise or to help with difficult cases. Always have, always will. And in this part of the world, Philip Jackson is the best upper abdominal surgeon.'

'That still doesn't allow him to break the rules. He could be leaking commercially sensitive information.'

'My God, that's true,' said Cassidy. 'He could have told them which magazines we have in Outpatients.'

Bennett's eyes narrowed. 'Do you think he went to do another of those "first in New Zealand" operations? Because if he has, he's way off limits. That operation is ours.'

'This needs fixing,' said Diamond.

'Don't you worry.' Bennett was writing on his pad. 'I'll make sure he understands, and if he doesn't promise to behave I'll dispense with his services.'

As people were standing up and packing their papers at the end of the meeting Russell shouted, 'Don't forget the fun run, people! Victoria Park at 11am this Saturday.'

CHAPTER TWELVE

Usually Cassidy enjoyed having his hair cut. Eric, a large, even-tempered man, did a good job and would discuss the news of the day or work in companionable silence as required.

Today was definitely a silent day, with vile weather to match Cassidy's hung-over gloom.

Bryce Bailey had scared him. Bryce had been on the inside at the RHA, one of their top people. And if he had no faith in the reforms, how could anyone else? And yet it was full steam ahead at Peachy with CCMAU stoking the boiler. They would force the Board to squeeze the senior managers, and the pressure would run down the management chain until it reached the hospital staff. And then God help the patients.

And clever Cassidy had strutted into the middle of all this, just assuming that he would make a difference, exactly as Zoe had said. And how was he getting on?

Sure, he'd got them to reconsider scrapping charge nurse positions, but that was probably temporary. He couldn't claim any real wins at all. Perhaps if he hadn't been there, it would have been worse. But look what he'd lost in the process . . .

'Steve,' said Eric gently, 'I've finished.'

'Sorry — er, it's great. Right.' Cassidy paid and put on his jacket.

'I hope it all works out OK, whatever it is.'

'Yeah. Thanks, Eric. See you next time.'

The wind bullied him as he walked towards High Street. He needed new shoes and had been putting it off for weeks, but today was the day. There was nothing else to do except go home and mope around the flat before heading off to the God-awful fun run.

He did one round of Dudding's shoe shop, then walked out and kept walking until he found a little café and went in to get a break from the wind. Eating was out of the question, but he got a coffee and sat near the window, warming his hands on the cup and trying not to think about anything.

There was a popping, crunching noise in the street and he saw Claudia Donaldson staggering and struggling with a wrecked umbrella. He ran out and grabbed her.

'Claudia, come in here.' Cassidy took the umbrella and dropped it into a convenient rubbish bin, then tugged the café door open and pushed her inside. The roar of the wind dropped away as the door slammed behind them.

She had to get her balance and brush the hair away from her face before she could see her rescuer. 'Oh, Steve, thank you. It's dangerous out there.'

'It certainly is. Would you like a hot drink?'

He went and bought her a coffee. 'I didn't get you anything to eat, after your callous rejection of the pink bun last time we met.'

'I'm sorry,' she laughed, putting away her comb and mirror. 'I'm sure I would have appreciated it if I'd been in a better mood.'

Cassidy's day had suddenly improved. 'Anyway, what are you doing over here? I assume you're a Warwick girl.'

'I am. But I need a dress for a wedding, and I can't find what I want in Warwick.' She sipped her coffee. 'Did you hear my news? I've joined a commercial law firm — I'm leaving the RHA.'

'They'll miss you. Bryce certainly seemed to think you were terrific, although that might have been more about the red leather jacket.'

She smiled, then picked up the salt cellar and tilted it from side to side. 'The job's not what I expected. The provider contract negotiations have become a sort of game, to see which side can win, rather than everybody working towards getting the best outcome for the country. And both sides are turning over staff so fast that there's lots of time lost as each new person has to learn their job. It's wasting huge amounts of time and money. The Core Services people have walked away—'

'Really? Why?'

'They didn't think it was possible to do what the Government wanted. And they're right, of course. We're driving at full speed into a tunnel that's blocked at the other end.' She watched the salt sliding about inside its prison. 'Did you know the RHA has admitted that it won't even be able to fund current services out of its own budget?'

Cassidy sighed. 'Yeah, Bryce told me that a while ago. But here's the real problem: to ninety-nine point nine per cent of the country, that's further evidence that the reforms have failed. But to the key players, it means that more reform is needed.'

'I know. But it's quite beautiful politically, because each agency can blame somebody else when it doesn't work.'

'And none of it's the Government's fault, somehow,' Cassidy agreed. 'Anyway, enough of all that.' He picked up his jacket. 'Would you care to join me for breakfast?'

'Breakfast?' Claudia looked at her watch.

'Yes, I know it's late but I was feeling unwell earlier on. But now my condition is improving, you'll be delighted to hear, and I need bacon and eggs. How about you?'

'We had breakfast at the normal time, thanks. But I've got a few more minutes.'

'Great,' said Cassidy. 'Call it brunch, and you could have something too. No, not here, Fraser's is where serious breakfast eaters go. It's just round the corner.' He waited as she buttoned up her coat, and they braved the storm together.

Fraser's was unusually quiet because of the weather, and they found a table upstairs straight away. Cassidy ordered the full mixed grill, and Claudia chose a salmon bagel and freshly squeezed orange juice.

'"We"?' said Cassidy after the food arrived.

'Pardon?'

'You said "We had breakfast."'

'Yes, we did. My fiancé Andrew and I had breakfast. Muesli and blueberries, coffee, toast with marmalade. What else do you want to know?'

'Fiancé?'

'Yes, Steve. The dress is for when we get married, in March.'

'Congratulations.' Cassidy drank coffee then suddenly said, 'I've got a girlfriend.'

'That's nice,' said Claudia. 'Does she live in Paxton?'

'I doubt it, but I don't know.'

She frowned. 'What does that mean?'

And so out came the whole story of Cassidy's relationship with Zoe Sorensen: the carefree early days, followed by his boorish and self-centred withdrawal from normal life, her frustration and her departure. Then the new era, hopeful but marred by her insistence on a platonic relationship while she considered. Her sweet personality, her high professional standards and her beauty.

He switched to orange juice, Claudia had a cup of tea, and the story continued. His inability to win her unqualified love, despite his scrupulous observation of the platonic requirement in the face of great temptation. His efforts in the kitchen. Her increasing anger at the damage done to the hospital, and finally her despairing departure for an unknown destination, with her need to be somewhere else outweighing her desire to be with him.

He sighed and sat back in his chair. 'Thanks for listening. It's good to have shared it with somebody.'

'I seem to recall you doing the same for me not so long ago,' smiled Claudia. 'But — is that it? Don't tell me you're giving up.'

Cassidy looked at the serviette he had shredded during the story. 'I don't see what I can do. I want to marry her, and I know I've changed. But how do I convince her?'

'Letters and phone calls won't work. You need propinquity,' said Claudia firmly. 'That means being close. Ask around, and the moment you know her address, get on a plane. Be there with her, and start becoming whoever you're both going to be, together.

'You can't do anything for Paxton Health, Steve, with respect, just as I couldn't do anything for the RHA. Liberate yourself, woo and win the lovely Zoe, and invite us to your wedding! Oops, wedding. I'd better go and start looking at dresses.'

'I've missed the fun run, unfortunately.' Cassidy tried to look sad. 'Never mind, I'm sure they had a great time.'

He paid and they went downstairs and stood looking out at the weather. The wind had dropped but steady rain was falling.

Claudia turned to him. 'Follow her, Steve, and value her properly this time.'

'Andrew is a lucky man,' said Cassidy.

She suddenly hugged him, and before he could respond she opened the door and walked away.

··

'It was a disaster,' said Turnbull on Monday morning. 'Where were you?'

'Sorry,' said Cassidy. 'I'd planned to come but I got caught up in town. Not that I would have made much difference to the numbers.'

'You would have, actually.'

'How many came?'

Turnbull considered. 'Fifteen, maybe. Most of them from Ricky's section. Three orderlies, Terry Goldsmith, somebody from Pharmacy. Not one doctor or nurse.'

'Out of over four thousand Paxton employees? My God. Was Jim there?'

'For about five minutes.'

'Poor old Ricky,' said Cassidy.

'Yeah, Ricky took it hard. He came along dressed as Mr Peachy, and—'

'What? How do you dress as Mr Peachy?'

Turnbull laughed. 'You wear a big round peach-coloured bean-bag thing, with your head, arms and legs sticking out, and a peach-coloured hat.'

'You're kidding.'

'No. Apparently he sometimes walks around the hospital corridors dressed like that. I don't know what happens when he needs to take a leak. Anyway, everybody was trying to keep warm in the tent, and Mr Peachy went out into the gale to try and get a race going. He pranced around and waved his arms, then he slipped and fell in the mud, and he couldn't get up again because of the big ball.'

'So no more Mr Peachy.' Poor Russell, but Cassidy started laughing, for the first time in months.

'We went out and picked him up and he sat sulking in the back of the tent. Until it blew over.'

'Oh my God. Was anybody inside?'

'We all were. We got out OK, but we'd put the barbecues right behind the tent for shelter, and now it's got a big hole burnt in its side.'

Cassidy stopped laughing. 'That's not so funny, is it? What a disaster. Still, I guess there won't be any record of it.'

'You obviously haven't seen the front page of today's *Globe*,' said Turnbull. He paused. 'Anyway, I've come to say goodbye. I've accepted a great offer from another sector.'

'That's sad, Gerald,' said Cassidy. 'But I expected it after Jim got the CEO job.'

'Yeah. But Jim's the right hire for the times. He's tough, and he's driven by a robust incentive scheme so I think he'll do very well. I'll miss seeing this thing through, though, now that we're getting towards the payoff for all the hard work.'

Cassidy grimaced. 'Really? Aren't we just getting deeper in the mud? We haven't seen any savings yet.'

'No, Steve. You don't expect world-class ground breaking to yield results immediately, this is work in progress.'

'An experiment, yes. That reminds me, where's Randy Steinberg these days? I haven't seen him for a while.'

'He went back to Chicago as soon as we started workout. He said his work here was over.'

'It would be interesting to read his report,' said Cassidy. 'But tell me about the new job.'

'I'll be heading up a new property development company. It's called QCB, Quick and Cost-Effective Builders, and it'll be huge. Are you familiar with the new Building Act?'

'No.'

'These days the builder just has to promise that the house won't fall down for fifty years and that the outer surfaces will stay intact for fifteen. It's going to kick-start the building industry, just as we're doing in health. There's a lot less inspection and other nonsense involved, so overheads are slashed because builders can vouch for the quality of their own work.'

Turnbull grinned at Cassidy. 'This Government is so good for business growth and wealth creation. It's the new paradigm: "Go away Nanny, I promise I'll make sure everything's done right and safe." Building, mining, electricity supply; you name it, development will be easier, margins will be higher and agile players will get very, very rich.' He was rubbing his hands together in his excitement.

'Harry Prattley came to see us. He's started up a finance company. They've deregulated finance too, and there are huge opportunities there for people with the right skills. So watch out for joint ventures between Prattley Finance and QCB.'

'Sounds good, Gerald,' said Cassidy. 'But I'll miss you around here, you've taught me heaps.'

'I've enjoyed working with you, Steve.' Turnbull stood up and held out his hand. 'You should start planning your next move. You're wasted in health, your inside knowledge holds you back from making the tough calls. But you get on well with people and you could succeed in whatever you felt like doing. Good luck.'

···

Cassidy tried to get back to his incident forms, many of which now featured the leaking roof. But he kept thinking about life without Gerald, then about poor Mr Peachy lying in the mud with his little legs kicking.

There was nothing he could do about the roof complaints after Gordon Diamond had placed it on the deferred maintenance list. But how long could that last? Deferring maintenance was crazy; the longer the repairs were delayed, the more expensive they became, in buildings or in human bodies.

There was a sharp knock on the door, and then CCMAU's favourite son stood before him.

'Good morning, Mr Boyle.'

'Good morning.'

'Did you have a nice weekend?'

'I worked on my spreadsheets,' said Boyle with an air of martyrdom.

'And after that you curled up on the couch with Ayn Rand?'

Boyle frowned. 'How did you know?'

Cassidy leaned over the desk. 'Be careful about working all hours, Mr Boyle. The rewards are transient, and the damage may be permanent.'

'What?'

'Never mind. What can I do for you?'

'CCMAU invites you to a confidential meeting to be held at the Paxton Grand Hotel, Room 235, at 1830 tonight. No-one must know where you are going, where you have been, or what happens. Are there any questions?'

'What's the meeting about?'

'I can't say,' said Boyle.

'Well then, why would I come?'

'The invitation comes from key players. That's all I can say at this point in time.'

'Hmm, it's intriguing.' Cassidy considered. 'Will food be served?'

'I don't know.'

'Is there a special knock to get in?'

Boyle frowned. 'I wasn't told anything about that.'

'And should I carry the pearl-handled Beretta in my shoulder holster? No, it doesn't matter. No further questions, Mr Boyle. I'll be there.'

Boyle left, and Cassidy stared out of the window. A secret meeting with key players? This job might be ghastly, and frustrating almost beyond endurance, but you could never call it dull.

Cassidy knocked on the door of Room 235. Boyle himself unlocked the door and showed him into the richly furnished and softly lit sitting room of a large suite. Bennett and Frankton sat on a couch discussing a spreadsheet. Diamond stood beside a silver-haired, three-piece-suit man, who looked over his glasses at the newcomer.

'Dr Cassidy,' said Diamond. 'Meet Dr Craig, from the Business Roundtable.' As they shook hands, Diamond explained that Cassidy was a medical doctor, there to provide supplementary knowledge if needed.

Craig nodded. 'Good. That's everyone then? Gentlemen, your attention, please.' He bowed his head, closed his eyes and clasped his hands together. Bennett and Frankton scrambled to their feet and everyone except Cassidy closed their eyes.

'The market is the mechanism that works. Amen.'

'Amen,' said Diamond loudly.

Frankton and Bennett sat down again, while Diamond and Boyle took the other couch. Cassidy sat in a large armchair, wondering why he was here.

Craig was still standing. 'Soon we will be joined by Mr Bismark J Pelham, the Chief Operating Officer of Health 4U, a health maintenance organisation working out of Reno, Nevada. Health 4U have been keeping a watching brief on our health reforms, and they are now declaring their interest.' He straightened his bow tie. 'The HFU jet touched down at Paxton Airport half an hour ago.'

The men on the couches exchanged glances.

'HFU are considering entering the New Zealand health provider market by buying and operating full-sized hospitals, staffed by their own people. We have recommended Paxton Hospital for the first purchase.'

All Bennett's birthdays had come at once. 'That's *fantastic* news. It's ready to go, it's even got a new paint job.'

Cassidy frowned. 'A lot of equipment needs repairing or updating. If I'd known I could have brought a list. Radiology alone—'

'For God's sake,' said Bennett. 'This is about a profitable hospital, not a bloody palace. The parameters change for the kick-ass commercial model.'

'But what about the boilers and the leaking roof?'

'It's spring now, it'll be summer before they carry out due diligence.' Bennett smirked. 'We'll make sure they only visit on sunny days, and we'll open the kimono once the contract's signed.'

'Will you tell them we're in workout?'

'Let's just accentuate the positive,' said Frankton, forcing a smile. 'But it would be more attractive to buyers if we had less debt.'

'I'm sure the Crown will fix that once we've had a word with them,' said Craig. 'This will be the first hospital of many to be sold, and they want a good outcome just as much as we do.'

Somebody knocked on the door. Boyle hurried to open it, and a waft of cigar smoke announced the arrival of Bismark J Pelham, followed by a young woman carrying a briefcase.

Pelham was broad and very tall, with a snowy white ponytail. He might have been a retired professional basketball player.

Craig rushed forward. 'Mr Pelham—'

'BJ. You must be Archie,' said Pelham in a deep, resonant voice.

'Archie Craig, yes. We've talked on the phone. Thanks for coming, I'm sure you won't regret it. How was your trip?'

'Long.'

'Yes, sorry about that, ha ha!' Craig looked as if he would get the Government to move New Zealand closer to the USA if that was what BJ wanted. 'Let me introduce you to some local key players.'

The woman put the briefcase down beside the armchair and went through to the other room, where she could be heard picking up the phone and asking for room service.

Cassidy found a smaller chair, and Pelham took over the armchair and the meeting.

He drew deeply on his cigar and mashed it out on the ashtray that Boyle had reverently placed beside him. After unbuttoning his brown suede jacket, he brought a note pad and a gold fountain pen out of the briefcase. 'All righty, then. Noo Zealand.'

No-one answered. Cassidy wondered if BJ was planning to buy the whole country.

'Tell me where your health reforms are at.'

Craig retold the key player view of the recent history of New Zealand's public health system — the Nanny State, health care costs blowing out, the Gibbs committee chaired by one of his Roundtable colleagues, and its report. Then the reforms set in motion and going well, despite predictable opposition from vested interests.

Pelham pulled the Green and White Paper out of the briefcase. 'This is the business plan, right?'

'It's the public version,' said Craig. 'You've seen the more detailed documents — one that the Roundtable commissioned from Professor Danzon and CS First Boston, and the CS First Boston report commissioned by the NIPB.'

BJ rummaged in the briefcase and brought out a folder of notes. 'Yeah. I liked the part about, let's see . . . yeah, "if restructuring proceeds, it will almost inevitably involve multiple business failures". That sounds promising for penetration by experienced players.

'But now your politicians have gone soft on the reforms. "Private health marketeers would be unwilling to enter the proposed new health system because of the Government's recent performance." What's that about, Archie?'

'They've got an election coming up,' Craig explained. 'Last time they won in the biggest landslide in recent history. They've weakened and made some silly health policy mistakes since then, but they should get the mandate again in November.'

'OK. And when they do, we'll be at the table, champagne on ice and ready to deal. Now let's — hold on a minute, Archie. Leanne!' Pelham shouted without turning his head. 'You got those spare ribs comin' along?'

'Sure, Mr Pelham,' came from the other room.

'I just felt like a big plate of ribs, I got the pilot to patch me through to the kitchens here. Special order. You boys good with ribs? Yeah? And Leanne, tell them to send up some beers as well as the Jack Daniels.'

'Sure, Mr Pelham.'

The evening was speeding up, and Cassidy wished that Boyle had given him a bit more warning. The last thing he felt like was a full-on night out with the boys. Or these boys, anyway.

Pelham consulted his notes. 'Now, let's go from the top. You got the market going, right?'

'The funder-provider split,' said Craig with a smile. 'Yes, that's been accepted.'

'And tax inequalities? Still in place, waiting for the, what's it, the CHEs to fall over?'

'Yes.'

'Good. Next is co-payments. Part charges, yeah. You got those going.'

'Yes and no, er, BJ.' Craig's smile faded. 'They started, but they stopped.'

'Why?'

'A lot of people refused to pay, and debt collection was uneconomical. There was political fallout.'

'Pardon me? They refused to pay — don't you have laws down here? A night in jail would fix that real quick.'

'Our jails wouldn't be big enough,' said Cassidy.

Pelham considered. 'Co-payments are part of perception management. But once we have control, consumer perception is irrelevant. It's not a deal breaker.' He consulted his notes again. 'Now, we'd be setting up as a Health Care Plan, right? Competing with the Regional Health Authorities for public money, then building revenue as public funding falls, dropping public sector quality and forcing more folks to insure.'

'Health Care Plans are on hold,' said Diamond.

'What's the deal there, Archie?' said Pelham. 'We need to be a Health Care Plan.'

'They're still on the statute books, they can start up tomorrow, if the Crown decides,' Craig smiled. 'Just waiting for your call, BJ.'

Pelham scratched his chin. 'Why are they on hold?'

After a silence Cassidy spoke up. 'The Minister said it was because of the complexities involved and the risk of cream-skimming. That means only taking the low-risk cases.'

'Cream-skimming — Jesus, who is this guy? How else would we make a profit? Leanne, when am I meeting the Minister?'

'Ten a.m. tomorrow, Mr Pelham.'

'It's a different Minister now, BJ,' said Craig uneasily. 'We don't know what he thinks about HCPs.'

There was a discreet tap on the door. 'Room service.' Leanne came out and unlocked the door, and a waiter pulled in a fragrant food trolley. She locked him out again after giving him an American bank note of jaw-dropping size.

BJ got up and lifted some covers. 'Hey, this is good. C'mon folks, help yourselves.'

Cassidy didn't want to be a wimp in a room as testosterone-filled as this one, but eating greasy meat from a plate in his lap was the last thing he felt like doing in a meeting of such importance. He took a token rib and a beer.

But Bennett was in his element. He wiped juice from his chin and took a sip of Jack Daniels. 'How do you manage doctors, BJ? Our doctors refuse to prioritise the interests of their employer.'

Pelham smiled. 'We had that problem early on, but we got it under control. You see, there are stages when you enter a market that's new to managed care. When the medics hear you're coming, they try grouping together so's none of them will work for you. But each of 'em expects to call the shots, and nobody'll compromise, so that fizzles out.' He chuckled and inspected the dripping rib in his hand. 'Damn, this is good.

'Then you arrive and run saturation marketing of your high quality and low costs, and you start recruiting docs. Some always join early for the best deal. And the rest suddenly find' — he burped softly — 'excuse me, that you're winning their clients away big time with your lower premiums. Steve, you're not eating. You want Leanne to call down for something else? Sure? OK.

'So yeah, then you have them. The docs want to stay put, but there's not enough work except with you on your terms, and they sign up or leave. But if they go interstate they face re-registration headaches, sometimes even exams. So that's not easy.'

'But they can still practise medicine the way they want to,' said Cassidy.

'Hell no,' laughed BJ, 'they work on our terms, remember? And we want consultations as short as possible and interventions as few as possible, so if somebody feels like referring a case for some procedure that's not on the schedule, well, "Uh uh Doc, can't do that!"'

'But they could still go ahead and treat the patient, if treatment was needed.'

BJ smiled. 'Sure they could. But then you show 'em the no-cause non-renewal clause in their employment contract.'

'What?' Bennett was deeply impressed. 'You can fire them, just like that? With no appeal?'

'Yup. They signed the contract, didn't they? So then maybe they go for a job with, guess what, another managed-care company, and the guy says, "So why did you leave your last job, doctor?" That's a bad moment for Doctor Know-it-all, believe me.' He wiped his face with a napkin. 'You make your docs choose to keep their jobs instead of spending shareholders' money on expensive treatment for folks who aren't entitled. It's about managing your medical loss ratio, all day, every day.'

'What's a medical loss ratio?' asked Frankton.

'A medical loss is when you have to spend money to provide some health care,' Pelham explained. 'We do everything we can to avoid spending money, to keep the ratio of medical losses to premium income as low as possible. That's how we maximise shareholder returns.'

'It sounds fantastic, BJ,' Craig beamed.

'Works for us.' The big man got up and checked the middle shelf of the trolley. 'Well, look what I found. Anybody like some cheesecake?'

Bennett stared at Diamond. 'A no-cause non-renewal clause for doctors is just what we need.'

'No doctor here would dream of signing a contract like that,' said Cassidy. 'With New Zealand qualifications, if things are hopeless here they can walk straight into jobs in Australia, in large numbers. And as we're already short of doctors, health services would collapse, followed by the government.'

Tension appeared above Pelham's snowy eyebrows. He put his dessert down untasted. 'It'll be tricky if you can't hog-tie your medics, Archie.'

The frown got bigger as time passed. The cheesecake was excellent and Cassidy had a second helping, but BJ had lost his appetite and everybody else looked increasingly uncomfortable as the questions and the unsatisfactory answers kept coming.

'Less than half the people have health insurance? Why? Because good hospital care is *free? Jesus!*

'No plans for compulsory insurance? HFU can't operate unless almost everybody has their own health money to spend, like Patty Danzon recommended. Why hasn't that happened?

'What's the population? Three and a half million? That's good. *Pardon me* — that's the whole country, you say? Well, what about in this region? Two hundred thousand? Archie, I need fifty thousand capitated, low-risk individuals, minimum, before I can guarantee a medical loss ratio that's acceptable to my shareholders. That's not good math for entering a new market, unless we take a loss for maybe five years. I would need more than a quarter of the local population, and that's after I'd declined cover for people who were already sick.'

'*What?*' said Cassidy. 'You'd turn away the people who need health care the most?'

'That's how you manage the medical loss ratio, Steve.'

Frankton wrung his hands. 'It's an attractive concept businesswise, BJ, but in New Zealand it would be political suicide.'

'I'm afraid I have to agree,' Craig whimpered.

'It's morally bankrupt too,' said Cassidy.

Pelham poured himself another whisky and sat staring into his glass between sips. The others sat quietly, some watching him, others with their eyes closed. Craig's lips moved silently, perhaps repeating the pre-meeting mantra. Cassidy's neglected spare rib stood accusingly in a pool of congealed grease.

'Shit, Archie.' Pelham stood up. 'I thought you had this all in hand. Frankly, I was expecting a little more sophistication. I was expecting people who understood what's good for the economy, and politicians who'd make things happen. Instead, what happened? You did the easiest parts, getting the market set up and pushing the tax thing under the rug, but you flunked out on every other piece of the plan.

'But even if it had all gone the way you planned, it was never going to work in a population this size.' His anger filled the room.

'The politicians have let us down,' said Craig, almost under his breath.

'You said you were leading the world with these reforms.' Pelham shook his head in amazement. 'My fault too, I guess. I didn't even think to ask about that basic stuff, I assumed you would know what was needed. Big mistake, huh? Big lesson for BJ Pelham, yes, sir.'

He sighed deeply and stared down at his boots for a moment. 'Well, good luck, gentlemen. Leanne, we're leaving now.'

Leanne reappeared, picked up the briefcase, and gave the room a neutral smile.

Then Health 4U's representatives started the long journey back to Nevada, leaving behind the wrecked healthcare dreams of Treasury, the Crown, and the Business Roundtable.

....

Claire sat on the couch in front of the television, mug of tea in hand, a neat little one-person scene of reasonableness and good humour. Cassidy felt like hugging her.

'Kettle's just boiled, if you'd like a cup.' She smiled up at him, then looked again. 'Are you alright?'

'Yeah, I'm OK thanks. I'll get some tea.'

He switched on the kettle and leant against the bench with his eyes closed, feeling uncomfortably full of strawberry cheesecake and secrets of national importance.

As the water came to the boil he opened his eyes and saw the postcard on the table. A picture of a tram, a Melbourne postmark and '*Wish you were here. XX*', in Zoe's unmistakable handwriting. That was all.

He would have to wait for the card with her address on it, but the game had begun. Cassidy suddenly felt a whole lot better.

As he was returning the hall phone rang, and he put the card on the table beside it. This could even be her now . . .

It was Bennett, almost incoherent with rage. 'Turn the TV on!'

'It's already on. A cooking programme.'

'I'm firing him! My office, first thing tomorrow. You too.'

'You're going to fire me?'

'You're meant to be controlling him!'

Cassidy went into the lounge. 'Do you mind, Claire? Apparently there's something I must watch.'

He changed channels and Tony Walsh's serious face filled the screen. 'They imply that the consultation for the reforms had to be done secretly because it was too complicated for people to understand. But they never published the Arthur Andersen report because it would be too *easy* for people to understand. Based on what we know, it has so little detail that it couldn't possibly be a serious basis for the massive change that has been inflicted on us. But it suits the agenda—'

'What is the agenda?' asked Langdon Doherty.

'The plan all along has been to turn the public hospitals over to private providers. It's part of *making government smaller*, which they want us to believe is a good thing for everybody. But it's really a way of getting money to pass into private hands, at the expense of people who can't do anything to stop it. That's an unacceptable cost to the country, in money and quality of life. And there's no way it's what New Zealand people want.'

Doherty nodded.

'Powerful people tell us how hopeless the old system was, how much better it would be if the private sector was in charge, and how market forces would give the people a better deal. They hope that if they keep saying it loudly enough, it'll become what people believe. But it's just a smokescreen for getting their hands on taxpayers' money and running things for shareholder profit rather than public good.'

'Surely there were inefficiencies in the old system?' said Doherty.

'They could have been solved for a fraction of the costs we're facing now.' Walsh leaned forward. 'Langdon, the people behind these reforms have two major credibility problems. Firstly the experiment has already failed, and remarkably quickly. Based on their promises we should be saving hundreds of millions of dollars by now, but instead every CHE has gone into debt and the Government is quietly bailing them out. Why?'

Doherty waited, with one eyebrow slightly raised.

'It's because they were so sure that the theory was right that they forgot about the business of implementation. They somehow ignored the massive extra costs of writing, negotiating and monitoring contracts. And the contracts have to be very strong, because these people live in a world without trust.

'But the people organising all this mostly have no health background, meaning even more time and money wasted as they try to understand what they're supposed to be doing. Zero benefit for patients there, but it's all being paid for out of the health budget.

'And the scale of it is huge. Each RHA will soon have two thousand provider contracts. How much do eight thousand contracts across the country cost to create, negotiate annually, and administer? And they told us they would *save* half a billion dollars.'

'You said there were two problems,' said Doherty.

'Yes. The second fatal blow to their credibility is their ridiculous arithmetic. For example, a senior public servant told us to expect thirty per cent savings, which of course would be great if it was going back into health services. But a week later he said twenty to thirty per cent, and at the same time the Minister said ten to twenty per cent. How can we believe anything they say?'

'Dr Walsh, before the programme we were talking about the hidden costs of the reforms. Can you tell viewers about that?'

Walsh nodded. 'The reforms are having an adverse effect on patients. Increasingly I'm seeing patients with heart disease at a later and more severe stage, when it's more difficult to treat successfully.'

'Why is that?'

'Staffing cuts mean that we can't do as much work as we used to. Perhaps they think that will reduce the number of people getting ill, I don't know. Our surgeons naturally have to treat the sickest people first.

But if you have less capacity than demand, people who are less sick go onto a waiting list.

'And then guess what, many of them get sicker and come back as an emergency case, displacing somebody else who's about to come off the list and get their treatment. So the lists get longer, but remember the Government promised to *reduce* waiting lists.

'The other cost is harder to see. It's the effect on skilled people who have been laid off. These people, and it's mostly nurses I'm talking about here, can't support their families after they lose their jobs. Many emigrate to Australia, taking with them the training that we've all paid for and the expertise they have gained. That's a huge loss. Or they stay here and many go on the unemployment benefit, another significant cost. Unemployed nurses and ballooning waiting lists? What's going on?

'And bear in mind, Langdon, that this is just the start. If our big hospitals are ever run solely for the benefit of business investors, things will get very rough indeed, especially for the elderly and the chronically ill.'

'You sound very anti-private sector,' said Doherty.

Walsh shook his head. 'A strong private health sector is vital. People with insurance can get care for simple problems quickly and conveniently, and that frees up public hospital space for everybody else. It also attracts specialists to stay here and work in both sectors, rather than going overseas. But privatising the whole sector is madness, socially and fiscally, for this country.'

'We're nearly out of time,' said Doherty. 'Can you sum it all up for us?'

Walsh nodded. 'A society is judged by how it treats its most vulnerable. Our health system needed improvements, but it's been hijacked by people who see it as a business opportunity and have no interest whatsoever in society's most vulnerable. It's a disgrace.'

'Thank you, Dr Tony Walsh. I'm Langdon Doherty, and you've been watching "Food for Thought". See you next week.'

'Hi Steve,' smiled Dawn, as if this was an ordinary day. 'Mr Bennett is with Mr Frankton and Mr Diamond at the moment. I'm sure he won't be long.'

'Thanks. Dawn, did you watch television last night?'

'Yes we did, it was those little cakes from France, very light and fluffy, they have them at weddings. Did you watch it too? I didn't know you were a foodie, Steve!'

They shared a smile, and Cassidy sat down to wait.

It was clear that HMS Paxton Health 4U had taken a torpedo in the engine room last night, and the reforms themselves must surely collapse after Walsh's onslaught. The only thing now was to see what Frankton and Bennett would do about it.

Bennett came out of Frankton's office. 'Come through.'

They sat down on each side of the CEO's glass desk. Bennett seemed surprisingly normal for a man who had recently loaded himself with whisky and fatty food before having his career plans destroyed.

'The Minister personally rang Ross Frankton last night and chewed him out. Walsh knows the rules about media contact. He's got to go.'

'I understand that this is annoying—'

'*Annoying*? It's bloody intolerable! I'm on the Minister's radar as a CEO who can't control his staff.'

'That's unfortunate for you,' said Cassidy. 'But there are more important things to discuss.'

'Like what?'

'Like last night's meeting.'

'What about it?'

'Wake up, Jim. There'll be no rivers of gold flowing off to investors here and in Nevada. The reforms are over.'

Bennett shook his head. 'Last night there was an informal, confidential conversation about a possible shared business initiative. A positive outcome was not achieved but both sides learnt from it, and that knowledge will inform our future thinking. It was disappointing, but that's all.'

'Really,' said Cassidy. 'Having watched old Bismark kicking Archie's bottom round the room, I'd say he was more than "disappointed" with the knights of the Roundtable. They got him to come all this way for something that couldn't possibly work. Doctors can't be pressured like that here. And deliberately excluding people from health care because they're ill, can you believe that? Sure it works in the States, but no politician would survive trying to introduce it in New Zealand.

'No Jim, the business is failing, the model has collapsed, and you can't privatise. It's all over. You should start putting the furniture back the way it was before the party.'

'All finished?' said Bennett after a moment.

'Er, yes.'

'Good. We were slightly premature last night, that's all. The key players need to develop some aspects, and we will.'

'More RD?'

'More RD.'

'There must be no more RD,' said Cassidy. 'The system can't take any more cuts. I keep saying this, but you don't listen.'

'More RD and less Doctor bloody Walsh! I've got a meeting now, but I'll see him and you here at 9:30. Go and tell him.'

'Alright,' said Cassidy, 'but I warn you, sacking Tony Walsh would bring a whole lot of consequences that you haven't thought about yet. You'd struggle to replace him at any time, but right now New Zealand's rotten employment contracts are being discussed in the *British Medical Journal* and people are telling doctors to get advice before applying for jobs here.'

'9:30, Butch. Now hop it.'

....

Walsh was in Coronary Care discussing an ECG with some students. He saw Cassidy and came over.

'Morning, Steve. Come to fire me?' He had not shaved and there were dark shadows under his eyes.

'No, I haven't,' said Cassidy sadly. 'But Jim Bennett wants to see us both at 9:30. I've warned him about the risks of firing you, but he's pretty worked up because a Minister has been shouting at Ross Frankton about last night's show.'

'OK. 9:30.' Walsh went back to the ward round.

When they met again on the seventh floor, Dawn told them Mr Bennett was running a few minutes late. She showed them into the CEO's office, and brought coffee.

Walsh looked around the gleaming black and white room. 'No uncertainties here, obviously. Did you watch the programme?'

'Most of it.'

'What did you think?'

'It was terrific, unanswerable I would have thought. I liked the bit about how society is judged. And two thousand contracts for each RHA, my God.'

'Mind-boggling, isn't it? Perhaps this will be the start of changing public perceptions.' Walsh wandered over to look at the view, then said, 'That's strange. Somebody's taken my car and replaced it with another one.'

The door opened and Bennett walked in, looking twitchy but determined. 'Morning, Dr Walsh.'

'We were admiring your new car,' said Cassidy.

'Which one is yours, Mr Bennett?'

'It's the black Destroyer, down there.' Bennett pointed to where his big four-wheel-drive bulged and towered over the cars next to it. 'I had to get somebody else's car towed before I could use my park this morning. Cheeky sod won't do that again in a hurry.'

'What sort of car was it?' said Walsh in a quiet, steady voice.

'It was a crappy old VW Beetle. Red.'

'My car, Mr Bennett. That area used to be the consultants' car park. I came in here to do an emergency procedure at five this morning, and I parked where I've parked for most of the last twenty-two years. I was in a hurry and I forgot that you had moved our parks to the far side of the car park to make way for managers.

'And when the emergency was over, the morning had started and I forgot about my car and got on with my work.' He stared levelly at the CEO.

Bennett's eyes seemed larger than usual. He swallowed. 'Don't worry, Dr Walsh, we'll sort it out. Steve will get onto it, won't you Steve? Dawn will find out where they took it. Did the, er, patient, survive, may I ask?'

'Yes he did.'

'Right. Good. That's very good. Now, let's sit down and talk about the television interview.' He was moving towards his desk chair, but changed course as the others sat down in the armchairs.

'Dr Walsh, only the Board Chair or myself are allowed to deal with the media, and last night's interview showed why this policy is in place. We can't have employees randomly criticising from within the organisation. It risks damaging public perceptions and it's unacceptable. You're entitled to your opinions, even if they are incorrect in the light of fiscal reality and political policy. But you are not entitled to share those opinions in the media while you draw a salary from Paxton Health.'

'Did I say anything that was factually incorrect?' said Walsh.

Bennett smiled. 'Well, a lot of what you said is just your opinion.'

'Like what?'

'I haven't invited you here for a debate, Dr Walsh.'

'A debate,' said Cassidy. 'Great idea. Why don't we talk to Langdon Doherty and get the two of you in the studio together?'

Walsh nodded. 'I'm on.'

Bennett smiled and shook his head. 'Sorry, I'm far too busy for stunts like that. Dr Walsh, what you did last night has put me in a difficult situation as your CEO. And it's not the first time, is it?'

'No, and it probably won't be the last, unless you fire me,' said Walsh in the scary quiet voice. 'Which would cause the cardiology service to collapse, as there are only three of us at the moment instead of the five we need, and the two left behind would not be able to cope.'

Bennett blinked. He tugged at a knuckle but it would not pop. He seemed to be grinding his teeth as he glanced at Cassidy.

'Although it might prevent annoying car park mistakes in future.'

Bennett swallowed and held up his hands in mock horror. 'Dr Walsh, who's talking about firing you? Let's move away from conflict and go forward together. We want to help you, to support you in your very valuable work.

'Through the reforms we're working to free up hundreds of millions of dollars, as you know. And while some of that will go into the general funds, we expect some to come our way around the extra contracts after the collapse of Warwick. So we'll be budgeting for incentives, like any modern business.

'I mean, what do you need? Some new equipment? Sounds like you could do with a few more colleagues, right? I can assure you that once the reforms kick in, things will improve very quickly.'

'How's it going so far?' Walsh asked in a neutral tone.

'I wouldn't be sitting here if I didn't believe the savings can be made,' said Bennett. 'We just have to unlock all the wastage that has built up over the years, and channel it back.'

'But nothing is being channelled back, is it? And so your debt grows larger every month.'

'Early days, Dr Walsh, early days.'

'I'll go and get the car,' said Cassidy. Either that or he would throw up on the nice new tiles.

'Thanks.' Walsh passed over the keys.

··

Cassidy went in a taxi to a fortified compound on the outskirts of South Paxton. Here a large dog barked ceaselessly at him while a heavily-tattooed man with poor personal hygiene insisted on cash payment before he would release the car. Cassidy had to walk for twenty minutes in light rain to reach the nearest cash machine, then twenty minutes back.

He drove to the hospital, parked the VW on the far side of the car park, then went up to see how his tough, no-nonsense CEO was getting on.

'Thank God he didn't resign,' said Bennett with a wan smile.

'I thought you were going to fire him.'

'Well, Steve, watch and learn. Sometimes you're a mighty oak, and sometimes you're a reed bending in the wind.'

'Did Sir Roger say that?'

Bennett grimaced. 'What was I supposed to do? Fire a guy who'd saved somebody's life before breakfast, plus bring down an entire service in the hospital? How would that play in the *Bugle*? Of course I wanted to fire the arrogant sod, I'm sick of him, but I'm not about to commit PR suicide. I'll find another way to shut him up.'

'What happened after I left?'

'I offered him a part-time job as an adviser. But he gave me some pathetic excuse about having too many other things to do.'

'And then you parted on good terms.'

'Yeah,' said Bennett bitterly. 'I saw his point of view: if I did fire him it would be a disaster for Paxton CHE clinically, fiscally and PR-wise, while he would get a better-paid job in any one of a dozen hospitals around the world and we wouldn't be able to replace him. And once he knew I understood that, he was OK.'

'Well, he's right. A hospital this big couldn't possibly run on just two cardiologists.'

'I suppose that's . . .' Bennett paused and stared at Cassidy for a moment. Gradually the early-days, confident Bennett face reappeared, and a triumphant smile spread across it. 'Wait a minute. They're running on three specialists, right?'

'That's what he said.'

'And two would make it unviable.'

'Yes.'

'He says they're meant to have five, but three are doing the work now.' Bennett jumped up and started pacing. 'So if we gave in to their whining and employed two more cardiologists, we'd waste two specialist salaries for no more output. That's a significant saving right there — that's what Gibbs and Andersen were talking about. And if we did that right across the CHE, my God!

'They really only need sixty per cent of the quacks they say they do. Bad mistake letting that little secret out, Tony.' He gave Cassidy another manic grin. 'How many specialists do we employ? Where's Dawn?'

'Jim, listen to me. Professional people need time to do non-clinical stuff, they can't do service work every single hour. They have to read, and teach, and do research and administration. All those things don't affect clinical output directly, but are critically important for quality.'

'But we don't measure that sort of quality, do we? We agreed it was too hard.' Bennett opened the door and yelled for Dawn. Cassidy glimpsed her startled face a few metres away before the door swung shut.

'This is madness. What about leave cover, for a start?'

'Dawn, I need a list of all the consultant doctors who work here. Yes, right now. Ring Payroll then, they'll know.' Bennett sat down and started scribbling notes.

Cassidy sat in one of the black and chrome chairs and slumped down as far as he could go. How nice it would be to lie down and forget about all this. 'Start laying off specialists, and even if you can get sixty per cent to stay, we'll soon be able to measure quality of medical care really well. There is that, I suppose.' He closed his eyes.

Bennett stopped writing. 'How come?'

'Staff who stay will get exhausted from trying to cover everything. They will undoubtedly make more mistakes, and there will be avoidable patient deaths. Then you'll have a really strong quality indicator.'

Bennett tried to return to his scribblings, then threw his pen down and glared at the apparently sleeping Cassidy.

'Look at you, sitting there so bloody smug. You can always bring out that stuff about deaths, and I'm supposed to say, "Oops, sorry, I'm wrong, you're right." I'm doing everything I can to improve this company, and all I get is negativity. I'm bloody sick of it.'

'Sorry, I can't help with that.' Cassidy stood up and stretched. 'By the way Jim, do you remember telling me about Hayek and markets the day we first met? Have you actually read his book, *The Road to Serfdom*? You should have a look at it.

'You see Hayek says lots about markets, but he also says it's appropriate for governments to provide universal social insurance for disease and accidents. So Hayek himself, the great guru for the Roundtable and all these politicians, recommends exactly the *opposite* of public hospitals making a profit and competing with each other. How do you explain that?'

Now it was Bennett who had his eyes closed.

'I'd better get going,' said Cassidy. 'And don't forget, you've promised to fire Philip Jackson as well.'

....

Cassidy had been staring at the same letter of complaint for twenty minutes, and he had no idea what it was about. He sighed and closed the folder.

After this morning it was only a matter of time before he was fired, so he may as well go home now. There might be another card from Zoe.

He yawned and stood up. For the hundredth time he remembered her at Scarlatti's all those months ago, saying "Is it too late to get out of it?", and for the hundredth time he wished he had listened to her. Maybe they could have avoided all the pain of the last ten months and somehow got back together. If you love somebody let them go . . .

He switched off the computer and snapped his briefcase shut. He was pulling on his jacket when the door crashed open and Gordon Diamond walked in, large and angry.

Cassidy sat down behind his desk, clutching the briefcase to his chest as adrenalin flooded his system. 'What do you want?'

Diamond leant over the desk, bringing his face close to Cassidy's. 'Your resignation is what I want. We've finished with your interference.'

'Interference? I've been helping you avoid disasters.'

'You've been whispering in Jim Bennett's ear and he's stopped holding the line. Next he'll be as wet as you are, and then he'll be history too.'

'Holding the line? What line?'

'This creep Walsh thinks he can defy Treasury and get away with it. We don't tolerate that attitude, and Bennett was told to fire him. But you talked him out of it.'

'I didn't talk him out of firing Tony Walsh,' said Cassidy. 'I warned him about the consequences of losing lots of highly skilled specialists. Jim made up his own mind about it, and thank goodness, he did the right thing for the patients.'

'The patients?' Diamond shouted. 'What about the shareholding Ministers?' He stared for a moment before sitting down and continuing in a calmer voice. 'I opposed your appointment from the start. But Richard Nesbit had already made up his mind, and that brown-noser Turnbull would do whatever Nesbit told him to.

'You told them in the interview you knew nothing about anything, but you still got the job. Unbelievable. And now look at the damage you've done.'

'Have you talked to Alex King recently?' said Cassidy.

'We know we're on the right track—'

'But you won't show anybody the evidence.'

'—so we can ignore the noise from vested people. Our job is to realise the savings by maintaining a high level of tension.'

'What do you mean by tension?'

Diamond rolled his eyes. 'My God, you're ignorant.' He sighed. 'Alright, I'll humour you. I'll explain tension, then you can write your letter of resignation.'

Cassidy said nothing.

'There's tension if you haven't got enough money to buy everything you want, right? Tension forces choices, so you prioritise spending and cut overheads.' Diamond was sounding almost matey now, probably because he was sitting between his prey and the door. 'But without tension, there's no need to make the tough calls. And that's how it was before we came in.'

'So by cutting the operating budget by ten per cent,' said Cassidy, 'you increase the tension to make everybody try harder.'

'Very good, Doctor, now you're getting the hang of it.'

'They'll never achieve that.'

'Doesn't matter. We know the efficiency gains are aggressive. But we won't relax them, because that would undermine Paxton's resolve to meet the target.'

Cassidy stared at him. 'That's truly horrible. By definition you'll keep going until clinical safety cannot help but be compromised.'

Diamond shrugged. 'It's not our role to consider how the plan might affect Paxton's ability to deliver services, that's for the purchaser to assess. But for your information, we did get a clinical consultant's opinion and there's no risk to client safety.'

'I don't believe you. No doctor would say such a thing — who was it?'

'You don't need to know that. But the point is, we will enforce optimal financial performance by keeping the tension high. And any clinical issues that arise are not our problem, they're for the Board to fix.'

'For God's sake,' shouted Cassidy, 'how can the Board do anything when you keep cutting their budget? If you've been told that people will die if you keep doing this, and you go ahead with it, then you are directly responsible for the consequences.'

Diamond shook his head. 'I don't see why.'

'You — don't — see — why.' Cassidy's head suddenly went clear and calm as cold, fearless anger flooded through his veins. 'We're done. You need to go now.'

'What?'

'Get out.'

Diamond sat back and crossed his arms with a menacing smile. 'Oh no, Doctor, we haven't finished our meeting yet. I'm here to get your resignation, remember?'

Cassidy grabbed the phone and moved well back out of Diamond's reach. 'Operator, put me through to Security please. Hello, I've got an intruder in my office. Dr Cassidy, room 205 in the managers' building. That's right. His name is Gordon Diamond . . . OK, thank you.' He put the phone down.

'Security will ring back in thirty seconds, and if you're still here they will come up and expel you. They record all calls so if you try anything primitive before they arrive or even in the next few days, you will be caught.'

Diamond's sneer faltered and he got to his feet. 'You haven't heard the last of this, you creep. I'll be making some calls this evening.'

Cassidy might have been carved from stone. Diamond gave him a last glare, and walked out.

....

Cassidy got home safely and made a few calls of his own. Then he packed his suitcase and loaded the Jaguar with all the other things from his room. He said an affectionate goodbye to Claire and gave her a note for Geoff, promising future delivery of a chocolate fish.

He went out to Oakville, had dinner with his parents, and slept in his old bed after storing most of his belongings in the garage.

After breakfast and sad farewells he drove back into Paxton. At 10:15 he parked near Kirk Street and walked into the *Globe* building, knowing he was burning his bridges and knowing it was right. He checked in at reception for his appointment.

For the next hour he sat with Clive Maxted and two colleagues in a meeting room on the top floor, with the peach-coloured hospital visible in the distance. Cassidy told them everything he knew about the events of the past ten months, and especially the past few weeks.

Finally the questions stopped, and the other journalists left to get started on tomorrow's front page story.

'*Tension.*' Maxted nodded thoughtfully. 'That'll make a good headline.' He looked at Cassidy. 'Where does this leave you, Steve?'

Cassidy patted his pocket and felt the crackle of the ticket. 'Out of here, that's for sure. I'm going to vanish.'

'Very wise. But give me your address so that I can contact you if I need to check anything.'

'I wouldn't do that even if I had an address to give you,' said Cassidy. 'It's over for me. Goodbye, Clive. Keep up the good work.'

Then he was back on the street, looking around at the shops and the people, storing up memories and wishing that things could have been different. But now the bomb was ticking and he had only hours before it exploded.

He shook himself, bought the biggest bunch of flowers from the stall outside the *Globe*, and put them carefully on the front seat of the car.

He drove out to Westmere and a lunch appointment with Isabel Sorensen.

Later he took his faithful steed to the Jaguar dealers on Cornell Street, where a deal was done. An apprentice came with him to the airport and Cassidy handed over the keys, took his luggage out of the boot, and walked away.

He was in good time for the afternoon flight to Melbourne.

POSTSCRIPT: HOW IT REALLY ENDED

This novel uses fictional characters and a contracted timeline to describe real events and attitudes during a turbulent time in the history of our health system.

The novel's ending, with our hero turning whistle-blower, does not reflect what happened. Instead the reforms were halted by a number of factors:

The proposed and then partly-implemented changes were the subject of sustained and energetic criticism from a broad spectrum of professionals, the public, and the media.

The National Party almost lost the general election in late 1993, with its majority cut from 19 (a record) to 1 in a 120-seat Parliament as the public indicated their displeasure at its deceptive election campaigning and its unannounced continuation of neo-liberal policies, including those in health.

The *Patients are Dying* report, written by courageous clinicians at Christchurch Hospital and published in December 1996, received wide publicity.

It was followed by an in-depth investigation of Canterbury's public health system by the first Health and Disability Commissioner, Robyn Stent. Her report, published in April 1998, was highly critical of the reformed system, from Treasury down to hospital senior management level.

I can only speak for Christchurch Hospital, where I work. But there at least, the hospital and the public health system are generally working well. We have been lucky in recent years to have two visionary CEOs who have worked with hospital managers and clinical staff to produce a system which, while inevitably not perfect, has high clinical standards and strong systems management.

Others have not been so fortunate. In 2013 the Francis report,[1] on levels of care at the UK's Mid Staffordshire National Health Service Foundation Trust (Stafford is in the West Midlands of England), described an underfunded and understaffed hospital with appalling standards of care, filthy wards and departments, dysfunctional professional staff and a patient mortality rate significantly higher than expected.

There had been an earlier enquiry into Stafford Hospital by the UK Healthcare Commission, whose report, was published in 2009. In a subsequent article[2] the report's author, Dr Heather Wood, highlighted managerial attitudes similar to those at this novel's fictional Paxton Crown Health Enterprise.

In pursuit of politically-set guidelines for maximum 'efficiency', which if achieved would have allowed the hospital to take in fee-paying patients, Stafford managers gave financial considerations priority over patient care and ignored the protests of their clinicians as clinical care suffered. By some estimates between 400 and 1200 more patients died at the hospital between 2005 and 2008 than would have been expected for a hospital of its size.[3]

Stafford Hospital has subsequently been renamed County Hospital following the dissolution of the Mid-Staffordshire NHS Trust.[3]

New Zealand escaped in the 1990s, but we must never forget.

Ian Cowan
April 2015

Postscript References:
1. 'The Mid Staffordshire NHS Foundation Trust Enquiry', chaired by Robert Francis QC. 6 February 2013. Available online at http://www.midstaffspublicinquiry.com/report.
2. Wood, Heather. 'Mid Staffs is evidence of all that is wrong with NHS management'. *BMJ* 2013:346:f774. Published online 6 February 2013.
3. 'Stafford Hospital', Wikipedia. Accessed January 2015.

REFERENCES

Abbreviations used in source list:
ASMS   The Association of Salaried Medical Specialists.
GHE   'The Government's Health Experiment – an overview of the health "reforms"'. Coalition for Public Health, Wellington, September 1992.
GWP   (Green and White Paper). 'Your Health and the Public Health, a statement of Government health policy'. The Hon. Simon Upton, Minister of Health. Wellington, July 1991. ISBN 0-477-07557-6.
HDC   'Canterbury Health Ltd'. A report by the Health and Disability Commissioner. Auckland, April 1998. ISBN 0-477-01824-6.
HRSO   'Health Reforms, a Second Opinion – a comprehensive critique by leading health commentators'. Wellington Health Action Committee, December 1992.
HRST   'Unshackling the Hospitals'. Hospital and Related Services Taskforce. 1998. Wellington. (Also known as the Gibbs Report). ISBN 0-477-04520-0.
Listener   The New Zealand *Listener*.
NIPB   The report of the National Interim Provider Board, Wellington, May 1992.
NZMA   The New Zealand Medical Association.
NZMJ   *The New Zealand Medical Journal*.
Press   The *Press* newspaper, Christchurch.

Sources:
Ansley, Bruce. 1998. Cut and run. *Listener*, 2 May, p. 18.
ASMS 1992a. Newsletter No. 13, p. 1. December.
ASMS 1992b. Information Bulletin no. 5, p. 3. December.
ASMS 1998. Newsletter No. 36, p. 1. October.

Birch, Bill. 1993a. What the Government wants health reforms to achieve. *Press*, 29 April.
Birch, Bill. 1993b. Health funding. Letter to the editor, *Press*, 2 June.
Bowie, Robert. 1992. Health expenditure and the health reforms – a comment. *NZMJ*, 11 November, p. 458.
Bowie, R and Easton, B. 1994. Vexation in the voluntary sector. *NZMJ*, 9 March, p. 76.
Brett, Cate. 1996. Clash of the Codes. *North and South*, September. p. 86.
Bridgeport Group. 1992. The core debate: review of submissions. Wellington. May. p. 5.
Campbell, Gordon. 1991. Rx for chaos. *Listener and TV Times*, 25 November, p. 14.
Canterbury Hospitals' Medical Staff Association. 1996. Patients are dying: a record of system failure and unsafe healthcare practice at Christchurch Hospital. December.
Chapple, Max. 1995. Get well soon. *North and South*, April, p. 102.
Corbett, Jan. 1990. Condition: serious. *Metro*, April, p. 58.
Coalition for Public Health. 1992. The health reforms, one year on. GHE p. 4.
Danzon, Patricia and Begg, Susan. 1991. *Options for healthcare in New Zealand*, report for the New Zealand Business Roundtable, CS First Boston NZ Ltd, Wellington.
Douglas, Roger. 1993. *Unfinished Business*. Random House, Auckland. ISBN 1-86941-199-4.
Easton, Brian. 1992a. Is health an economic commodity? 1992 Nordmeyer memorial lecture. GHE p. 8.
Easton, Brian. 1992b. Economy column, *Listener*, 2 March, p. 37.
Easton, Brian. 1993. Behind the health hype. *Listener*, 29 May, p. 60.
Easton, Brian. 1997. *The Commercialisation of New Zealand*. Auckland University Press.
Easton, Brian. 2010. Crisis point. *Listener*, 20 February 2010, p.54.
Gauld, Robin. 2001. *Revolving Doors: New Zealand's health reforms*. Institute of policy studies and health services research centre, Victoria University of Wellington. ISBN 0-908935-58-7.
Gray, Alan, 1992a. Funding of health services. From 'The ethical implications of health sector reform', Wellington School of Medicine, November 1991. GHE p. 21.
Gray, Alan, 1992b. 'Untested theories' threaten health care. *Evening Post*, 9 June 1992. GHE p. 2.
Hazledine, Timothy. 1998. *Taking New Zealand seriously: the economics of decency*. Harper Collins. ISBN 1-86950-283-3
Hayek, Friedrich August von, 1944. *The Road to Serfdom*. Routledge Classics 2010. ISBN 0-415-25389-6.
Hewlett, Sylvia Ann. 1993. Child neglect in rich nations. UNICEF. ISBN 92-806-3026-1
Holmes, Anna. 1992. An unethical experiment? HRSO p.15.
Hopkinson, Glenys. 1992. There's large writing on the wall for the public health system. *National Business Review*, 31 January. GHE 27.
Hornblow, Andrew. 1997. New Zealand's health reforms: a clash of cultures.

British Medical Journal 314, 28 June, p. 1892.
Howden-Chapman, Philippa, 1992a. What do the recently released consultants' reports tell us about the Government's intentions? GHE p. 26.
Howden-Chapman, Philippa, 1992b. Doing the splits: Contracting issues in the health service. GHE p. 19.
Hubbard, Anthony. 1992. Gray's Elegy. *Listener*, 17 April, p. 28.
Hubbard, Anthony. 1993a. Losing our patients? *Listener*, 20 February, p. 29.
Hubbard, Anthony. 1993b. Corporate surgeon. *Listener*, 13 March, p. 34.
Kassirer, Jerome. 1995. Managed care and the morality of the marketplace. *New England Journal of Medicine*, 6 July, p. 50.
Keenan, Diane. 1992. Blow-out in health budget angers PSA. *Press*, 23 December.
Klein, Naomi. 1997. The Shock Doctrine: the rise of disaster capitalism. Penguin/Allen Lane. ISBN 978-1-84614-028-0.
Klinkman MS 1996. Episodes of care for abdominal pain in a primary care practice. *Archives of Family Medicine*, 5:279–85.
Light, DW. 1991. Embedded inefficiencies in health care. *Lancet*, 13 July 1991, p. 102.
Loughlin, Michael. 1996. Rationing, barbarity and the economist's perspective. *Health Care Analysis*, 4: 146–156.
Mackenzie, Helen. 1992. The devaluation of nursing care. HRSO p. 33.
McCrone, John. 2011. Reaping the past. *Press*, 20 August, p. C4–C5.
McLoughlin, David. 1993. Simon Upton's leap in the dark. *North and South*, March, p. 64.
McLoughlin, David. 1996a. How bad is our health? *North and South*, September, p. 68.
McLoughlin, David. 1996b. What becomes of the broken hearted? Trauma at Green Lane Hospital. *North and South*, December, p. 108.
Morrison, Alastair. 1992. Government reforms chase health and wealth. *Dominion* 28 August. GHE p. 5.
Morton, John. 1992. Tied up with contracts. HRSO p. 23.
Munro, Robin. 1992. Reforms in health are 'bound to fail'. *Press*, 7 December.
Munro, Robin. 1993. Public care for private patients attacked. *Press*, 18 March.
Murray, Dennis. 1995. The four market stages, and where you fit in. *Medical Economics*, 13 March, p. 44.
Notman, Mark et al. 1987. Social policy and professional self-interest: physician responses to DRGs. *Soc. Sci. Med*, vol 25, no. 12, p. 1259.
Neutze, John. 1993. Health reforms and the public hospitals. *NZMJ*, 27 January, p. 17.
NZMA 1992a. NIPB report is a dismal failure. *Newsletter* 27 May, in GHE p. 28.
NZMA 1992b. An 'exercise fraught with uncertainty.' *Newsletter* 22 July.
NZMA 1995. Telling it as it is! Nelson doctors speak out. *Newsletter* 12 April.
Patel, Raj. 2009. The Value of Nothing. Black, Inc. ISBN 9781863954563.
Pearce, Neil. 1994. Economic policy and health in the year of the family. *NZMJ*, 28 September, p. 379.
Powell, Ian. 1992. Health restructuring has major restraint of trade implications. GHE, p. 25.
***Press* 1992.** Topsy-turvy about health. Editorial 28 November.

Press 1993a. Healthy instincts. Editorial 24 March.
Press 1993b. 'Modern' health system promised. 13 February.
Press 1993c. Profit a key measure, CHEs told. 19 January.
Press 1993d. 'Sunny personality' costs anger nurses. 5 June.
Press 1993e. Labour and health policy. 2 June.
Press 1993f. CHEs debilitated by debt – Shipley. 17 December.
Press 1993g. No cover-up, says Minister. 17 August.
Press 1994a. Health reforms critic. Editorial 14 November.
Press 1994b. Unhealthy absurdities. Editorial 8 February.
Rand, Ayn, 1957. *Atlas Shrugged*. Signet Books. ISBN 0-451-16828-3.
Ray, Pauline, 1998. The business of caring. *Listener*, 9 July, p 38.
Rentoul, Michael. 1993a. Health adverts success argued. *Press*, 27 August.
Rentoul, Michael. 1993b. Problems abound in selling co-operation in health care. *Press*, 21 August.
Roberts, Peter. 1998. A question of respect. Presidential column, ASMS newsletter. March, p. 5.
Roberts, Jennifer. 1993. Managing markets. *Journal of Public Health Medicine*, vol 15 no 4, p. 305.
Southern Regional Health Authority. 1993. Contracting with the SRHA: a guide for providers. February. ISBN 0-477-01648-0.
Stiglitz, Joseph. 2012. The Price of Inequality. Penguin Books. ISBN 978-0-718-19738-4.
Vaithianathan, Rhema. 1999. The failure of corporatisation: public hospitals in New Zealand. *Agenda*, volume 6, number 4, p.325.
Walker, Martin, 1997. 'Greenspan's brave new capitalist world', *Guardian Weekly*, 20 July, p 6.
Webb, Olive, 1992. End of 'another bucket of money' era for health. *Press*, 2 January 1992.
Welch, Denis, 1991. Social illfare. Political Diary, *Listener*, 14 January, p. 8.
Welch, Denis, 1992. Welch's Week, *Listener and TV Times*, 4 May, p. 38.
Welch, Denis, 1999. A good de Cleene man. *Listener*, 11 September, p. 24.
Wignall, Keith. 1992. Why health care should be completely privatised. *Press*, 10 October.
Wilkinson TJ, Sainsbury R. 1995. Diagnosis related groups based funding and medical care of the elderly: a form of elder abuse? *NZMJ* 22 February, p 63.
Williams C. 1996. Doctors warned over New Zealand jobs. *British Medical Journal* 313, p.578, 7 September.
Williams G. 1993 Health quality v dollars. Letter to editor, *Listener*, 3 April

14 Gibbs committee's report ... 'Unshackling the Hospitals – Report of the Hospital and Related Services Taskforce', Wellington 1988. Commissioned by Roger Douglas and Michael Bassett, Ministers of Finance and Health in the Lange government; businessman Alan Gibbs was the chairman. The Gibbs committee commissioned the Arthur Andersen report which was

the origin of the claimed potential savings of $451–601 million per year, based on comparison of the 'most efficient' and 'least efficient' hospitals. The methods used and the specific hospitals studied were never revealed publicly. Areas for improvement were length of patient stay, hospital facilities, greater efficiencies within the hospital and its supporting facilities, and staff incentives. The Gibbs committee proposed the separation of funders and providers.

14 **who's given the ethical approval?** ... nobody. See Holmes 1992; Gray 1992a.

18 **Green and White Paper** ... see GWP. The Minister of Health's document setting out the problems and the proposed reforms, with limited options for public feedback.

20 **National Interim Provider Board** ... 'The NIPB was set up by the Government to make recommendations on the optimal structuring to help public hospitals and their related services function efficiently and effectively in this new health system.' NIPB p. 7. The report proposed the formation of new committees to do the actual setting-up work and produced some splendid verbal meringues (a few used by characters in this book), but was otherwise 'a dismal failure', NZMA 1992a. See also Gray 1992b.

22 **Six hundred and one million dollars** ... HRST p. 13.

28 **We have had to draw on the skills** ... Howden-Chapman 1992a provides examples.

29 **Way too much control over how public cash is spent** ... see Gibbs p. 29.

30 **Simon Upton** ... The Minister of Health after the 1990 election. Intellectual, Rhodes scholar, and when he entered Parliament directly from university aged 23, at that time the youngest MP in New Zealand history. He was subsequently one of its youngest cabinet Ministers. A disciple of Hayek, he won the Mont Pelerin Society's Hayek essay prize in 1987. See reference to page 185.

30 **they just throw money at it** ... see Webb 1992.

31 **people will be expected to take responsibility** ... see Webb 1992.

33 **ram the changes through as fast as possible** ... see Douglas 1993 p. 220.

33 **the Department of Health's budget had risen** ... GWP p. 7.

44 **A total lack of proper costing information** ... HRST p. 21.

45 **They're either an RGU or an RLU** ... See Wilkinson and Sainsbury 1995. This was a medical paper warning of the dangers to elderly patients of being assessed solely in terms of the cost of their care.

48 **Absolutely extraordinary lack of costing** ... HRST p. 20.

48 **over-centralised, bureaucratic, inflexible and confused** ... HRST p. 18.

48 **despite the demonstrable fact** ... HRST p. 8.

49 **based on proven principles that work** ... NIPB p. 8. The proof was never made public.

49 **All the recommendations are from business people** ... see Hopkinson 1992.

49 **Discouraging public submissions** ... See Gauld, p. 82.

51 **Paxton Hospital would take in about 8 million dollars a year** ... see Coalition for Public Health 1992. A total of $26 million was removed from area health boards' budgets.

52 **To make them mindful of the most economic use of health resources** ...

see Campbell 1991. 'Now that prescription charges have trebled and it costs more to visit the doctor, people will be less inclined to get ill. Alternatively, from a menu of illnesses they may choose the one that best suits their pocket. And knowing there's no super increase next year is a positive disincentive to growing older. Smart players in fact, will read the market signals right and grow younger.' Welch 1991.

52 **They don't choose to come into hospital** ... Easton 1992b.
52 **People are visiting their GPs less** ... Hornblow 1997.
52 **Community Services Card** ... see Gray 1992a.
52 **Not in the changes themselves, but in the speed of it** ... see Dr John Dobson, in Munro 1992.
53 **Nobody could get away with anything like this** ... see Gauld, p. 79.
58 **a third of the fee** ... Danzon & Begg, p. 14.
59 **And then going bankrupt** ... 'CHE's that make a loss will do what businesses that make a loss normally do', Simon Upton, in Morrison 1992.
59 **if some services were still not viable** .... NIPB p. 64.
61 **He's observing the experiment** .... 'It is impossible to anticipate the shape of NZ's health care system after the reforms; the programme is entirely experimental; ... the exercise is fraught with uncertainty.' CS First Boston report for NIPB, quoted in NZMA 1992b.
61 **The whole world's watching** ... 'The New Zealand experience will be seen by countries around the world as a marker for the future in the delivery of public health [services].' Prime Minister Jim Bolger in Parliament, 27 April 1993, quoted in Gauld p. 79.
63 **the cost of the reforms so far** ... Keenan 1992.
63 **content free** ... 'At a meeting in late 1995, a senior administrator in the health sector described the skills needed for the work in his agency. References to knowledge about the health system were notably absent. When questioned about the omission he said that sort of knowledge was unnecessary. One of the audience said: "It helps to know what you are talking about." He replied: "I dispute that."' Easton 1997, p. 181.
63 **Of the twenty-three new CHE CEOs around the country** ... Gauld, p. 89.
67 **Because the insurance companies won't pay** ... Southern Cross, New Zealand's largest medical insurer, declined the invitation. Munro 1993.
67 **Most Kiwis still believe we have a pretty fair society**... *Press* 1993a.
67 **The theatres and equipment belong to the public** ... see Munro 1993.
68 **the Warwick CHE Board-designate had apparently tried to buy Paxton Hospital** ... This possibility was raised in a CHEAC report. See *Press* 1993b.
72 **A raft of KPIs** ... Williams 1993.
80 **The staff just keep on treating as many units as they can** ... Graham Scott, former Treasury chief and head of the Health Funding Agency formed in 1999 by amalgamation of the RHAs: 'the reason that the expected savings were not realised when the market was reformed was that the doctors just kept on treating patients and that was not what they were supposed to do in response to the signals which were being sent.' Roberts 98.
80 **Did you notice that they've changed 25(a)** ... *Press* 1993c.
82 **painted the colour of a peach** ... Wanganui's CHE (Good Health Wanganui)

	led the way in managing public perception. See Chapple 1995, p. 102.
83	**Accident and Emergency – such negative words!** ... Wanganui again. *Press* 1993d.
86	**We will require from providers a firm undertaking** ... HDC, p. 249.
87	**It has 467 basic items** ... the original (1987) list, later greatly enlarged. Source: Wikipedia. There is no evidence that wholesale adoption of USA DRGs was considered, but I include it here to highlight the number of DRGs compared to the roughly 2,000 contracts each RHA finally had to negotiate and maintain (Gauld p. 116).
87	**'Don't worry, we're hiring plenty of people!'**... see Gray 1992a.
87	**The Green and White Paper said that RHA's would consult** ... GWP p. 34.
87	**The Bill requires only that we consult** ... Health and Disability Services Bill 1993, section 22.
87	**unless you incentivise them the docs don't co-operate** ... see Notman et al 1987.
88	**We'll be using a cost-and-volume model** ... see Roberts 1993.
88	**Roll the client over to the next year** ... The chairman of the Board of the Canterbury Health Ltd CHE suggested that cancer patients would have to wait for surgery for up to 12 weeks while operating theatres were kept closed to save money. See HDC p 99.
89	**But isn't the new system going to be more flexible and responsive?** ... That certainly was the expectation. See GWP, p. 19.
90	**the figure of twenty-seven per cent** ... Hubbard 1993a. This had emerged the previous November, see Bowie 1992.
90	**A curious piece of arithmetic** ... Dr Alister Scott, chairman of the NZMA. Hubbard 1993a.
91	**Simon Upton talked about it** ... Easton 1997, p. 153.
92	**It got people thinking there was a crisis** ... see Klein 1997.
94	**Warwick must have a chance to come back in** ... see Light 1991.
94	**But we can't innovate competitively** ... see Howden-Chapman 1992b.
96	**It's about one person in three with abdominal pain** ... Klinkman 1996.
101	**financial pain for us** ... see Light 1991.
101	**message from the Crown's communications strategy group** ... see Gauld p. 91.
102	**above economic and fiscal reality** ... 'You are I think developing a theme that has been run before, namely that the health service should somehow be above the economic and fiscal realities of New Zealand. That is not a proposition with which I can agree.' Simon Upton, quoted in NZMJ, 23 September 1992.
104	**The first commercial featured** ... I saw this at the time and found it a distinctly unsettling experience.
108	**Roadblock, they call it** ... Gauld p. 91.
109	**Running a hospital is no different than** ... I heard a manager shout this in a noisy meeting similar to the one described; I don't know his name and I never saw him again but that moment was the genesis of *Not Our Problem*.
109	**Soon we will know how many** ... David Troughton, director of the CHE Establishment Unit. In Hubbard 1993b.

110	**What about personal details** ... 'In theory CHEs should not share information about patients. This limitation can only be added to the long list of things about the health reforms which can only be described as bizarre. If a patient is brought unconscious to one hospital, it is useful for a doctor to know whether that person is allergic to penicillin, and not to have to depend on that information being on the hospital's records.' *Press* 1994a.
110	**Competition will help managers develop and reinforce** ... NIPB p. 34. The pick of the quotes from the NIPB report, for the sheer grandeur of its misunderstanding.
111	**My whole day is taken up with meetings** ... response from a CEO to whom I once made this suggestion.
113	**Simon Upton had been replaced** ... Gauld p. 96.
115	**Information asymmetry** ... see Easton 1997, p. 30–33.
115	**The employers have to trust doctors too** ... see Vaithianathan p. 331.
116	**He said we need lots more doctors** ... see Vaithianathan p. 331.
116	**They're setting up a Health Commission** ... Birch 1993a.
117	**when Hong Kong becomes part of China** ... NZMA 1995.
123	**Or we could do the operations that need to be done** ... 'If these guys feel strongly that patients are missing out, then why don't they pay for the operations themselves?' Ian Frame, departing CEO of the Christchurch CHE, Canterbury Health, on orthopaedic surgeons wanting to exceed the negotiated quota for hip replacements. Brett 1996.
124	**But they must be used up before** ... This suggestion was made by a manager in a hospital overseas, without success.
126	**New Zealand proportionally spends less per person on health** ... Bowie 1992.
127	**people are dying because of these policies**... see Christchurch Hospitals' Medical Staff Association 1996.
128	**Keeping a cardiac patient alive and out of hospital** ... Neutze 1993.
128	**People upstairs wanted us to review his contract** ... 'The CHEAC recommended that the contracts of clinicians who spoke out against 2 CHEs in Christchurch should be reviewed.' HDC p. 78.
129	**The Crown has brought in external consultants** ... Gauld, p. 107.
129	**We can't even get them to commit to service definitions** ... Gauld, p. 107.
129	**holding back two per cent** ... Birch 1993b.
131	**You can always cash in on the comorbidities** ... See Roberts 1993.
132	**The collective contract has expired** ... See ASMS 1992a.
136	**we'll be down at around 6.5 per cent** ... percentage of Gross Domestic product spent on health in 1992: New Zealand 7.6, USA 13.9, Australia 8.6, UK 7.0. OECD figures quoted by Gauld, p. 233.
138	**Seventy-seven per cent of New Zealanders were dissatisfied** ... Bill Birch in *Press* 1993e.
140	**We're already past the deadline for inking the contracts** ... NZMA 1995. HDC p. 47.
141	**Yes, I believe it's a world first** ... It was. See Gauld p. 110.
141	**When we have the right solution we go for it** ... see Douglas 1993, p. 217.
141	**But that was eight years ago, and since then** ... 'Long regarded as one

of the world's most enlightened social democracies, New Zealand has, since 1984, demolished its cradle-to-grave social welfare system in the name of economic efficiency. Nevertheless, untrammelled markets have not produced vigorous growth. On the contrary, eight years of stringent monetarist policies have produced massive unemployment, rising crime rates, a widening gap between rich and poor, and a declining GDP. Between 1985 and 1990, New Zealand's GDP fell by 0.7%, the worst record of any industrialised country, while unemployment more than doubled. The fall in living standards has been particularly severe among families with children.' Hewlett 1993, quoted in Pearce 1994.

'Between 1989 & 1991 official unemployment figures increased from 7.1% of the labour force to 10.6%, and ... numbers below the poverty line increased from 360,000 to 510,000 ... Cuts in public spending on social security eventually incur increased expenditure on health, unemployment, & law & order.' Pearce 1994.

'In 1991/2 welfare benefits were reduced and state house rents raised, reducing the disposable income of the poor. The cost of user part-charges, transport, prescription charges and loss of access to public hospital and support services selectively affect the poor... Between 1980 and 1991, before user part charges, the government contribution to health expenditure fell from 88% to 81.7%... In the year ended 31 March 1992 household expenditure on health rose 18% and on medical goods 13%, while food spending reduced by 5%. There are now record numbers of social welfare beneficiaries and working poor who rely on the charity of voluntary agencies to avoid destitution.' Holmes 1992.

141 **Trickle down never happens** ... See Stiglitz 2012, p. 8.
143 **start owning the problem** ... see Easton 1997, p. 170.
150 **That's disgusting** ... Sentiment expressed on TV by the leader of striking hospital workers in a hospital where I worked in England, regarding volunteers helping in a strike-bound hospital.
154 **Both bags were now overflowing** ... This was done by a TV crew during the same strike, and shown on the BBC news that evening.
157 **How you get the results is a blend** ... David Troughton, director of the CHE Establishment unit, on being asked whether nurses' jobs would go in the reforms. Hubbard 1993b.
158 **Is it fair that forty-two percent of people** ... see HRST, p. 7 and p. 14.
159 **Arthur Andersen is a highly respected** ... They were at that time; the founder, Arthur Andersen himself (1885–1947), was renowned for his integrity. The company was found guilty of criminal charges related to the accounts of Enron when the latter collapsed in 2001, and voluntarily surrendered its licences to operate as Certified Public Accountants in 2002. Source: Wikipedia.
166 **setting up a branch in Saudi Arabia** ... 'The interesting thing about the Dunedin CHE venturing into Saudi Arabia and setting up a cardiothoracic unit in Christchurch is not that these moves are bizarre – which they are – but whether the government will acknowledge how bizarre these and other aspects of the health reforms have become.' *Press* 1994b.

167 **Instead they're getting longer** ... see Gauld p 120.
167 **As soon as the RHA know** ... *Press* 1994b.
169 **Evolving Business Opportunities** ... There were several lavish conferences like this, with agendas emphasising business opportunities rather than patient care. See Welch 1992.
175 **From Labour we inherited massive debt** ... Gauld, p. 81. National inflated the size of the deficit by adding in Labour's new policy promises: see Easton 1997, p.52.
175 **put the consumer in the driving seat** ... '[Despite reforms in 1989] The area health boards had conflicting objectives, and users were not put into the driving seat – the position they hold in more businesslike systems of providing goods and services.' NIPB p. 26.
176 **they'd return health administration into** ... Birch 1993a. The Minister of Health attacking the opposition by suggesting they would do exactly what his government was doing.
176 **We have cut something under one hundred million dollars** ... Campbell 1991, p. 16.
177 **from 64 to 199 dollars a day in a small hospital** ... HRST report, p. 14.
180 **Our leaders blew 2.8 million dollars** ... Rentoul 1993a.
183 **evidence worldwide makes it clear** ... NIPB p. 53.
184 **Is this based on some God-given guidance? ... mysterious revelations of some kind?** ... Annex to Treasury Government briefing papers, 1987: background papers on Social Policy, p. 413.
184 **Relying on everyone to do 'the right thing'** ... 'In health care you have complex and hard-to-cost processes and technologies, and producers – nurses, therapists and doctors – who know a lot more about those processes than the patients or their ostensible bosses. This means that the rest of us have to trust the professionals to behave honourably and not abuse the power of their information advantage.

But rationalism has no place for trust. Outputs and inputs are tightly specified and enforced contractually, with no discretion for people to behave well or badly. Unfortunately, because the information asymmetries are so fundamental, only a part of the process can actually be rationalised ... If you want to trust people you have to trust them all the time, and not just when you can't supervise them.' Hazledine 1998, p. 195–196.
185 **Hayek** ... Friedrich August von Hayek (1899–1992), an Austrian economist who promoted unregulated markets as the best way to run an economy, with government responsibilities reduced to a minimum. He was one of the founders of the Mont Pelerin Society, which keeps the flame alive. Roger Kerr, for many years the executive director of the Business Roundtable, was a member, as was the Minister of Finance in the Bolger government, Ruth Richardson. Simon Upton won a Mont Pelerin Hayek essay prize in 1987. Alan Gibbs was 'a keen follower of ... Hayek' (McLoughlin 1996a), and Roger Douglas's rules for introducing reform against resistance were first presented at a Mont Pelerin Society meeting (Douglas 1993).
185 **Atlas Shrugged** ... A novel by Ayn Rand (1905–1982), published in 1957. The entrepreneurs and industrialists who make America run are under attack

from politicians and bureaucrats with their increasing demands for taxes and compliance. One by one the noble capitalists quietly flee to a sanctuary high in the mountains where they can all live simple lives together. As the last one leaves, America completes its descent into anarchy and despair. But perhaps they will return . . . A fairy tale, cartoonish in the goodness of the goodies and the badness of the baddies, and without a sniff of irony in its 645,000 words, it promotes the concept that looking after your own interests is the best way to make a better world (Rand equated altruism with servility). It remains widely-read, and hundreds of thousands of copies are distributed free in American schools each year by the Ayn Rand Foundation. *(Word count and sales data from Wikipedia.)* Allan Greenspan, who was for many years the Chairman of the USA's Federal Reserve and who saw no need to stop the fraudulent behaviour leading to the 2008 global financial crisis (Patel 2009, p 4) used to re-read this book every two years (Walker, 1997).

185 **it's unfair that my tax money should be spent** ... see Wignall 1992. Keith Wignall was at that time a lecturer in economics at the University of Canterbury.
186 **The CEO's package is incentive based** ... *Christchurch Mail*, 31 January 1994.
187 **Two months into the financial year** ... NZMA 1995. The contracts for the 1994/95 financial year, starting in July, were given to the Nelson CHE by the RHA in December.
187 **Average length of hospital stay** ... Ministry of Health figure quoted by Gauld, p. 78. It had been 10.6 in 1982–83.
188 **caring for them will put an extra burden** ... Bowie and Easton 1994.
188 **Arthur Andersen predicted savings** ... HRST, p. 13.
188 **If we start doing something** ... see Brett 1996.
189 **They're the hospital volunteers** ... Bowie and Easton 1994.
191 **You've been told to find more savings** ... see HDC p. 236.
195 **The public of Oregon** ... Campbell 1991, Neutze 1993.
197 **They do all sorts of tricks** ... providers can generally dominate purchasers via information asymmetry. See Roberts 1993.
197 **But the legal side is a quagmire** ... see Morton 1992.
198 **eliminating charge nurse positions** ... see Brett 1996.
199 **Another ten per cent!** ... CCMAU required efficiency gains from Canterbury Health representing 10% of current operating cost. HDC p. 53.
199 **CCMAU may recommend replacement** ... Ansley 1998.
200 **a contract with another RHA** ... Rentoul 1993b.
200 **We'll be sending a team to assess unit quality** ... Rentoul 1993b.
200 **Patients will go from here to another part of the country** ... NZMA 1995.
201 **But it was improving** ... Gauld, p. 67.
201 **Before the election you promised to keep the status quo** ... see Gauld, p. 80.
202 **If people are stupid enough to believe parties' promises** ... Trevor de Cleene, Welch 1999. De Cleene was Associate Finance Minister in the Lange government elected in 1984; Minister outside cabinet in 1987, with Customs and Revenue portfolios. (sources: Welch 1999, Wikipedia).
202 **Food is supplied by private companies** ... see Wignall 1992.

206 **All the contract forms we'd drawn up** ... see Southern Regional Health Authority 1993.
207 **The external surgery contract is cancelled** ... see Vaithiananathan 1999.
207 **So many surgeons have terminated their employment** ... see Hubbard 1992.
209 **The National Interim Provider Board proposed this** ... NIPB p. 57.
209 **Workout** ... In December 1994 CCMAU placed the Canterbury Health CHE in workout as described. See HDC p. 52.
210 **There will be weekly meetings with CCMAU** ... HDC p. 81.
210 **Yesterday we had twenty-one patients on drips** ... This was happening at Christchurch Hospital. Brett 1996.
211 **Trevor Hoskins had cancelled Mr Richards' operation** ... 'a Disneyesque world in which contracts are won and lost overnight; where operating times vacillate wildly from week to week; ... where surgeons walk into theatres to find a manager has added an extra patient to their operating list thinking they ought to be able to whip hips in and out a bit faster; where surgeons are told to stop performing certain types of operations because they don't fit into any purchasing category.' Brett 1996.
212 **Choosing random patients off the waiting list** ... Brett 1996.
214 **a public relations backlash** ... see HDC p. 12.
215 **The new plan will remain strictly confidential** ... *Press*, 1993g.
215 **You will re-negotiate your teaching contracts, and you may withdraw from contracts** ... HDC p.81–82.
215 **All the CHE's are in debt** ... *Press* 1993f. In their first financial year the CHEs returned a combined deficit of $189.4 million. See Gauld p. 117-8.
215 **Several have received equity injections** ... HDC p. 54.
215 **Five CHEs are borrowing** ... *Press* 1993f.
220 **The provider contract negotiations have become a sort of game** ... 'An elaborate and costly game of brinkmanship played out between CHE managers and the SRHA which, far from ensuring efficiency and cost effectiveness, actually promotes price increases, internal cost transferring and petty interpersonal conflicts.' Brett 1996.
220 **lots of time lost as each new person has to learn their job** ... Gauld p 115.
220 **The Core Services people have walked away** ... see Gauld, p. 99.
220 **the RHA has admitted that it won't even be able to fund current services** .... HDC p. 241.
220 **none of it's the Government's fault, somehow** ... 'The Minister is nowhere in the Health & Disability Services Bill made accountable. Nor even are the RHAs; the accountability clauses in the bill are discretionary rather than mandatory. It is instead the provider who will be held accountable for the failures of an under-funded system.' Allen Fraser, ASMS National president, ASMS 1992b.
224 **Are you familiar with the new Building Act?** .... 'New Zealand's economy was over-protected, over-regulated, in the Muldoon era. And so we leapt to the other extreme. In a revolution quietly fomented by a clever clique of Treasury officials and led in blitzkrieg fashion by Labour's incoming Minister of Finance Roger Douglas, New Zealand took the neoliberal textbook and swallowed it whole. We deregulated everything in sight,

slashing government controls to allow markets to self-regulate, and now some 20 years later, we are still picking up the pieces.' McCrone 2011. 'Our leaky-home problems began in 1991, with market extremists still triumphant, when the system of construction changed dramatically ... construction [became] regulated through a building code that set out performance criteria to be achieved, rather than prescribing the precise manner in which buildings were to be constructed ... Little thought seems to have been given to answering such questions as, "if the cladding falls off after 14 years, what redress does the house owner have?"... Our leaky-home crisis will cost $11.5 billion, in proportion roughly 10 times the cost to the USA of the global financial crisis.' Easton 2010.

224 **mining, electricity supply** .... Mining: 'Twenty-nine dead in the Pike River explosion. Reforms to the Health and Safety in Employment Act in 1992 resulted in the disappearance of specialist mine inspectors and mining-specific safety laws as New Zealand switched almost overnight to generic performance-based standards. Market theory said this was how to both save public money and encourage business innovation – unleash the productivity tiger. The nanny state could be rolled back by allowing workplace safety to be controlled by a single, simpler set of pan-industry rules. Just tick the boxes to ensure compliance ... Firms would be set general health and safety targets, but left considerable choice about how they went about meeting them. Bosses could make the cost/benefit decisions about how much they actually needed to do to meet their legal obligations.' New Zealand went from seven mine inspectors to two for the whole country, including gold mines and quarries. '"People's approach, was that well, you know, it's the employer's responsibility, not yours, to identify their own hazards. You just go and audit them." – Department of Labour mine inspector Michael Firmin at the Pike River enquiry.' McCrone 2011.
Electricity: Mercury Energy, supplier of Auckland's electricity, was privatised and devoted itself to raising cash to acquire rivals. It gave this priority over continuity of supply, and so did not install any back-up transmission capacity. All four cables failed simultaneously in February 1998 leaving Auckland's central business district without power for several weeks. See 'Darkness at the heart of privatisation', *Guardian Weekly*, 15 March 1998.

224 **They've deregulated finance too** .... 'Around $8.6 billion of life savings of 200,000 Kiwi investors frozen, and potential losses of perhaps $3 billion even with Government bailouts and guarantees, following the domino collapse of some 60 weakly-regulated deposit-takers and investment trusts ... the industry was largely self-regulated, relying heavily on the sign-off of trustee and auditor firms that the finance companies hired themselves ... it was all a cosy arrangement that for a few years generated spectacular growth until ... they fell with a loud bang.' McCrone 2011.

226 **Health 4U, a Health Maintenance Organisation** .... 'At a 1996 international gathering of health businesses including HMOs in Mexico City, New Zealand was one of a small number of countries singled out for aggressive profit expansion. This was motivated by both increasing difficulties in extracting health profits in the United States and developments conducive to

privatisation in this country.
One New Zealand participant, Ian McPherson representing Aetna's 'down under' subsidiary, reportedly advised that New Zealand was already halfway to the goal of moving the government out of the business of running public hospital systems. Implicitly the role of Aetna was to complete the move, fill the vacuum and rake in the profits.' ASMS 1998.

228 **The CS First Boston report commissioned by the NIPB** ... This does not appear to have been published but according to Campbell 1991 it took six person-days to prepare. It advocates full commercialisation of the health system.

228 **if restructuring proceeds, it will almost inevitably involve** .... See NZMA 1992b.

228 **Private health marketeers would be unwilling** ... see NZMA 1992b.

229 **because of the complexities involved** ... Simon Upton 29/7/92, quoted in Coalition for Public Health 1992.

230 **You see, there are stages when you enter a market** ... Murray 1995.

231 **We want consultations as short as possible** ... Kassirer 1995.

231 **No cause non-renewal clause** ... Kassirer 1995.

231 **a medical loss is when you have to spend money** ... Kassirer 1995.

232 **fifty thousand capitated, low risk individuals, minimum**... see Campbell 1991.

232 **after I'd declined cover for people who were already sick** ... see Kassirer 1995.

234 **The plan all along has been to turn the public hospitals over to private providers** ...
'The Green and White Paper ... advocates commercialisation of the health system so that profit-centred private agencies would dominate the supply side and private payment and insurance would dominate the demand side. Some see this commercialisation as a lead up to privatisation, the pure form of the US system.
Suspicions were raised when Sir Ronald Trotter was appointed to chair the National Interim Provider Board which is overseeing the reforms. Trotter does not have much experience in health, but no business executive in New Zealand has been more involved in privatisation and, as chairperson of the Business Roundtable, he has been advocating the nostrum of privatisation elsewhere as a solution to our economic ills. Suspicions were confirmed when his board appointed consultants with little experience in health, but who had advocated and participated in privatisation.
The Minister of Health swears that privatisation is not his intention. I believe him, just as I believed the Labour ministers who swore that corporatisation of state trading assets would not lead to privatisation. But it did.' Easton 1992b.
'[Upton's] colleague Paul East, the new Minister of Crown Health Enterprises, does not rule out privatisation as the ultimate destination of the reforms. In Parliament during October [1991], East merely said this was not the Government's intention. Those familiar with the fate of state-owned enterprises elsewhere in the public sector – first corporatise them, then

sell them off – will know the value of such assurances ... It is, as Nurses' Association Lyndon Keene explains, a step-by-step process. The reforms corporatise hospitals. User charges make private insurance seem essential. Government funds can be taken out of health authority budgets to subsidise alternative (ie private) health care plans. Once private sector medicine has been bolstered in these ways, Keene concludes, it would then be feasible for government to sell off the hospitals and other health services.' Campbell 1991.

Alan Gibbs: 'In the long run I foresaw hospitals being privatised. There are lots of *private* hospitals out there. They are a service industry like a restaurant. Imagine the Government running restaurants!' McLoughlin 1996a, italics added.

235 **they were so sure that the theory was right** ... 'Competition at the provider level of service is potentially a major stimulus to efficient performance and its introduction is likely to generate gains that exceed any costs arising from separation of funding and provision.' Danzon and Begg p. 42.

235 **Each RHA will soon have two thousand provider contracts** ... Gauld p. 116.

235 **For example, a senior public servant told us** ... Peter Troughton, the director of the Crown Health Enterprise Establishment Unit, was the civil servant. Brian Easton wrote to Dr Troughton and Mr Birch but received no satisfactory answers about the basis of these claims. See Easton 1993. Earlier, Alan Gibbs had said that $720 million a year could be saved, out of a public hospitals' budget of (then) $2.4 billion. Ray 1998. That's 30 per cent; Arthur Andersen had estimated 25.

Simon Upton, addressing the (then) $82 million blowout in setting up the new structure, thought that 'it would be worthwhile if $50 million a year was saved'. McLoughlin 1993.

235 **Increasingly I'm seeing patients** ... John Neutze, Green Lane Hospital cardiologist, in McLoughlin 1996b. Also HDC, p. 49.

236 **It's the effect on skilled people who have been laid off** ... Loughlin 1996.

238 **New Zealand's rotten employment contracts** ... see Williams 1996.

239 **You had moved our parks** ... This was instituted at Wellington Hospital for a brief period during the reforms.

243 **do you remember telling me about Hayek** ... Hayek saw 'social insurance' for health care as the role of the state rather than a competitive market. It would seem that the reformers overlooked this. See Hayek p. 125.

245 **A high level of tension** ... 'I acknowledge that the tension between services and funding is explicitly recognised by the Health and Disability Service Act 1993 which refers to the provision of health and disability services that are *reasonably achievable within the amount of funding provided.*' (Italics original). HDC 53.

'The aggressive business plan which CCMAU urged on Canterbury Health Limited for cost saving reasons and CCMAU's drive to develop tension in the system did not take adequate account of human or structural factors that required a reasonable time-frame, good information and adequate resources to work through the process of change.' HDC p. 53.

245 **We know the efficiency gains are aggressive** ... 'In a revealingly cynical

letter to shareholding ministers, including then Health Minister of Health Shipley, CCMAU said Canterbury Health's business plan was unrealistic, and aggressive efficiency gains were unlikely to be achieved. "More realistic" targets should be set. But Canterbury Health should be kept in the dark about this because "it will likely undermine their resolve to achieve the targets set". So, fully aware of the risks, knowing the targets were unattainable, CCMAU nevertheless sent the CHE on a course that at its worst ended with patient deaths. When it saw this letter exposed in the Stent report, CCMAU defended it as entirely appropriate and said it was under no obligation to advise the CHE of its reservations ... One letter from CCMAU even complained of 'insufficient tension between management and clinical staff.'" Ansley 1998.

245 **It's not our role to consider how the plan might affect** ... 'CCMAU advised the HDC: "it is not its role to consider how the plan might have affected CHL's ability to deliver services.... It is not required to advise Ministers on the risk to service quality of CHE business plans."' HDC p. 238.

245 **that's for the purchaser to assess** ... 'it is "the purchaser who has the responsibility to understand, measure, contract for and ensure delivery of service volumes and quality."' CCMAU advice to the HDC, HDC p. 238. This is incorrect: the RHAs were protected from any responsibility for provider quality or safety; the Southern RHA asked Canterbury Health to assess its own performance and report to it, HDC p.51. Because Canterbury Health never raised these problems, the SRHA thought monitoring was unnecessary, HDC p. 249. The SRHA never obtained a copy of "the Patients are Dying" report despite major media debate, the prospect of a ministerial enquiry and questions being asked in Parliament.' HDC p. 51. Not its problem!

245 **We did get a clinical consultant's opinion** ...'In the event that it became apparent that a business plan presented an unacceptably high level of risk including clinical risk, then CCMAU would advise the minister accordingly. It is for this reason that we appoint clinical reviewers.' HDC p. 238.

246 **No doctor would say such a thing – who was it?** ... When the Commissioner asked to see the clinical reviewer's feedback, 'neither Treasury nor CCMAU were able to locate the clinical assessment of the 1995/6 business plan ... CCMAU advised that they remain unsure whether any actual document in fact existed and that it appeared the review may have been done verbally.' HDC p.238.